DAGGER'S DESTINY

LINNEA TANNER

BOOK TWO IN THE CURSE OF CLANSMEN AND KINGS SERIES

Book 2: *Dagger's Curse*
Curse of Clansmen and Kings Series by Linnea Tanner

Books may be purchased by contacting the publisher or author at:
www.linneatanner.com or
linnea@linneatanner.com

Cover Art, Cover Layout and Interior Design: Priya Paulraj
Map: D. N. Frost, maps@DNFrost.com
Editor: Jessica Knauss
Publisher: Apollo Raven Publisher, LLC

ISBN: 978-0-9982300-5-4 (paperback)
      978-0-9982300-4-7 (e-book)

1) Historical Fiction   2) Fantasy   3) Ancient Rome and Britannia
4) Celtic Mythology

First Edition: Printed in the USA

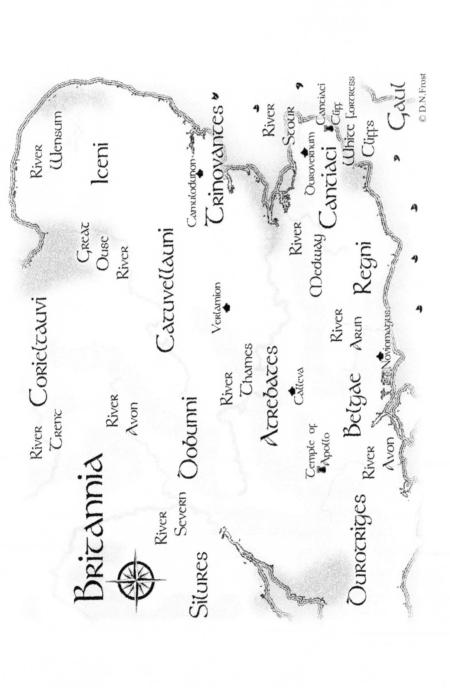

Britannia

River Severn

River Trent

River Avon

Corieltauvi

River Wensum

Iceni

Great Ouse River

Dobunni

Catuvellauni

Camulodunon

Trinovantes

River Stour

Canciaci Cliff

White Fortress

Gaul

Cliffs

Ourovernum

Canciaci

River Medway

River Thames

Verlamion

Atrebates

Calleva

River Arun

Regni

Belgae

Noviomagus

Temple of Apollo

River Avon

Durotriges

Silures

© D.N.Frost

This book is dedicated to my husband, Tom Tanner, for his lifelong support

I

TREASON

July, 24 AD, Southeast Britannia

The image of her father being wounded at the prisoner exchange haunted Princess Catrin as she entered the cave's dank womb where warriors had secretly carried the casualties. Under the illumination of a flaming torch, she found several men hovering over the king's motionless body. She feared the decision to use the dark forces of the Ancient Druids to alter the future could doom her father and people.

Catrin trembled as she knelt by her father and studied his blood-smeared face. A chill of foreboding sliced down her spine. Just that morning, she had made love with Marcellus on what could be her father's death-bed. She placed the palm of her hand on his forehead. His skin was cold and clammy, but he was still alive.

Feeling the bloody streaks on his tunic, she pulled her fingers away and turned to Cynwrig, the king's most-trusted guard. "Help me remove the tunic. I need to stop the bleeding!"

Cynwrig supported the king as Catrin cut the fabric from his chest. The ghastly crisscross cuts and deep abdominal gash made her cringe. A stench like rotten eggs assaulted her nostrils.

King Amren fidgeted. "Fetch my Druidess."

"No!" Catrin snapped. "Agrona is a traitor. We can't risk letting anyone know we've rescued and are tending you. There are herbs near the wall that will help reduce the swelling."

Catrin clasped her father's icy hands and noticed his sunken, bloodshot eyes. She looked to Cynwrig. "Heat a knife so I can seal his wounds. I also need water from the river."

"Do what my daughter says," rasped Amren.

Cynwrig pointed to the cave's opening. "I'll start a fire over there and get someone to fetch the water."

While Cynwrig prepared the fire, Catrin rummaged through several pouches, searching for the proper herbs. After a warrior returned with a bucket of water, she soaked several strips of willow bark in the container, then crushed dried blackberry, borage, and sage stems in a ceramic mortar. She finally added vinegar to the powder and stirred the contents with her finger into a green paste.

She looked at Cynwrig. "Is the knife ready?"

Cynwrig pulled the glowing red blade from the flames. "It looks hot enough."

"Then bring it to me."

Catrin took the knife from Cynwrig, who then restrained the king's arms. She pressed the searing blade on the wounds, methodically moving downward. The king writhed in agony, his eyes as wild as a wounded animal's as he fought Cynwrig's restraint. Concentrating on her task, Catrin swallowed the bile in her mouth and handed the dagger to Cynwrig to reheat the blade. Light-headed and in a cold sweat, she leaned into the hard wall to brace herself, then applied the paste dressing over her father's reddened wounds. Even with her gentle touch, his muscles flinched. Observing the anguish on his face, she placed a blanket under his head and gave him chamomile and poppy in water to ease his pain.

She continued the treatment by placing bark strips on the dressing until the king's grip around her wrist stopped her.

"We need to speak about Marcellus," Amren said with a growl from deep within his throat.

Catrin winced, apprehensive her father knew about her relationship with the Roman hostage placed under her charge. She warily studied the king as he closed his eyes and breathed deeply. He waved Trystan, his second-in-command, over and whispered to him. With a nod, Trystan ordered everyone away.

The hairs on Catrin's neck prickled. The only reason her father would order warriors away would be to reprimand her. She wilted under the king's burning glare as he began questioning. "Trystan told me when we were imprisoned together that Cynwrig found you unconscious in Marcellus's arms. I want to know what happened between the two of you."

Catrin hesitated, fearing her revelation would anger her father and cause his condition to deteriorate. "You should rest now. We can discuss this later."

"No. Tell me now!" Amren snapped.

Catrin could feel the king's eyes probing her like a sharp-edged scalpel for the truth. She bit her lower lip to stop it from quivering. "When I was stricken with the falling sickness, Marcellus came to my aid."

"Trystan said the Roman was found naked with you, and Agrona accused him of bewitching you with an amulet!"

"Marcellus had just finished bathing," Catrin answered, suddenly feeling queasy.

Amren cocked an eyebrow. "Bathing?"

"Yes."

"And that is all that happened?"

Catrin froze under her father's cold stare.

"Answer me!"

"You can't trust what Agrona says," Catrin replied.

"And why is that?"

"She is a druidic spirit from your past."

"Get to your point," Amren grunted.

"Remember Rhan, your former Queen? She possessed Agrona at the time you executed her for treason."

Amren's brow furrowed. "How do you know this?"

Catrin nervously shifted her weight. "I had a vision. Under the blood moon, you walked on a pathway of red-hot rocks around a towering fire. A woman with a wolf pelt draped over her shoulder approached you between two lines of people chanting, "Rhan, Rhan, Rhan.""

"What did this woman look like?"

"She had coppery hair and wolf-like eyes just like Marrock's. He was also there, just a few feet in front of her. He looked to be about eight years of age."

A lump formed in Amren's throat. "What did you see next?"

"You accused the woman of treason and cut off her head with your sword. Her head flew off and through the arms of a girl standing next to Marrock."

"The girl was Agrona," Amren interjected, his face now as pale as a corpse. "How do you interpret the vision?"

"When Agrona touched the severed head, Rhan's soul entered her. When I confronted Agrona about it, she drugged me so I wouldn't tell others. She also wanted to steal my powers." Catrin cringed, recalling the slimy feeling of Rhan's thoughts crawling in and out of her mind like a maggot.

Amren mumbled, as if struggling to comprehend what Catrin had just told him, and then continued. "I believe the gods speak through Agrona. She was born mute but spoke for the first time after Rhan's execution. Agrona declared me to be the king of truth and light. I implicitly trust Agrona on all spiritual matters. She has told me things only Rhan would have known."

"She tricked you just like she tricked me," Catrin said.

"I'm not so sure . . ." Amren squeezed his eyes shut and groaned. "Give me more poppy for the pain."

Catrin brought the cup with the poppy mixture to her father's lips. Moments later, he relaxed and asked her to help him sit more comfortably. She helped him lean against the stone wall. Though he spoke more slowly, his voice seemed stronger as he continued his questioning.

"What are your feelings toward the Roman?"

Catrin couldn't answer, her stomach twisting into knots from dread of what her father might do.

Amren narrowed his eyes, targeting on the truth. "Trystan told me that your mother questioned Marcellus about what he had done to you before you were found stricken with the falling sickness. He confessed that he loved you and that you had both . . . had . . ."

With a sob Catrin blurted, "Yes, I love Marcellus."

Amren frowned. "You did this knowing I was negotiating your betrothal to Cunobelin's son?"

A wavering shadow cast by a burning torch seemed to descend on Catrin. Shaking, she said, "Yes. I felt betrayed you did this without telling me."

"What in the name of the gods have you done?" Amren grimaced. "Your mother showed Trystan the dagger inscribed with Rhan's curse. The blade glowed as if it had just been pulled out of a furnace. Words melted away as others were being formed. Your mother, afraid the curse was again altering, locked the dagger away to stop the transformation."

This revelation stunned Catrin.

Amren then accused, "I believe you altered the curse when you slept with the enemy."

Dumbstruck, Catrin shook her head in denial. *No. No. This can't be. Our love is blameless. Something else caused the curse to alter.*

"Speak!"

Catrin knew that no matter the consequences, she had to tell her father what shifted the curse. "Altering the curse has nothing to do with Marcellus. When you were gone, the Raven—my raven guide— explained how the powers of the Ancient Druids worked."

"What powers?"

Catrin drew in a long breath and exhaled slowly. "I can travel to other spiritual realms in the Raven's mind. One place is a transitional barrier where the mortal world and the spiritual Otherworld join. It is called the Wall of Lives. On its surface, life threads for every living human weave in and out of a fluid tapestry. This is where the Past, the Present, and the Future merge into one. I discovered that I could change the Future by manipulating the life thread."

"How is that?"

"When I pulled the life thread of a person fated to die out of the portal leading to the Otherworld, I extended his life," Catrin explained.

"No mortal has that power," Amren said incredulously.

"I have that power. But I don't know how extending a person's life will impact the Future."

"Whose life did you extend? Mine?" asked Amren.

Catrin's voice cracked with emotion. "I saved Marcellus."

"Cursed gods!" Amren's eyes blazed with fire as he pointed to the gash in his belly. "This wound was inflicted by your lover's blade. He almost killed me!"

A sense of dread overcame Catrin.

Marcellus couldn't have done this! He knows how much I love Father. Why hadn't I foreseen this?

She averted her eyes from her father. "I never meant to harm you!"

Amren snarled. "But I just saw Marcellus fall with an arrow in his chest."

"No, Father, he is alive. I rewove his life thread so the death arrow wouldn't pierce his heart."

Amren sunk his fingers into the cave's dirt floor. "This is the disloyal act of a stupid girl blinded by love—not a noble princess I raised to put family and kingdom first. I must now go to war against my banished son, Marrock, and King Cunobelin. The Romans will likely join their cause after what we did to their soldiers today at the prisoner exchange. Just when I needed you, you betrayed me and my people when you helped the Roman enemy. Your act of changing the future might have altered Rhan's curse. In what way, I can't be certain until I inspect the dagger's inscription. You've left me with no choice but to charge you with treason."

Catrin felt as if a mule had kicked her in the stomach. She gasped. "Father, you can't do this."

"I can and I will," Amren said coldly. "I will serve you the same justice as any subject who betrays me."

"Have mercy on me," Catrin implored, grasping her father's hand. "I will do anything you ask to regain your trust!"

Amren's face softened for an instant, but then his glacier-blue eyes hardened. "Trystan!"

The commander walked from the shadows. Amren's face turned leaden. "Detain Catrin as a prisoner until her trial . . ."

Amren went limp as he rolled over on the cave's muddy floor.

Conflicting emotions of shock, fear, love, and hate whirled inside Catrin as she pressed her trembling fingers on her father's neck. Feeling no pulse, she pressed harder.

Suddenly, the king swatted her hand away. She recoiled in terror when his eyes fixed on her like a venomous snake. "Trystan, take my daughter away now!"

Horrified, Catrin pleaded to the commander for mercy. In his scowl, she could see none.

Trystan clenched her arm and dragged her to the cave opening.

Once outside, Trystan ordered a warrior to bind her to a tree until the next morning, when they would return to the capital. In the long night's gloom, unforgiving rain washed the tears away from Catrin's face. Branded as a traitor for loving the Roman enemy, she must share Rhan's fate for treason unless she could find a way back into her father's heart.

2

BETRAYAL

At times feverish, Marcellus had languished during the arduous five-day wagon ride to the Roman encampment near the Catuvellauni capital of Camulodunon. The constant jostling aggravated the pain in his chest wound. The soldiers' open contempt for him grated like salt on a lanced boil. After he had first been injured, one soldier spat on a bandage before applying it, disregarding that Marcellus was a nobleman from a powerful family.

Another cavalryman with two swollen black eyes also offered Marcellus another round of sputum on his bandage earlier that morning before saying, "Why did you save that Celtic cunni after she led our men into an ambush at the prisoner exchange?"

If his chest hadn't hurt so much, Marcellus would have knocked the foul-mouthed horseman off his mount and whip-fisted him. Weakened, his mobility limited by stabbing pain, he only had enough rage to grumble, "Keep your nose out of my affairs."

The badger-eyed horseman gave the ugliest scowl Marcellus had ever seen. "The other day, I buried five of my companions. Two had their eyes gouged out by those demonic ravens." As the cavalryman reined his horse away, Marcellus overhead him mumble, "Traitor."

The word "traitor" disquieted Marcellus still. He couldn't explain why he had attacked one of his own men who had hurled Catrin on the ground and stomped her abdomen. At that instant, his only thought was to protect her from harm. He never even considered this as treason. He drew in a deep breath and sighed.

Love can make a man lose all reason.

Not until he met Catrin had he understood how the unbridled passion of his great-grandfather, Mark Antony, for Cleopatra could make him forsake his Roman heritage. Even his grandfather, Iullus Antonius, had been forced to fall on his sword for his scandalous affair with Augustus's daughter, Julia. As a consequence, Marcellus's father, Lucius Antonius, was banished as a young man to Gaul for the sins of his forefathers.

Marcellus recalled his father's excitement after Emperor Tiberius pardoned him and allowed his family to return to Rome when he was a gangling twelve-year-old boy. Marcellus never quite meshed with his more sophisticated peers in Rome. Loneliness plagued him despite the city's bustle of one million inhabitants.

That all changed when he immersed himself in weapons training, military strategy, and oratory skills. He ultimately caught the eye of Eliana, the consul's wife, twice his age. An exotic, dark haired beauty, she invited him over to her villa so they could read poetry together. In her bedchamber, she undressed him and stroked his hardened shaft in elegiac couplets as she read Ovid's *Ars Amatoria* aloud:

Woman cannot resist the flames and cruel darts of love, shafts which, methinks, pierce not the heart of man so deeply. Pluck, then, the rose and lose no time, since if thou pluck it not 'twill fall forlorn and withered, of its own accord.

Once, during the Lupercalia Festival, Eliana's drooling, silver-haired husband with crippling gout almost caught Marcellus in bed with her. Hearing the consul's shuffling feet entering into the bedchamber, he scrambled to hide behind a large vase.

Even though Marcellus barely escaped with his life, he still believed he was invincible until death almost claimed him in Britannia. The image of Catrin's father lunging at him during the conflict at the prisoner exchange flashed into his mind. He had no choice but to defend himself against the king or be killed. Just when he had lost all trust that Catrin could alter his fate to die at the prisoner exchange, she summoned the raven to take the blunt force of a death arrow aimed at his heart. Just as he realized he had found his true love, she was snatched away. Their relationship was now impossible.

With the dark clouds billowing above, Marcellus's mood spiraled into a vortex of gloom. Loneliness dug into his soul. His chest stabbed with relentless pain; his head throbbed with the constant clack-clack of wagon wheels on the rough roadway. Upon further reflection, he acknowledged he had given little thought to his mortality and the consequences of his reckless actions. He lifted his eyes toward the parting clouds, and the sun's brilliance shone through. Believing this was an omen that he had another chance to fulfill his destiny with honor, he silently prayed.

Apollo, show me how to rise out of the ashes of my ancestors and ascend to the heavens.

No longer willing to wallow in his glum thoughts and listen to the wooden wheels, Marcellus shouted to the driver, "Stop. I need to get out!"

"No need," the driver said. "We're almost there."

Marcellus pulled himself up against the wagon's side to look over. Ahead was the rectangular Roman encampment on top of a rolling hill. Riding beside the wagon was Decimus, who wore a perpetual scowl on his scarred face. The close-lipped tribune was an enigma. Rumors abounded in Rome that his political career had suffered as a result of his marrying a Gallic commoner who died giving birth to their daughter—a tale of caution for any nobleman considering marriage with a foreigner beneath his status. Marcellus had to admit he had grown to respect the commander's rock-solid demeanor since their initial confrontation with King Amren. Still, the tribune's silence on the journey to the Roman camp roared disapproval of what Marcellus had done to save Catrin. And shortly, he would face his own father, whose soldiers accused him of treason.

Decimus reined his horse closer to the wagon. "You look pale as a corpse. What did those savages do to you back there?"

Marcellus hesitated revealing what he had endured as a prisoner; it could disrupt the political balance and endanger Catrin. He shrugged. "Not much worth speaking of. The bleak weather puts me in a bad mood."

Decimus cocked an eyebrow. "Weather? The bruises on your face tell me otherwise."

"It happened at the prisoner exchange," Marcellus said, looking away from the tribune's probing eyes.

Decimus pressed further. "Those bruises were already there before the conflict broke out. I'm baffled as to why you attacked Priscus to save that sorceress."

Marcellus bristled. "Catrin helped me to escape."

Decimus spat on the ground. "Those Cantiaci warriors who ambushed us tell me otherwise. As I recall, you shouted the alert."

Marcellus grasped the side of the wagon as it jerked over a rough area of the pathway. "Catrin didn't know this would happen. Besides, the Romans were ready to do the same."

"You mean ambush?"

Marcellus nodded.

Decimus's jaw tensed. "As the military commander, I must prepare for any surprise. Don't fool yourself. That Briton siren knew exactly what she was doing. She lured us into a trap. It's best we got you away from her wiles. The only reason I can think of why you turned on Priscus is she bewitched you."

Marcellus glared at Decimus. "She never bewitched me. I saved Catrin because she helped me to escape. I betrayed no Roman."

Fidgeting with the horse reins, Decimus said, "She blinded you to what she is—a sorceress with dark powers. She summoned the ravens that attacked our soldiers at the prisoner exchange. I've never seen so many demented birds dive into midst of battle like that. Two of my soldiers were pecked to death by these creatures. Catrin is just as deranged as her brother, Marrock."

"Her half-brother," Marcellus corrected. "You malign Catrin, but my father and you bargain with that monster, Marrock. He ignited the firestorm while I was held hostage. He must have stolen my father's insignia ring and imprinted our family's wax seal on the fake message that the queen intercepted. She only threatened to kill me when she read the lie that my father had imprisoned Amren and threatened to attack her. Didn't you consider this when you broke the agreement at the exchange?"

"Of course, I did," Decimus grumbled. "But anyone could have sent that forged letter."

"It was Marrock," Marcellus insisted. "You're a reasonable man. I'm surprised you support my father in his dealings with that barbarian."

"As a loyal servant to your father, I do what I'm told," Decimus said bitterly. "Between the two of us, this cursed island should sink in the ocean along with its brutal warriors and sorcery. We should not be dealing with any of them."

"Oh, I see. You are of the same mind as I," Marcellus said, suspecting a falling-out between his father and Decimus. "Is there something I need to know?"

Decimus pressed his lips together and stared straight ahead at the Roman encampment. "Let me just say, your father's friendship depends solely on how well I serve him to elevate his political standing. If anything goes wrong here, I will be the scapegoat."

Marcellus winced from a sudden pain in his chest. Gripping the edge of the wagon side, he cursed, "Damn the gods! I can't let Father see me helpless like this."

"Perhaps a good meal and some wine will put you in better spirits," Decimus said in a lighter tone.

"I almost forgot how I missed Roman comforts." Marcellus grimaced in pain as he leaned on the wagon's edge to ease his discomfort. "Is there a horse I can ride into camp? I would like to present myself as a nobleman, not a barnyard cat."

Decimus cracked a smile and barked at a nearby cavalryman. "Give this patrician your horse."

A lanky horseman climbed off his black-spotted gray pony about fourteen hands high. Marcellus gingerly crawled out of the wagon and lumbered to the pony. Mounting, he felt a sharp pain shoot through his chest. For good measure, he cursed the gods again and reined his horse closer to the tribune.

Decimus sniffed and wrinkled his nose. "You are starting to stink like piss and shit."

Not sure how to take the tribune's comment, Marcellus scratched his bristly beard that had incessantly itched the previous three days. He decided to explore further the possible discord between his father and Decimus.

"I need a shave," he said off-handedly. "Have any other envoys from Rome joined my father at the headquarters?"

Decimus frowned. "Senator Marcus Crassus Frugi is there. He has the same mind as your father regarding Britannia."

"Which is?"

"Now is the time for Rome to invade this god-forsaken island."

Concerned that Catrin could be slain in an invasion, Marcellus felt his stomach clench into a knot. "Invasion is a bad idea. The sooner we leave the better."

"I've argued this point with your father. His response is that I'm only here to serve him. He can as easily bring me down as he raised me up."

"Did you confront him and say that we should leave?"

"Yes. That is when I learned Tiberius has the same opinion as mine. Ask your father about the emperor's mandate. Right now, I could use some of your support."

"What mandate?"

Decimus shook his head. "No matter . . . I don't want any further troubles with your father."

Without saying another word, Decimus kicked his horse and galloped toward the encampment.

What Decimus had said troubled Marcellus. If his father disobeyed the emperor's mandate, it would be construed as treason. He had to convince his father otherwise or their family's legacy could be destroyed forever.

3

CHIMERA

Marcellus dismounted and handed the reins of his horse to a stableman at the center of the Roman encampment. With the approach of nightfall, a misty chill hung in the air as he walked to the tented pavilion headquarters where his senator father was waiting outside. He noted his stern glare but nonetheless opened his arms to embrace his father.

Lucius, stiffening the arms at his side, spurned the warm gesture. He instead greeted Marcellus with a sarcastic tinge in his voice, "Thank the gods you are alive. Your mother would never forgive me if I left you dead in Britannia." He cast a glance at Decimus. "We need to talk before I speak to my boy."

Marcellus glowered. *You call me "boy" after what I've been through!*

He begrudgingly followed his father into the main chamber, which was sparsely furnished with two tables, foldable stools, and multiple shelves. Behind the elongated table was a scarlet tapestry with an embroidered gold eagle.

Lucius pulled back the tapestry to reveal a smaller bedchamber. "You can clean up in here while I speak with Decimus."

Marcellus avoided his father's eyes as he entered the room about half the size of the main quarters. At the back were two couch-like beds, end tables, and corner shelves. He took off his tattered tunic and inspected his chest bandage near the light of a flaming oil lamp on an end table. He winced from the pain of touching the pink-tinged cloth and cursed, "Sons of Hades!"

Retrieving a wash cloth from a shelf, he rinsed it in a bowl of water and cautiously lifted the bandage to wipe the yellowish discharge off his swollen wound. Once he finished the painful task, he noticed a platter of cheese, bread, and berries set on another table. With his appetite returning, he gobbled the food down and rummaged through shelves of folded clothes, brushes, strigils, razors, and jars of cleansing oil until he found a scarlet military tunic to wear. As he slid the garment off the shelf, a scroll dropped at his feet. He set it on the bed while he finished dressing.

Marcellus picked up the scroll to inspect the broken wax seal of what appeared to be the imprint of the intaglio portrait of Emperor Tiberius. He wondered why his father had placed such an important document with his personal effects. Considering it further, he surmised it was the emperor's mandate that had caused the disagreement between his father and Decimus. To confirm his suspicion, he unrolled the parchment on the table and read:

Emperor Tiberius Caesar Augustus orders all diplomatic negotiations in Britannia to cease immediately. Return to Rome for further instructions. All cohorts under the command of Tribune Decimus Flavius must report to the military fort at Gesoriacum, Gaul, for further assignment.

Marcellus felt his mouth drop. He couldn't fathom why his father and Senator Frugi were still planning an invasion if the emperor had recalled them. The ramifications of his father disobeying an imperial mandate rattled in his head. Defying the emperor was treason. Nobles had been banished—even executed—for such acts. No wonder Decimus had been so disgruntled with his father.

A sudden movement of the tapestry divider caught the corner of Marcellus's eye. He hastily rolled the parchment and tucked it into his sleeve.

Lucius walked in. "It looks like you found something to wear."

Marcellus nervously readjusted the scroll into his sleeve to conceal it better. "Yes, but most of my belongings are still at the Cantiaci capital."

"I will have my body slave find you some other clothes," Lucius said, rubbing the back of his neck. His eyes froze on Marcellus. "Tell me what happened when you were held hostage."

The cold tone of his father's voice made Marcellus bristle. "No warm greetings . . . just an interrogation?"

"You expect a warm greeting after your misbehavior?"

"Misbehavior?"

Lucius's jaw clenched. "King Amren told me you had been found naked with his youngest daughter. He accused you of rape and ranted your Apollo's amulet cursed her with the falling sickness."

After the ordeal of Cantiaci warriors brutalizing him for defiling their princess, Marcellus was in no mood to defend himself again with his father.

"That is an utter lie!"

"Did you seduce her to get the information I asked for?"

"No, I befriended her. That is all it took to learn that Marrock is a debauched man whom you should not be dealing with."

Lucius glowered. "I deal with any barbarian who serves my ambition! Why did you help Amren's daughter to escape at the prisoner exchange? I wanted to capture her to use as a bargaining tool after you were released."

"I thought the exchange was to calm the political storm between you and the Cantiaci. It appears you never intended to honor your agreement with Queen Rhiannon to release Amren."

"She betrayed us," Lucius snorted. "Decimus told me the conflict broke out after the queen's warriors ambushed us. Even so, you assaulted a centurion so that whore could escape. You did this without any regard for the safety of our troops. The soldiers accuse you of betraying them!"

Marcellus stepped within a few inches of his father's face. "She is no whore, and I betrayed no one. The centurion was trying to kill Catrin. She had no knowledge of her mother's plans to ambush us."

Lucius huffed. "You idiot, she lured us into a trap!"

"If the queen had trusted you, none of this bloodshed would have occurred," Marcellus retorted.

Lucius roughly grabbed Marcellus by the arm. "No one threatens my family and lives!"

Marcellus jerked away, but his father continued ranting. "That queen wanted to butcher you—to sacrifice you to her war goddesses. I swear to Jupiter above, that bitch will pay dearly!"

"What do you plan to do?"

Lucius pounded his chest with a clenched hand. "I want vengeance! I want that pompous king and all his family to suffer for what they have done to me!"

"The queen acted like any prey cornered by a predator," Marcellus lashed. "You would have done the same—defend your family in any way you could."

"You imbecile! I had to grovel like a mangy dog to that mad bitch. I should have trampled her beneath my heels! Why didn't I do this? Let me tell you why . . ."—Lucius raised his fist at Marcellus—"To save your ungrateful arse!"

Marcellus knew by the fury in his father's eyes that he was determined to destroy Amren and his queen. He recalled another heated dispute between his father and a political rival. A few days later, the patrician's bloated body was found floating in the Tiber. At the time, he believed his father had no connection to this man's death, but now he wasn't sure. Standing before him was a three-headed chimera speaking from whatever head served him best.

Determined to stop his father from going down a destructive path, Marcellus pulled the scroll out of his sleeve and waved it at him. "Tell me about this! How can we remain in Britannia when the emperor ordered you back to Rome? You can't ignore his decree so you can avenge King Amren for what he did."

Lucius reached for the scroll. "Where did you get this?"

Marcellus pulled it away. "It was in plain sight with your personal belongings."

"You impudent boy!" Lucius shouted. "I brought you here so you could learn how to deal with foreign rulers. But you threw it all away on a foreign whore."

Marcellus shoved his father. "As I said, Catrin is not a whore! I owe her a debt for saving my life."

Lucius shot a seething glare. "And you paid that debt by fucking her! Don't think you were her first. Marrock claims she bewitches men."

"Why should that monster's opinion matter? The issue before us is the emperor. If you defy him, you will be charged for treason."

Eyes ablaze, Lucius slammed Marcellus into the table, knocking scrolls and goblets all over the red-carpeted floor. "You ungrateful bastard, you know nothing of my plan to convince Tiberius otherwise. Who are you to challenge me, boy?"

Marcellus raised his fist. "Back off or I will lay you flat on your back!"

Lucius answered the challenge with a hammer punch to his son's chest. Marcellus gasped from the burning pain in his lungs. He crumbled to the floor, the scroll dislodging from his fingers.

Lucius scooped the scroll into his hand and waved it over a burning candle, setting it afire. The edges of the parchment charred. Smoke filled the room, exacerbating the burning pain in Marcellus's lungs. He pushed himself up to a sitting position, leaned over his knees, and hacked until he spewed bloody mucous.

A bone-chilling growl from the adjacent chamber rumbled into the room, startling Marcellus and his father. They both gawked at the tapestry swaying between the chambers.

Large red-furred paws appeared beneath the fabric. Loud barking and snarls mixed with stomping footsteps and banging metal erupted from the other chamber.

Fear overcoming his pain, Marcellus sprang to a defensive stance.

"Who's out there?" Lucius shouted.

The paws disappeared beneath the tapestry but were soon replaced with leather-strapped boots shuffling back and forth. The emblazoned gold eagle on the crimson tapestry appeared to fly as the fabric whipped back and forth.

A soldier yelled, "Jupiter's balls!"

"Look at the size of that wolf!" another man shrieked.

Decimus's voice shouted, "Corner him and spear him!"

The creature's red-furred muzzle appeared beneath the bottom of the tapestry.

Lucius tapped Marcellus on the arm and handed him a dagger. Marcellus scanned the room for more weapons and cast a glance at his father. "Get me the spear at the back."

Just as Lucius scrambled to retrieve the weapon, the tapestry shot up. A massive beast with bared fangs and eyes glowing like red embers pounced into the room. Panic sheared into Marcellus as the mammoth wolf leapt at him like a red flame of fur.

The next instant, Marcellus found himself under the wolf's lead-heavy paws. Sharp pain spiked through his lungs and he almost passed out.

But then, a powerful force shot into Marcellus like a burning ember. His hand now had a will of its own as he thrust the dagger blade into the beast's underbelly.

The wolf's jaws snapped within inches of Marcellus's face, its demonic eyes devouring him. He felt his hand jerk from the force of stabbing the creature's belly again. A supernatural force controlled his hand's movement as he stabbed the beast over and over again.

When Marcellus heard Catrin's voice cry, "Get away from Marrock," he realized she was the force in his hand.

No time to ponder.

The wolf's fangs lunged for his throat. Panic shot into Marcellus as he imagined his body being shredded. Then suddenly, to his amazement, the creature's weight lifted and its massive body hurled back as if caught in a whirlwind.

With renewed energy strengthening his muscles, Marcellus sprang to his feet. About ten feet in front of him was the dazed, gargantuan beast struggling to get up as two soldiers and Decimus surrounded it.

One of the soldiers threw a javelin at the creature's side. The direct hit did not stop the beast. It jumped upright on its paws. Before anyone could hurl another weapon, the wolf leapt into what looked like fog and disappeared.

Mystified, Marcellus blurted, "What just happened?"

He impulsively looked up to find Catrin floating over him like a translucent cloud. It dawned on him then her prophecy that he would escape Marrock's attack had been fulfilled. Reaching for her hand, he felt her essence radiate into him, but she faded into a hazy mist and her warmth dissipated.

4

WEREWOLF

A bright white light flashed in Marrock's mind. The next instant, he ricocheted off a boulder, tumbled over the ground, and smacked the trunk of an oak. Dazed, he vacantly stared at the crescent moon filtering through the thin clouds as he returned to his human form. Not only did his skin burn as if a thousand wasps had stung him, but his body ached from the pounding of the fall. Raw pain sheared from side to groin. The transformation was more agonizing than usual.

A night breeze finally cooled the fire in his skin, but pain wrenched his belly where Marcellus had stabbed him. Lightheaded, he pushed himself up to a sitting position and squinted, adjusting his eyes to human night vision. The nearby trees looked like shadows of wild-haired crones encircling him. Darting his gaze all around, he had a sick feeling in his stomach when he didn't recognize where he had transformed. His clothing, weapons, and a torch to light his way were left in the forest glade near his home. He must have become disoriented in the magical fog that made him invisible during his escape from the Roman encampment.

The reality that he had to wait until sunrise to ascertain his location made him feel helpless. He clawed some sharp-pebbled dirt into his palm and hurled it. Without a stitch of clothing on, he began shivering in the night's crisp air. Goose pimples erupted on his skin and his teeth chattered.

Looking down, he inspected the swollen abdominal wounds under the light of a silver moonbeam that had escaped through the fog. Blood seeped from the lacerations. Racked with pain, he wearily leaned his head against the tree trunk and reflected on what might have gone wrong at the Roman encampment.

After he had overheard Roman soldiers remarking that King Amren had been secretly exchanged for the son of Senator Lucius Antonius, he couldn't believe his ears. The senator had promised to support Marrock's claims to the throne and retain the king as prisoner. Agrona's scheme to sacrifice Marcellus to the war goddesses—the final act to incite a war between the Romans and his step-mother—must have failed.

Marrock decided to confront the senator about the prisoner exchange. Earlier that afternoon, he had presented his credentials to a Roman guard at the entry gate and asked to speak with Lucius. An idiotic sentry by the name of Quintus, whose face festered with boil-like pimples, told him the senator was indisposed. When Marrock inquired further, the sentry scrunched his face in disgust. "Savage, you don't need to know. Get your hideous face out of my sight!"

Enraged, Marcellus decided to shapeshift into a wolf and snoop in Lucius's headquarters later that night. His wife, Ariene, had described his transformation as colored particles of his human body disappearing into a vortex then reappearing and coalescing into the wolf's form. Using the magical fog to make himself invisible, he crawled alongside the tented walls to the front corner near the flapped entry door. He waited for the opportunity to leap on the unsuspecting Roman soldier guarding the entryway. When the guard leaned his pilum against the tent's front panel to adjust his sandaled boots, Marrock leapt off his hind legs in a burst of gale speed, knocked the soldier on his back, and sank his fangs into the guard's throat. With a fierce wag of his head, he shredded the man's tissue from the spine until he went limp.

Savoring the sumptuous blood in his mouth, Marrock peeked through the entrance flaps. Though he didn't see anyone, he heard the pitched voices of men behind a tapestry at the back.

Marrock dragged the soldier's body inside with his fangs to the shadows of a corner. He hid under the table near the tapestry and listened to the heated discussion of two men. The argument confirmed his father had been released, but to his shock he also learned of the emperor's mandate for all Roman forces to leave Britannia. Even so, Lucius seemed bent on avenging King Amren, giving Marrock some hope the senator would follow through on his promise.

But Marcellus fervently argued against staying in Britannia. Apprehensive that Marcellus might convince his father to leave, Marrock decided then and there to kill the young noble in the disguise of his wolf form. He rammed through the tapestry, but Marcellus was waiting with dagger in hand. Sniffing pus and blood on him, Marrock was confident the young Roman was wounded and at this mercy.

To his dismay, Marcellus stabbed him with a force like no other. He sensed Catrin's essence clamp his jaws shut. Unable to open his mouth, he was helpless as Marcellus repeatedly thrust the dagger into his belly. A hurricane force finally hurled him off. The only way he could escape the onslaught of Roman soldiers was to disappear in his magical fog.

Becoming woozy, he now realized he was losing too much blood. He could barely discern the shadowy trees under the storm clouds as cold rain began spitting on his exposed body. Violently shivering, he thumped his head hard against the tree. The rain came down harder, like shards of ice on his wounds. Panic seized him when he saw rivulets of blood streaming down his groin. He needed to summon his wife to seal the wounds, but was too weak to get up.

Hoping his wolf companions were in earshot range, he howled, yipped three times, and howled again—a signal for his pack to gather at his side. The only sound he could hear was the rhythmic drumming of raindrops against the forest tundra.

Moments later, Marrock finally heard the faint call of his silver she-wolf. In desperation, he lifted his head and howled, but the sound sputtered from his mouth and fell silent. Weakening, he couldn't muster the strength to howl. A deep sadness filled every sinew of his body that he would never be accepted by his kinsmen with his monstrous, pitted face that had been sculpted by Catrin's demented raven warriors. The anguish of his father banishing him dug into his soul. His mind floated into a delirium of chants.

Howl on. Howl on to the faceless moon.
Join me and sing my song of sorrow.
Gather around and heal me with your wet kisses.
Howl on under night's unforgiving fury.

Drifting in and out of consciousness, Marrock saw lustrous silver fur shimmer under a moonbeam. A rough tongue licked his face, and he nestled into the warmth of his she-wolf. Her heat radiated into his icy body. The relentless pain eased and black tranquility overtook him.

When Marrock awoke to loud squeals of children, he slowly opened his eyelids to find his wife hovering over him. Her red-rimmed eyes were filled with tears as she lowered to kiss him.

"Oh, my sweetheart," she said softly, her silver-blonde hair gently falling on his chest. "I thought you were dead when your wolves came to get me."

Looking around, Marrock knew he was safe in his dome-shaped home. He weakly stroked his wife's face and asked, "How long have I been here?"

"I found you yesterday morning," she replied, her voice choking with sobs. "When . . . when you did not return . . . two nights ago, I searched for you. Three wolves approached me, and . . . and . . . I knew you were hurt."

"Something went wrong when I shapeshifted. I didn't know where I was," Marrock muttered, his voice weakening to a whisper.

The sudden appearance of both his sons' ruddy faces and wild red hair over him made him smile. They burst into giggles, but Ariene raised a stern eyebrow and pushed the boys toward two she-wolves that picked them up by the scuff of their necks and took them outside the curtained-off sleeping area.

"How did you get me here?" Marrock rasped.

Ariene gently stroked his eyebrows with her fingertip. "Two she-wolves watched over the boys while I followed your Black through the hard rain. When I found you about a mile from here, the Silver was atop you, shielding you. I treated your wounds as best I could and covered you with blankets. I then got help from our clansman, Alfrid, to lift you on his pony to carry you back."

"What did you tell Alfrid about my injuries?"

"I said you had been wounded by a wild boar," Ariene said, creasing her brow. "But I'm at wit's end as to what really happened."

Marrock explained that he had shapeshifted into his wolf form and was wounded after he overheard Lucius Antonius arguing with his son about invading Britannia.

Ariene shook her head in bewilderment. "I don't understand. I thought the senator's son was being held prisoner at the Cantiaci capital."

"The prisoner exchange was done without my knowledge," Marrock grumbled. "I fear the senator will not help me overthrow my father as he promised. I wanted so much for you to be queen of this kingdom."

"My dear husband," Ariene said softly, "this is only a momentary setback."

"Are you sure?" Marrock said, clasping his wife's hand. "Do you foresee I will still become king?"

Ariene told him of a vision she saw after she had stitched his wounds. "Lightning flashed between three skulls. You placed an antlered crown on your head with bloody hands in front of my father and the senator. They both humbly bowed before you."

"What meaning did you take from this?" asked Marrock, feeling more uplifted.

Ariene held Marrock's head between her hands. "Embrace the powers from your family's skulls and crown yourself with their glory. You must shed blood to take the kingdom that is rightfully yours. Only then will my father and the Romans acknowledge your sovereignty."

Marrock considered what his wife had told him, but still could not fathom how he could do this alone. "I don't know how to do this."

Ariene smiled and rubbed honey balm over his lip. "You will know what to do at the time you must act. For now, I'll give you some herbs that will heal you. Don't shapeshift until you are completely better. The stress of changing into your wolf shape might harm you."

Marrock nodded slightly. "Tell my wolves to stay close by and wait for my next command. Meanwhile, visit the Roman encampment and offer your healing services. Find out as much information as you can about the senator's intent for me."

5

FERREX THE LION

The dread of Rhan's curse had loomed in King Amren's thoughts ever since he had returned to the Cantiaci capital of Durovernum. For almost a week, the image of his headless body, which the dark prophecy had foretold, besieged him with nightmares and denied him restful sleep. Yet the incessant pain from his wounds made it almost impossible for him to bide his time lying in bed to heal despite his wife's scolding, the arch in her eyebrows more fearsome than any warrior he had fought.

A battle-hardened ruler, Amren was resolved to get up and to see how the inscription of Rhan's curse had transformed on the dagger blade. How could he judge Catrin fairly without knowing if, or how, the curse had altered as a result of her changing Marcellus's fate? Even if the curse had not been changed, the fact remained the Roman rogue had almost killed him during the conflict at the prisoner exchange. How could he ever forgive his daughter for allowing herself to be misled by an enemy who only wanted to gratify his lust with her? It was his duty as king to punish every traitor the same. For any other subject in his kingdom, he would show no mercy.

Yet he had also felt the obsessive power of first love for Rhan, who ultimately vowed to destroy him. Tears misted in his eyes with the prospect that he would have to execute Catrin, a daughter who had filled the void in his heart with warmth.

Does cold justice require I overturn my basic instinct to protect my daughter?

Sweeping away his self-approach, he bitterly muttered, "My own flesh and blood betrayed me. Do your duty and get out of bed."

Slowly breathing in and out, he braced himself for the gut-wrenching agony of getting up. As he struggled to a sitting position, nausea hit him like a fist. He retrieved a bowl from the table next to his bed and spewed acrid mucus onto the polished brass surface. After the stomach spasms eased, he scooted to the edge of the bed, dangled his legs over, and took a few more deep breaths to ease the queasiness. He scanned the torch lit bedchamber for furniture he could use as support for his trek to the doorway. Beside the bed was a shoulder-high chiffonier that stored his personal belongings. A small but sturdy table was about five steps in front of the bed. Near the doorway was a spear that he could use as a staff to maneuver down the corridor to his council chambers. There, he could inspect the dagger blade to determine if the etched curse had transformed.

Putting full weight on his bare feet, he pushed himself off the bed to a standing position. He twitched a self-satisfied smile. He took another step, but his bandy legs gave out, and leaning over to grasp the table, he awkwardly fell forward on hands and knees like a toddler learning to crawl. Aggravated with his clumsiness, he cursed the gods through clenched teeth. With great effort, he rocked himself backwards to sit on the wooden floor, muttering, "Damn, damn, damn," as pain surged down his side.

Amren was startled as strong hands lifted him to his feet. He regarded Ferrex, a farm boy turned warrior with the strength of an ox. The young man resembled a lion with his broad-tipped nose and shoulder-length, coppery hair and beard. This lion of a man was reputed to be one of his fiercest warriors.

"My lord, are you hurt?" Ferrex asked.

"I'm fine," Amren grumbled, again frustrated with his helplessness. "Why are you here?"

"The queen asked me to watch over you," Ferrex said, wrapping the king's arm over his shoulder. "Here. Let me help you back to bed."

"Do I look helpless?" Amren snapped. "Get me that spear."

"To do what?" Ferrex asked tentatively. "The queen will have my head if she finds you out of bed."

"I'm the king here! Let her wrath fall on me," Amren grumbled, annoyed the warrior would question his command. "On further thought, you can walk me to my council chamber and we can talk."

"All right then," Ferrex said, furrowing his brow as though it was a bad idea.

Amren disregarded Ferrex's hesitancy and leaned against him for support. He felt Ferrex's strong clasp around his arm as he shuffled one foot in front of the other. The walls spinning around him didn't help his balance as he took the second step on bedridden legs. One foot slipped beneath Amren, but Ferrex stopped his fall by almost yanking his shoulder out of joint. Amren bit his lower lip to muffle his agonized cry as pain stabbed through his belly where he had been wounded.

Ferrex's eyes gaped at Amren. "My lord, are you sure you want to do this?"

"Get me to my chamber!" Amren barked, anger swelling in his chest that the strapping warrior dared question his resolve. He shifted his arm more comfortably around Ferrex's broad shoulder and planted his right foot on the floor to take the next step. After a few more strides, they reached the black oak door, which Ferrex opened. They both straggled through sideways into the arched corridor. The one-eyed resident cat that Amren called Heartless greeted them and dropped a headless rat at their feet.

The last thing Amren wanted to see was a gristly reminder of Rhan's curse that he would meet the same fate as the rodent. He gave the gray-and-black striped cat a weak kick. The fur rose on the creature's hunched back. The mean-spirited cat hissed and bared its teeth. After a few more vicious snarls, the pernicious beast picked up the rat with its teeth and scampered down the corridor with its tail puffed up.

Wide-eyed, Ferrex slowly shook his head. "That is the last thing I would ever want to meet in a battle."

Amren chuckled grimly. "It takes a cunning feline to keep the vermin at bay."

"Aptly said." Ferrex snickered.

Once the cat disappeared, Amren continued his sojourn down the corridor with Ferrex's aid. The shadows of torch flames flickered on the stone ceiling with each of his painful steps. Amren, determined not to show any weakness, pressed his lips together and mumbled, "How's your family?"

"Much better," Ferrex grunted, readjusting the king's weight on his shoulder. "My sister and her husband help my mam on the farm since Pa died. I should be there for the harvest. But my duty is to serve you."

Amren recalled Ferrex's father, Bladud, a skilled swordsman who fought alongside him in the Germanian Roman auxiliary. Slighter than Ferrex, Bladud nonetheless had the speed of a gale storm on his feet and a quick blade that struck like lightning into his foes.

Amren gave Ferrex a smile of approval. "You are just like your father—strong, one of my best fighters. I'll grant your leave when the time comes."

A broad grin broke out on Ferrex's face. "Thank you, my lord . . . my king. Thank you, you are most kind."

They continued down the corridor lined with bedchambers and entered the council chamber. Ferrex steadied Amren as he seated himself at the pentagram-engraved table. Finally settled, Amren waved for Ferrex to leave, but the warrior stood steadfast and opened his mouth like a fish out of water, as if trying to speak.

"What is it, man?" Amren asked impatiently.

Ferrex cleared his throat and lifted his shoulders as if gathering his courage. "I want to speak to you on behalf of Catrin."

Taken aback, Amren fought back his anger that the farmer-warrior had the audacity to approach him about his daughter. Rumors of the warrior's affection for Catrin abounded in the village. Amren was not in a mood to speak with the love-stricken commoner about a political matter as delicate as Catrin's situation. He waved Ferrex off.

The Lion remained steadfast. "My king, I urgently need to talk with you."

Amren frowned. "About what?"

Ferrex shifted his feet. "I was with Cynwrig and his brother when we found Catrin with the Roman . . . after she was stricken . . ." Ferrex paused, his forehead creasing with obvious apprehension.

"Say it!" Amren barked.

"I've always thought highly of Catrin. It pains me to say we found her in the Roman hostage's arms. He was naked, but to her credit she was fully dressed."

"You are speaking of Marcellus?" the king said with contempt.

"Yes, if that is the Roman's name."

The image of the Roman rogue wounding him at the prisoner exchange put Amren into an even fouler mood. He glowered at Ferrex. "Your words do not speak well for my daughter. Is that all?"

Ferrex straightened his shoulders as if emboldening himself to say the next words. "I at first believed the Roman had roughly used her. I found a pelt near where we found them. It was besmeared with blood. Based on this evidence, Agrona accused the Roman of raping her. The Druidess further accused he had given Catrin an amulet that cast a curse on her, making her go mad. Sire, I beg to refute Agrona's claims."

Ferrex lowered his eyes, waiting for permission to continue.

Everything that Ferrex had said reaffirmed Amren's conclusion that the Roman lecher had taken advantage of his virgin daughter. And now, she must suffer the consequences of the rogue bedding her.

Amren seethed. *Why does Ferrex have to prick me with details I already know?* His impulse was to dismiss the young man, but the warrior's persistence piqued his curiosity. "Do you dispute my most trusted advisor's accusations?"

Ferrex swallowed hard, keeping his eyes fixed on the king. "Agrona ordered me to hold Catrin down as she poured a strange-smelling concoction in her mouth. I did as the Druidess commanded in the belief this would help Catrin recover from the amulet's curse. My guts wrenched when I heard Catrin wail as if evil spirits were tormenting her."

Amren grimaced and resituated more comfortably on his stool. "Nothing you have said disproves what Agrona has accused."

"There is more." Ferrex lowered his eyes and his voice cracked with emotion. "It was only after Agrona gave her these elixirs that Catrin went into these mad rants. She was chained like a wild dog and forced to eat food thrown on the floor."

Recalling Catrin's warning about Agrona, Amren felt his stomach twist into a knot. "When did you see this?"

"I was charged with guarding Catrin at the time the queen agreed that Agrona could take her to a secluded cottage in the woods. It was more like a lair where Agrona performed her rituals. She ordered me to shackle Catrin, but I at first refused. Then she explained that Catrin had to be restrained so she wouldn't hurt herself. When I was left alone to guard Catrin, she begged me to free her. She claimed Agrona was trying to steal her powers. Most disturbing, she also told me that Rhan's soul lives inside Agrona."

"Rhan lives inside Agrona," Amren muttered to himself, incredulous his daughter had also told Ferrex this.

"Yes. That is what she said, word for word," Ferrex confirmed. "That is when I began to question Agrona's intent."

"If you were so concerned, why didn't you help my daughter?" asked Amren, anger boiling to the surface that the warrior had waited so long to tell him.

Ferrex contorted his face into a pained grimace. "My Lord, I regret not doing so. But it was my duty to guard Catrin as the queen demanded. I was taught to obey and not question orders."

Amren slapped the table with his hand "And now you risk my wrath by revealing this? Have your feelings for Catrin overtaken your reasoning? Is that why you are trying to sway me to show her mercy even though she betrayed me?"

"My Lord, I do this because I believe you should know all the facts before you judge her too harshly."

"You didn't answer me. What are your feelings for my daughter?"

"I admire her from a distance," Ferrex answered, his face coloring to a bright red.

Amren could not help but admire Ferrex's courage for standing up for Catrin. The warrior, in many ways, was like him as a young king—duty-bound by honor and naïve about power's duplicity. If only this lion had captured Catrin's heart instead of the Roman enemy, Amren would not now be forced to judge his daughter for treason. He shook his head at the irony of how love chooses each person at its whim. Considering what Ferrex had told him, he decided to probe Agrona's loyalty to him. Still, it didn't change the harsh reality that Catrin had recklessly bedded the enemy.

"I will give your words more consideration," Amren finally said. "Now, summon the queen and have her meet me here."

Ferrex gave a thin smile, saluted, and turned on his heels to leave.

6

RHAN'S CURSE

Left alone in the meeting chamber, Amren turned his attention back to Rhan's curse. He gingerly rose to his feet, placing the palm of his hands on the tabletop for support, and lumbered to the back, where he opened the hinged door of the oak cabinet. He rummaged through the shelves until he found the dagger case wrapped in a plaid woolen scarf. He carefully removed the cloth from the case and carried it in both hands to the table. As he leaned over to set the case down, it slipped out of his hands and dropped sideways on the tabletop. The gut-wrenching effort of such a small task almost brought him to tears—a harsh reminder that he yet lived in spite of the Roman's attempt to kill him. He fought through the agony, gritting his teeth to muffle his groans.

Perhaps, summoning Rhiannon was not such a good idea, he thought. She would certainly nag him about his stubbornness of his getting out of bed despite her advice for him to rest. But, if he had gotten this far, *by gods,* he would carry out his inspection of the dagger.

He sat down at the table and turned the dagger case upright to examine the raven inlays on the front panel for any discernible movement. Rhiannon had told him the raven's wings appeared to flap as she had opened the lid to inspect the dagger at the time Catrin had been discovered with Marcellus. The blade had glowed orange-red as if it had just been pulled out of a furnace. Letters began mysteriously etching on its surface. Rhiannon, terrified the curse was altering again, had slammed the lid shut and locked it.

However now, Amren found nothing out of the ordinary on the case's panel. Taking a calming breath, he studied the lid's carving of the three ravens intertwined in a triskelion, symbolizing creation, preservation, and destruction. He tried to lift the lid, but it wouldn't budge. Somewhat light-headed, he couldn't figure out why it didn't open. His gaze shifted toward the brass-winged deadbolt that clasped the lid to the front panel.

"My wife must have the key," he muttered to himself.

Feeling weary, he rested his head on the table while he waited for her. Closing his eyes, he again recalled the anguish he felt for sentencing Rhan to death for conspiring to assassinate him and to take sole sovereignty of his kingdom. He had every right as a king to carry out the judgment and execute her and to force Marrock to witness his mother's death. But the agony of passing a similar judgment on Catrin besieged his heart. No father could love a daughter more than he. He had treasured her like the enigmatic white raven and had done everything in his power to protect her. Yet, her betrayal stabbed deeper into his heart than Rhan's treachery. For any other subject in his kingdom, he would not hesitate to exact the ultimate punishment—death by beheading or fire.

The sound of clicking footsteps into the chamber startled Amren out of his grim thoughts. He lifted his head to find Rhiannon standing in front of him. Her dark hair, plaited and coiled on top of her head, made her seem taller. The clasped azure cape that cascaded over her pearl-white tunic highlighted her royal beauty and elegance—a goddess towering over a mortal king.

"Husband, why are you here?" Rhiannon asked, cocking a stern eyebrow. "Look at your tunic. You've reopened your wounds."

Amren looked down at the tunic's fabric, now tinged yellowish-pink from seeping pus and blood. He smiled stoically at his wife.

"It's only a scratch."

"Only a scratch?" she said, her voice grating with irritation. "You should thank the gods you're alive. What am I to do with you, Amren, tie you up?"

Amren could feel the heat of anger flush into his face. "Woman, don't scold me like a child. I'm useless in bed. The kingdom needs my attention. Besides, I can't wait any longer to inspect the dagger."

Noting his wife's glower, Amren decided to tread more lightly for his next request. "Do you, by chance, have the key to open the case?"

Rhiannon frowned and stretched out the palm of her hand to reveal the key. "Here, take it. Do you still want me to stay?"

A foreboding sense of dread sank into the pit of his stomach as he stared at the case. Even though he didn't want to admit his trepidation of inspecting the dagger, he needed his wife's strength so they could together confront his fate.

"Yes, please stay."

Rhiannon pulled a chair next to Amren and gave him the key. "It is best you open it."

Amren nodded and inserted the key to unlock the bolt. They both simultaneously leaned over and looked in. The dagger was snugly tucked in a cloth-covered groove in the case. The multicolored gems on the dagger's curved handle sparkled in the candlelight.

Amren's heartbeat quickened when he observed that the etching of Rhan's curse now covered more than twice the blade's steel surface than it had before. With shaky hands he carefully lifted the dagger and read the Latin inscription aloud.

"The gods demand the scales be balanced for the life you take today. If you deny my soul's journey to the Otherworld by beheading me, I curse you to the same fate as mine. When the Raven rises out of Apollo's flames with the dark powers of the Ancient Druids, Blood Wolf will form a pack with the mighty empire and fulfill this curse. The Raven will then cast liquid fire into the serpent's stone and forge vengeance on the empire's anvil."

A stark silence fell over Amren as he quietly reread the inscription. Not only had the curse reset that Marrock would behead him, it added that the Raven would forge vengeance on the empire's anvil. The meaning of the altered curse confounded him. He grimly frowned with the acceptance that Catrin had indeed altered the curse by changing the Roman's fate at the prisoner exchange.

After several awkward moments, Rhiannon broke the silence with a shaky voice. "Almighty gods! What does this mean?"

Amren set the dagger on the tabletop. "It is as you feared. The curse has reset that Marrock will behead me." He brushed his forefinger over the blade's etched surface. "I'm not sure what it means that the Raven will forge vengeance on the empire's anvil and how this connects to Marrock."

"Vengeance . . . empire's anvil," Rhiannon said in a hushed tone. "Is Catrin the Raven?"

"It seems so," Amren said with profound sadness.

Rhiannon clutched a hand over her breast. "This can't be. Not our Catrin. She foolishly succumbed to a foreigner's sexual desires, yet I can't believe she would wittingly betray us and carry out the Roman Empire's vengeance on us, if that is what it means."

Amren also could not fathom Catrin becoming so vile she would ally with Rome to exact vengeance on their kingdom with no compunction. "Perhaps we are making false assumptions about what the curse means."

The king paused again to study the inscription, rubbing his forefinger over each etched word, hoping to decipher the truth. "There is a change from the original curse that gives me hope. It doesn't say the Raven will join forces with Marrock to overthrow me. What if Catrin is not the Raven, but it is someone else? We could be wrong assuming Apollo's flames represent Catrin's all-consuming passion for the Roman. Until we know for sure, we should cling to the hope that we can still stop this dark prophecy."

Rhiannon gave him an anguished look. "If that is so, do you still plan to accuse Catrin of treason?"

Amren gazed at the burning candle, his thoughts wrestling again over how he would judge Catrin, a daughter he still held close to his heart. "This makes my decision even harder. But how can I forgive Catrin for sleeping with the Roman enemy? The words, 'The Raven will forge vengeance on the empire's anvil' could actually mean that Catrin has taken the first step to side with the Romans against us. She could have unknowingly revealed secrets to Marcellus that could aid the Romans in attacking us. As far as I'm concerned, her actions are treasonous—plain and simple."

Rhiannon's face paled. "It breaks my heart that her blind loyalty to Marcellus could incite her to betray us."

Amren gave a heavy sigh. "It also tears at my heart. As I think more about the curse, it makes sense that Catrin is the Raven. Did you know she has the ability to change the Future?"

Rhiannon's eyes widened. "No. She only told me that her raven guide had given her new powers. She also said Rhan had possessed Agrona, but I thought that was impossible. Everyone had seen you execute Rhan."

"I also didn't believe Catrin when she told me about Rhan," Amren said. "But now, I think otherwise. Ferrex just revealed to me that Catrin also told him that Rhan lives in Agrona. I remember Rhan's head flying into Agrona's outstretched arms. Rhan could have possessed her then or shapeshifted into her form."

Amren paused, considering about what Ferrex had revealed. "Did you know about Agrona's cruelty after she took Catrin to her cottage?"

"I never visited her," Rhiannon said with a tinge of bitterness to her voice. "Instead, I assigned Belinus and Ferrex to guard Catrin while Agrona performed her healing rituals to remove her evil spirits. Right before the prisoner exchange, Catrin mentioned Agrona had drugged and chained her. But then, Catrin and I had a nasty argument. I told her that she might have to kill Marcellus to save you at the prisoner exchange. She refused to do so, saying she loved him. I was so enraged by her blind loyalty to the Roman that I didn't give the notion that Rhan possessed Agrona any further thought."

Amren frowned. "I also didn't give any credence to what Catrin said about Agrona. Yet, when Ferrex confided in me that Agrona had drugged Catrin to make it appear as if Marcellus had cursed her, well, I . . ." The hairs on Amren's neck prickled as he mulled over the possibility his most trusted spiritual advisor was the essence of Rhan.

"What were you about to say?" Rhiannon asked after a few awkward moments of silence.

"I must find the truth as to whether Rhan possessed Agrona. And if so, did Rhan alter the curse and not Catrin?"

Rhiannon clasped the king's hand. "If that is so, you can't judge Catrin for treason. You need to condemn Agrona . . . or Rhan, whoever she is . . . for treason instead."

Amren hesitated. "We need more proof that Rhan embodies Agrona. I will question Belinus and Ferrex further about what they observed in Agrona's domain. As for Catrin, the facts speak for themselves. She betrayed me!"

Tears swelled in Rhiannon's eyes. "Oh, Amren, now that we suspect this about Agrona, I beseech you not to judge Catrin too harshly. It would tear me apart if you condemned her to death. Let me remind you our eldest daughter, Vala, is still held as a prisoner by the Romans." She clasped Amren's wrist and pled, "You can't execute Catrin. I couldn't bear losing two of my daughters!"

Reminding himself that it was his duty as king to execute all traitors, Amren wrenched his wife's fingers off his wrist. "Catrin's actions thunder treason. Not only did she betray us when she slept with Marcellus, but she also altered my fate when she saved him. Her decision almost cost me my life. She showed more loyalty to the Roman enemy than she did for me."

"It was never Catrin's intent to betray us," Rhiannon argued. "She is young and foolish. I beg you to show her mercy."

Amren could feel his jaw tighten with the rage unfurling inside him that his wife would reproach him for performing his god-given duties as a king. "I will judge Catrin the same way I judge any traitor in my kingdom. I can show no weakness as a king. Not for my daughter . . . not even you. If that means I condemn Catrin to death for her treason, I will do so! It is my right as the king."

Angry tears rolled down Rhiannon's reddening face. "I can't believe how your heart has turned to stone."

The queen's words troubled Amren, but he would not compromise his obligations as the rightful king. He pounded his fist on the table to emphasize the point. "I will not show Catrin any mercy unless she grovels before me in complete submission. She must beg for my forgiveness and swear her fealty to me. She must demonstrate her loyalty through actions . . . not through empty words!"

"Then, my king, how do you judge Agrona, if she is indeed Rhan?" Rhiannon said sharply. "She is a Druidess with dark powers. Have you not considered she bewitched Catrin and Marcellus to fall passionately in love with one another, so she could recast the curse?"

Pain shot into Amren's belly from the stress of arguing with his wife, inflaming his anger further. "Gods above, do you think that has not crossed my mind? Rhan escaped death once . . . she could do it again."

Rhiannon glared. "What? Are you afraid of Rhan?"

"Of course not," Amren snapped. "But we can't let Agrona suspect we are digging out the truth about her."

A painful spasm in his belly almost brought Amren to tears. Not wishing to argue further, he clicked his fingers and rasped, "Enough! Go fetch Ferrex."

Rhiannon shot a nasty glare. With deadly silence, she stood up and stamped out of the chamber.

Amren was left in utter misery that he would have to contend with her again. Thankfully, Ferrex poked his head through the doorway and inquired, "Do you need help back to your bed?"

"What do you think?" Amren grumbled, feeling decrepit.

7

APOLLO AMULET

For over a fortnight, Catrin had been held as prisoner in her bolted, windowless bedchamber. A single candle dimly lit her makeshift cell. The musty room reeked of fumes from the chamber pot that was emptied only once daily. Isolated, she reflected night and day on what she had told herself before making love to Marcellus.

I would rather burn in the moment than live the rest of my life in the cold ashes of a loveless marriage.

Her desire was momentarily fulfilled with Marcellus, but at what cost? She was now like a caged animal living in its own filth, awaiting sentence. After the shame and humiliation she had experienced, death was now a welcome guest. Banishment would be worse than death. She would be a blight that had to be eradicated from everyone's memories in her kingdom. Her ill repute as a traitor would follow her everywhere. The prospect of losing her family's love and respect tore at her heart. Had her choice to love Marcellus been fated in Rhan's curse? She often wondered. Agrona had, after all, admitted sprinkling aphrodisiacs on the wolf pelt upon which they had made love.

Even now, she couldn't block her memory of Marcellus. Every time she visualized his eyes burning the hottest of blue flames when he proclaimed, "I choose you, Catrin," her heart raced. The pit of her stomach still fluttered as she reminisced about the pledges they made one to another to be husband and wife before Mother Goddess. The power of his kiss as they consummated their marriage would be forever etched on her lips.

Marcellus was her soul mate and she could sense whenever he was in danger.

A fortnight ago, she had dreamt Marrock in his shapeshifted wolf form attacked Marcellus. Even though the Ancient Druids regarded the ability to change the Future as dark magic, she had done so again and had travelled to the Wall of Lives in the Raven's mind and pulled his life-thread out of the portal leading to the Otherworld. As she rewove his life-thread into the fluid tapestry, she empowered Marcellus with superhuman strength to escape Marrock's deadly jaws.

Catrin pulled the amulet out from beneath her tunic to gaze upon its features. She sighed ruefully. The marble figurine of Apollo, armed with bow and arrow, had been chiseled in the likeness of Marcellus. He had given her the Apollo amulet as a gift, saying "Keep Apollo close to your heart. Whenever you look at him, remember it is I who loves you and will protect you."

Though he had pledged his love for her, he cautioned, "Our families will never accept our marriage."

She never considered the consequences of giving herself to Marcellus in the throes of passion. Her heart had always overruled reasoning. Yet, her father's revelation that Marcellus had wounded him fractured her heart. Her decision to alter the Future so she could save Marcellus almost cost her father's life.

Tears welled in Catrin's eyes and the Apollo's white-stone face blurred. "Marcellus, why aren't you here to protect me from my father's wrath?"

A sudden click of the bolt on the door jolted Catrin out of her grim muse. She fumbled to hide the amulet beneath her tunic as her mother, Queen Rhiannon, appeared at the doorway. Behind the queen was a shadow of a man cast on the corridor's stone wall.

Rhiannon spoke to someone behind the door. "Let me speak with my daughter before you escort her to the king."

A man's voice quavered, "You must hurry, my queen. You know how impatient the king is."

Rhiannon whispered something incomprehensible to the man on the other side. Catrin, anticipating her mother was the bearer of bad news, slowly rose like a ghost from her chair. She folded her hands to stop them from shaking and squeezed her fingers until they became numb. After her mother finished speaking with the man, Catrin asked, "Am I to be executed now?"

"No, but your father wants to speak with you before your trial tomorrow," Rhiannon replied. "This will be your only chance to redeem yourself in his eyes."

Dumbstruck, Catrin didn't know how to respond.

Rhiannon closed the door and moved closer. "Your father doesn't know I've come here. Listen closely if you want to live. Approach your father with utmost humility. Show him remorse for what you have done. Blame Marcellus for seducing you. Say he took advantage of your youth. Plead with your father that you will do anything to win his favor back. He needs something tangible from you to show he can trust you again."

"How can I do this?" Catrin asked.

"Despite his anger that he believes you betrayed him by sleeping with the Roman enemy, he is a man driven by reason. He will bend if you offer him a way to get Vala back."

"I've been so concerned about what will happen to me that I didn't think about Vala still being imprisoned by the Romans," Catrin said, ashamed.

"Think of a way you can tug Marcellus's heartstrings to get her back," Rhiannon said with urgency in her voice as footsteps could be heard coming down the corridor from outside. She clasped Catrin's shoulders. "Promise me that you'll not tell Father I've spoken to you."

"I promise," Catrin said, "but do you trust the guard outside?"

"It's Trystan," Rhiannon assured. "He won't tell your father I've spoken to you."

Catrin gave a slight nod, keenly aware of her mother's earlier affair with Trystan, who had fathered Vala.

"Know this, more people support you than you realize," Rhiannon added. "But alas, the king is your final and sole judge. Give him a reason to grant you mercy."

The voices of two men conversing outside the room sent a shudder through Catrin. Her mother looked wide-eyed at the door and whispered, "Someone is with Trystan. I'll hide in here until I'm certain no one sees me leave."

Trystan announced from outside, "The king has summoned you, Catrin."

Rhiannon hid behind the door as it clicked open.

Catrin swallowed hard to release the tightness in her throat. She stumbled on her first step toward the door. Struggling for composure, she entered the arched corridor and followed another king's guard while Trystan waited beside the chamber's door.

As she walked between the lines of burning torches on the stone walls, she noticed the striped resident cat proudly displaying its new victim beneath it claws.

A baby raven!

Catrin felt her stomach drop. A sense of dread crawled down her spine as she approached the king's meeting chamber at the end of the corridor. The guard opened the door for her, and she tentatively entered the chamber.

The king was seated on a high-backed chair at a round table. He greeted her with a nasty scowl. Recalling her mother's instructions, Catrin dropped to her knees and spread the palms of her hands forward as a gesture of supplication.

Amren considered her for a moment. "I summoned you so we can speak before your trial tomorrow. As king, my first loyalty is to my people. They expect me to administer a just penalty for anyone who commits a crime against the kingdom. As you are well aware, the sentence for treason is death. What do you have to say before I judge you tomorrow?"

Catrin lowered herself face-down on the floor and humbly pled, "My king, my father, grant mercy on your foolish daughter. I fell for the wiles of Marcellus. I never intended to betray you."

"Rise, my foolish daughter," Amren said with sharp edge to his voice. As Catrin rose, the walls spun around her. She lowered her eyes to the floor that appeared to be moving under her feet.

"Did you honestly believe this Roman had true feelings for you?" Amren asked, frowning. "He is from a foreign empire where men consider women chattel."

Catrin hesitated, carefully considering her next words. "Please forgive me. He took advantage of my youth. My only desire now is to regain your trust and love."

"Look at me!" Amren snapped.

Catrin looked at her father's narrowing eyes.

"As you know, the Romans hold Vala," Amren said. "I fear for her life. Even though Senator Lucius Antonius planned to ambush us at the prisoner exchange, he blames me for the conflict. He would like to spike my head in vengeance for the loss of his soldiers. I'm in a dilemma. We have five Roman soldiers we can exchange for Vala. I'm leery that the senator can be swayed to barter his men for Vala."

Following through on her mother's advice, Catrin said, "Marcellus can help us."

Amren's brow creased. "Why should he help? He almost killed me."

"I'm baffled he did this," Catrin admitted. "Yet Marcellus saved me from a deathblow from one of the commanders. I know he still loves me . . ." She bit her lower lip, recognizing her words could be used against her.

Amren's eyebrows perked up. "Can we use this love as an advantage to get Vala released?"

Catrin took the Apollo amulet off her neck and handed it to her father. "Marcellus gave this to me as a symbol of his love. Return the amulet to him and press the demand that if Vala isn't released, you will execute me for treason. I know in my heart he will do everything he can to save my life."

Amren studied the marble figurine. "This is the Apollo amulet that Agrona insists the Roman bewitched you with?"

"He gave it to me, promising he would protect me. He doesn't share his father's ambitions to invade our homelands."

Amren winced. "Why didn't you tell me about the senator's plans to invade our homeland sooner?"

"You didn't give me a chance," Catrin said more bluntly than she had intended.

Amren gave a thin smile. "You have a point. Even so, you've confirmed my suspicion that the senator has loftier ambitions than placing Marrock on the throne." The king lifted the amulet and studied it for a moment. "Would Marcellus go as far as defying his father to spy for us?"

"Yes . . . I think so. But you are asking him to betray his people."

Amren grimly chuckled. "Would you gamble your own life on the bet that Marcellus will betray his father to save you?"

"My life is already a thin thread in your hands," Catrin retorted. "You have nothing to lose, but everything to gain if you take the bet that Marcellus will do anything we ask to make sure I'm not harmed."

"Indeed." Amren paused, lifting his eyes in deep thought. His stare then pierced Catrin. "Every ruler is forged by the choices he makes on whom to trust. If you judge Marcellus correctly, this could sway how I judge you."

"If Marcellus releases Vala, will that be enough to regain your love and trust?" Catrin asked, a glimmer of hope lifting in her chest.

"Once you lose love and trust, it can't be earned back with the snap of fingers," Amren said sharply. "There is still the matter of Rhan's curse. Tomorrow, I will show you how the inscription of the curse transformed on the dagger. You must reflect on how your choice to change the Future to save Marcellus impacted the curse and the fates of others. You used a forbidden power reserved for the gods. Your pathway to redemption will be based on the next choices you make and your ability to assess a person's true character. As a ruler, if you make one wrong decision, you may not be given another chance. You must not only convince me you deserve mercy, but you must also persuade my people to take you back."

Emboldened she had been given another chance to redeem herself, Catrin said with conviction, "I will do everything to win back your love."

"I'll hold you to that promise," Amren said with a glum smile.

8

TRAITOR'S WALK

"Bring in the prisoner accused of treason," the king's guard announced, opening the massive door for Catrin to enter the Great Hall. As she entered the wood-beam vaulted chamber, she noticed the spiked skulls on the stone walls looking down at her with empty eye sockets. She had not given the skulls much attention before. They were nothing more than wall decorations that greeted visitors. Some of the jaws of the skulls gaped open with fear while others gritted their teeth in pain. The various skulls were once heads of formidable rivals from other tribes or treacherous nobles within her father's circle.

Catrin wondered how her small skull would look among the others.

Her eyes shifted to the pathway opening for her in the midst of nobles, warriors, Druids, metalworkers, craftsmen, mothers, children and elderly—townspeople she had counted as friends, who now viewed her as a traitor. She could feel the weight of their judgmental eyes crushing on her chest as she slowly approached the royal thrones elevated on a dais. Her parents were waiting for her there.

The long skirt of her emerald-bodiced dress made it cumbersome for Catrin to put one foot in front of the other without tripping. She studied her parents' faces. They were like iron masks of hard justice that made her pause before taking the next step forward.

At least, she tried to reassure herself, *I'm not shackled as a common criminal.*

The crowd was as quiet as a grave, unlike at most trials, where the people clamored for justice. The spectators gazed at her with grim faces similar to the skulls on the wall. She could sense their quiet rage of disapproval for her betrayal. She could not deny the charges she had slept with the enemy. How could they ever understand how strong her love was for Marcellus? Their bond had been forged by the gods.

Approaching the thrones, Catrin reflected on the conversation she had earlier with her father. She shuddered, not knowing if and how she had altered Rhan's curse.

In the corner of her eyes, Catrin caught a glimpse of Agrona shuffling out of the crowd toward the thrones. The despicable Druidess ascended the three stairs and stood beside the king. Bitterness gnawed at her that Agrona, the embodiment of Rhan, still served as her father's spiritual advisor at her trial.

Agrona should be on trial for treason. Not me!

From the back of the chamber, a child's voice shrilled, "Cut off her head!"

A chill struck down Catrin's back as other voices from the mob rumbled in the chamber like claps of thunder.

"Traitor!"

"Sorceress!"

"Trollop!"

"Whore!"

Catrin felt like an insect trampled under the wrath of her people. With growing angst over how the king would judge her, she felt paralyzed, barely able to move one foot in front of the other. Looking down, she realized that she was wearing the same dress she'd had on when she first met Marcellus earlier in the spring. She pulled the heavy fabric off the floor with her trembling hands. *Just three more steps*, she told herself. *Don't let Father see any weakness.*

Squaring her shoulders, she tightened her calves and clamped her heels on the wood plank floor so she would not waver but present a stoic mien. The shadows of torch flames cast up the gray walls like the quavering arms of hooded executioners. She inhaled deeply and steadily took her final step to the front of the dais to await her father's next command.

King Amren, a broad-shouldered man of short stature, rose like a colossus from his throne. He stepped to the front of the platform and said nothing.

Catrin warily lifted her eyes to meet her father's ice-cold stare.

Amren's baritone voice thundered, "Catrin, you stand accused of treason. Every person in my kingdom is held accountable for his or her actions—most of all, anyone in my family." The fiery torches near the skulls on the wall reflected on the king's eyes as he grimly announced, "Witnesses gathered here will attest that you willingly slept with the Roman enemy called Marcellus Antonius. This Roman gave you a marble figurine of Apollo, his patron god. This talisman struck you down with the falling sickness. My spiritual advisor claims this is a sign evil spirits possessed you. You assaulted the queen before you were taken away by Agrona to cast out these demonic forces. Princess Catrin, come up here and stand beside me to face your accusers."

Catrin hadn't adequately prepared herself to hear the gut-wrenching accusations. The mob appeared to wave back and forth as she climbed the first step to the thrones. Her legs felt weighed down as she cautiously ascended the second step, firmly planting the sole of her shoe before lifting herself onto the third step.

On the dais, Catrin noticed the raven-inlaid wooden case that her father held. She recalled seeing the hand-crafted container when the king first revealed the inscription of Rhan's curse on the blade. At the time, he revealed the curse had changed shortly after she fought off Marrock's attempts to transform her into a wolf to join his pack. He also told her that the original curse had foretold she would join Marrock in his quest to overthrow him. The altered curse prophesied she would rise out of Apollo's flames as a raven with the powers of the Ancient Druids. The original dark prophecy foretelling she would join forces with Marrock had been obliterated. The king had previously told her that this change had given him hope that Catrin could break Rhan's curse by conjuring powers of the Ancient Druids.

Catrin pulled out of her thoughts when her father again addressed the assemblage of villagers.

"Before I bring forth the witnesses to testify, I order Catrin to kneel before me and kiss the dagger I present to her."

As commanded, Catrin dropped to her knees and humbly lowered her head. She almost crumbled under the weight of the cold metallic blade on her head. Deeply ashamed, she wanted to disappear into the depths of her anguish. Lifting her gaze to the king, she could tell by the deep crease on his pallid forehead that he was in significant pain. She wondered if the pain was due to the wound Marcellus had inflicted or she was the cause.

Amren leaned forward and spoke to Catrin in a softer voice that nobody could hear. "I want you to kiss the blade and silently read the inscription. Only you and I will know how Rhan's curse has altered. No matter how harsh my sentence is today, the judgment you place on yourself will be far worse."

Catrin's eyes filled with tears. "Please, Father."

As Amren extended the dagger for her to kiss, his face remained expressionless as stone. The blade felt hard and cold on Catrin's lips.

"Take the dagger from my hand and make the curse your own," Amren said.

Catrin clasped the dagger by the blade and pressed its razor-sharp edge into the palms of her hands until it cut into the skin. Overcome with shame, she pressed the blade's tip against her throat as a gesture she would take her own life if the king so commanded.

"Lower the blade and tell me what it says."

9

RISE OF THE RAVEN

Choking back her sobs, Catrin dropped her bleeding left hand aside and clasped the jewel-crusted pommel with her other. She lifted the blade to her eyes and silently read the entire inscription. Taken aback by the changes in the curse, she again read it line by line, trying to interpret its meaning before moving to the next. The first lines directed to the king remained the same as the day of Rhan's execution, when she cast the curse.

The gods demand the scales be balanced for the life you take. If you deny my journey to the Otherworld by beheading me, I curse you to the same fate.

Catrin shifted her gaze toward Agrona, now standing behind the king. She knew the Druidess was the vessel for Rhan's soul. Looking at the blade again, Catrin could not stop her lips from quivering as she mouthed the words of the new lines that were directed at her.

When the Raven rises out of Apollo's flames with the dark powers of the Ancient Druids, Blood Wolf will form a pack with the mighty empire and fulfill this curse. The Raven will then cast liquid fire into the serpent's stone and forge vengeance on the empire's anvil.

Catrin felt her temple throb as she mulled over how the curse had altered this time. The original prophecy that Marrock would behead their father had reset. Although the curse was now unclear as who was the Raven, Catrin assumed it was she. It was not until she was consumed in the fiery passion of Marcellus that her raven guide revealed how she could foresee and alter the Future on the Wall of Lives—a forbidden power of the Ancient Druids.

Yet there was still hope. The prophecy she would join Marrock to overthrow their father had not reset to the original curse. Catrin surmised she broke that part of the curse when she thwarted Marrock's attempts to transform her into one of his wolves.

The king gently touched Catrin's head and leaned closer to whisper, "Put the dagger in the case. You must accept the consequences for your decision to sleep with the enemy. The past is locked in place, but I believe you can still change your fate by the decisions you make today."

Change my fate, Catrin repeated inwardly, wondering what choice the king expected her to make that day. Encouraged, she grasped the dagger's curved, jewel-crusted pommel and set it on the gold brocade cloth in the case. The inlaid ravens on the case seemed to flap their wings as she closed the lid. Lifting her head, she stared steadfastly into her father's eyes and awaited his next command.

"Rise and face your accusers."

Catrin searched for familiar warriors she had fought alongside at the prisoner exchange. She wondered if Cynwrig, with the tattoo of a blood-red bolt of lightning striking down his arm, would testify against her. Renowned for cutting off heads of his enemies with one swing of his battle axe, he was known as the Red Executioner. Most warriors painted their bodies with blue woad, but Cynwrig had artisans tap ochre dye with sharp-bone needles into his arm. His chest and back were brightly decorated with depictions of the thunder god, Taranis, hurling bolts of lightning at sea monsters and stick-figured warriors.

Next to Cynwrig was his cousin, Belinus, a sun-tattooed guard engaged to Catrin's sister, Mor. The warrior never hid his disdain for Marcellus, admitting he would have enjoyed killing the "Roman scum" slowly. Catrin thought it odd that Mor was not there. Neither was the king's second-in-command, Trystan.

Amren announced, "The first witness is Queen Rhiannon."

As her mother rose from the throne, Catrin felt as if her heart splintered apart. She couldn't believe her own mother would testify against her.

"What light can you shed on the charges against Catrin?" Amren queried.

Rhiannon cleared her throat. "It is with a heavy heart that I must tell the truth that Catrin slept with the Roman enemy. More than once, she begged me to allow her to escort the Roman around the countryside when he was our guest . . . uh, I mean hostage. I could tell by the way he leered at Catrin that she should be on guard for any entry into her gates."

Laughter broke out in the crowd. Catrin lowered her head in humiliation. A sob caught in her throat.

Amren raised his voice, calling for order. The chamber fell silent.

Catrin nervously watched her mother brush some dark strands of hair from her forehead before she continued her testimony.

"I told Catrin that you contracted her to marry Adminius. I emphasized you had made this pact so Cunobelin would hand over Marrock to us. She pleaded I allow her to ride with Marcellus outside the fortress walls one last time. I agreed only if Belinus was with them. But alas, she tricked Belinus and rode off alone with the Roman."

A soot-faced blacksmith in the crowd blurted, "And where did Belinus venture off—to be with Mor?"

Bright red with anger, Belinus lunged into the crowd and punched the blacksmith in the face.

The king stomped his foot and roared, "Enough of this! No more interruptions!"

After Cynwrig pulled Belinus off the blacksmith, the spectators settled down.

Rhiannon turned to the king and said with a sigh, "Thank you." She continued her testimony with a glint of determination in her eyes. "Cynwrig told me he found Catrin in Marcellus's arms. She had been struck down with Apollo's affliction. Marcellus was dressed like a newborn."

Laughter erupted from the crowd at the back, but the king's icy glare silenced them. He turned to the queen. "Explain to everyone what Apollo's affliction is. Tell us if Catrin was clothed."

"Agrona told me Marcellus's patron god, Apollo, cursed Catrin with the falling sickness," Rhiannon answered, clasping her hands and averting her eyes from Catrin. "Cynwrig can address how Catrin was dressed."

"He will have a chance to speak after you," Amren affirmed. "What happened next?"

"When I questioned Marcellus about what happened between Catrin and himself, he confessed that they had pledged their love as husband and wife before Mother Goddess. I imprisoned him, suspecting he had forced himself on her. Just before the prisoner exchange, Catrin also admitted she loved Marcellus."

The crowd's voices buzzed like flies on a rotting carcass. King Amren raised his voice above the loud chatter and called Cynwrig to the platform to give his account.

With his red hair tied back like a horse's tail, Cynwrig clomped up the stairs, bowed to the king, and turned to the audience. In a loud, gravelled voice he said, "On the day we found that Roman scum and Catrin, I was hunting boar in the forest with Ferrex and Gavin. I heard Catrin shout, 'Get away.' I thought she had been attacked by some kind of predator. Moving in the direction of her voice, I found two horses grazing. Nearby, we finally found the Roman with his cock hard and growing."

The reaction from the crowd was a mixture of gasps and chuckles, but the noise died down when Amren glowered at Cynwrig.

"Leave your opinion out of this. Just give me the facts."

Cynwrig grimaced. "Forgive me, my king. That is what I saw." He again faced the crowd and his voice grated with anger as he continued. "The Roman was naked. Catrin was clothed but white as fresh snow. The idiot Roman couldn't speak our tongue, so I didn't question him. Needless to say, I suspect the Roman raped Catrin."

"Do you know this for a fact?" Amren growled.

"No. That is my opinion . . . my king!" Cynwrig said, straightening his shoulders. "After that, I returned Catrin into the loving hands of the queen. That is all I have to say."

Amren irately dismissed Cynwrig with a wave. Cynwrig descended the stairs with the same heavy footsteps as he had climbed them.

When the king announced, "The last witness is my spiritual advisor, Agrona," Catrin felt as if her stomach was sinking in a bog from which she couldn't escape.

10

AGRONA'S TESTIMONY

Catrin watched Agrona slink to the front wearing a silver wolf-headed pelt over her shoulders. She was sure the sorceress would lie so her father would sentence her to death. Agrona met Catrin's eyes with a sneer. She then turned to the audience and spoke in a deep, smoky voice.

"On the day Catrin was brought to me, I knew by her ranting that she had gone mad. I found the figurine of Apollo around her neck—a sure sign the Roman cursed her with his god. I told the queen that I needed to take Catrin to my domain, where I kept my strongest herbs, to remove the evil spirits. Despite my efforts, these demons used her voice to rant that fire-breathing eagles will burn down our village. Catrin insisted her Roman lover would descend as the sun god and rescue her from the firestorm. Further, Catrin admitted she hated her parents for demanding she marry Adminius. She slept with the Roman in revenge for what they had done. In doing so, she revealed secrets to him that would aid the Romans in pillaging our kingdom."

The people began chanting, "Off with her head. Off with her head."

Amren raised his hand to calm the spectators and asked Catrin bluntly, "Did you have sex with the Roman enemy known as Marcellus? Tell the truth."

Catrin nodded, her throat constricted with fear that telling the truth would lead to her doom.

"Did you disclose any information that could threaten our kingdom?" Amren asked with a frown.

"No. I did not," Catrin answered resoundingly.

Amren creased his brow, as if considering his next move. "Are you now cursed?"

"I was never cursed," Catrin said adamantly. "Agrona drugged me so it appeared that evil spirits possessed me."

Amren pressed his lips into a firm line. "Even so, you consented to lie with the Roman enemy. You did this knowing I was negotiating your betrothal with Adminius in exchange for Cunobelin's agreement to hand Marrock over to me."

Catrin nodded and nervously wiped the beads of sweat off her forehead.

The king pointed a finger at her. "By your own admission, you slept with the enemy. Though it may not have been your intent to betray me or your people, your actions nonetheless have harmed us. This is an act of treason, plain and simple."

Catrin met her father's stare with teary eyes. "I have convinced Marcellus that our cause was just. He promised to speak to his father about Rome forging an alliance with you instead of Marrock."

"Nonetheless, by sleeping with the enemy," the king said with fevered pitch, "you unleashed a series of unfortunate events that could ultimately lead us to war against Cunobelin, the Roman Empire, and Marrock. Your intentions do not save you; your bad decisions condemn you."

Gasping for air, Catrin felt as if she had been spiked in the chest. She dropped to her knees and fell face down, her arms spread like wings before her father's feet. Following her mother's instructions to submit completely to her father for any hope of clemency, she pleaded, "I beseech you, my king, grant me mercy. My heart ruled my decisions, not my head. If you must condemn me, condemn me for my human frailty. But know this, I did not betray you."

King Amren said nothing, but Catrin could feel his steel-cold eyes probing her for the truth. She rose to her feet so she could look him in the eye when she addressed him.

"You said I would be judged by my actions. Give me another chance to prove my loyalty to you. I will forsake all men and serve as a warrior in your army. I will protect you with my body and die by the sword, if need be.

I promise you my complete fidelity so long as you live. Let the gods decide my fate and strike me dead if I ever waver on my oath to you."

The king gave a sly smile and stepped to the front of the podium. "Is there any champion who will train my cursed daughter as a warrior on the condition he will suffer the same fate as her if she fails to keep her oath to me?"

Catrin gaped at her father. It was as if he had steered the proceedings for this outcome.

The room became as silent as a forest at dusk just before a storm. King Amren paced back and forth, looking over the crowd. "Is there no warrior brave enough to accept my challenge?"

A man's voice rose above the crowd. "I accept that challenge."

"Step forward and identify yourself," Amren commanded.

Catrin looked toward the direction of the sound of boot steps striding heavily on the chamber's wood-plank floor. The people parted like a wave to allow a pathway for someone to come through. To her utter surprise, a warrior called Ferrex swaggered out of the midst of the throng. Wild, coppery hair bounced off his shoulders like a lion mane as he bounded up the stairs and landed as quiet as a cat on the platform. The hard-bodied warrior grasped Catrin by the arm and slightly bowed his head to the king. Dumbfounded, Catrin stared at Ferrex, a man she hardly knew. Warm blood surged into her face when she met his feral, hazel eyes. She acknowledged him with a nod.

After the clamor died down in the chamber, the lion-faced warrior proclaimed, "I am Ferrex, the son of Bladud. I accept your challenge to train your daughter. I do not condone her misdeeds with the Roman but can say with certainty that she is not cursed. I am here to claim Catrin's innocence on this charge. Agrona ordered me to hold her down while forcing a foul-smelling mixture down her throat. It was only then Catrin ranted and appeared mad. You have been deceived by a spiritual advisor with whom you've placed your full trust."

At the base of the dais, Belinus declared, "I attest what Ferrex said is true. In a secluded cottage in the woods, Agrona shackled Catrin like a wild beast and forced her to drink elixirs smelling of blood and shit. At the time, Catrin tried to convince me that Rhan lived in Agrona's body. I thought her crazed and did not believe her. I reconsidered her story after Agrona ordered me to sacrifice Marcellus while the queen was away negotiating your release. After the prisoner exchange, I asked Trystan if anything strange had occurred at Rhan's beheading. As you know, he had witnessed the execution as a boy on the verge of manhood."

"And what did Trystan say?" Amren asked.

Trystan strode from behind the throne and joined Belinus at the front to proclaim, "My lord, I told Belinus that after Rhan was executed, her severed head slipped through Agrona's arms before it fell on the ground. I also informed Belinus that Rhan was a shapeshifter and thus everything Catrin had told him must be the truth."

Overcome with emotions of gratitude that these three warriors supported her, Catrin choked back tears. These warriors had previously expressed their disdain for Marcellus yet supported her testimony that Rhan possessed Agrona.

The final surprise was that Mor strode out of the crowd to stand beside Belinus. Attired as a warrior in a chainmail shirt and trousers, she proclaimed, "Everything that the king's guards have said is true. Catrin may have foolishly given her heart to a foreigner, but she never betrayed the king or our people. It was Agrona who tried to stop Catrin from revealing who she truly is."

Wild-eyed, Agrona pounced at the king like a wolf and clenched him by the arm. "These are blatant lies. I'm not the one on trial here. It is Catrin who betrayed you. She confessed that she has learned the black magic of the Ancient Druids to bring you down. She has cast spells on these warriors so they will lie for her."

Amren wrenched Agrona's hand off his arm. "No, it is you who stands condemned. You held my daughter as prisoner so she would not reveal the truth of who you truly are. I know the eidolon hiding behind your eyes is Rhan. And for years, you have lured me into your web of deception. It is Catrin who opened my eyes as to who you truly are. I sentence you to death." He gestured toward his guards who had supported Catrin's claims. "Trystan and Belinus, apprehend Agrona. Shackle and imprison her until her execution."

Stunned by her father's swift judgment, Catrin felt her jaw drop as the men trampled up the stairs and restrained Agrona by her arms. The Druidess fought back, kicking and shrieking, "You will regret this, Amren! The curse is set in stone. You will die headless . . . a butchered animal, a sacrifice on my altar. You can't stop the curse. Catrin cannot save you! Only I can!"

"Take her away," Amren snapped.

Belinus and Trystan dragged Agrona down the stairs as she continued to fight fiercely against her restraints and to shriek curses. After they disappeared through the entrance doors, Catrin noticed her father's hard stare as he charged Ferrex, "Train Catrin to defeat every warrior in the kingdom. Teach her a ruler is bound by duty to her people."

Amren then shifted his glacial blue eyes toward Catrin. "Your pledge to be a warrior has determined your fate not to die today. But make no mistake. I will not grant you any mercy for your reckless liaison with the Roman enemy. The repercussions of what you did will haunt you for the rest of your life. Today, I banish you from my sight. Ferrex will train you at his family's farm until such time I deem you ready for my final judgment. Before I take you back, you must first prove you are worthy of my respect and love."

Just at the moment Catrin believed she had won back her father's love, she felt her heart wrench from the anguish that he had betrayed her even though she had told him how to maneuver Marcellus into releasing Vala. The king must have known she feared banishment more than death. She would be isolated and shunned from everyone she loved just as Marrock had been. With tears in her eyes, she wanted to shout this was not fair, but something inside told her to be strong. Accept her father's punishment with dignity. Demonstrate she was worthy of his love again.

Catrin cringed when her father clenched her wrist and handed her over like an animal to Ferrex. "Take my daughter and train her. I will summon you when needed."

As Catrin followed Ferrex down the stairs, she resolved to prove her father wrong about her loyalty. She would do whatever was needed to earn his trust again.

II

KING AMREN'S MESSAGE

Marcellus entered the new officer's tent where his father had banished him to avoid any further escalating arguments about invading Britannia. The musky-smelling tent had been furnished with a cot, a shelf for storage, a small wooden table, and a couple of foldable chairs. He sat at the table and nervously inspected the wax imprint on the rolled parchment that a local merchant pitching his wares had just secretly handed him. Recognizing King Amren's family insignia of the triskele of horses, he apprehensively broke the seal and unrolled the scroll near the flaming lamp on the table.

As he read the king's proposal for him to meet with his commander, Trystan, to negotiate the release of Vala for five Roman prisoners, he wondered if it was a ploy to murder him. After he reread the king's message two more times, he racked himself with guilt because he had endangered Catrin with their intimate liaison. He recognized the king was using the threat to execute Catrin for treason as leverage to force him to comply with the conditions of the proposed clandestine meeting.

The message was blunt. Only Marcellus could negotiate the exchange of Vala for the five captured Romans. The king openly mistrusted his senatorial father. And who could blame him? Even the soldiers in the encampment grumbled about his father's blunders with local rulers and his penchant for angering them.

Marcellus had to act quickly, though. His father had ordered him to sail back to Rome before the fall equinox in a fortnight. The king's demand for Vala's release would be almost impossible without the aid of Tribune Decimus, who oversaw her imprisonment. With the widening chasm between his father and Decimus, perhaps Marcellus could take advantage of the situation and convince the tribune to carry out the prisoner exchange, even if it meant deceiving his father.

A battle-hardened military commander, Decimus had disclosed to Marcellus that he was torn between his conflicting loyalties to his father and Emperor Tiberius. If Decimus didn't obey the emperor's mandate to return his forces to Gaul by the fall equinox, he could be reprimanded for insubordination and stripped of his military command. Conversely, Marcellus's father had repeatedly threatened Decimus, "I can easily find commanders in camp who will serve me as loyal and obedient dogs."

Further, the tribune had openly expressed his apprehension that the soldiers held captive under Amren would suffer horrific deaths. A highly religious man, Decimus had sacrificed an unblemished lamb earlier that week and beseeched, "Most powerful Apollo, god of light and divination, I offer you this succulent lamb in return for a sign of how I can obtain the release of my men."

Later, the highly superstitious Decimus remarked that a raven perched on Marcellus's tent was an omen that Apollo would soon answer his prayers. Perhaps, Marcellus thought, he could show Decimus the way.

An announcement, "The local healer is here," jolted Marcellus out of his contemplation. A guard entered the tent with a noticeably pregnant woman with a strawberry-colored birthmark over half her face.

Surprised to see the healer, Marcellus asked, "What happened to the Greek medicus?"

"He told me this local healer could help the swelling on your wound with magical herbs," the guard replied.

Marcellus raised an eyebrow. "Can she speak our language?"

The guard shrugged. "I don't think so. Do you want me to send her away?"

"No, have her stay," Marcellus snapped, annoyed the medicus had not come. "Did you summon Tribune Decimus to my quarters?"

"I did. The tribune will be here shortly after he talks with your father."

"Tell the guard outside to let the tribune in when he arrives."

The soldier saluted and left the tent.

Marcellus took off his tunic and sat on the cot for treatment. The silver-haired woman spread out an assortment of supplies on the table and prepared a greenish mixture in a bowl. Leaning over Marcellus, she removed his bandage and carefully applied the pasty ointment on his bruised chest. He flinched from the burning sensation of the dressing, but the discomfort gradually eased by the time she finished.

Pleased with the treatment, he asked, "What is your name?"

The diminutive woman smiled at him but did not seem to understand. Marcellus pointed to himself and said his name. The ivory-complected woman said, "Ariene."

"You have a nice touch," Marcellus said, trying to gesture his meaning.

She nodded and smiled.

Just then, Marcellus recognized the voice of Decimus outside, announcing, "I'm here to see Marcellus Antonius."

"Tribune, he is with a local healer," the sentry replied.

"It doesn't matter," Decimus snapped. "I'm in a hurry."

The entrance flaps flew back as Decimus entered the tent. He acknowledged Marcellus with a nod and regarded the healer for a moment.

"Why did you summon me here?" Decimus said gruffly.

"I need to talk with you in private."

Decimus pointed to the woman. "Do you know who she is?"

"A local healer the medicus sent," Marcellus said.

Decimus looked at the woman. "Do you speak our tongue?"

"A little," she said in a childlike, squeaky voice.

"Finish your task. Then leave us," Decimus demanded with a glare of suspicion.

Marcellus gave Decimus a quizzical look, but the tribune stayed quiet as the healer finished bandaging his wound. After she collected her supplies and exited the tent, Decimus repeated, "Do you know who she is?"

Marcellus shrugged. "I was told she is a local healer with magical abilities."

"She is Marrock's wife," Decimus said curtly, "And I doubt she is here for your benefit."

"Well . . . if that is the case," Marcellus said, inspecting his bandage, "I'm glad she's gone. I have to admit, though, the dressing she put on the wound helped the pain. It's hard to fathom a woman with such gentle hands could be married to that monster."

Appearing jittery, Decimus silently stepped to the entryway and pulled back the flap.

Ariene was there with a shocked look.

"Why are you still here?" Decimus barked.

The words fell out of Ariene's mouth like thick honey. "I wait. Help Masulas. Need me heal."

Decimus waved over an infantryman from outside. "Escort this woman out of camp. Then go find Quintus and tell him to get back now to stand guard. Is that understood?"

The soldier snapped his heels together and saluted. "Understood."

Decimus stared through the doorway as Marcellus cautiously put the tunic over his bandaged chest. The tribune finally looked at Marcellus.

"What's this secrecy about?"

Marcellus, hearing some men's voices from outside, gestured for Decimus to move closer and told him in a hushed tone, "A local merchant delivered a message from King Amren to me."

Decimus's eyebrows perked up. "Why was it delivered to you?"

"That is why I summoned you here. The king is concerned about the safety of his eldest daughter. He wants to exchange her for five of your men he captured."

Decimus squinted. "Have you discussed this with your father?"

Marcellus rubbed the corner of his mouth, considering how to broach the subject of his plan to deceive his father. "Normally I would follow standard procedures, but King Amren demanded I keep this from Father. And he has good reason."

"Explain."

"Father blames Amren for the conflict at the prisoner exchange, but I know it was his intention to break the agreement and recapture the king and Catrin. He holds you culpable for failing to do this. He also accuses you of disloyalty because you've confronted him about disobeying the emperor's mandate to leave Britannia."

Decimus glowered. "Get to your point."

"I know you to be an honorable and loyal commander," Marcellus flattered, "and that you would do anything to get your men back. But as you know, my father stands in the way. He wants to start a war with Amren. This war has nothing to do with the glory of Rome. This war is about my father's pride. Amren also knows this about Father and that is why he approached me about getting Vala back."

Marcellus paused, regarding Decimus's stone face. "I need your help."

"What do you want?" Decimus asked bluntly.

"I would like you to make the honorable choice," Marcellus said, grasping the tribune's arm. "Exchange Vala for your men without my father's knowledge."

Decimus's eyes widened. "You are asking me to betray your father. There must be another way to convince your father to do the prisoner exchange."

"How do you think my father will react if I tell him Amren secretly approached me about the prisoner exchange? He will take this as an insult. You know him. He is vindictive and will stop at nothing to avenge those he believes have humiliated him. What do you think Amren will do to your men if we don't make the arrangements?"

Decimus shook his head. "I can't imagine."

"Oh yes, you can," Marcellus said, looking Decimus straight in the eyes. "The Cantiaci will sacrifice them to their war goddesses. They will first cut out their guts while they're yet alive. Then the king's Druids will study how their victims' bodies jerk in the throes of death for omens. Is that what you want?"

Decimus fingered his sword hilt and said with a biting tone, "Lucius would feed his own mother to the wolves if it served his ambitions."

"Exactly."

"There is a complication," Decimus said. "Your father has ordered me to crucify Amren's daughter. You need to convince him otherwise so we have time to make the arrangements."

Marcellus sighed. "Father is ready to disown me. He may not listen to what I have to say."

"Despite what you think, you have influence over your father," Decimus insisted. "If I don't carry out the execution, he'll have others do it."

"Why don't you trick my father instead?" Marcellus suggested. "Tell him you killed Vala but burned her body. He pays little attention to details. He won't even know when your freed men have returned."

Decimus nervously scratched the back of his neck and looked away. "Lucius can see through me when I'm lying. His wrath will fall as fast as an executioner's axe on me if he ever discovers the deception."

"All right then. I'll find a way to convince him or divert his attention elsewhere. If he finds out, I'll take the blame for all of this."

"Are you sure about this?"

"Yes."

Decimus seemed more reassured. "How do we move forward?"

Marcellus finally revealed, "Amren demands I meet with his commander tonight."

"Tonight? So soon?"

"We need to move quickly," Marcellus said. "Further, you need to accompany me. The message said Trystan would meet us just after sundown at the same location where you and my father previously negotiated with Queen Rhiannon for the king's release."

Decimus lifted his eyes. "Jupiter's bolts! What have I got myself into?"

Marcellus thought the same about the tribune but masked his concern with a smile. "I can think of no one else better than you in negotiations."

Decimus stared at Marcellus with deadly silence.

"Well, it appears you agree," Marcellus chuckled. "Why don't you arrange for the horses?"

The tribune nodded and muttered beneath his breath as he exited the tent.

12

ROMAN SPY

Just before sunset, Marcellus rode alongside Decimus through the tower gates of the Roman encampment. A thin veil of fog hovered over the landscape—a sign for more evening rain. The stabbing pain had returned to Marcellus's chest, making the ride difficult. As they rode on the sodden pathway, Marcellus wrestled with his gnawing guilt that he had jeopardized Catrin's life.

After a while, they veered their horses onto a pathway into the dense eastern woods. Hearing an ominous raven's shriek, Marcellus glanced at the thickening fog swirling above him like a crone-faced wraith. A chill pierced his bones, making him shiver. He tightened the cloak around his shoulder and remarked, "The fog is a bad sign. It will be hard to see Trystan."

"I'm sure he'll let his presence known. What do you know about this Trystan?" asked Decimus.

Marcellus reined his horse closer to Decimus. "Do you mean can he be trusted?"

"That and how we deal with him."

"I've seen two sides of him," Marcellus replied. "He can be as loyal as a hunting dog to Amren but has a quick temper. If you recall from our first meeting with the king, Trystan was ready to rebel if Amren agreed to our demands."

"I do remember that," Decimus said with a nervous chuckle. "I mostly recalled the sun-tattooed guard who was eager to take your head as a trophy."

Sensing that someone was watching them, Marcellus reined his horse to a halt and stared through the darkened trees for any movement.

"Do you see him?" Decimus asked in a hushed tone.

"I thought I heard something, but it was probably nothing but some animal," Marcellus said, urging his horse forward.

"I found it odd how frequently Trystan glanced at the queen during our first meeting with the king," Decimus mentioned.

"Do you think they are lovers?"

Decimus shrugged. "Who knows?"

A gigantic oak towering over the other trees came into view and Marcellus halted his horse. "I think this is where we are to wait for Trystan's signal."

Not long after, an arrow whizzed within inches of Marcellus and startled his horse. He gently pulled on one rein to turn the horse's head, to settle it down, then looked in the direction from where the arrow had been released.

A figure strode through the fog now tinged pink from the setting sun. Unsure if it was Trystan, Marcellus unsheathed his gladius and shouted, "I am Marcellus Antonius."

A man's voice echoed, "Who's that with you?"

"Tribune Decimus Flavius," Marcellus replied. "He is aiding me in the prisoner exchange."

"The king never agreed to this," the man shouted. "Why should I trust you?"

"We'll drop our weapons," Marcellus offered, then turned to Decimus and said, "Be on guard."

After they dropped their weapons, Trystan approached them through the trees. Marcellus noted the commander's chestnut-brown hair was shorn in the Roman style, but his bare chest displayed a warrior's ferocity with blue-tattooed raptors and lightning bolts striking from their talons down his belly.

Trystan greeted them with a nod and gestured for them both to follow him. They dismounted and pulled the reins of their horses as they trailed

Trystan into a thick, wooded area. The fading crimson light of the setting sun barely filtered through the treetop canopy, making it difficult for them to see clearly. Their boots slipped on the moss-covered tree roots that undulated like serpents above the ground. A campfire in a glade soon came into their sight.

Decimus and Marcellus seated themselves on a fallen log before the crackling flames while Trystan sat across from them on a tree stump. In the illumination of the fire, Marcellus noticed Trystan's eyes frequently shifting from Decimus to him as he initiated the conversation.

"King Amren sent me to negotiate his eldest daughter's release," Trystan announced. "The king does not trust Senator Lucius Antonius to keep his promises. That is why he asked you, Marcellus, to be here instead."

Trystan's eyes blazed from the flames as he shifted his stare to Decimus. "You were not invited."

"As the commander of the soldiers you hold prisoner, it is my utmost duty to make sure they are released unharmed," Decimus said firmly. "I oversee Vala's imprisonment and will escort her to the prisoner exchange."

Trystan regarded Decimus for a moment, then stepped around the fire to hand Marcellus the marble figurine of Apollo. "My king asked me to return this to you."

The image of Catrin's blue-green eyes lighting up after Marcellus gave her the Apollo amulet came to his mind. He swallowed back his emotions as he fingered its leather straps.

Decimus leaned over to inspect it. "Isn't that yours?"

"Yes," Marcellus said, hesitant to say anything about the special meaning it held for him. How could he explain to a battle-hardened soldier that he had given his family heirloom to a foreigner as a symbol of his love?

"My king accuses you of giving this to Catrin to bewitch her so you could seduce her," Trystan said brusquely.

Marcellus heaved with anger at the accusation. "If your king believes this, why did he ask me here to negotiate?"

"A good question—one I asked myself," Trystan admitted. "But I serve the king and do whatever he commands. Amren wanted me to press upon you that Catrin has been condemned to burn at the stake for her liaison with you. If you love her, as you confessed to the queen, you will agree to spy for us in exchange for her life."

Dumbstruck by the demand, Marcellus felt his mouth drop like the tribune's. Before he could respond, Decimus lashed out. "This is an insult! We are here to arrange a prisoner exchange, not serve as your spies."

Trystan said evenly, "I'm only the messenger. And this message is meant for Marcellus."

Decimus opened his mouth to argue, but Marcellus clenched his wrist and glared at him, shaking his head not to say anything. Decimus pressed his lips into a firm line.

Marcellus then turned to Trystan. "You tell the king I know about his curse inscribed on a dagger. I gave the amulet to Catrin to protect her from its dark spell. We are both victims of its dark prophecy. I am also branded as a traitor for having saved her life at the prisoner exchange. You tell your king that Catrin is falsely accused. The blame lies with the curse that his former queen cast at the time he executed her. Nonetheless, I love Catrin and will do anything the king demands to make sure she is not harmed."

Marcellus could feel the tribune's disapproving stare and turned to meet his probing eyes.

Decimus spat at the fire and mouthed, *"What are you doing?"*

Marcellus could imagine Decimus thinking that he was heading down the same self-destructive path as his great-grandfather, Mark Antony. Only this time, a Celtic princess would bring him down.

"The king expects you to keep that promise, Marcellus," Trystan said.

"Only if he spares Catrin," Marcellus said, emphasizing each word. "If any harm comes to her, I will personally carry out Rhan's curse on your king. Is that clear?"

Trystan smirked. "Understood."

Decimus ripped the amulet from Marcellus's hands. "What are you doing? You can't agree to this. This amulet is making you say these things. Throw it away and let us leave now!"

Trystan scowled and rose to his feet. "I should have never trusted either of you two."

As the commander began walking away, Marcellus said, "Wait while I speak with Decimus."

Marcellus grasped Decimus's arm and pulled him away. He blasted hot air into the tribune's ears as he said, "You want your men back, don't you?"

Decimus nodded, clenching his jaw.

"Trust me on this!" Marcellus demanded.

Decimus looked down at the amulet as he rolled it in his hand. "At least have a priest inspect the amulet for any sign of blemish that an evil spirit possesses it."

"If that will ease your mind, I'll have a priest bless it," Marcellus said, struggling to temper his voice.

"Agreed," Decimus said hesitantly, giving the amulet to Marcellus. "But I want words with you about this afterward."

The tribune then walked up to Trystan and leveled his eyes at him. "What guarantee do you give that there will not be any surprises during the prisoner exchange?"

Trystan smiled. "Right now, five warriors have arrows pointed at your heads. If I had sensed any treachery, you would both be dead."

Marcellus interjected, "And that is your guarantee?"

"No. This is the king's warning," Trystan retorted. "No one has more reason to kill you than my king. Yet today, he showed his mercy by not killing you. Be forewarned. He will not show that mercy again if you don't meet his demands. As for you, Marcellus, you must leave Britannia and never contact Catrin again after you release Vala."

"Marcellus wounded the king in the heat of battle," Decimus barged in with fevered pitch. "Marcellus was also seriously injured, but he came here at the risk of his life to advocate my men's release."

Trystan bared his teeth like a wildcat ready to pounce on his prey. "And here we are . . . arguing over nothing. How do you say it in Rome? *Quid pro quo*: Vala for your men. This time, you must keep your promise."

Decimus finally relented. "I am only doing this because my men are like brothers to me. Bloodshed will not help anyone's cause. But if you betray me, I promise we will meet again."

Trystan scowled. "I look forward to it. Now for the terms—"

"First, these are my terms!" Decimus blurted. "I want utmost secrecy on what we agree here. I'm risking my career, even my life if Senator Lucius Antonius finds out. He has ordered me to execute Vala. And if I release her, as you demand, I could be crucified for my insubordination!"

"I support Decimus on this," Marcellus added.

Trystan leveled his eyes at Marcellus. "Fine, we are in agreement on this. Now these are my conditions. You must release Vala at the next full moon. I'll send you word of where the exchange will take place. But before we free your soldiers, you must first release Vala unharmed to us."

Decimus again asked, "What guarantee do I have you will release my men?"

"I leave you no other choice," Trystan said. "And further, Marcellus must be at our beck and call to soothe any hostilities between Senator Lucius Antonius and my king, and to spy for us."

Marcellus could feel the tribune's eyes probing him for an answer. He knew Decimus wanted him to say no to Trystan's demands. His throat clenched, as if a noose had tightened around his neck, as he agreed to what Trystan demanded.

Later that night, Decimus confronted Marcellus in his quarters. "Why did you agree to spy for Amren? It's bad enough we are deceiving your father to get my men back."

"No one asked you to spy for Amren," Marcellus said.

"What you are doing is outright treason," Decimus accused. "The only reason I can think you agreed to Trystan's demands is because the amulet cast a spell on you."

"This has nothing to do with the amulet," Marcellus insisted.

"Then why did Amren return it?

"He must have taken it from Catrin to sway me."

The tribune's eyes widened. "Then it is the Celtic princess who bewitches you through the amulet. What else can explain why you would betray Rome to save her?"

Marcellus glowered. "Catrin befriended me and saved my life. I accept the blame for what happened to her. I want to return the favor."

"You lovesick fool!" Decimus blurted. "You already returned that favor when you attacked Centurion Priscus at the prisoner exchange to save her. By your own admission, you would do anything—even betray Rome—to save that sorceress's life."

Marcellus came within a few inches of Decimus. "Careful, Tribune, we are both traitors in this together. If we are to work together, we need to be truthful with each other. I know you fear Catrin's mystical abilities, but can't you understand how a man can lose his heart to such a woman?"

Decimus unexpectedly wrapped his arm around Marcellus. "I understand how a man can lose his heart to the right woman. But Catrin is no ordinary woman, is she? She is a sorceress, as I warned you."

"She is an oracle who can see into the future," Marcellus revealed.

"Did you ever see her do magic with that raven?" asked Decimus.

"Raven?"

"The raven perched on her arm at the ritual when we first met Amren," Decimus clarified. "Is that Apollo's raven that sends messages directly to her? Does she have a special connection with the sun god through the amulet you gave her? Can she harness Apollo's powers? I am told Druids call upon their guide animals to help them from the spiritual world."

Marcellus gave a nervous chuckle, realizing the superstitious tribune might have a more self-serving interest in Catrin. "I must admit her powers sometimes confound me."

Decimus's eyes grew big. "Did she summon those demonic ravens that attacked us at the prisoner exchange? I've never seen forces of nature like that."

Marcellus pulled away from Decimus, growing uneasy with the tribune's obsession with Catrin's powers. "You are probably right. She must summon forces from the Underworld. Why are you asking me these questions?"

"I've been wondering if the large wolf that attacked you and disappeared into a fog was not of this world."

"That was Marrock," Marcellus admitted, hoping the tales of monsters in Britannia would reinforce the tribune's decision to deceive his father so they could leave the fantastical isle. "He most likely summons dark forces from the abyss of Hades itself."

Decimus's jaw tightened. "Tell me what kind of sorcery we're dealing with Marrock."

"Catrin told me that he could shapeshift into a massive wolf that can snap a person's neck in one crunch of his jaws."

"Does Catrin have these mystical powers?"

Becoming disconcerted with Decimus's continued questioning, Marcellus said, "As I said, she can see the future through raven-sight."

"Did she ever do this in your presence?"

Marcellus nodded. "When we hunted together, she spotted the prey first. Not only is she an oracle, she is a formidable warrior. She can best most men with the accuracy of her spear throws. Why do you ask?"

"Just curious, that's all," Decimus said, lifting his eyes as if in deep thought. "What a deadly combination, a woman who is both a sorceress and warrior."

"I'm not sure where this conversation is going," Marcellus finally said. "Do I have your support or not?"

"Yes. You have my absolute support."

13

BANISHMENT

Every muscle in Catrin's body ached. For a fortnight, she had conditioned and sparred with Ferrex using a sword, spear, or battle-axe and had harvested waist-high wheat with a scythe, swinging it to and fro to cut the base of the stems. The daily warrior's ritual began by waking at dawn and eating gruel for breakfast. After sunrise, she jogged the perimeter of the farm, then halted to draw circles in the air with the point of the sword: first clockwise, then counter-clockwise, each circle becoming smaller and smaller. After that, she practiced swinging her sword at a pole: overhead, sideways, and undercut. The morning session ended by sparring with the ox-strong Ferrex who chanted his mantra: lunge and thrust, step back and defend. Just when she was ready to collapse from exhaustion, she renewed her energy with a noon meal of cheese, bread, and berries. From afternoon to sunset, she cut wheat stalks, bundled them, and heaved the bales into a wagon.

The repetitive motion of sword fighting and harvesting made her muscles cramp and lock up at night, often waking her. Adding to her misery were the pungent odors of urine from freshly dyed wool and smoke rising to the thatched ceiling of the round house.

Quarters were cramped. Ferrex, his younger brother, and older sister's family, consisting of her husband and three children, slept together in the back. Their loud snoring, talking, and grinding teeth often woke Catrin in the darkness of early morning. She most dreaded the nighttime, when she was alone with her thoughts. She longed for the comforts of her previous life, when she slept on a straw mattress in the privacy of her bedchamber and the sweet scent of lavender calmed her to sleep. Though she should be grateful that her father spared her life, she missed Mor's giggles, her father's warm embrace, and mother's gentle kiss.

But most of all, she missed Marcellus.

She should despise him for almost killing her father at the prisoner exchange, but she was now drowning in a shipwreck of conflicting emotions over him. She did not know how to stop loving Marcellus without destroying herself. Their love had been forged into a hardened bond when they had pledged themselves as wife and husband before the Mother Goddess. Now that she had altered his fate to die young, wasn't she still obligated to keep her promise to be with him whenever death tried to claim him again? She had already saved him twice, the first time at the prisoner exchange and the second when Marrock's jaws were clamped around his throat. Her essence had guided his hand as he thrust the blade into the underbelly of Marrock's wolf form.

Saving Marcellus's life had catastrophic consequences, condemning Catrin as a traitor and banished. The shame would follow her for the rest of her life, unless she redeemed herself in her father's eyes.

And the only way she could do that was to forsake Marcellus.

She exhaled ruefully. *Move on. Accept I'll never see him again.*

To escape her melancholy, Catrin decided to sneak out before anyone awoke so she could bathe at the river without Ferrex there. Her father had given him strict orders to guard her at all times, as tensions between the Romans and the Cantiaci were escalating. Although Ferrex's gruff voice and hard slaps on the back were meant as encouragement during practice, his lingering gaze disquieted her. She didn't want to deal with his attraction for her.

"The Lion," as everyone called Ferrex, was as different from Marcellus as a wild beast from a gallant stallion. Ferrex was crude while Marcellus was eloquent and a considerate lover. She loved Marcellus's soft skin and fresh, musky smell after he shaved. Ferrex was disgustingly hairy. She cringed at the assortment of cheese particles, bread crumbs, and meat chunks often trapped in his beard. Most of all, she could not stand his awful, sweaty stench that made her gag, particularly after a hard day of weapons training and harvesting.

The only good thing about him, she conceded, was he was a stern, supportive mentor and spoke the truth as sharp as a razor-edged sword. She had learned sound battle tactics from him and ways to regain her father's respect.

But she needed to be away from his eagle eye.

Making sure everyone was asleep, Catrin tiptoed across the room and escaped through the flapped doorway. As she walked briskly to the river about a half-mile away, the cold gray clouds flamed to a fiery crimson as the sun began its ascent in the eastern horizon.

Finally reaching the river, she gazed at the shimmering blue water, which reminded her of Marcellus's deep-set eyes, so piercing that he could disarm her every time he gazed at her. His eyes were the hottest of blue flames whenever he drew her into his arms. He had a strong chin and dimpled, boyish grin. Though she had publicly proclaimed to forsake all men and to defend her father's kingdom, she broke that vow whenever she relived their intimate moments in daydreams. A profound sadness weighed on her chest as she recalled the bittersweet moment at the prisoner exchange when he accused her of betraying him. How could she have known that her own mother didn't trust her and had warriors ready to ambush the Romans? She sensed he knew that she had saved him from the death's arrow. Nonetheless, she had to endure the consequences for altering the future. She had to focus on winning back her father's approval and becoming his champion.

Feeling grimy, Catrin pulled down her plaid trousers and scrunched her face in disgust as she noticed the dirt-caked splotches on her calves. At least her legs were toned and her belly rock-hard from training.

Ready to bathe, she dipped a foot in the frigid water and began shivering. At home, the servants had always poured hot water into a tub, a luxury she had taken for granted. Bracing herself for the plunge, she dove into the water and bobbed up, clutching her chest with crossed arms. With goose-pimples erecting on her skin, she quickly rinsed off any visible dirt and dunked her head to rinse her hair. She then waded back to the shore, dreading the prospect of getting back into her soiled clothes.

After she stepped on shore, she closed her eyes from the glare of the bright sunlight, stretched her arms upward, and wiggled her hips to capture every drop of sunshine on her skin. She bent over to retrieve her clothes, but then to her embarrassment, she caught sight of Ferrex gazing at her. He must have caught full sight of her womanly backside. With warm blood surging into her face, she abruptly lifted and yelled, "Ferrex, what are you looking at?"

Ferrex mischievously smiled and turned his back on her.

"Hmm . . . the birds and the bees."

Catrin put on her soiled woolen trousers while keeping a close eye on him. "You shouldn't have followed me."

Ferrex shrugged. "I had the same mind as you . . . to bathe in the river." His back muscles appeared to wink as he chuckled.

Catrin felt her face broil with anger. "That is not funny." She quickly put her tunic on and brushed the wet hair back from her face. She moaned at the thought that the Lion had seen her perform a "twisty dance" for his entertainment.

"Don't worry, Raven," Ferrex said brusquely, "I've seen plenty of naked women, old and young, bathing here. There's nothing special about you."

Catrin mumbled to herself, "Why does he call me 'Raven'?"

Finally composed and fully dressed, she told Ferrex to turn around. He burst into laughter and swaggered with a big grin toward her. She seethed at his arrogance. He treated her like one of his cattle.

Reaching Catrin, Ferrex narrowed an eye and scolded, "You know I'm to be with you at all times. You are bait for the Romans, who would like to snatch you for ransom. If you want to wash up, have me escort you."

"I wanted to be alone," Catrin said sharply. "Besides, I don't like being cooped up like a chicken in your home. Everyone snores and clicks their gums, keeping me awake."

"Get used to it, Raven. This is how peasants live. During times of war, you'll be stuck in close quarters with other warriors."

Catrin blazed. "Call me by my name. I'm not your raven."

Ferrex smirked. "Don't you get your magic from the raven above us?"

Catrin heard her raven's shrieks, but she did not respond to it. She demanded, "You will call me Princess Catrin, is that understood?"

Ferrex cracked a smile and said with a tinge of sarcasm, "Whatever you want . . . most gracious highness, Princess Catrin. Milady, what weapon would you like to strike me with today . . . tongue or sword?"

Realizing her snide comment would only result in harsher training, Catrin tempered her voice. "Let us talk with civil tongues."

Ferrex cocked an eyebrow and regarded her for a moment. "What do you want to talk about?"

"You've put me through a gauntlet of warrior's maneuvers, but you've never told me what qualities a commander must have to lead an army."

Ferrex pointed to a fallen tree. "All right, then, I'll answer your questions over there."

Catrin sat on the rough-barked log, but as Ferrex sat too uncomfortably close to her, she scooted sideways from him.

He gave her a wicked grin. "I won't bite. We might as well be friends. We're together day and night."

She glared. "I'm not your friend! You have one task, and that is to train me. I don't know why you volunteered to do this. Sometimes I wonder if Father and you made these arrangements before my trial."

Ferrex chuckled. "Your tongue is as sharp as a whetted blade. In answer to your question, I spoke to your father before the trial. I told him how Agrona had drugged and mistreated you. I felt badly that I had not helped you escape her cruelty. I thought training you to be a warrior would be a way to redeem myself."

Catrin dropped her eyes, regretting she had been so rude to Ferrex, but she did not want to admit this to him. "You should be ashamed of yourself. I will always resent that you held me down as Agrona forced potions down my throat. There is nothing more humiliating than to be proclaimed mad. I felt the whole world was against me."

Ferrex frowned. "What did you expect? You never denied coupling with the Roman, what's his name?"

"Marcellus," she snapped.

"Why should anyone trust you after you slept with a foreigner?"

The bitterness in his tone made it sound as if she had personally betrayed him.

"It was never my intention to betray my father. And I don't believe Marcellus meant to hurt him."

Ferrex bit his lower lip as if clipping off sharp words. She could see the longing in his eyes but didn't want to encourage his affection. Though he was crude and sharp-tongued, she had to admit that he was loyal to a fault—definitely a warrior she would want at her side in battle. Averting her eyes from his gaze, she said, "Why should it matter to you what happens to me? I've been harshly judged but have accepted my punishment."

"Your father is still judging you," Ferrex retorted. "He asked me to watch you for any sign that you have forsaken Marcellus as you pledged at the trial."

Catrin felt a deep heaviness in her heart as she again thought about the Apollo amulet entrusted with her father to sway Marcellus. Becoming melancholic, she scooted further away from Ferrex and looked the other way.

Ferrex touched her arm. "I've seen your sadness at night. Is this because of the Roman?"

Disquieted with his question, Catrin shrugged. "There are many reasons I'm sad. I've accepted I will never see Marcellus again. My only purpose now is to win back my father's favor and prove to him I'm worthy of his love."

"Let me answer your original question of what I value in a leader," Ferrex said. "The first quality I look for is courage. I want a ruler who is willing to die with the warriors he leads. The last thing I want to see is a king, a queen, or any noble retreat from battle in fear."

Curiosity piqued, Catrin asked, "What other qualities must a commander have?"

"I want a leader who inspires me and gets in ditches with me, enduring the same hardships as me. A commander should also have good wits and make wise decisions. I don't want a leader cowering in the outer wings of his army in defeat because of bad choices he made."

Catrin perked her head up. "What about me, a woman? Would people follow me?"

"People follow rulers with visions of greatness for their kingdom and for them. Even though I'm a commoner, your father elevated me in his royal guard. I would do anything for that man to pay back his generosity. He treats me with respect, yet he demands great things of me. He listened when I approached him about granting you mercy."

"Do you expect me to respect you as well?" asked Catrin.

Ferrex grimaced. "Yes, but you treat me with disdain. You should show me more respect for my loyalty to you."

"And how do I do that?"

Ferrex inched closer to Catrin. "Acknowledge I've given you a chance to redeem yourself by training you. Show me that you can reach your full potential."

"Have I not taken the first step?" Catrin asked, tilting her head back. "Have I not trained with you without complaint?"

"There is more you can do," Ferrex said. "I've been told you have magical powers and can see the future. People follow anyone who can speak with gods for guidance. Whenever I see you with your raven guide, I know you are communicating with these divine forces."

Catrin smiled, thinking Ferrex had more insight into her magical abilities than what she had first assumed. "I can join my thoughts with the Raven's and see everything it does as it flies over the countryside."

Ferrex's eyes widened with awe. "That is quite something. What else can you do?"

"I can travel to other places in the Raven's mind," Catrin replied. "There is a place that is like twilight before day transforms into night. It is a liquid tapestry dividing the mortal world and spiritual Otherworld called the Wall of Lives. Here, everyone has a life thread and the Past, the Present, and the Future merge into one time. This is how I can prophesy."

"Have you seen my life thread?" asked Ferrex.

"No, but I've seen other life threads weave in and out the tapestry."

"Whose?"

"I saw Agrona's life thread," Catrin said, her fingers moving back and forth as if weaving. "This is how I discovered that Rhan possessed Agrona as a little girl. I've even twisted someone's thread so I could extend his life."

"Who was that?"

Catrin hesitated. "Marcellus."

"You saved him, so he could kill your father," Ferrex spewed with disdain. "What were—"

"Don't scold me!" Catrin said, raising her voice. "No one knows more than me the consequences of changing the future. I'm now afraid to connect with the Raven and use its magic. Even so, the Raven follows me everywhere and tries to connect with me. At times, it mimics my voice. It even imitates your commands."

Ferrex regarded Catrin for a moment, and then asked bluntly, "Did you still foresee a future with the Roman?"

"I don't have to answer that question," Catrin snapped.

"I deserve to know," Ferrex demanded.

The truth was Catrin didn't know how to answer. How could she explain the spiritual connection she still had with Marcellus? She somberly confessed, "I no longer want to foresee anyone's future and have forsaken this ability. When I change the Future, it harms others. If I reweave the life thread of one person, the other threads momentarily disjoin and the tapestry ripples. At that moment, I don't know how the life threads will rejoin and reshape the Future."

Ferrex grasped Catrin's hand. "You must learn how to control these forces. You must also learn how to ignite your people with the hope that you can make their futures brighter. They will give you their solemn loyalty and follow you anywhere."

"I can't do this. If I change the future for one person, I may doom others."

"You talk to the gods and goddesses, don't you?"

"I talk to the Raven," she corrected.

"Is your raven a god or goddess?" he asked.

Catrin shrugged. "My raven often speaks with a man's voice, almost like thunder. That is why I believe the Raven may be a messenger from Apollo."

"You mean Apollo, the Roman god?"

"What does it matter if the sun god is called Apollo or Bel, as our tribe calls him?"

"I suppose it doesn't make a difference," Ferrex admitted. "Yet I've always known you were more than a mortal. You can harness forces that only the gods have. If you can alter the future, you can do other magical feats—call on the forces of nature to help farmers like me. You can use your divine gift to inspire our people and win their trust back."

Catrin didn't know how to respond. "Everything you say puts my mind in a spin. I am but a mortal. These divine powers can have calamitous consequences. And I don't want any part of that."

"As I said, learn to control these forces," Ferrex said fervently. "Show others how you can use these powers to overcome the impossible."

"What makes you believe I can do this?

"I've heard bards sing of heroes transforming into gods to perform great feats. If you see this in yourself, others will see it in you."

"I'll consider your advice," Catrin finally said, "but I must first win back the respect of my father and family."

Ferrex rose from the log and slapped Catrin hard on the back, almost knocking her off the log. "Then let's get back to training, Raven."

14

GATHERING OF WOLVES

Marcellus rode with the Roman contingent—his father, other Roman dignitaries, and legionary guards—through the fortress entranceway into the Catuvellauni oppidum of Camulodunum. With the heavy downpours the past few days, the central dirt road between the thatched-roof structures leading to the Great Hall was saturated with water. The horses' hooves kicked mud on the boots and the braccae Marcellus had borrowed from an infantryman. The miserable weather dampened his mood, as did his father's nasty disposition since Cunobelin had announced he wanted to reach a peaceful settlement with Amren. His father still refused to answer Marcellus's questions about when they would sail back to Rome. The unpredictable gale winds and tides could wreak havoc on their ships if the crossing was delayed much longer.

Decimus had warned Marcellus that his father had held clandestine meetings with Marrock during the week. Knowing how ruthless and calculating his father was, Marcellus suspected he had schemed with Marrock to convince Cunobelin to go to war against Amren.

The night's meeting couldn't have had worse timing.

Decimus had told his father that he could not attend the night's festivities. He gave the excuse that he had to search for some men missing from a hunt. In truth, the evening's gathering gave Decimus the diversion he needed to get Vala out of the encampment without notice. Marcellus could now tell by his father's furrowed brow that he was angry that Decimus was not there.

Approaching the Great Hall, Marcellus studied the stone façade of the rectangular building that was more reflective of Roman architecture, unlike the other primitive round Celtic structures in the fortress. He wondered if he should speak up to support Cunobelin's proposal for peace, but with the widening chasm between his father and him, he decided to wait and see how the meeting proceeded.

Marcellus halted his horse in the courtyard, dismounted, and handed the reins to a stable boy. The king's guards then escorted the Romans into the high-beamed Great Hall that had been set up for dining. Attendants, balancing platters of roasted pheasant, venison, and lamb, scurried back and forth between tables. Marcellus was seated midway at a long table perpendicular to the king's table elevated on a platform. His father climbed three stairs and sat to the left of Cunobelin while the queen was seated on his right. Cunobelin's three sons were seated across from Marcellus. Glancing around the chamber, he thought it odd that Marrock and his wife were not among the Celtic nobles intermixing with Roman dignitaries at the tables.

Boisterous chatter filled the chamber as everyone began feasting on meats, black pudding, breads, fruits, and cheeses. Marcellus took a bite of the lumpy pudding and scrunched his face with the unsavory taste of rust. *Britons like everything bloody.* He spat out the half-chewed piece of sausage in his hand.

Desiring some wine, Marcellus waved over a hunched servant whose pale blue eyes glinted with mirth. The wrinkled woman poured wine into an ornate chalice. Marcellus whiffed the aroma of the wine and recognized a fine vintage from Pompeii. He found it fascinating that the glass etching of King Lycurgus entwined by vines on the filled chalice changed from green to berry-red, depending on the light. The Greek-made vessels were highly valued possessions of the Roman elite—an obvious display by Cunobelin to impress his Roman guests.

He raised his chalice to Cunobelin, but the king seemed distracted, conversing with his father. He then lifted his chalice to the king's three sons sitting across from him. The brothers were as different from each other as vinegar and wine. The firstborn of Cunobelin, Adminius stood out from his brothers and other Celtic nobles. He was clean shaven and elegantly attired in a violet Roman tunic and white toga. His dark chestnut hair was cut short in the Roman style. His wide-set, hazel eyes looked almost green in the candlelight.

Decimus had told Marcellus that Adminius's mother died in childbirth. The prince was educated as a boy in the home of a Roman patrician—the result of a policy adopted by the former emperor, Augustus, to acculturate the offspring of British client kings. Augustus believed they would adopt Roman traditions and beliefs, hoping to gain their allegiance when they returned to their homeland.

Marcellus recalled Catrin bemoaning she had been betrothed to Adminius. That was also the moment he impetuously pledged himself as her husband. He knew then their consummation would never be recognized as marriage by either family. Nuptial contracts were hammered on the anvil of tough negotiations to assure the family's line and status. Nonetheless, the image of Adminius putting his hands all over Catrin ignited an irrational jealousy inside him, although he recognized that a political marriage would be the best way to prevent a war between the Cantiaci and the Catuvellauni kingdoms.

The clamor in the room quieted as Lucius rose to make an announcement. Marcellus noticed the black-spotted lynx pelt now draped over his father's shoulders—most likely a gift just given by Cunobelin, who was similarly caped.

Lucius raised his gem-studded goblet. "I toast Cunobelin, our most gracious host, client king, and ally. I am here to proclaim Rome's support of his claims to the Cantiaci territory that King Amren stole from his family."

Marcellus noted his father's forced smile as Cunobelin clinked his horned drinking vessel against the goblet.

"Tell me," Lucius asked Cunobelin, "how can Rome aid you in getting back your rightful lands?"

Marcellus flinched. His father was forcing Cunobelin to acknowledge his long-time grudge and declare war against Amren. Should he speak out so his father didn't go down this treasonous path?

Cunobelin gave a terse smile. "I am grateful for your offer, but I can deal with Amren without any intervention from Rome. I understand why you want to avenge the loss of your soldiers at the prisoner exchange, but if you had sought my advice—"

"I did this to save my son's life!" Lucius barged in. "I explained this to you. Still you question me and reject my offer. You are the vassal king of Rome, am I not mistaken?"

The king twirled the ends of his mustache with his fingers and said in a more conciliatory tone, "Let us not argue about this but move forward to peace. I believe all of my political differences with Amren can be resolved without a war. As you are aware, I sealed a marital pact with Amren for Adminius to marry his youngest daughter before you had imprisoned him. He swore by his blood and honor—"

"I thought Amren was our enemy!" Lucius interrupted. "Has something changed that I'm not aware of?"

Cunobelin shook his head. "No . . . no, I am loyal to you and Rome. To ease the loss of your men, I will give you one thousand gold coins."

Cunobelin's offer was a clever move, Marcellus thought, but he doubted his father would accept it. His father had a singular purpose: reclaim the Antonius family's legacy by conquering Britannia. Cunobelin had surely caught a waft of Lucius's ambitions. The king had been educated in the mire of the politically scheming court of Augustus. With his upbringing, Cunobelin had gained a reputation for being as savvy as any Roman politician. He would do whatever was necessary to promote his standing as *Britannorum rex*— the king of the Britons—to the Emperor Tiberius.

But Cunobelin stood in the way of his father's lofty ambitions.

Lucius gave a disingenuous smile as he replied in a grating voice, "A most gracious offer, but how can we have peace with Amren? He murdered my soldiers! This is an affront to the Emperor Tiberius. As our client king, you are obligated to go to war with us against Amren. My spies have said that Amren publicly denounced you as a traitor. He proclaimed that he would rather have his limbs chained to four horses and torn from his body than to negotiate—"

The loud slam of a door from the back of the room diverted everyone's attention. Five heavily tattooed warriors strutted into the dining area,

Marrock in the midst of them. His cratered face shone like a blood moon under the illumination of burning torches lining the walls. One edge of his lip appeared melted in his jaw. The scar on the left cheek resembled a red-orange imprint of a duck's webbed foot. Marrock's disheveled coppery hair and amber-gold eyes had an eerie similarity to the gigantic wolf that had attacked Marcellus.

Three of the warriors gathered around Marcellus while Marrock and the others swaggered up to Adminius. Marcellus studied Cunobelin to ascertain how he would handle his son-in-law's abrupt appearance. Cunobelin scowled which Marrock returned with a snarl.

Marrock's words, "Why wasn't I invited?" resonated throughout the chamber.

Before Cunobelin could respond, Marrock smacked Adminius hard on the back. "Am I not a family member through my marriage to Ariene? Who are you to steal my birthright as king of the Cantiaci? I will not be left with only scraps from the king's table like a dog."

Everyone in the dining area gaped at the two men as they shouted Celtic words at each other. Adminius abruptly bumped into Marrock's shoulder, ending the altercation, before joining Cunobelin at the head table.

Marrock then narrowed his eyes at Marcellus and lowered his jaw like a wolf ready to attack. "Stay put, Roman! I want you to hear what I am about to say." The pounding of his fist on the table made Marcellus flinch.

"I demand the floor," Marrock shouted.

Cunobelin's eyebrows furrowed together. "Who do you think you are, stomping in here like a crazed boar? Your words can wait!"

"Not if you are plotting to bring me down," Marrock said with a snarl. "I just learned from Ariene that you didn't invite me to this meeting. Quite an oversight, don't you think, considering you promised to support my claims to the Cantiaci kingdom. Let me remind you of your pledge to me in exchange for my fealty. You swore your daughter, Ariene, would rule as my queen over the Cantiaci territory. Yet, behind my back, you propose Adminius steal my rights through his marriage to Amren's whore daughter.

I am here to make sure you keep your promise to me that you will deliver my father and his family for my swift justice."

Cunobelin's face colored bright red, while Lucius had a smug grin as if he had conspired with Marrock. Marcellus feared his father was spinning a web around Cunobelin to force him to reach the same conclusion as him—destroy King Amren and ignite the firestorm to convince Tiberius to invade Britannia.

Cunobelin leaned over to whisper something into Lucius's ears and then scowled at Marrock. "Back down. We'll speak of this later, as I said!"

"No, we will speak about this now!" Marrock shouted, reinforced with another pounding fist on the table that made the platters and goblets shake and clatter. "Adminius will not marry that sorceress whore and steal my birthright!"

Cunobelin stretched out his hands in a conciliatory gesture. "Calm yourself. I have glorious plans for you that we can discuss privately."

Marrock jerked his head back and his nostrils flared. "What plans? You already know what I want. I want my father dead. I want his bitch queen dead. I want his bastard daughters dead. I demand my inheritance!"

Lucius turned to Cunobelin. "Listen to what Marrock is saying. He speaks the truth about King Amren. Not only is he a threat to your kingdom, he is anti-Roman. The only viable political solution is to overthrow him."

Cunobelin broke in. "It's not in anyone's interest to go to war. The best way forward is forge a peace by having Adminius wed Catrin."

Marrock's face flushed to crimson. "At what cost to me? I heard you want to serve my head to Amren in exchange for peace."

"That is a blatant lie!" Cunobelin bellowed, finally losing his composure. "I only want peace. There are other ways you can share my powers."

Lucius again interceded. "Hear me out, Cunobelin. I know Amren. With everything that has happened, he will never agree to marry his daughter to Adminius . . . but I have a possible solution that you and Marrock might agree with."

Cunobelin stared at Amren. "What do you propose?"

"Go to war," Lucius said without hesitation. "You can settle your family differences by splitting the kingdom into half. Give Adminius power over the northern territory while Marrock rules the capital and surrounding territories. If Adminius wants Catrin to warm his bed, let him take her at his will. The marriage could soothe the Cantiaci rage for the loss of their king."

Marrock hit his chest with his fist. "I want it all! You know this, Lucius. You promised that I could be Rome's vassal king in exchange for supporting your ambitions to invade Britannia."

Cunobelin's face turned white as a corpse. "Nobody advised me of this!"

"Lucius assured me in private that he would work this out with you," Marrock asserted.

Cunobelin glowered at Lucius. "What is this about?"

Lucius glared at Marrock. "I never promised you anything. I came here as the emperor's agent to settle political differences directly with Cunobelin."

"You are lying!" Marrock lashed. "You promised my father's head if I did your bidding."

Marcellus could see the panic in his father's eyes, though his face was emotionless as stone.

"You are the one lying," Lucius accused and abruptly turned to Cunobelin. "In Rome, this type of behavior and disrespect would be condemned."

Cunobelin paused and regarded Lucius, then motioned to his guards at the back. "Take Marrock out of here!"

"You don't need to set your attack dogs on me," Marrock said, placing his hand on the pommel of his longsword. "I'll leave of my own accord."

Marcellus felt the table rattle as Marrock leaned over the top. "Later, Roman, you'll pay for turning your father against me!"

Cunobelin motioned to his guards to let Marrock pass as he stomped out of the room with his warriors.

Marrock's threat shook Marcellus to the core.

15

DARK PRINCE

The chatter in the Great Hall rose like a thunderclap after Marrock's intrusion. Thoughts as to what he should do next bombarded Marcellus. His father had obviously bungled his political maneuverings with Marrock behind the scenes. Even though Marcellus felt some relief Cunobelin had not budged on his demand for a peaceful resolution with Amren, Marrock should be feared as a wounded animal ready to lash out. He could potentially disrupt the delicate political balance. The prospect that Marrock could act alone as a "lone wolf" to destroy Amren ran a shiver down Marcellus's back. He had to find a way to stop him.

And the only way was to kill Marrock.

With the fallout between Cunobelin and Marrock, Marcellus came to the grim conclusion that it was in Catrin's best interest to marry Adminius to assure peace. It felt as if fate were juggling knives, and he had to make the blades land such that his father had no choice but to depart Britannia.

Marcellus studied his father's expression to discern his mood. His jaw was clenched and his face glistened from sweat. As his father conversed with Cunobelin, Marcellus observed that his eyes appeared vacant as though he were somewhere else. He found it curious that Adminius, standing behind Cunobelin, now seemed calm, almost jovial, after the disruptive events. An idea grew in Marcellus's mind that he might be able to influence the dark prince to champion peace with Amren.

Adminius met Marcellus's stare and acknowledged him with a slight nod. The prince left the side of Cunobelin and strode back to Marcellus. He leaned over and asked quietly, "You want to speak with me?"

Marcellus nodded. "In private."

The dark prince pointed to an isolated area at the back of the Great Hall. "No one will hear us there."

Marcellus picked up his chalice and followed Adminius, who had a flagon of wine in one hand and a gem-studded goblet in the other. In the shadows at the back of the chamber, Adminius poured some wine into Marcellus's chalice and toasted familiarly, "Salutaria!"

Marcellus smiled disingenuously.

"How do you find the wine?" Adminius asked cordially.

"It tastes Pompeian, a fine vintage," Marcellus commented.

"A taste I acquired when I was in Rome." Adminius drank some more, keeping his eyes steady on Marcellus. "What did you want to say to me?"

Rubbing the edge of his goblet, Marcellus said, "As we've not had a chance to talk, I thought it would be to our benefit to know each other better. I assume by your demeanor and taste in wine that you were educated in Rome."

Adminius grinned. "I was educated as a young boy in the household of Emperor Augustus until his death ten summers ago. I returned to my homeland after Tiberius came to power."

"Did you ever regret being forced to leave your homeland?" Marcellus asked bluntly.

"Well, let me say," Adminius said with a glint in his eyes, "I have a better appreciation of your politics and understand what is needed to win patronage from nobles such as yourself."

Marcellus stroked his chin, mulling over what the prince might want. "How could my patronage help you?"

Adminius twisted his lips into a half smile. "Advance my standing as a client king to Rome."

Curiosity piqued, Marcellus said, "Ambition is a two-edged sword that could wield its purpose for both of us. But what I don't understand is why you seek my patronage without Cunobelin's knowledge."

Adminius paused and slowly lifted his goblet to his mouth to sip. "Every son of a great king has his eye on a higher prize. My ambition is to rule the Cantiaci kingdom and welcome Romans to its shores."

In Marcellus's mind, Adminius was no different than any other zealous young man lusting for power. He cringed at the prospect of Catrin marrying the dark prince, who was as smooth as olive oil, to seal peace between the two kingdoms.

"Is that why you insisted on marrying Catrin instead of Mor so you could take her kingdom?" Marcellus impulsively asked.

"Catrin's kingdom?" Adminius humphed and threw his head back to gulp down rest of his wine. "I thought we were talking about my kingdom. Was I not clear?"

"Perfectly so, but you could have married Mor and still fulfilled your ambition of ruling the Cantiaci."

Adminius narrowed his eyes. "Is there something more between Catrin and you?"

Marcellus bit his lower lip to stop his thoughts from slipping out of his mouth.

Why should Catrin marry a snake like you? You are nothing more than a savage dressed as a Roman nobleman.

"Well, is there more?" Adminius repeated.

Though the prospect of the dark prince marrying Catrin grated at Marcellus, he had to quell his jealousy and think only of her safety. No doubt Adminius would protect her as his queen. Masking his contempt, Marcellus replied in an even tone, "As you probably know, I was put under Catrin's charge when I was held as a hostage. She told me that you had refused to marry Mor, but chose her instead, causing disruption in the negotiations. It struck me as brash for you to defy your father's orders."

"I got what I wanted, didn't I?" Adminius said with a smirk. "Wouldn't you defy your father to marry the woman you love?"

Feeling a sharp pang of jealousy in his heart, Marcellus jerked his head back. "You love Catrin? She told me that she hardly knew you."

"Oh . . . did she?" Adminius said with a cock of his eyebrow. "I was a ward of King Amren a few summers back and lived in their household. Why would she say something that personal to you . . . a foreigner?"

Struggling to temper his anger, Marcellus said, "I'm not trying to start an argument with you. I understand that the best way to settle political differences between Amren and your father is through a political marriage between you and Catrin. As you said, every son has his eye on a different prize. Unlike my father, I only seek peace between the kingdoms. I'm not here to interfere with your politics."

"You say this, even though the Cantiaci imprisoned you?"

"Yes. That's why I'm eager to return to Rome."

The dark prince eyed Marcellus for a moment. "As Marrock and my younger brothers are too eager to dispose of me, I believe we could both benefit from an alliance."

Marcellus felt a tap on the shoulder and turned around. The hunched female attendant gave him a parchment that he opened and read:

Meet me outside.

"Who gave this to you?" he asked.

"Marrock," she whispered into his ear.

Marcellus winced.

Once before, Marrock had tried to kill him in his shapeshifted wolf form. Perhaps he should return the favor and stick a knife through his throat. If he killed him, the dispute between Amren and Cunobelin would then easily resolve.

Marcellus ended the conversation with Adminius, saying, "I will give your offer further consideration. If you would excuse me, I have unfinished business to attend to outside."

16

REVELATION

The sweltering heat from the boisterous dignitaries blasted Marcellus like a furnace as he strode through the Great Hall. Marrock's threat, "Later, Roman, you'll pay for turning your father against me," rattled in his head. Passing the main table, he saw his father raise a brow at him as to say, "Where are you going?"

Marcellus fanned himself to indicate he needed fresh air. His father nodded, seemingly satisfied with his explanation, and turned to Cunobelin to converse. Somewhat relieved his father was now preoccupied with the king—most likely trying to smooth out misunderstandings from the night's events—Marcellus focused on ways he could counter Marrock. He had not brought a weapon. Even if he had, he questioned how effective it would be against the shapeshifter. He had barely escaped Marrock's previous deadly attack, even after stabbing his underbelly several times—not from his own strength but with the force of Catrin's essence. The invisible fog into which Marrock disappeared was another factor Marcellus hadn't considered in his unbridled compulsion to kill the monster.

Am I on a fool's mission?

It didn't matter. He'd figure how to kill Marrock and deal with his father's repercussions later.

Marcellus stepped into the crisp, misty night and looked around for Marrock. Near the Great Hall's entryway, Roman guards were talking with each other while curious villagers milled around them to inspect their weapons. Not seeing Marrock, Marcellus asked himself whether he should wait at the Great Hall or venture into the confines of the fortress to look for him. He answered his own question when he spotted Marrock at the outer perimeter of the courtyard. He felt his heart pound with anticipation as to what the shapeshifter might do next.

He approached a burly Roman guard and said in a hushed tone, "Give me your dagger. Keep a close eye on that hideous barbarian at the fire pit. If he makes a false move while I speak to him, strike him down."

The guard furtively handed a dagger to Marcellus, who then slipped it into the sleeve of his tunic. After the burley guard waved his fellow soldiers over, Marcellus cautiously walked over to Marrock, who was warming his hands over a fire in a stone-lined pit. The smoke rose like a black shadow into the night sky.

Marrock stared at Marcellus with feral eyes that glowed like amber gemstones in the light of the flames. He scrunched his elongated nose and sniffed as Marcellus approached.

Unnerved by the barbarian's facial tics and wolf-like gestures of scratching the back of his ears, Marcellus asked, "Why did you want to meet me?"

Marrock answered with an ominous growl to his voice, "What were you and Adminius discussing in the Great Hall?"

"Who told you this?" Marcellus asked, wondering if one of the servants or a warrior from inside had informed the hideously scarred barbarian.

"I have my spies," Marrock grunted.

"We exchanged pleasantries . . . the weather, the food and wine," Marcellus said, wondering if the barbarian's upturned mouth was a smile or a snarl.

Marrock's brow crevassed like a fractured rock. "Did Adminius talk to you about Catrin?"

The mention of Catrin made the hairs on Marcellus's neck erect. He slid the dagger out of his sleeve into the palm of his hand. "Adminius told me he wanted to marry her."

Marrock cocked an eyebrow. "Did he now? You must know what he really wants, don't you?"

"I assume it is to forge a peace between the Cantiaci and Catuvellauni tribes," Marcellus said, glancing at Marrock's hand to make sure he didn't have a weapon.

"Bahh!" Marrock hacked and spat into the fire pit. "Adminius wants my birthright. And he lied to Cunobelin to get it."

"Did my father talk to you about Cunobelin's change of plans on how he would deal with Amren?"

Marrock leveled his eyes at Marcellus. "My wife told me. Your father never said a word about this. Did Catrin mislead you about my claims to the throne?"

"I came to the conclusion myself that you have no right to Amren's throne," Marcellus said firmly.

"Did you persuade your father to the same conclusion?"

"He makes his own conclusions."

Marrock flung his head back like a wolf and sniffed. "I smell a temptress in the breeze."

Not sure if he had heard Marrock correctly, Marcellus said, "The sky looks clear to me."

A corner of Marrock's mouth curled up. "How did you find my half-sister, Catrin?"

Taken aback by the abrupt switch in topic, Marcellus snapped his eyes at Marrock. "What do you mean?"

"I find it odd I can sniff Catrin's scent on you. Don't think you were the first man she lured into her warm waters?"

Marcellus felt his jaw clench. "What are you implying?"

"Let me explain what Catrin is," Marrock said with a wry smile. "She appears as unblemished as a newborn lamb. I remember her playing as a little girl in the woods and singing to the birds. Her hair glittered like spun gold under Apollo's sun. Her pale skin . . . hmm . . . so soft like lamb fleece. Did she say anything to you about me?"

Marcellus adjusted the dagger's blade in the palm of his hand. "Nothing of worth."

Marrock pick-up a nearby stick on the ground and jabbed it into the fire. The flames crackled and shot higher. "Pity that. I thought she had feelings for her poor banished half-brother." He vigorously scratched behind his pointed ears, then remarked, "Oh, by the way, did you know Adminius was a ward of King Amren a few summers back? He had salacious intentions for Catrin even though she was a prepubescent girl. He didn't know she could bewitch men with her sorcery."

"I found Catrin shy and reserved," Marcellus said through gritted teeth.

"Did you?" Marrock smirked. "First impressions often deceive—"

"Get to your point!"

Marrock burst out laughing. "I didn't mean to pluck your fine feathers, Roman. I only wanted to tell you a tale of what Catrin truly is." Marrock paused and the light of the moon escaping the clouds flashed on his eyes. "When Catrin was eight summers, I took her on a quest to find the white raven in the woods. She had no breasts then. Does she have them now?"

Anger boiling to the surface, Marcellus could feel his jaw tighten. He recalled Catrin's anguish when she revealed that Marrock had done something so vile, it had repressed her memory of the act. He questioned whether he could bear to hear the truth that Marrock might have raped her.

"Don't let my question ruffle your feathers," Marrock scoffed. "Let me finish my story."

"I don't want to hear any more," Marcellus said with a growl.

"You will, once you realize that I was Catrin's first." Marrock snarled and pointed to his hideous face. "Do you know who sculpted this?"

Marcellus glowered.

Marrock smiled with a glint of evil in his eyes. "Of course, you do. In my youth, I had a comely face just like Catrin's. We were seeded by the same father, you know, not like her two bastard sisters. You must get closer so only you can hear the naked truth about her."

Hot embers shot from the fire pit at Marcellus. Readying himself to strike the debased barbarian, he gripped the dagger's handle as Marrock continued the tale.

"Catrin has a nefarious raven that protects her like a jealous lover. I'm sure you've heard the Greek tale of the sirens' attempts to lure Ulysses into treacherous shores with their enchanting songs. Even as a little girl, Catrin entranced me with her sweet melodies. That was before"—Marrock lifted his eyes as if reliving the memory—"she summoned her feathered warriors to peck out half of my face, revealing her evil nature. But before she did this, she made me do something vile."

"What was that?" Marcellus said, his voice shaking with anger.

Marrock contorted his lips into a macabre smile. "Fuck her!"

Uncontrollable fury struck Marcellus like a bolt of lightning. With Herculean strength, he charged Marrock with his dagger aimed at the monster's heart, but the sharp point of the stick Marrock was holding jabbed Marcellus in the throat first, followed by a swift kick at his ankle that brought him down. The hard impact crushed the air out of Marcellus's lungs and the dagger flew from his hand.

No longer armed, panic sliced through Marcellus. He quickly bounced to his feet but was attacked by another warrior from the back. Rage unfurled in Marcellus like the sails of a ship in a tempest. "Let the *Keres* rip out your soul," he shouted, struggling to free himself of the warrior's restraint. "Burn in Hades!"

Breaking the warrior's hold, Marcellus charged Marrock with a lethal fist aimed at his throat. Marrock gripped his wrist, flipped him on his back, and put a headlock on him, squeezing his throat. Four Roman soldiers ran to Marcellus's aid and yanked Marrock off. Gasping, Marcellus staggered to his feet as Marrock fought fiercely against the Romans' restraints.

Marrock spat at Marcellus. "I am Blood Wolf, the rightful Cantiaci king. No one takes that away from me. Not Lucius! Not Cunobelin! Not Adminius! Not you, a Roman who fucked my sister—a sorceress and her demon raven—no one, do you hear me, no one! I swear on the souls of my ancestors and the bond of my wolf pack that I will slaughter everyone who stands in my way!"

Another wave of rage erupted in Marcellus. He hurled his anvil-hard fist into Marrock's nose with a bone-crunching noise. Blood splattered everywhere. As Marrock howled in pain, one of his warriors leapt on Marcellus with a knee to his lower back, hurtling him to the ground. Sharp pain spiked through his skull from the hard smack on the courtyard's cobblestone. Blood clogged his nostrils. Colored dots danced before his eyes.

"Calm down!" Lucius's voice thundered into Marcellus's ears, which was followed by Cunobelin's sharp words. "Enough, Marrock! Stand your ground!"

The weight lifted off Marcellus, allowing him to get up to meet the blazing eyes of his father.

"You idiot!" Lucius yelled. "What in Vulcan's fire made you do this?"

Ignoring his father, Marcellus prepared to punch Marrock again. He held back, though, as he watched three of the king's guards drag the crazed monster away. Marcellus's fiery rage finally cooled down under the gentle mist of rainfall, making him shiver.

He knew Marrock would never forget this encounter.

17

CARNAGE

Imprisoned in a metal-barred cage, Marrock felt like a wild animal ready to lash out at those who had betrayed and injured him. He could barely breathe through his blood-clogged nose. His right eye was swollen shut. His temple throbbed as if a hammer was pounding against his skull like an anvil. He spat out a loose tooth in disgust. The humiliation of the Romans manhandling him made his blood boil.

Shapeshifting into a wolf would not help him escape the metal constraints of his cell. The sentry guarding him had fallen asleep, but he was beyond Marrock's reach to retrieve the latch key to unlock the cage. He was at the mercy of Cunobelin. Even his wife, Ariene, could not intervene on his behalf. If he didn't acquiesce to his treacherous father-in-law, he could be held in his caged quarters for days to serve as an example of what happens to those who didn't lick the arse of their ruler.

The misty cold of the morning's darkness dampened his hopes of ever fulfilling his mother's curse. He had not received any word from Agrona since King Amren imprisoned her. He now dreaded Catrin could have broken the curse. If so, his thirst for avenging his sorceress half-sister would never be quenched. Her raven warriors had ravaged his face, making him into a hideous monster. The final assault on his pride and dignity was that everyone he trusted had plotted against him to steal his rightful claims to the Cantiaci kingdom. Even Senator Lucius Antonius had turned against him at the meeting. Everyone was now against him except for his beloved wife, Ariene, who had cared for him like a she-wolf, and his mother, Rhan.

Marrock felt utterly alone in the morning's darkness just before dawn.

He wearily sighed. His face hurt too much to get any sound sleep, so he stared vacantly through the metal-rimmed cage. A thin line of fog approaching the sleeping sentry caught his attention. An instant later, a dagger thrust out of the fog through the guard's throat.

Senses heightened, Marrock clasped the metal rods and closely watched the fog envelop the guard. The thick mist floated away from the motionless body and slithered like a snake toward Marrock. The only other person besides himself who could disappear into a fog was Agrona.

To his surprise, a shadowy man stepped out of the fog. The man's black silhouette was hunched as he limped with the aid of a staff toward the cage and unlocked it. Marrock couldn't discern the man's face, hidden in the cowl of his hood.

"Who are you?" he asked.

"I am known as the Wild Druid. Rhan summoned me in a vision to help you," the man declared with a gravelly voice. "Enter the tunnel of fog that will render you invisible and escape through the fortress gates. Outside, your wolf awaits you with news of Vala."

Marrock noticed the top end of the wooden staff in the Druid's hand was shaped like a serpent's mouth biting a crystal orb. He recognized the crystal globe as that used by the Ancient Druids to look into the future. On its pearl-like surface, he saw an image of himself astride a horse, holding Vala's head.

"Is this what I must do?" he asked, "Take Vala's head?"

"Yes, if you are to be king. Go now." The Wild Druid mysteriously disappeared into a fog.

Emboldened, Marrock lowered his head and crawled through the narrow opening of the cage. He entered the tunnel of fog and followed its pathway until he met his silver she-wolf at the eastern perimeter of the forest. The first tinge of crimson light from the rising sun was filtering through the trees. The she-wolf barked, warning him that a detachment of Roman soldiers had left the encampment with Vala. The unexpected transfer of Vala under the cover of darkness raised Marrock's suspicions that Lucius had broken his promise to crucify her in retribution for the slain Roman soldiers at the prisoner exchange. He angrily recalled the night when he had shapeshifted into a wolf and overheard the heated argument between Lucius and Marcellus about the emperor's mandate to leave Britannia. Marrock now surmised the senator planned to release Vala to avoid a war and to return home.

In need of a horse to ride, Marrock rushed about a mile home and quickly gathered his weapons and supplies. He would later find a way to deliver a message to Ariene to seek the aid of her younger brothers, Togodumnus and Caratacus, for his next moves to overthrow Amren.

Marrock mounted his plough horse and followed the silver wolf into the woods bordering the Roman encampment. A pack of three other she-wolves, a red alpha male, and a younger male were awaiting him. He directed the wolves to track the Romans and their prisoner, Vala. The wolves lowered their muzzles and sniffed the area until they found the scent. They excitedly scurried alongside the main roadway as Marrock followed on his horse.

At the sun's zenith, Marrock caught sight of six infantrymen led by Tribune Decimus Flavius on horseback. Vala was in the midst of the Roman contingent with her hands tied behind her back. The possibility of a conspiracy shook Marrock to the core. His stomach felt as if it had twisted inside-out with uncontrollable rage that Lucius might have conspired to hand him over to Amren.

"I won't let this happen," Marrock grumbled.

The wolves reacted to Marrock's growing agitation with loud barks and snarls. Struggling to regain his wits, he lowered his hand to silence them. The wolves quieted, their eyes intently focused on him. He motioned for his wolves to trail the Romans. For any hope of them overtaking seven armed men, he had to wait until the darkness of night to ambush them.

Marrock and his pack trailed the Romans for about ten miles until they halted in the woods near the Blackwater estuary that emptied into the ocean. As the Romans set up camp, Marrock and the wolves hid behind some scrub. He watched a guard yank Vala down to the ground and shackle her ankles near a fallen tree before joining the other soldiers gathered around Decimus, astride a chestnut brown horse.

Marrock was at too great a distance to clearly hear the commander's instructions, but he caught the tribune's final words, "Don't fail me. Your brothers depend on you."

Ariene had told him that she had overheard some Roman soldiers say that five of their brothers had been captured by the Cantiaci savages. They feared the imprisoned soldiers would be tortured to death.

Marrock wondered if these Romans were to be exchanged for Vala.

Decimus galloped off like a whirlwind on the pathway from which they had travelled, leaving the six soldiers at the campsite. Marrock was tempted to follow Decimus, but the tribune's steed would outpace his gray pony. Besides, he didn't want to lose sight of Vala. He motioned for the gray male wolf to follow the tribune while he and the other wolves kept guard of the other Romans.

Marrock sat on a fallen log and waited for nightfall. He vigorously scratched his itchy scalp with sharp fingernails as he mulled over where the prisoner exchange would take place and whether his father would partake. If so, it didn't make sense for the king to arrange a location so deep in Catuvellauni territory. A neutral zone south of the river estuary bordering the kingdoms made more sense. Not knowing where Decimus had ridden made him feel anxious and out of control. He nervously chewed a hangnail until it bled. Sucking the blood off his finger, he tried to embolden himself with his wife's prophecy that he would embrace the power from his family's skulls and crown himself with bloody hands. The Wild Druid's orb foretold he would take Vala's head. Only then, Cunobelin and Lucius would recognize his right to rule as Blood Wolf.

A firestorm of fury broiled in Marrock's chest.

They have all played me as a fool. They will soon learn I am the master of my fate. I will turn their schemes upside down.

He now understood the orb's meaning that beheading Vala would drive Amren to war against Cunobelin and the Romans for revenge. He had to overcome six armed Romans with the aid of his wolf pack. Vala was a skilled warrior and would likely put up a fierce fight. He decided not to shapeshift so he could cleanly cut off her head with a sword to enshrine it in the Gateway of Skulls. He knew his human eyesight would be a disadvantage, but he could meld his thoughts with one of his wolves and see through its eyes as he unleashed his bloody deed in the darkness of night.

The long wait for nightfall grated at Marrock's nerves. To calm himself, he rubbed the red alpha wolf between the ears to imbue his predatory essence and courage. The other she-wolves became jealous and crowded around him for attention. One by one, he stroked the soft fur of each of his wolves. The alpha wolf's sister, Silver, was his favorite. Each time Marrock shapeshifted into a wolf, he imagined Silver as Catrin. He could easily overpower Silver and experience the vicarious thrill of imposing his will on Catrin as he mated with her, stealing her mystical powers with each thrust.

He smiled affectionately at his white wolf as she nudged his hand. She was the most beautiful of his she-wolves. He could smell she was in heat. He would also mate with her and seed pups to grow his wolf pack.

The black wolf with earth-brown eyes reminded Marrock of the bitch queen, Rhiannon. She spurned him and only mated with the red alpha male. Nonetheless, he needed the Black's cunning and strength to bring down the prey. He smiled, envisioning his beloved wolves cracking open the Romans' skulls with their powerful jaws and shredding the tissue away from their bones.

The long day finally ended as the clouds flamed like fiery tongues in the western horizon. The ascending moon being swallowed by thickening fog from the sea was a sign that nightfall would soon arrive. Marrock's heart pounded with predatory anticipation of mercilessly killing the soldiers. He sliced his finger over his sword blade. Blood seeped from the cut, and he licked and savored the metallic taste. The six Roman soldiers huddled like a herd of deer with ears perked up, listening for predators. Occasionally, a group of three soldiers ventured to the camp's outer fringe. One of them would gather firewood while the others protected him with their swords extended. At least three soldiers always stayed close to Vala.

To gain advantage, Marrock knew he had to pounce on them one by one if any strayed from the others. He mumbled beneath his breath, "Piss-sucking Romans, always huddling together like rabbits." He had to remind himself to be patient, to be in control, and to make no mistakes. Taking a few deep breaths, he relaxed his shoulders as he watched the Romans prepare their supper.

An idiot soldier managed to club a hare that had wandered into camp. The soldier haphazardly skinned the animal, thrust a spit through its belly, and propped it on forked sticks to roast over the fire. The aroma of dripping juices tantalized Marrock' nostrils as he gnawed on some dried pork strips he had brought to eat. He spat the stringy pieces on the ground. His wolves greedily lapped up the chewed pieces and restlessly paced around him for more morsels.

A little later, the gray male wolf finally returned with news that Decimus and another man had boarded a ship moored on the eastern coastline. The report spiked a chill down Marrock's spine. He wondered if Decimus was arranging to transport Vala by ship. He quietly stepped closer to the Roman campsite so he could overhear their dinner conversations to gain insight into their plans.

The air filled with loud chatter as soldiers bit off meat from the rabbit bones and loudly smacked their lips. Marrock listened to the soldiers' conversations as they huddled around the crackling fire. A gangly soldier handed a roasted leg to Vala, who managed to hold it to eat, despite her bound wrists.

"How'd we get so lucky to escort such an ugly dog?" a soldier sitting near the fire blurted.

"Shut up, Quintus," another soldier at the fire said gruffly. "I'm sick of you taunting the bitch."

Quintus, whom Marrock recognized as the ill-mannered sentry he had earlier confronted at the Roman encampment, said, "It gives me pleasure to tease the ugly cunni while we wait here with nothing else to do. Besides, I don't understand why Cunobelin's men aren't escorting her instead of us. They know the coastline better than us."

A different soldier burst in. "Dimwit! Didn't you hear what Decimus said? Our brothers are at the mercy of those Cantiaci cannibals who are ready to burn them alive and eat them. The Catuvellauni could care less what happens to them. It is up to us to make sure our fellow soldiers are released!"

"So the Cantiaci can ambush us again like they did before!" Quintus spat on the fire. "Why don't we just slit the bitch's throat and put an end to this? Why risk our lives?"

"That is why no one will protect your sorry arse!" a soldier barked.

Quintus poked a stick at the fire. "It's not only my arse. I've heard rumors the emperor has ordered us all back to Gaul. Before we lose any more men, let's put an end to the bitch."

"If we kill her," a man with a husky voice countered, "we'll incite a war. Those barbarians will swarm us like flies on rotting meat before we can sail away in our ships. We are outnumbered at least ten to one. We'll never get off this cursed island alive. Didn't you see the spiked skulls when we first met King Amren at his reception hall?"

Another soldier laughed. "They will cut off our balls before spiking our heads."

The soldier's comment gave Marrock a savory idea of how he could further inflame the Romans. At any other time, he would only gladly remove the idiots' heads to enshrine them in his Gateway of Skulls. Yet there was nothing more grisly than a soldier's defiled corpse to deliver the message that he was a force to be reckoned with.

Hearing Vala call out, "Guard, I need go to forest," Marrock paid closer attention.

"To do what?" Quintus shouted.

"What you think?" Vala snapped.

Another man's voice ordered, "Quintus, unshackle the prisoner and take her out of camp to shit. While you're at it, do the same. You're starting to stink."

This was the opportunity Marrock needed. Drawing his sword, he quietly skulked behind a clump of bushes near where Vala was taken. A few feet from her, Quintus was trumpeting gas. He directed the alpha to attack Quintus and bring him down.

The twigs crunched beneath the alpha's paws as he jumped off his hind legs and knocked Quintus to the ground. With his legs entangled in his dropped breeches, Quintus looked like a hapless snapping turtle as the alpha's jaws chomped his genitals. The soldier's screams of agony rumbled through the forest.

Marrock motioned for the alpha to get off Quintus. He lowered his sword on Quintus and cleanly sliced off the head, sending him to the grim underworld the Romans called Hades. The headless body convulsed for a few moments as blood spurted everywhere. With a self-satisfied grin, Marrock bent down to stroke the slick blood over the face like a grim reaper. He glimpsed Vala's shadowy figure scooting away but let her go, hearing the sounds of crunching steps and clinking metal. Turning, he observed the shadows of three men. He whistled for his wolves to bring them down.

In the stillness, the shadows of both men and wolves faded in and out of the trees. A chill clawed at Marrock's neck when he sensed someone approaching him. He squinted but couldn't see anything in the darkness. He regretted not having the wolf's keen eyesight as the sound of the footsteps quickened and became louder.

A shadow lunged at Marrock. He twisted sideways and slashed his sword into the man's leg for the cripple. The soldier dropped face down on the ground. With both hands on the pommel, Marrock drove the blade into the man's shoulder. Before he could yank the blade out to cut off the soldier's head, a ball of snarling white fur leapt past him and knocked down another Roman, loosening a javelin out of his hand.

Marrock quickly clasped the wooden shaft of the javelin and thrust the metal tip through the man's back, impaling him to the ground.

Three men down!

He then heard the agonized whelps of one of his she-wolves close by. He yanked the sword out of the other fallen Roman and blindly rushed toward the noise. By the time he reached his wolf, it was too late. Silver was motionless on the ground. Nearby, the Black was crunching the neck of a fourth soldier with its powerful jaws.

Heart-sickened with the loss of Silver, Marrock struck the soldier's head over and over with the sword blade until the skull split open, spattering blood and brain. Gasping, he fell to his knees in exhaustion and crawled over to his beloved she-wolf to touch her head. A tear formed in his eye when he sensed her soul had already left the skull.

Racked with grief, Marrock threw his head back and released a howl.

The night breeze replied with a mournful echo above the treetops.

Marrock raised his arms to the heavens and prayed, "Take my beloved wolf to join her sisters in the Otherworld."

After a moment of somber silence, Marrock perked his ears for the movement of potentially more Romans, but he only heard the soft whoosh of a breeze. He considered shapeshifting into a wolf for keener eyesight to find the remaining two soldiers. However, he decided to meld his thoughts with the alpha's mind and see through its eyes.

A light flashed in his mind as he connected with the alpha. Now seeing through the wolf's eyes, Marrock directed the alpha to move toward the Roman camp. As the alpha approached the site, he didn't see any soldiers by the fire but detected movement behind some trees near the camp's periphery. He discerned three red shields moving deeper into the forest. He wondered if Decimus had returned and had brought additional men.

Thinking now of Vala, Marrock reconsidered his plan to attack the Romans and ordered his wolves to search for her instead.

18

VENGEANCE

With darkness giving way to dawn's light, Marrock observed the estuary's shoreline coil around the waterway like a giant serpent. Vala had eluded both him and his wolf pack. With last night's chaos, he feared she might have discovered the Roman bodies and taken their weapons.

Astride his plough horse, Marrock scanned the thick woods behind him but saw no signs of her. He then stepped to the edge of the forest to look for movement in the tall marsh grass that sloped to the estuary. Three obscured figures lumbering through the marshlands came into his vision. The silhouette of a ship on the waterway was steadily moving toward the shoreline.

With the brightening day, he discerned his wolves were crouched in the reeds beside a platform dock. As the figures stepped from the tall grass onto the platform dock, Marrock recognized them as the Romans who had escaped his attack. They appeared to be waiting for the hull-shaped ship gliding toward them. Assuming they were Decimus and his two surviving men, Marrock whistled to his wolves not to attack so he could further study their maneuverings. He dismounted and tethered his horse to a low tree branch.

The hairs on his neck prickled with a feeling that something was lurking close by. Gripping the sword pommel at his side, he warily glanced over his shoulder. A black-bellied duck waddled out of some red-berried bushes and loudly quacked with annoyance.

Marrock quietly chuckled, relieved it was nothing more. He again focused on the Romans standing on the platform. He recognized the triskele of horses on the sail of the incoming ship as the insignia of King Amren. Marrock's heart pounded with growing anticipation that his father was on board. On the ship's deck were five Romans with their hands shackled behind their backs.

A sudden crunch of twigs startled Marrock. He glanced back to find a blurry figure catapulting at him. With only a heartbeat to react, he jerked sideways and barely averted the glimmering blade aimed at his stomach.

He unsheathed his longsword and positioned to face his opponent.

Vala.

She was statuesque and as muscular as any male warrior. Her eyes pierced him like a wild falcon's. She flew at him and sliced his shoulder before he could counter with his sword, throwing him off balance. Her speed shook him. He had to outmaneuver her lightning agility with strength and cunning.

Pretending to be injured, Marrock staggered. Vala took the bait and lunged forward, thrusting the sword at his chest. He jumped back to escape her blade. She again lunged and thrust her weapon, but this time he parried her blade with his longsword and quickly shifted sideways to take her off balance. As she stumbled, he grabbed her shoulder with his left hand, pulling her closer, and smacked his forehead against her nose, dazing her. He swung his sword overhead for the final deathblow, but she wheeled around and only the tip of his sword slashed her shoulder as she dashed toward the estuary like a crazed doe, shouting, "Help me! Help me!"

Fearing that the Romans and the Cantiaci warriors on shore would reach her, he climbed onto his gray horse and kicked it into a full gallop. The pounding of horse hooves filled his ears as he chased her down. He bellowed a war cry as he gained ground on her. She glanced back, her eyes white with fear. She pumped her arms harder and harder, screaming, "Trystan, help me! Help me now!"

Marrock shifted his eyes toward the ship approaching the dock. He recognized that Trystan was on deck with sword in hand. Next to him were the shackled Romans.

Fury again engulfed him like a firestorm that both the Romans and his father had conspired against him.

Finally reaching Vala, Marrock swung his sword at her neck. Her head flew off and her headless body crumpled on the reed grass. He howled with glee, hot blood rushing into his head and making it spin. He reined his horse to a halt, jumped off, and quickly grasped Vala's head by her blood-smeared hair. Mounting his horse again, he lifted the severed head and gloated, "Look what I have. Marcellus betrayed you! Lucius betrayed you!"

The frightened horse reared on its hind legs, but Marrock held the reins with one hand while clasping Vala's hair with the other, refusing to let her head drop. Finally taking control of his spooked horse, he turned the animal toward the ship to observe Trystan's next move.

One by one, Trystan lobbed off the heads of all the shackled Romans on the deck of the ship. Other warriors pushed the bodies and heads like butchered animals into the rippling water.

Marrock observed the three Roman soldiers on the dock retreat back into the tall reeds.

Wild with delight with the havoc he had fueled to incite Amren to war, Marrock tied Vala's head to his saddle as a trophy. Though he could slay the Romans on shore, he decided to leave them as witnesses to report his brutal act to the treacherous senator. He contemplated what he should do next.

The curse's prophecy that he would ally with the Romans had steered him wrong. He could no longer rely on them or the support of Cunobelin after what they had done. He must take control of his destiny and recruit rebel warriors from his kingdom and the neighboring Dobunni tribe, who would gladly follow him into battle and glory.

He whistled for his wolves to return so they could find the Roman bodies and add to the horror of what he had done.

19

WANDERING DRUID

Catrin and Ferrex set their shields, swords, and spears next to a red-berried Rowan tree. She was weary from full day of training and harvesting wheat, but her spirits had lifted with the news that the king would allow her to return for Mor's wedding in a couple of days. Even though the coos of the doves roosting in the tree invited her to rest with them, her task master insisted they practice with weapons in the remaining light.

Ferrex cuffed metal bands around his wrists and motioned for Catrin to do likewise. He handed her a spear and shield. He strapped a shield to his left forearm and clasped the sword with his other hand. "Counter my sword with your spear."

He pushed forward, thrusting his sword over his shield. Catrin countered his blade with her spear, stepping back to avert the tip. He again lunged, but this time drove his sword underneath his shield toward her stomach. She blocked his sword with her shield and thrust the spear at his legs. He stepped over the shaft and pushed her shield back with his.

"Strike me now!" he ordered.

With all her strength, Catrin pounced at Ferrex and whirled her spear at him, but he jumped back as the wooden tip nicked his chest. She stumbled and Ferrex wacked her on the back with the flat of his sword. She slammed face down on the ground. Tasting grass in her mouth, she spat it out.

Ferrex pressed the tip of his sword against her shoulder. "Get up and do it again. You attack without thought. Think with your head. Be cunning as a raven. Look for any weakness. Anticipate my next move. Distract me and strike me like a hawk."

Catrin pushed herself to a sitting position and brushed the loose grass off her trousers. As she prepared to spar with Ferrex again, a neighboring farmer ran up to him and asked for help with a wagon stuck in a rut. Ferrex told Catrin to wait until he returned.

Catrin gingerly sat at an oak and leaned against its trunk. Fatigued, she closed her droopy eyes. For the last few nights, she had dreamt of disguising herself so she could run off with Marcellus to escape her father's judgment. Yet the somber thought that her sister was still imprisoned made her emotions vacillate between the overpowering love she still held for Marcellus and her duty to her family. She hoped her father had sought Marcellus's aid to release Vala.

An owl's hoots pulled Catrin out of her reverie. She looked overhead and found a barn owl perched on a high tree branch, gawking at her. Its long white face and pointed beak between two black eyes reminded her of an old man. She sensed the bird telling her to watch closely. The owl then flew from the tree and landed in the marshes near the river.

Curiosity aroused, Catrin walked to the riverbank and found the owl with a mouse in its beak. After the bird gulped the rodent down, she heard the grass rustle.

A stoat jumped at the owl, intent on snatching it as a meal, but a blinding light flashed, making Catrin close her eyes from the glare. When she opened them again, she was shocked to see what looked like dust in a globe of white light coalescing into the shape of a human. A wrinkled man, whose features strikingly resembled an owl, came into focus. His disheveled gray-speckled white hair and beard hung from his face to chest like a bird's nest. His pot belly thankfully concealed his shriveled male parts.

The owl-faced man, who looked a century old, chuckled with a glint in his amber eyes. "Oh dear, I'm inappropriately attired to meet a young maiden such as you."

"You gave me quite a startle," she remarked. "I could have sworn you switched from an owl to an old man."

"You have keen eyes, my dear. Sadly, the world is a blur to me with my old eyes," the Druid said with a grimace. "I am a shapeshifter."

Catrin looked at him in awe. "A shapeshifter? How is that?"

"I can change back and forth between an owl and old man, but must be naked to do so or I get tangled in my clothes. You didn't happen to notice if I have any feathers on my body?"

Catrin looked at him in bewilderment. "What!"

"Sometimes shapeshifting goes awry, and some of my feathers remain intact," the Druid clarified with a wink.

"Has that happened before?"

"Yes. It's quite annoying. I have to go through the process of shapeshifting again to get rid of all of the feathers."

"Doesn't it concern you to shapeshift if this occurs?" asked Catrin, unsure what to think of the Druid who also seemed to have misplaced his wits.

"No, I've done this for more than a century now." The Druid pointed to some garments flung over a boulder. "Would you mind?"

Catrin retrieved the cape and tunic. Averting her eyes, she handed them to the old man; he was not a pleasant sight to behold.

After dressing in the ankle-length tunic and hooded white cloak, the Druid twitched a smile. "Thank you, maiden. What are you called?"

"I'm Catrin, the daughter of King Amren. What is your name?"

"Some call me the wandering Druid. I venture from village to village, from tribe to tribe, or from wherever to a place of strife."

"Where are you headed now?"

"Wherever my feet go," the Druid said with a wry smile.

"There is no strife here except for some unruly pigs that escaped their pens. The Cantiaci capital of Durovernum is a half-morning ride from here."

The Druid shuffled around. "Did you see my staff?"

Catrin searched the area and found a wooden staff. One of its ends looked like a carved serpent's head biting an egg.

"Are you an Ancient Druid?" she asked, handing the staff to the Druid.

"I've been called that. Are you a Druidess?"

"I've never considered myself as such. Is it hard to shapeshift?"

"It is a difficult magic to master," the Druid said. " I only use it when I need to escape a predator or conceal who I am."

"Sometimes I wish I could take another form and be someone else. How do you do it?"

The Druid cocked an eyebrow. "Why do you want to know?"

"At one time, I asked my father if I could train as a Druidess so I could learn magic such as changing forms. He denied my request, saying the powers are too unpredictable."

"Shapeshifting is a powerful magic," the Druid said, shaking his staff until the orb in the serpent's mouth began glowing. "You must balance forces of creation and destruction."

"Please explain," Catrin urged.

"For me to shapeshift from an owl to a man, I had to disintegrate the stoat and use its mass to create a larger form. There can't be duplicates of the form you create at the same time. A rule of nature."

"Can more than one soul inhabit a body," Catrin asked, pondering how Rhan could have possessed Agrona.

"That is quite a dilemma, more than one soul inhabiting the same body. Though it is possible, there is a cost."

"What cost?"

"A body struggles to provide sustenance to more than one soul." The Druid thumped his head. "It can make your mind feel like a spider web. Pieces of your memory get tangled in a big glob of thread. It can also diminish your mystical powers."

"Tell me how you shapeshift."

Myrddin raked his beard and pulled out some food crumbs. "You visualize yourself latching onto an image and melting into its form. It's like casting liquid fire into a mold to form a sword blade. This is unlike the fluid soul that can wander in and out of minds of other living beings. The soul is like a wave that embraces a beach but must return to the ocean."

"Can you teach me how to change forms?" Catrin asked, thinking she could be as powerful as Marrock with the ability to shapeshift.

"Only a few select persons can master this magic. It is an ability that best serves you at the time you need to conceal yourself from an enemy or deceive family or friend.

"Could I shapeshift into another person?"

"As I said, there cannot be duplicate forms at the same time. Like any skill, it takes practice."

The Druid shuffled to Catrin and regarded her face. "It's possible you already have this ability."

She gave the Druid a bewildered look. "I do?"

"Perhaps so." The Druid stomped his staff on the ground. "If you would excuse me, my feet are itching to wander."

"Why don't you fly to your next destination?"

"The slower it takes me, the more I enjoy the journey," the Druid said, hobbling down the pathway along the river.

Considering what the Druid had said as he lumbered down the pathway, Catrin took it as a challenge to shift into another form. Following his instructions, she visualized herself as a white raven, then felt herself lifting out of her body as she imagined her human form melting and reshaping into a raven. Her heart raced with excitement with the prospect she was changing into a raven, but her exhilaration turned to panic when her body began burning with excruciating pain and it felt as if large needles were piercing into her skin. She drew out of her vision to escape the agony and found herself lying on the ground, with Ferrex kneeling next to her. Somewhat disoriented, she touched what felt like a couple of feathers on her arm.

"What happened to you?" Ferrex asked with concern.

"I met a confused wanderer who could not find his way," Catrin said, plucking out two feathers.

"I met an old Druid on my way back here. Did he do something to you?" asked Ferrex.

"No. I had a vision," Catrin said, although in the back of her mind she wondered if the Druid was a foreboding sign of her return home.

20

FOREBODING SHADOWS

On the ride to the Cantiaci capital, Catrin was still troubled by the wandering Druid's unexpected appearance. Upon entering the fortress, she became disheartened when the villagers glared at her with contempt. None of her family was there to greet Ferrex and her at the Great Hall's courtyard. The stablemen silently took their horses.

Ferrex accompanied Catrin to her former bedchamber, where she could dress for the ceremony. At the doorway, he told her, "Servants have been instructed not to help you. I'll be back to escort you to the wedding. Be forewarned, most of the villagers will shun you during the festivities."

Feeling utterly alone, Catrin choked back a sob as she entered the room. After the all-morning journey on horseback, she felt disheveled. To her dismay, no water had been poured in the bowl on the end table. Unable to wash herself, she rummaged through the shelves. Finding a jar of oil, she dripped a few drops of the lavender fragrance on some cloth and wiped her face with it. She removed her dusty clothing and cleansed herself the best she could with the oil-saturated cloth. Somewhat refreshed, she pulled out a pearl-white linen dress from a wooden chest. Over her dress, she put on a bodice-fitting cloak that tightened at the front with leather bindings. With her muscle gain from conditioning, Catrin grimaced from the constriction of the emerald bodice below her breasts and the tightness of the dress's long sleeves around her arms.

"Just as well," she sighed, acknowledging this was the only formal attire she owned for the occasion. Hearing a knock on the door, she knew Ferrex was ready to escort her to the ceremony.

"The king has summoned you to meet him in his chamber," Ferrex said as she exited into the corridor.

Taken by surprise, she asked, "Do you know why?"

"He said it was about Vala but gave no details."

Catrin wondered if her father had approached Marcellus about releasing her sister. Could it be possible that the night's festivities would celebrate the return of two daughters and the marriage of the other?

A foreboding sensation made her think otherwise.

The trek to the king's chamber now seemed arduous, unlike the joyful skipping she had experienced as a child to greet him. Was she deluding herself with the hope her father would welcome her back into the family fold without further testing her, even if Vala were released?

Approaching the king's chamber with Ferrex, she reminded herself to put on a brave face and show her father utmost reverence. She should not call him "Father," but greet him as her sovereign.

Ferrex tapped on the dark oak door. "My king, Catrin is here to see you."

The door creaked open to reveal her father resplendently attired in a fur cape clasped over his gold-trimmed blue tunic and trousers with the distinctive turquoise-and-gold family plaid. He was bejeweled with a massive torc around his neck and gold bracelets. Even so, his face looked grim as he acknowledged her with a nod. He pointed to the pentagram-engraved table in the center of the room. "Sit with me over there."

Catrin did not detect any harshness but rather a sad timbre in his voice. She clumsily curtsied, holding her stomach in. The king extended his hand for her to kiss—a formal gesture, not the warm embrace he usually greeted her with. The austere welcome made Catrin teary-eyed, but she held back a sob, sensing the meeting might not bode well for her.

Lifting her heavy skirt, she stepped to the table and cautiously sat down. A single burning candle on the tabletop lit the bleak chamber. The flame flickered as the king heavily sat himself down.

A woman's shadow holding a severed head at the doorway startled Catrin. She gasped and closed her eyes. When she opened them again, the shadow had disappeared. Shaking, she turned her gaze to her father, whose eyes were as wide as hers.

"Did you see something?" he asked with a quavered voice. "You looked as if you had seen a wraith."

Clutching her trembling hands, Catrin hesitated to tell him, not sure what the foreboding vision meant. "I saw a shadow. It could have been a trick of my eyes when the candle almost blew out."

"Did you foresee something in the future?"

Catrin could feel her father's eyes probing her. She shifted in her chair to get more comfortable. "I no longer have visions. I swore off these powers, as you commanded."

"That may be what you swore, but I sense you can still use these powers. Did you see Vala?"

Catrin anxiously shook her head. "Has something happened to her that I should know about?"

Not answering her question, the king slowly rubbed his lower lip. "I thought, perhaps, you had seen her just now in a vision or in one of your dreams."

Catrin studied her father's face, which reminded her of a death mask concealing a dark secret. Unsettled, she hesitated to say more until she could glean more information from him. "I've not seen Vala, but I sense you fear for her safety. Did you approach Marcellus about releasing her, as I suggested?"

Amren drew in a heavy breath and leaned forward on his elbows. The reflection of the candle flame wavered on his blue eyes as he confided, "You must promise me that no word of what I am about to say leaves this room."

The hairs on Catrin's neck prickled. "I promise."

Amren straightened on his high-backed chair. "Based on your claims that Marcellus loves you, I put your faith in him to the test. After my spies informed me that his father planned to execute Vala, I followed your advice. I had a message secretly delivered to Marcellus, saying you had been accused of treason for his affair with you. Trystan secretly met with Marcellus and a Roman commander about exchanging Vala for the five soldiers we captured. At the meeting, Trystan gave Marcellus the Apollo amulet and demanded he spy for us to save you from the ultimate punishment of being burned to the stake."

A breath caught in Catrin's throat. "When did you do this?"

"About two weeks ago."

"Marcellus agreed, didn't he?" she rasped, suddenly anxious that something had gone wrong.

"Just as you foretold, he readily promised to free Vala," Amren said. "He promised to meet my condition that she be released prior to Mor's wedding. Trystan was dispatched three days ago to exchange prisoners."

Noticing the glum look on her Father's face, Catrin swallowed hard. "Has Trystan returned?"

"No, not yet." Amren leaned back into the chair, his stare remaining frozen on her. "I thought of postponing the wedding until Trystan returned with Vala. But my people might become alarmed that something is afoot. That is why I asked if you had seen any omens to explain why they had not returned."

Catrin felt her stomach drop in dread that she had seen harbingers of Vala's demise. She confessed, "When I first entered the room, I saw a shadow holding a head in the back corner. It was just for an instant, so I thought it was an illusion, as I said earlier. After what you've told me, I now fear it is a bad omen. But there is more. I've had vivid nightmares of lightning boring holes through three human skulls lined up in a row. Marrock stood behind these skulls and manipulated the lightning between the palms of his hands. Each time I dreamt of this, I awoke in a cold sweat, terrified that one of the skulls was mine."

Amren's eyes grew bigger. "Was Vala's skull among them?"

A shiver streaked down Catrin's spine. "I'm not sure. When I have these nightmares, I don't always know what they mean."

The king considered Catrin for a moment. "When I banished you, I beseeched the gods to show me a sign of what my final judgment should be for your relationship with the Roman. Your omens have just shown me what to do. My final sentence will be based on whether Marcellus fulfills his promise to release Vala, as you swore he would. If he breaks that promise, he has shown his true nature. He has abandoned you and willingly accepts you will be condemned to death. Remember what I said. Your pathway to redemption is based on the next choices you make. As a ruler, if you make one wrong decision, you may not be given another chance. As such, if Marcellus betrays us, I will be hard-pressed to rescind your banishment—a punishment far worse than death, would you not agree?"

Catrin froze under her father's cold stare. She wanted to throw herself into the candle flame like a moth. How could Marcellus turn on her when she needed him most?

He loves me. He promised to protect me! In my heart, I know he'll do everything to save me. He won't betray me. He can't betray me.

Catrin felt her chest heave with angst. Her path to redemption depended on Marcellus. She had to cling to hope that he had released Vala.

Amren's voice shook Catrin out of her ruminations.

"Look at me, Catrin. Look at me!"

Still in denial that Marcellus could betray her, she shifted her eyes toward her father, now standing next to her.

"Now that I have your attention," Amren said sternly, "I want you to know that before you came in here, Ferrex barged into my chamber. He fell on his knees and pleaded I grant you mercy and take you back. He said he would follow you into banishment if that is my final decree. No man has shown you greater love or loyalty than Ferrex. Treat him kindly tonight. He may be your only friend tomorrow. Your Roman lover is nothing more than a fleeting memory of when he seduced you at your weakest. You've paid a great price for giving him your virginity. Love is forged in duty and honor. It is hammered into shape by decisions and commitments a man and a woman pledge to one another. Ferrex can give you that loyalty. Marcellus can't."

Catrin recognized Ferrex was an honorable man, but how could she throw her love and loyalty for Marcellus away?

She couldn't.

She would keep her pledge to her father. She would swear off all men and serve her father as a warrior to win back his love and respect.

Catrin gazed at the burning candle until her father snuffed it out. Left in total darkness, she heard him say sharply, "We need to go."

21

MOR'S WEDDING

Leaving the chamber with her father, Catrin was surprised to see Ferrex waiting in the corridor for them. She almost didn't recognize him. His coppery mane was shorn to shoulder-length and his face was clean shaven. Why hadn't she noticed his transformation before, when he had escorted her to the king's chamber? There was a glimmer in his hazel eyes, which looked almost gold in the torch light as he acknowledged her with a slight nod. She was disquieted with her father's sly smile as he placed her hand into Ferrex's palm.

"Ferrex will be your escort at the wedding," Amren declared. "As such, both of you will follow me in the procession as part of my family to the sacred oak grove."

Catrin's first impulse was to pull her hand away, feeling guilty that she was betraying Marcellus. Her father's stern brow warned her to adhere to his wishes. Nonetheless, she pulled her hand out of Ferrex's sweaty palm and folded her arm into his. Ferrex seemed agreeable to this, but her father creased his brow.

Thankfully the king said no more as they walked outside to the courtyard, where celebrants had gathered around Queen Rhiannon and the betrothed couple. Amren offered his hand to the queen, and everyone followed them in the ceremonial procession to the sacred grove about one half-mile from the fortress.

Mor and Belinus stood in front of a crackling bonfire in the midst of towering oaks. The flames lit up their faces as they faced each other. In the bittersweet moment, Catrin recalled her marriage vows with Marcellus before Mother Goddess. She forced back a tear, trying to accept that their ill-fated love was doomed. She slipped her arm out of Ferrex's and stood stiffly as she witnessed the remaining ceremony.

Amren raised his hand and proclaimed, "Queen Rhiannon and I recognize and bless the marriage between Belinus and Mor. They will now publicly declare their vows as husband and wife."

The king wrapped a blue-and-gold plaid cloth around the couple's wrists to bind their hands together. Belinus smiled and said his vows first.

"Mor, daughter of King Amren and Queen Rhiannon, I give you my heart, body and soul to join yours. As your husband, I vow my fidelity to you in times of both bounty and famine. I am the sun. You are Mother Earth. My light shines on you as we journey together from sunrise until we part at sunset."

Mor wore a loose teal-green dress, the color signifying the fertility of Mother Goddess. She beamed in loving affection. "Belinus, I give my heart, body, and soul to you. I promise my fidelity to you in times of both health and sickness. You are the sun that warms the love I have growing in my belly. I join you in the circle of life that connects darkness until dawn's light."

The bonfire illuminated the love radiating from Mor's face. Belinus's pale blue eyes appeared to flash in the flames as he pulled her into his arms and gave her a lingering kiss. Catrin could hardly breathe, realizing she would never know this moment with Marcellus . . . or with any other man. Looking around the gathering, she caught sight of a headless shadow clutching a bundle and wandering just outside the perimeter of celebrants. She trembled with an inexplicable dread that the vision was a portent that she would never see Vala and Mor's child, cradled in the shadow's arms.

As the celebrants broke into cheers and song, Catrin felt Ferrex's hand reach for hers, awakening her to his presence.

"Let us sit down by the bonfire," he said amiably, "and enjoy the festivities."

How could she enjoy the festivities with her mind filled with grim images and gnawing doubts that Marcellus would fulfill his promise to release Vala?

Is Vala dead because Marcellus betrayed me?

She quickly buried that possibility, rationalizing that Trystan would return with Vala unless he had met an ill fate.

The tightening of Ferrex's hand around hers drew Catrin out of her thoughts. She could tell by the longing in his eyes that he had other amorous plans in mind for her. He was ready to celebrate—drink, dance, and feast on roasted boars—and do what lusty couples do in drunken glee.

Looking all around, she noticed some of the warriors were already gulping down ale from ram horns and bellowing their distinctive war chants. The loud beats of the drums were inviting young couples to perform Bel's fire ritual under the full moon.

Catrin reluctantly followed Ferrex to a wooden bench near a fire pit but away from the ruckus. Hot beads of sweat dripped between her breasts from the fire's intense heat. Aware that Ferrex was looking where he shouldn't, she looked down at her caped bodice and readjusted the leather bindings to release the pressure beneath her chest. Averting his stare, she fiddled with the thin braids woven in her long golden hair until she felt Ferrex's hard tap on her arm. She looked at him. His eager grin and feral eyes glinting with high expectations made her feel queasy.

"Would you like to dance?"

Catrin folded her hands and looked straight ahead. "No, I'd rather watch."

Averting Ferrex's stare, she watched Mor and Belinus dance with each other. Mor mimicked a doe while Belinus pranced like a stag near the main towering fire. She could feel Ferrex's eyes all over her as she gazed at the tongued flames licking the silver moonbeams.

After a long, awkward silence, he asked, "Are you enjoying the feast?"

What a stupid question? Of course, I'm not.

She scooted away from him. "Yes, very much."

Ferrex nervously glanced at her. "Me, too. Umm . . ." The bench shook as he bounced his legs up and down.

Catrin couldn't tell if he was moving in rhythm to the drumbeats or was uneasy with her cold response. Nonetheless, his attempts to be friendly annoyed her. Besides, she had other concerns on her mind.

"Cynwrig says you like to ride horses," Ferrex blurted.

Catrin gawked at him.

What a stupid comment. You trained me to throw a spear on a horse.

Noticing some dirt underneath his fingernails, Catrin decided to end the conversation then and there with a curt response. "Yes."

Without saying another word, she pushed herself up and left Ferrex sitting alone on the log. She made her way to the pathway leading back to the fortress but was halted by her mother's tight grip around her arm.

"What did you say to Ferrex?" Rhiannon said sharply. "Look at him. He looks as unhappy as a barnyard cat whose prey just got away."

Avoiding her mother's hard stare, Catrin looked in the direction of where Mor and Belinus were dancing their ritualistic fertility dance. Their hips provocatively undulated back and forth as they circled each other. She said curtly, "Ferrex can find someone else to dance with. Right now, I want to be alone."

She stepped away, but the harsh tone of her mother saying, "Young maiden, do not walk away while I'm talking to you," halted her. She turned and regarded her mother's raised eyebrow.

"You need to treat warriors who will defend you with their lives with more respect. Or you will not find any of them at your side in the heat of battle."

Catrin seethed. *You can't force me to love another man, if that is your game.* She glanced at Ferrex's downcast face and suddenly felt ashamed, recalling her father's words: *Treat Ferrex kindly tonight. Tomorrow, he may be your only friend.*

She couldn't understand why she had treated Ferrex so rudely. Perhaps it was the dread that Marcellus had betrayed her and Vala was dead. Even so, Ferrex had been her most loyal friend and ardent supporter. He deserved a better woman. She could never open her heart to any man and be hurt again.

Catrin took a deep breath and assured her mother, "I'll get Ferrex something to eat."

She walked to the open pits where the meat was roasting. The village butcher handed her a platter of boar ribs, which she knew were Ferrex's favorite. She walked over to Ferrex, who was brooding. She handed him the plate.

"Here, something for you to eat."

Ferrex's eyes brightened. "Thank you. Please sit down and share this with me."

Catrin nodded. Sitting next to him, she noticed a dimple on his chin that gave him a boyish charm. She had never observed this feature with his full beard. She had to admit he was handsome, yet the dirt underneath his fingernails distracted her as he pulled strips of meat off the bone to offer her some. She forced a smile, taking a smaller piece. Chewing cautiously, she picked out some gritty particles which she hoped were nothing more than specks of burnt meat.

A hatchet-throwing contest between Cynwrig and another warrior caught her attention. Rumors abounded in the village that Cynwrig's wife was pregnant, about as far along as Mor.

Catrin shifted her eyes toward the bonfire and watched her mother and father dancing together near the newlyweds. She could tell by the way they gazed at each other that they were truly in love with each other. A sense of guilt washed over her that she had accused her mother of not loving her father at the time she divulged she loved Marcellus.

Then, to her dismay, a mist swirled upward from the ground and transformed into the shape of Marcellus. He had a tear in his eye as he fingered the Apollo amulet in his hand.

A chill iced down her back.

A light nudge on her shoulder jolted Catrin out of her vision. She found Ferrex staring at her with concern.

"Are you alright? You appeared to be in a trance."

"I was caught in a dream," she said, her hands trembling.

Ferrex swallowed hard. "Would you give this warrior the honor of dancing with you?"

At that moment, Catrin sensed he would play an important role in her destiny—not as a lover, but as a protector and guide who would always stay at her side no matter what. He rose and offered his hand to help her up. The touch of his fingers elicited a vision of him standing in the midst of a multi-tier structure with a red loincloth covering his hips. He was heavily armed with leg greaves, a leather manica on a shoulder, and sword. Not sure what her vision meant, she followed Ferrex to a circle of celebrants slowly dancing to the melody of a bard's tragic song about lovers throwing themselves into a fire rather than being separated.

As she circled Ferrex, he lifted her arm to twirl her underneath the star-lit sky. Mesmerized, she closed her eyes and listened to the bittersweet melody of the instruments. At that moment, she longed to be with Marcellus, but Ferrex's hard kiss swept her out of the moment. After he released the wet kiss, he uttered, "I love you."

Angered by his bold move, Catrin pushed Ferrex in the chest. "Don't touch me like that again!"

The rejection on Ferrex's face momentarily tugged at her heart, but she suddenly sensed the Raven's essence warning her that something evil was approaching.

She looked beyond the bonfire and saw a figure racing toward them. The blood-stained face of Trystan came into focus as he frantically screamed, "Get your weapons! He's coming. He's coming."

The sound of Trystan's voice faded into the rumble of barks, growls, and howls rising like thunder out of the dense trees. The clinking of metal swords against shields grew louder and louder like a building tempest.

An instant later, wolves of all colors leapt through the oaks and cut down men, women and children who were in the line of their attack. The grove filled with a cacophony of snapping jaws, crunching bones, and screams. In the confusion, everyone scrambled to grab rocks, knives, cleavers, swords, and spears to ward off the beasts.

"Take this!" Ferrex tossed a sword to Catrin. With fighting instincts surging through her veins, she ran alongside Ferrex, joining other warriors to counter the wolves attacking children.

The grotesque specter of Marrock riding a coal-black steed came into sight. The bonfire lit up his moon-cratered face as his horse reared. Other mounted warriors circled their wolfish leader. At his command, the blue-faced demons threw severed heads at the charging villagers.

Marrock shoved a headless body off his horse.

As swiftly as the pack of wolves and horseman had appeared, they disappeared into dark woods.

22

Aftermath of the Wedding

Amren looked at the deadly carnage under the moon's illumination. Severed heads were strewn on the blood-soaked pasture near the trees. Women cradled screaming children while others inspected the motionless bodies for life. Weapon-wielding warriors on horseback were sweeping the area for Marrock and his warriors. Stunned, he felt like the walking death in the midst of a nightmare. He staggered to the severed heads and body thrown on the ground like butchered animals. As he knelt to inspect the headless body, he almost collapsed, recognizing the blood-soaked garments of Vala, whom he had accepted and loved as his own daughter.

For several moments, he gaped at the headless corpse and placed a shaky hand on her cold body. He scanned the immediate area for other casualties. There were at least five decapitated heads in the midst of mutilated bodies. He recognized the faces of two warriors who had accompanied Trystan to the prisoner exchange.

He moaned in despair.

This was supposed to be a time to celebrate . . . not a time to mourn the senseless slaughter of his people. How could Marrock and his warriors strike like lightning and disappear as shooting stars in the moonlit sky?

The swelling emotions of revulsion, grief, and rage finally overwhelmed him. He threw his head back and wailed—a cry so mournful that the moon disappeared behind a shroud of clouds. His cry transformed into a roar, a raging roar that pervaded every pore in his body and soul.

Strong hands lifted Amren from the grassy ground as if he were a helpless child. The torch lights whirled around him until the anguished faces of

his people gathering around him came into focus. His warriors were looking to him for his next command. How could he give the order? His heart
was too racked with grief and guilt.

Amren's thoughts then turned to Rhiannon. He could not let her see
their daughter like this. Not only had Vala been decapitated, she had been
dismembered and disemboweled like a butchered animal at a sacrifice. He
vaguely recalled Belinus whisking his wife and Mor away from the fray, but
what about Catrin? Did Marrock's wolves shred her apart?

He frantically looked around and yelled, "Rhiannon, where are you?
Mor . . . Catrin!"

The assemblage around him parted to let Catrin and Ferrex through.
Overcome with relief to see her, Amren impulsively pulled her into his
arms. He reassured, "You are safe . . . you are safe now," though the dread of
Rhan's curse hovering over him haunted his mind.

Ferrex looked at Amren with concern. "Are you injured, my king?
Your hands are bloody."

Amren released Catrin and gawked at his smeared hands. Fearing the
putrid-smelling stain was eating his skin away, he frantically wiped the
body fluids on his tunic. A sharp pain stabbed into his abdomen. He gritted
his teeth, realizing his wounds had re-opened. He fought for composure.

*I am the king. Get hold of yourself. You must be strong for my family and
people.*

"How many warriors have given chase?" Amren asked Ferrex.

"Cynwrig and several of his men are searching the area," Ferrex answered. "The others await your command."

With the darkness of storm clouds now closing in, Amren knew
it would be foolhardy to risk losing any more warriors by searching for
Marrock at night. But he had to reassure his people. He looked at Ferrex.
"Gather the people around me. Find my queen and Mor so they can stand
with me as I address them all."

Ferrex saluted and left.

As Amren waited for his people to assemble, he knelt beside Catrin,
who was touching Vala's corpse. He placed his hand on the headless shoul-

ders. Rigor mortis had set in. A putrid rotten odor assaulted his nostrils. Vala must have been dead for at least two or three days. How could he give proper funeral rites without the head, where Vala's soul resided? She could not journey headless to the Otherworld.

Amren joined Catrin in the ritual of waving his hands over Vala's desecrated body to remove all evil spirits. She removed her cloak and respectfully covered Vala's body.

Catrin's vacant gaze concerned him, as did her tearless eyes. He had often observed this empty stare in surviving warriors who wished they had died instead of their companions or family members.

Seeing Rhiannon approaching, he embraced her and said over and over, "I'm so sorry, I'm so sorry, my sweet wife."

Yet his words sounded as empty as a dried river bed robbed of its life-sustaining water. The queen trembled within his arms, but her eyes stayed as dry as Catrin's.

When all of the people congregated around him, Amren pronounced with a metal-hardened mien, "We gather here not as nobles, warriors, farmers, blacksmiths, or peasants . . . but as one beating heart. This evening, I celebrated the marriage of my daughter, Mor, but now must burn my eldest daughter, Vala, on a funeral pyre tomorrow. And yet, I do not celebrate and suffer alone. Everyone here has lost a loved one at some point. Our life journey is a circle interconnecting life and death. Life always springs forth from destruction."

Amren paused and studied the fear-struck faces of those before him. He sensed they needed more from him. They needed his strength. He walked around the circle of people and spoke to each of them in a firm but comforting voice. "Let us return to the safety of our fortress and grieve. Tomorrow, we will ignite our vengeance in the fires of the funeral rites."

A dead silence sliced through the crowd as they disassembled and walked to the village. Amren held Rhiannon's hand as Mor, Belinus, and Catrin walked quietly behind him as a united family. The night's events rumbled in Amren's mind as he restlessly slept and his rage swelled that Marcellus had not safely released Vala.

The following evening, Amren carried Vala's shrouded, headless body to the site where the wedding celebration had taken place the previous day. He set her body on the funeral pyre and took a burning torch from Rhiannon. He raised it to signal to the female archers who had been under Vala's command to release their arrows. The archers shot their flaming arrows into the pyre that then burst into a fiery inferno. Vala's body was consumed in the flames and transformed into black, choking smoke.

Deeply grieved, Amren watched Catrin and Mor embrace their sobbing mother. He unsheathed his sword, pointed the blade to the starlit night, and proclaimed, "We stand together as one beating heart. I refuse to cringe from the fire's blaze. And neither should you. Tonight, I ignite my grief into the fires of my fury. Join me and forge our grief into a sword of vengeance. I sacrifice my daughter to the gods so they will arm us with their wrath. I ask you to avenge those who murdered my daughter as I celebrated the wedding of another. Vala's defilement is the defilement of every Cantiaci who holds his daughter close to heart. I put my trust in the Catuvellauni king and the Romans to negotiate a just peace. Instead, they chained me, beat me, and cut my flesh. They butchered Vala like a spring lamb. My banished son's vile acts demand justice. What shall we serve our enemies at our war fest?"

Ferrex lifted his sword. "Death and destruction!"

Belinus did likewise and shouted, "Death to our enemies."

Others lifted their swords and chanted, "War, war, war."

Amren's voice rose like thunder over the cries of his people. "I hear your cries for justice. I hear your cries for vengeance. I hear your cries for war. We will thrust our swords of vengeance into the black hearts of our enemies!"

23

TRYSTAN'S TALE

The day after Vala's funeral, Amren told the servant to fetch Trystan. The calamity of Marrock's attack had finally sunk into him. His insides were ready to split open with unanswered questions that barraged his mind since he had been given the scroll found near the location where Vala's headless body had been dropped on the ground.

He again unrolled the scroll and reread the message written in bold Latin lettering.

Negotiations over! The Raven flies out of Apollo's flames as a harbinger that you can't escape Rhan's curse.

Amren slapped the papyrus parchment on the table. He retrieved the dagger case and inspected the blade's etching. The curse had not changed since he had last revealed the inscription to Catrin at her trial. The dark prophecy festered in him like an inflamed boil. He could no longer deny the truth. The instant Catrin succumbed to the fiery passion of the Roman enemy, she reset the curse that Marrock would ally with the Roman Empire to destroy him.

He slammed the lid closed. As far as he was concerned, his daughter was a whore who had spread her legs for the Roman Apollo who besmeared her honor. In a moment of weakness, Amren had shown Catrin mercy and believed her Roman seducer could save Vala. He should have done his duty as king and executed Catrin on the spot.

His anger did not stop there. He wanted to tear out Trystan's heart for failing to protect Vala.

Even though Amren acknowledged and loved Vala as his own daughter, Trystan was her biological father and Rhiannon's lover before they married. Trystan should have died fighting to save his daughter.

The images of his enemies suffering horrible deaths spilled into his mind like burning acid. The flames from the Underworld the Romans called Hades would melt Lucius's face from his skull like dripping wax. Cunobelin's headless body would slither like a snake on the ground after Amren struck off his head. He would castrate Marcellus with the cursed dagger for defiling Catrin as Apollo had forced himself on Daphne. He wished he had yanked out his monstrous son as a babe from the womb and hurled him over the white cliffs to be washed away by the tides.

And now, he had to face his most formidable enemy—Agrona, the embodiment of Rhan. He had already executed Rhan once, but she had escaped death by possessing Agrona. And she could do something similar again. He had dreamt that Catrin and Rhan chanted over a cauldron in which green-brown ooze bubbled over its rim. The prospect that Rhan had also possessed Catrin haunted his every waking thought. He questioned if his daughter's pledge of loyalty was a charade to win back his trust, so she and Rhan could combine their powers to destroy him and everyone he loved.

Conflicting emotions of love, hate, rage, and fear overwhelmed him. For his kingdom to survive, he must rule with a brutal fist. He must strike down any one who betrayed him, including those closest to him.

A gravelly voice yanked Amren out of his whirling thoughts.

"My king," Ferrex said, "Trystan is here to see you."

Ferrex and Cynwrig carried Trystan on a stretcher into the chamber and laid him on the dark oak floor. Amren could tell by Trystan's sunken eyes and pallid face that his commander was in significant pain. Amren showed no pity as he coldly ordered, "Trystan, stand before your king."

"But, my king . . ." Ferrex began to protest.

"I will do what my king commands," Trystan declared.

Ferrex lifted Trystan from the stretcher and helped him to a table, where he gripped its edge for support. Amren told Ferrex and Cynwrig to wait outside. After they left, he stepped to within a few inches of Trystan's face. "What do you have to say for yourself? You were charged to protect Vala—your own daughter whom I adopted and loved as my own—but you failed miserably. Why is your head not rotting alongside Vala's corpse?"

Trystan's eyes watered and his voice cracked as he said, "We were betrayed by Marcellus."

Amren glared. "What happened?"

"Marcellus promised to be there. Only a tribune and two soldiers were on shore." Trystan grimaced and closed his eyes for a moment, as if pushing through the pain.

"The Romans waved us to shore, but I didn't see Vala. It didn't feel right, so I halted the boat a little way offshore. Vala suddenly ran out of the woods north of the estuary. She screamed for help, but Marrock was galloping on a horse behind her with a sword in hand."

Tears swelled in Trystan's eyes as he uttered, "He . . . he cut . . . off her head and taunted, 'You fools, Marcellus betrayed you! Lucius betrayed you!'"

Trystan stumbled against the table but grasped its edge for balance and pressed on with his horrific tale. "My guts felt as if they had been ripped out. I ordered my men to behead every Roman prisoner and throw their heads and bodies into the river. We then rowed away, fearing a Roman attack."

Amren heaved with anger. "So you made no attempt to recover Vala's body! Were you too afraid to lose your own head?"

"We did make an attempt," Trystan replied. "We sailed to the opposite bank to disembark. We tried to pick up Marrock's trail, but we couldn't find him after searching all day. At nightfall, I decided to return and tell you what happened. After we landed our ship near the white cliffs the following day, we gathered horses and galloped them at full speed to get here. About a mile from here, Marrock, his pack of wolves, and warriors were waiting—"

"How could he have gotten so many warriors here in such a short time?" Amren blurted.

"I don't know," Trystan said, his face turning as pale as a corpse. "My men died fighting so I could escape . . . to warn you. My horse collapsed. I ran . . . Marrock . . . closed on me . . ."

Trystan's eyes rolled up and he crumpled to the floor.

Alarmed, the king turned him over to check his neck for a pulse. His heartbeat was weak. His skin was clammy. His bandages were soaked with blood.

"Someone get a healer!" Amren cried out.

Ferrex rushed into the chamber. "Cynwrig is fetching a Druid. Do you want me to carry Trystan to another bedchamber for treatment?"

"Wait to see what the Druid wants to do."

As Amren covered Trystan with his cape, he grappled with his remorse for treating his loyal commander so harshly. He swept away the emotion as Trystan clasped his wrist and rasped, "I didn't want this to happen. Give me a sword. I'll follow you into battle to avenge my daughter's murder."

Amren nodded. "You'll be at my side."

Trystan closed his eyes and seemed more at peace, but Amren's mind whirled with thoughts of the hurricane forces racing toward him. He refused to yield to Rhan's curse. He would face his fate with courage and honor. If need be, he would defy the gods and obliterate the curse into a thousand pieces.

24

SEARCH FOR DECIMUS

Marcellus rolled to his side and confirmed his father was still asleep on the other bed. Sitting up, he clutched his rumbling stomach and regretted the late-night drinking. Yet it had taken a copious amount of wine to calm his father, who kept asking, "What has taken Decimus so long to find his men missing from the hunt? He's been gone more than four days. He should be here by now, serving my needs."

"He'll be here soon," Marcellus said, though he had the same concerns as his father.

"This should be a one-day venture," Lucius insisted. "What if something went wrong?"

"Other soldiers are with him," Marcellus reassured. "They would have returned by now if something went wrong."

After the effects of the wine had taken hold that night, his father relaxed and spoke to Marcellus almost as a confidant. Surprisingly, he reminisced about meeting Marcellus's mother for the first time. "After I tragically lost my first wife in childbirth, I met your mother at a banquet hosted by my mentor, Gaius Druses, at Massilia. When he introduced me to his daughter, her name played like a song in my mind: Drusilla . . . Drusilla. I was surprised that Gaius, a swarthy and portly man as grotesque as a tusked boar, could sire such a goddess. Your mother's skin was as translucent as a white pearl. Her blue eyes looked violet in the soft light of a candle. I wanted to discover the mystery behind those eyes. We escaped to the garden under a full moon. I remembered the fragrance of roses that intoxicated me when I took her into my arms and kissed her for the first time. I later asked myself if I had foolishly fallen in love."

At that moment, Marcellus felt a rare connection to his father, who seldom cracked his shell to reveal his inner feelings. His father had never openly talked about his affection for his mother, whose comely features Marcellus had inherited—deep blue eyes, aquiline nose, thick eyebrows, and blemish-free, olive skin. With his reasoning doused with alcohol, Marcellus thought, perhaps, his father would eventually understand his affection for Catrin.

But his father's mood changed after he drank another goblet of wine. His words slurred with a grating bite to his voice.

"After we first married, Drusilla had those same fragrant roses planted at our villa in remembrance of the night we first kissed and . . ." Lucius furiously threw the goblet at the tapestry that divided the sleeping quarters from the main headquarters. "Don't think I married your mother out of love. Her father paid me a huge dowry to get her off his hands. After I discovered her dark secret on our wedding night, I roughly seeded her. And she had you." His words then transformed into snorts and gasps as he slumped in a wine-induced stupor.

The bitterness in his father voice when he said "she had you," made Marcellus burn with resentment.

Is that what I am? A mistake? A disappointment?

Now noticing the smoke rising out of a dying candle on the end table, Marcellus turned his focus to the grim reality that Decimus had not yet returned. A twinge of panic struck him that his father, upon wakening, would surely dispatch soldiers to look for the tribune. Marcellus now dreaded that something calamitous had occurred at the prisoner exchange to explain Decimus's delay.

The urgency of finding Decimus before their scheme came to light jolted Marcellus into action. If something went awry, he needed to execute their next plan to take command of the legionary forces from his father to prevent a war.

But first, he had to confirm what happened to Decimus before he took such a drastic step.

Gods forbid he's dead.

Marcellus skirted his father's bed and pulled the tapestry aside to enter the main headquarters. When he rushed through the flapped entryway, he was greeted by a sentry with the girth of a bear and chest hair that looked like fur.

"Did you sleep well?" the sentry inquired, snapping his boots to attention.

Marcellus forced a smile, even though the rancid wine in his stomach was ready to eject onto the soldier. He pressed his mouth with a hand and released a loud belch, giving him some relief.

"That's better. A little too much to drink, I'm afraid," Marcellus said. "Father is still feeling the effects of the wine from last night. I would not wake him if I were you. He's in a foul mood. Have you seen Tribune Decimus this morning?"

"No sir," the guard replied, shaking his head. "Some of his men are concerned that it has been more than five days since he left with six of his soldiers."

Marcellus had the same sentiment, but he didn't want to belabor the tribune's disappearance. "Prepare a horse for me to ride out of camp," he demanded.

"For what purpose?" the sentry asked, narrowing his eyes.

Disquieted with the sentry's tone, Marcellus snapped, "For whatever reason I choose. Soldier, you forget your place."

The sentry dropped his eyes. "I meant no offense. I'm only doing my duty. With Decimus gone so long, your father ordered me to keep track of anyone who leaves camp. And that includes you."

Marcellus nodded uneasily. "If that is the case, tell my father I've gone to Camulodunon to purchase some berries from a local vendor. I'll be back early this afternoon."

The sentry looked up. "The sun is almost at its zenith now."

Marcellus also looked at the cloud-covered sky and became annoyed with himself that he had slept so late. "I can't tell if it's morning or afternoon with this gloomy weather. Just tell my father that I'll be back by dinner. Now get me a horse."

The sentry rushed off and came back with a gray horse about fourteen hands high. Marcellus climbed onto the mount and rode between the legionary barracks and out the encampment's main gate. He directed his horse onto a rutted road and descended a grassy hilltop full of grazing cattle. At the bottom, he weaved in and out of natives driving chariots and carts conveying goods to and from the Roman camp to Camulodunon. He continued riding between plots of wheat, barley, and corn for about a mile, then veered southeast on a narrower road that meandered through the woodlands. Based on what Decimus had said, the horse path led to the river estuary where the rendezvous with Trystan was to take place. The tribune had planned to travel in the cover of trees, so his troops didn't draw undue interest.

Continuing southeast, Marcellus searched through the thick brush and trees for any movement of Decimus and his men. After awhile, the cackling ravens soaring overhead caught his attention. He looked up and noticed one of them flying to a nearby grove of crimson-berried trees. He halted his horse and focused on the location where the scavengers were landing. He noticed what appeared to be a soldier wandering between the trees. The glint from metal armor hinted he was a Roman officer, but the shadows from tree branches swaying in the breeze obscured the man's features.

Marcellus waved his arms to draw the man's attention.

As the man approached the clearing, Marcellus recognized Decimus. To his shock, the tribune's hair was blood-smeared and matted; his forehead was discolored reddish-purple from heavy bruising. One eye was swollen almost shut while the other was opened wide in fear.

Marcellus's stomach clenched as he asked, "What happened here? Where are your men?"

The tribune, who usually had a rock-solid demeanor, appeared disoriented and terrified. "I need to show you something, but prepare yourself. You will see something that will turn your guts inside out."

25

MARROCK'S VILE DEED

Decimus appeared to be choking back sobs as he gestured for Marcellus to follow him. Marcellus nudged his horse deeper into the woods and toward the ruckus of ravens. The shrieking birds evoked thoughts of Catrin, who could see the future through the Raven's eyes. He didn't need her prophetic ability to know what lay ahead—ravens gorging on corpses.

Beyond the dense trees, he found tens of ravens atop an open wagon, dancing to and fro on its rim like demented demons. The scene reminded Marcellus of the conflict that broke out at his prisoner exchange. Catrin had summoned ravens as thick as a dust cloud to attack the Romans. The birds gouged out the eyeballs of two Roman soldiers and shredded tissue from their bones.

As Marcellus apprehensively approached the wagon, he inhaled a foul odor that smelled like rotting meat. He watched Decimus furiously jab his sword at the ravens, but most of the disgusting birds escaped his blade and darted to the trees overhead.

As Marcellus finally peered inside the wagon, the putrid stench hit him like a catapult and he gagged. The sight was even more horrific than what he could have imagined.

Human body parts were piled in a bloody mass like butchered meat. Legs and arms crisscrossed between severed heads. Intestines oozed out of corpses like slithering snakes. His face suddenly drenched with hot sweat. He leaned over and vomited the rancid wine in his stomach. Still nauseated, he straightened himself up and wiped the acrid-tasting drool from his mouth with his sleeve.

"Merciful Juno, what happened here?"

Decimus picked up a head with one of its eyes gouged out and wiped the gelatinous blood clot out of the socket. He rambled, "Nine . . . nine men are dead. They're all here . . . I made sure of that. They need to be sanctified before their final journey."

Tears filled the tribune's eyes as he placed the mutilated head back into the wagon. "They were waiting . . . what they were, I'm not sure. Waiting for us . . . ambushed us . . . screams everywhere. I failed, I failed them . . ." The tribune's words tumbled into incomprehensible mutters.

Marcellus reined his horse closer to Decimus, but the stench from the corpses again overwhelmed him and he retched. When his stomach finally emptied, he felt as if his belly had been twisted out of him. He resolved to get past the horror so he could calm the terrified tribune and learn what had caused such a spectacle.

"Take a deep breath," he told Decimus. "Did Trystan ambush you?"

Decimus looked at Marcellus with fear-struck eyes as words tumbled out of his mouth in spurts. "Last night . . . the other night, I can't remember. I woke up . . . here. Someone must have hit me"—Decimus looked around, as if gathering his bearings—"Something out of this world, not here but near the river, attacked us. Only I and two men survived. We crawled on hands and knees. It was dark . . . so dark to see what the creature looked like. For the first time, I was afraid, truly afraid"

Decimus paused, his mouth slowly dropping. "Then we heard wraiths, shapeshifters, all around us, hunting us down . . . but I pushed on. I couldn't get to my fallen men. At first light, we dashed to the river. Trystan was in a ship with my captured men. I screamed 'Don't harm them!' It was to no avail—" The tribune's breaths rattled and his eyes pierced over Marcellus's head, as if he was reliving the horror again.

Marcellus raised his voice to get Decimus's attention. "Were the Roman prisoners with Trystan?"

"Yes. And Marrock," Decimus said with glassy eyes.

Marcellus shook his head in bewilderment. "Marrock? Why would he be in the ship?"

Decimus's voice quavered. "Behind me, hooves clomped. I turned and Marrock was ahorse with Vala's head in his hand—"

Unable to fathom why Marrock was even there, Marcellus snapped, "You are not making sense, man. Slow down and tell me what happened to the prisoners on the ship."

"One-by-one . . . off with their heads!" Decimus mimicked a sword cut with his hand. "They threw their bodies and heads overboard like slaughtered animals." The tribune's throat formed a large lump. "There was nothing, nothing I could do . . . but beg for a wagon and carry the bodies back for funeral rites."

Marcellus tried to piece together what Decimus had said, but nothing seemed to fit together. "What happened to Marrock?"

"He tied Vala's head to his saddle, threw her headless body on the horse, and rode off."

Marcellus could feel his heartbeats throbbing in his temple. "What about the other two soldiers with you?"

Decimus looked all around and suddenly gave a panicked look. "They're gone! The horses, too. They were just here, with me. They . . . they helped load the bodies." He scratched his head. "No. No. That was yesterday."

A sense of doom sank into Marcellus. The repercussions of what had happened could start a war and condemn Catrin to death—the outcomes he and Decimus had tried to thwart. Considering the tribune's irrational behavior, Marcellus could only conjecture the surviving soldiers had hit Decimus over the head with a blunt object, leaving him unconscious. The cowards must have run away. He wondered if the men would find the courage to return to camp and tell their tales of woe.

Then there was Marrock to contend with.

Who knew what the monster was capable of doing next. Marcellus had no choice but to warn his father about what had happened.

Sweet Clementia, have mercy on us.

Marcellus dismounted and clasped Decimus's forearm. "Help me hitch my horse to the cart, so we can take the bodies to camp."

"Back to camp?" Decimus muttered. "Your father . . . what will he do to me?"

Marcellus drew in a long breath. "The damage is done. All we can hope for now is to avert another disaster. You need to get a hold of yourself before my father questions you."

Shaking his head, Decimus said in a pathetic voice, "I should open my stomach."

Marcellus snapped, "Get your head on straight or I will do the favor for you. You need to tell father what has happened. I'll take responsibility for your involvement. I'll say King Amren sent the message directly to me that I had to release Vala without my father's knowledge. Then we'll see where the axe lands."

Marcellus looked over the wagon's edge and knew the grotesque sight would incite the soldiers' wrath. They had previously grumbled that they had left the known Roman world to the island of magic and sorcery. He turned to Decimus. "We can't let the other soldiers see this. Do you have something to cover the bodies?"

"A blanket," Decimus replied. "But it will not completely conceal the bodies."

Marcellus blew out a deep breath. "We can start with that." He looked around and spotted some tree branches on the ground. Then to his surprise, the tribune's horse walked through the trees. He gestured toward Decimus. "Gather your horse. Help me cover the bodies with the fallen tree branches."

By late afternoon, Marcellus hitched his horse to the wagon as Decimus concealed the bodies. Marcellus climbed onto the wagon's narrow seat and flicked the reins, but the small horse strained on the harness. The wagon would not budge.

Marcellus jumped off and assessed that the wheel was stuck in some mud. With Decimus coaxing the horse forward, Marcellus leaned his body into the wheel and pushed with all his might to move it forward. The wagon jerked forward on the decline. He jumped into the front seat to drive the horse while Decimus climbed on his horse. When they reached the main roadway, the traffic of vehicles carrying goods had abated, but the remaining travelers scrunched their noses as they passed.

At dusk, Decimus and Marcellus rolled through the Roman encampment's gate, where they were met with curious soldiers asking questions about what was in the wagon and where had Decimus been. A couple of men pulled off the tree branches to reveal the bodies inside, drawing a swarm of other soldiers anxious to see the mutilated heads lining the back of the wagon.

Decimus, who by then had found his wits, barked orders. "Take the bodies and do the right thing. *Justafacere*. Tonight, we send them off to the underworld as fallen brothers bonded in death."

26

SON'S CONFESSION

Lucius Antonius rubbed his temple to soothe his throbbing headache. What was he thinking, drinking so much wine at his son's insistence last night? His senses had been so dulled in a drunken stupor that he hadn't noticed Marcellus leaving the bedchamber that morning. More troubling, his son disobeyed orders and had left unescorted to buy some berries from a local vendor at Camulodunon. With the disappearance of Marrock and Cunobelin's defiant son, Caratacus, from the village, Marcellus should have known not to travel alone.

"This does not make sense," Lucius muttered to himself. "He doesn't even like berries."

Most bewildering, Decimus had been gone for so many days, after giving the flimsy excuse he had to find some soldiers missing from a hunting expedition. The last thing Lucius needed to worry about was the whereabouts of his son and commander, particularly with the political situation falling apart. So deep in thought, he was startled by the appearance of a cloaked man across the table from him in his headquarters.

"Who are you?" Lucius barked.

The man pulled the cowl of his red cloak back to reveal his face. The cross-eyed man extended a scroll. "I'm the emperor's courier with an urgent message."

Lucius grabbed the scroll and inspected the emperor's seal. He motioned for the courier to leave. "Wait outside until I've had a chance to write a response."

"I've not eaten for two days," the courier said.

"Ask my guard to scrounge some food for you."

After the courier left, Lucius nervously unrolled the scroll and spread it on the table to read. The emperor's mandate was blunt. He was not to interfere in the political differences between Cunobelin and Amren.

Taken aback, Lucius read it again and grumbled, "That backstabbing weasel, Cunobelin! He must have contacted the emperor."

All of his efforts to convince Tiberius the wisdom of invading Britannia because of the political turmoil between the kings had failed—plain and simple. The audacity of Cunobelin to covertly send a secret message asking the emperor to call him back to Rome made his head ache even more. Why had Cunobelin even bothered to petition Tiberius in Rome to support Marrock's claims if his goal had always been to marry his eldest son to one of Amren's daughters?

Lucius surmised Cunobelin finally realized Marrock was a lone wolf who could easily turn on anyone who threatened his rights to the Cantiaci throne. This was something, unfortunately, Lucius had discovered too late. And now, his long-life desire to restore his family's legacy—his grandfather, Mark Antony, and father, Iullus Antonius, brought down as a result of their scandalous liaisons with women—was slipping away. His ambition to match Julius Caesar's military power by conquering Britannia seemed a lost dream.

Incensed by the turn of events, Lucius slammed his fist on the table, causing a burning candle to fall on the parchment. His heart almost stopped when the papyrus caught fire. He frantically patted the parchment to extinguish the blaze, but the flames leapt at his face. He recoiled from the intense heat, grabbed a jar of water by the handle, and doused the burning scroll. Specks of blackened paper whirled around him like feathers. As the smoky haze cleared, he gaped at the emperor's message, now in ashes. Was this an omen from Apollo for him to heed, he wondered.

Lucius sat gingerly on the curule chair at the table to consider his options. He surmised Cunobelin's appeal to Rome to interfere on behalf of Marrock was a political maneuver to leverage more concessions from Amren in the marital contract. Cunobelin clearly desired that more of Amren's sovereignty be conferred to Adminius. The only way to incite Amren to war, Lucius finally concluded, was to carry out his plan to crucify Vala and to place the blame squarely on Cunobelin.

The sound of a man's clearing his throat drew Lucius out of his ruminations. He glanced up and found Centurion Priscus Dius snapping his heels at attention.

"Senator, are you all right?" Priscus asked. "It smells as if there was a fire."

"A mishap, nothing more," Lucius said. "Did you check on Amren's daughter as I ordered?"

Priscus hesitated. "Senator, I couldn't find her."

"What?"

"She's not in her cell. I asked the guard where she was, thinking she might be in the latrines. He told me Decimus moved her several nights ago to another location, but he didn't know where."

"Why were you not informed of this? You report to the tribune. Shouldn't you know such things?" Lucius asked, trying to make sense of Decimus's disappearance and the inconsistencies in the stories of why he had left.

"Pardon me, sir. I apologize. The tribune left without telling me. He only told me of his plans to hunt fresh game for the camp."

Lucius shook his head in puzzlement. "Decimus told me he would be searching for some soldiers who had not returned from a hunting trip."

Priscus swallowed hard. "Forgive me, senator, but that is not what he told me."

Suspecting a connection between the mysterious disappearances of both Marcellus and his commander, Lucius inquired, "Do you know where my son went?"

"No sir, I thought he was with you. Do you want me to check on both of them?"

"Yes. Order a search party to find both of them."

Priscus saluted and was ready to leave as another guard charged into the headquarters, blurting, "Senator, Priscus—you need to see this!"

Priscus glowered. "What happened to your salute?"

The lanky soldier snapped a fist to his chest. "Sorry, sir, I forgot . . . this couldn't wait."

"What is it, soldier?" Priscus demanded.

The guard's mouth gaped as if he had just seen some kind of evil apparition. Stumbling over his words, he said, "I . . . I don't know how, how to say this . . . something horrible has happened."

Priscus turned to Lucius. "I'll see what has happened?"

Lucius nodded. He stroked his forehead, trying to soothe his headache, as he watched Priscus pull the entrance flap away to leave. Loud voices from outside rose like a thunderstorm.

"Vulcan's fire!" one man shouted.

"They've all been beheaded," a gruff voice cried out.

"Who did this vile act?" Priscus's voice exclaimed.

No longer able to withstand the suspense of what had happened, Lucius pushed his chair back to get up but sat again, seeing Marcellus and Decimus rushing through the entryway. He noted the guilt written on his son's face. Marcellus had only appeared that way when he, as a boy, had accidentally started a fire in one of the stables at their family's villa in Gaul.

Lucius frowned. "Where have you two been? I was ready to send troops out to search for both of you. Do you think I have nothing better to do than watch you like children?"

Marcellus stepped forward. "Father, I don't know how to say this. King Amren sent a message to me that he wanted to negotiate a prisoner exchange—Amren's oldest daughter for five Roman soldiers he held as prisoners."

Lucius jerked his head back. "What?"

Marcellus regarded his father and swallowed hard. "Decimus and I secretly met with his commander, Trystan, to work out the arrangements. The king ordered me not to speak with you about this. He feared you would not agree to his conditions."

Lucius could feel his eyes burn as he silently glared at Decimus.

What in Hades have you done!

The tribune flinched.

"You met with Trystan today?" asked Lucius, his anger ready to erupt that his idiot son and commander would do such a reckless act without first consulting him.

"No," Marcellus said with what sounded like a gulp. "We met with Trystan a fortnight ago."

"You what?" Lucius said, incredulous.

"I ordered Decimus to come with me to meet with Trystan. I agreed to exchange Amren's oldest daughter for the soldiers. The hostage exchange took place five days ago."

"Why in the name of the gods did you not tell me this?" Lucius lashed.

"I was afraid you would defy the emperor's mandate to leave Britannia and start a war by killing Vala."

Lucius bore his eyes at Marcellus as he struggled to mask his fury. "I may rant and rave with you about the emperor in confidence. But don't take me for a fool. I would never disobey the emperor. I've almost convinced the emperor we need to keep a military presence here to calm the hostilities. Is there more you need to tell me? I heard men yelling that something horrible happened."

Marcellus dropped his eyes. "There are dead soldiers outside."

"Dead soldiers?" Lucius repeated, trying to wrap his mind around what his son had just said. "What happened to them?"

"Decimus will explain."

The tribune's face paled. His words seemed to catch in his throat before he spat them out. "Six of my men and I escorted Vala to the prisoner exchange."

Lucius could feel his face flush as he fought back his impulse to bash his commander for insubordination. "What happened?"

The tribune's voice quavered as he recounted the story of being ambushed in the darkness, leaving four of his men dead. He ended by saying, "We heard loud noises—something out of this world. The natives tell me shapeshifters lurk in the forest and eat hapless humans at night."

"You actually believe shapeshifters ate the four soldiers and Vala?" Lucius mocked.

Decimus's face colored. "Well, it was dark . . . we couldn't see a thing. We didn't know what we were up against so we hid."

"Bravely done," Lucius said with a sarcastic tinge in his voice.

Decimus glanced at Marcellus, as if seeking advice.

"Tell Father everything," Marcellus urged.

Lucius gave a dark chuckle. "Oh, I see, the story gets even better."

A lump formed in Decimus's throat. "At first light, we rushed to the riverside because Trystan made it clear that he would kill my men if Vala was not with us. It happened so quickly. Marrock suddenly appeared holding Vala's head. Then Trystan beheaded my soldiers and threw their bodies into the river. We retrieved my men's bodies and brought them back for proper funeral rites."

Lucius's first impulse was to severely punish Decimus and his son. Yet, upon further consideration, he realized they had accomplished what he had not. Their bungling of the prisoner exchange would surely incite Amren to declare war on Cunobelin for the brutal slaying of his daughter. This was the political firestorm Lucius needed to convince Tiberius for keeping the troops in Britannia to prevent a war that threatened Roman trade ways. This would be his first step to invade Britannia and match the military triumph of Julius Caesar himself.

"Congratulations! You've ignited a war! Tell me, how do you propose to stop this calamity?" Lucius said sardonically,

Without hesitation, Marcellus proclaimed, "I'll go back to King Amren and tell him the truth of what happened. I will convince him that this was out of my control."

Lucius gave Marcellus a flabbergasted look. "Are you that crazy? He'll cut off your head off!"

"I believe he will honor my banner of truce."

Lucius seriously considered sacrificing his son to the barbarian king. That was a lesson he would not soon forget, albeit short lived. If Marcellus went so easily behind his back to strike a deal once, he would do it again. Until that moment, Lucius couldn't have fathomed considering his own son as an enemy, but now he wasn't sure. Marcellus must have convinced

Decimus to join him in such a despicable scheme—a scheme that could nonetheless incite Amren into war. What was the loss of a treacherous son for him to gain the emperor's favor and rise to glory?

Am I that heartless?

It was, after all, Marcellus's decision, not his. Besides, his eldest son, Brutius, was the rightful heir to his inheritance. Why shouldn't he abandon his unfit offspring for the sake of elevating the family name of Antonius, which his forefathers had mired in the cesspool of their scandals?

Lucius gestured for Decimus to go. "Leave me. I want to speak with my son in private."

After the tribune exited the tent, Lucius told his son, "The emperor has given me leeway to handle the political unrest here."

"He did?"

"Yes, the emperor's message arrived this afternoon. To maintain utmost secrecy, I burned the scroll so it didn't get into the wrong hands," Lucius said, pointing to the ashes on the table. "With everything that has happened, I can't trust any of the barbarian kings. But what hurts me most is that I can no longer trust you. Did you really have so little faith in me, your own father, that I would actually defy the emperor's decree?"

Marcellus didn't answer.

Lucius sniffled, trying to appear as if holding back a sob. "When Amren's queen threatened to murder you in a most horrific way, I reacted as any father who loves his son. I wanted to avenge her for threatening your life. You underestimate me. I've always understood how important it is to maintain peace."

Lucius regarded Marcellus, who seemed moved by what he had said. "Would you risk your life to barter peace with Amren after the disaster at the prisoner exchange?"

"Yes, I would."

Lucius could see by Marcellus's distressed expression that there was something else driving his son's decision. "Is there something you're not telling me? Has Amren threaten you with something else that made you go behind my back? Tell me the truth, son, because I can always tell when you're lying."

Marcellus stared at him with grim silence. Lucius surmised that the only reason his son would risk his life would be for a woman. "Does this have to do with Amren's youngest daughter?"

"I want to atone for what I have done," Marcellus said, dropping his eyes.

To confirm his suspicion that the sorceress still had a hold on him, Lucius remarked, "You must realize that the only way to bring peace now is through a political marriage between Catrin and Adminius."

Marcellus nodded slightly, his face reddening.

Lucius, detecting a tinge of jealously in his son's expression, decided to move forward with his son's self-destructive plan. "You must approach King Amren alone. If you can convince him not to go to war, you will atone for the distress you've caused me. To help you succeed, I will prepare a document stipulating terms I believe Amren will agree to stop the conflict. Present him with the nuptial pact he already signed with Cunobelin as a way to tempt him back into negotiations."

Marcellus gazed vacantly at the wall, as if adrift in disturbing thoughts.

"Did you hear me, Marcellus?"

"I hear you," Marcellus said. "I will do all that is required."

For an instant, Lucius felt some regret that he might be sending his son into the jaws of death. He had to remind himself that his son's sacrifice could resurrect the Antonius's legacy that Augustus stole when he was banished to Gaul for the sins of his forefathers.

Lucius could never forgive his son for betraying him—the paterfamilias. For other formidable foes, he had slit their throats. Marcellus would share their doom in his political rise in Rome.

27

FOOL'S MISSION

Marcellus's decision to barter a peace settlement with King Amren was impetuous, he had to admit. As he scanned the hilltop to the Cantiaci fortress, he wondered if his plan to get through the entry gate would succeed. Once in, would he get caught?

The Roman merchant called Cato, sitting next to him on the front of the box-shaped wagon, was another concern. Although Decimus had recommended him as someone the Cantiaci trusted as a merchant, the leathery-skinned man had the tongue of a slippery serpent in his dealings with customers. Cato had frequently assured Marcellus on the one-week trip that the Cantiaci eagerly bought his wares and would not give it another thought that he had taken a new partner.

Marcellus was not so sure.

Cato pulled on the reins of his oxen team to halt the wagon and spat out some green grass he had been chewing. "Let me do the talking when we're at the gate. If they address you directly, I'll say a thief cut out your tongue. Only grunt when spoken to. Understand, boy?"

Marcellus nodded, disgusted by the greenish drool escaping the corners of the merchant's mouth.

"Will any of those savages recognize you?" asked Cato.

"A few of the king's guards know me."

"What are you plans after I get you through the gates?"

"I'll climb off this wagon and head toward the king's Great Hall."

"No, you won't," Cato grunted and spat another wad of green sputum. "Stay in the coach until dark, then make your way to the king's bedchamber. Remember, if you get caught, I don't know you. I'd hate to have my eyes gouged out. It's bad for business, you know."

Marcellus gave a dark chuckle. "Agreed."

"All right then." Cato flicked the reins on the oxen's backs, urging them to plod up the hilltop.

Marcellus pulled the cowl of his cape over his head to conceal his face. He leaned against the front of the wooden coach Cato used for sleeping quarters at night. The jerky movements of the wagon made Marcellus jostle and his head bump against the wagon's panel. The wheels creaked as the beasts lumbered up the narrow, hillside road. The clouds hovering over the fortressed settlement looked like tongues lapping up the remaining sunlight.

As the wagon approached the gate, Marcellus grimly remembered the open stall next to the pig pens where he had been imprisoned and shackled. At the time, the pot-bellied boar in the next stall humored Marcellus with snorts of mirth whenever he cracked jokes about their malodorous living conditions.

When Marcellus noted the piercing glare of the heavily tattooed warrior at the gate, he pulled the hood over his eyes to conceal his face. The wagon jolted to a stop. Cato spoke to the guard in Celtic, most of which Marcellus could not comprehend. After Cato exchanged some more words, Marcellus felt a nudge at his side. He peered at Cato and raised a brow in confusion. The merchant leaned over and whispered for him to grunt his name.

Pushing his tongue to the back of his mouth, Marcellus gurgled. The warrior, whom he could barely see beneath his cowl, asked in Latin, "Haven't I seen you before?"

As Marcellus tipped the bottom of the hood up so he could better see the guard, he felt his stomach lurch.

Jupiter's balls! Trystan!

He let out a pathetic, wheezing grunt, his throat constricted with panic.

"As I told you, he can't talk," Cato told Trystan, "but he's good with numbers."

"What are you selling, some of your snake wine again?" Trystan asked.

Marcellus raised his eyes to regard Trystan, who then cocked an eyebrow at him.

Cato spat and answered, "The usual—wine, glassware, mirrors . . . luxuries from Rome."

"I'm surprised, Cato, that you took on a partner. I didn't think you liked the company of people, except for the affections of loose women," Trystan remarked.

"With all the unrest between the tribes, I need more protection from thieves," Cato answered, fiddling the reins in the palm of his hands.

"Even so," Trystan said, "I want a closer look at your new partner. You never told me his name."

"I call him a cut-lipped snake 'cause he speaks with a hiss," Cato said, turning his head to Marcellus. "Reveal who you truly are and greet the guard."

Taking the hint from Cato's smirk, Marcellus abruptly pulled his hood back, gnarled his lips into a contorted half-smile, and hissed, spraying spit all over the merchant's face.

Cato angrily waved a fist in front of Marcellus's face. "Look what you did, you idiot!"

Trystan stepped back but kept his eyes fixed on Marcellus. Apprehensive that the commander might recognize him, Marcellus pulled the cowl forward on his face again. Without a clear vision of Trystan through the fabric of his hood, Marcellus couldn't tell if the spitting diversion had worked.

"Well, does that satisfy you now?" Cato asked. "Plain and simple, he can't talk without a tongue. I've had a long journey and need my sleep before the big sale tomorrow."

Trystan studied Marcellus a little longer, then finally said, "For tonight only, you can keep your wagon near the pigsty. Feed your oxen in the stalls next to the pens."

"I usually station my wagon near the marketplace in the middle of town," Cato began to argue.

"Not tonight," Trystan snapped. "You stay where I tell you to go. Or you don't sell anything."

"Put that way," Cato grumbled, "I accept your invitation to sleep by the swine."

Familiar with the pig pens, Marcellus smiled grimly. As the queen's shackled guest, he was acquainted with several of the sows' piglets and some white cattle.

Trystan's eyes narrowed on Marcellus as he spoke some incomprehensible Celtic gibberish to Cato. The merchant patted Marcellus on the head and said something snide in Celtic. He handed Marcellus the reins and stepped down from the wagon. Gripping the oxen's harness, he gave it a hard tug. The beasts finally lumbered through the entrance and followed Cato to an open stall to the left of the gates. A strong odor of hay mixed with dung greeted them.

Marcellus scrunched his nose and jumped from the wagon onto a fresh pile of pig droppings. He bit off a curse as he scraped the excess dung off his sandaled boots and dropped it on the ground. He helped Cato unhitch the oxen and tether them to poles. As the oxen chewed on their hay, Marcellus grabbed a handful of straw and wiped the remainder of the smelly gift off his leather soles.

Cato filled the trough with water for the oxen, then motioned Marcellus to the wagon. There, they ate some unappetizing salted meat strips and stale bread as hard as a rock. Finishing his meal, Marcellus glanced around to make sure no one was in hearing distance.

"Do you think Trystan suspects who I am?" asked Marcellus. "What did he tell you in Celtic?"

Cato chuckled softly. "He told me I'd be wise to choose better friends. It's best we not talk here. Let's go inside the carriage."

They both climbed into the inner darkness of the windowless carriage. Marcellus sat cross legged and leaned his head against the wooden backboard. Up to this point, he had felt no trepidation about what awaited him, but now his heart was pounding. If he managed to sneak into the royal sleeping chambers, the guards would surely greet him with their swords.

Somehow, he had to find a way to get past them. If he remembered correctly, the king didn't sleep with the queen. Even so, Amren would not welcome him with open arms.

Marcellus then wondered if Catrin could sense he was close by. He looked all around in the darkness, thinking she might appear to him in a vision and connect with his thoughts, as she had after Marrock's attack. A chill crawled down his back when he didn't sense her. He wrapped the cloak tighter around himself to get warm, but the prospect that he might be too late to save Catrin made him feel queasy. Should he first search for her to make sure she was alive before he sought the king out?

Get the thought out of your head that she might be dead, he chided himself and focused his mind on the setup of the village.

After a while, the ear-piercing snorts from the sleeping Cato jolted Marcellus out of his concentration. He decided it was a good time to leave. He slowly turned the door's latch and pushed the carriage door open. It took a few moments for his eyes to adjust to the thick fog swirling around him. In the distance, he could see a few flickering torch flames fading in and out of the haze. He looked in the direction of the fortress gate and didn't detect any movement. He knew the town's layout, but he was blind in the night's fog that shrouded the cone-shaped structures around him.

Maneuver like a sightless man, he told himself, *and keep your ears open to any sound.*

He took a step toward what he believed was the direction of the town's center. His boot sank into what he hoped was only mud. Swaying his other foot forward, he heard the squish of his back boot lifting up. He took another step forward and his boot sank again. *One step at a time*, he told himself, listening for any unexpected sound.

He suddenly felt something sharp jab into his side. Startled, he stumbled forward and bumped into a reed-like structure. He glanced back, fearing Trystan had followed him with a sword in hand.

Nobody was there.

He again felt something sharp jab against him. He darted his eyes all around for the culprit. Then he heard something metallic clacking against the structure as a breeze picked up. He stretched out his hand and felt the sharp tongs of a blacksmith that had been left hanging off the structure. Relieved, he blew out the breath he'd been holding.

Pressing the palm of his hand on the reed-like structure, he slowly maneuvered around its outer wall and saw a narrow road ahead of him that was illuminated from nearby torches. He cautiously walked to the next round house, again hiding until it was safe to continue, then moved from one structure to another. The fog lifted then settled on the ground like a ghost looking for its grave. His legs began cramping as he balanced himself whenever his boots sank into thick mud.

At one point, he panicked, fearing he had retraced his steps. But then, he caught sight of torch flames lining the courtyard of the Great Hall. He held his breath and listened for any sound. Hearing a footstep, he froze, then looked over his shoulder and glimpsed a shadow disappearing into the fog.

He shuddered. Someone was following him.

Marcellus decided to hide in the darkness of the king's stables across the alley from the Great Hall. He hastened his pace toward the horse stalls. The sound of approaching footsteps became louder and louder. With fight instincts taking hold of him, he reached for the dagger inside his cloak, but a strong grip on his arm stopped him.

"You are my prisoner," the man's gravelly voice declared.

The tip of a sword against Marcellus's back emphasized the point as other warriors surrounded him. He glanced over his shoulder and recognized Trystan.

The commander jested ominously, "The king will be glad to see you, Roman. He has something special in mind for you."

Marcellus felt his arm yank back as Trystan shoved him into a thatched-roof, domed structure. Other warriors spat at his face as they shackled and chained him like a wild beast.

As Trystan slowly unsheathed his knife, he gave a malevolent grin as he yanked Marcellus's head back by the hair and pressed the sharp blade against his cheek.

"The gods have answered my prayers. I get to butcher you like the traitorous swine you are!"

Marcellus thought his pounding heart would crack his ribs as the blade cut into his face. "I didn't betray you. Let me explain!"

"Explain what?" Trystan growled as he cut a little deeper.

"Marrock killed four Roman guards before he killed Vala!" Marcellus burst out. "He acted alone. I risked my life to come here, to broker a peace with the king! I swear by the gods above, my father and Cunobelin promise to punish Marrock for his vile deed."

Trystan released the blade. "Why should I trust you, Roman?"

"Would I risk my life if it were not true?"

Trystan narrowed an eye, at first appearing skeptical, but then another warrior entered and said something incomprehensible to him. They both dashed outside, leaving Marcellus alone in the mold-scented hovel. He frantically tugged on his shackle in the fading hope he could escape and find the king.

28

BLOOD MOON

King Amren rotated the dagger in his hand and studied the etched curse on its blade. Each inscribed word gleamed under the illumination of the candle light. That night, blood would cover the moon. The visiting Druids from the Isle of Anglesey predicted the portal from the Otherworld would open at the height of the blood moon. Souls could then wander into the mortal world. The Druids had summoned the ancestral spirits to drag Rhan's soul to the Otherworld after Amren executed Agrona. That would break the curse, he believed, and put an end to her skullduggery.

The longer Amren gazed at the blade, the more it glowed as red as a blood moon. Becoming emboldened, he reminded himself that he had overcome other formidable foes, some of whom were considered more cunning than him. Their skulls lined the Great Hall as a warning to his subjects of why he was the war king and took power from his vanquished enemies.

I'll be damned if I allow Rhan to defeat me! I'd rather die in battle than cower like a frightened rabbit.

This time, Amren would slay Agrona without any witnesses. Rhan wouldn't have the opportunity to possess another human being at her last breath. He rubbed his thumb over the etched metal of the blade and slid it over the steel tip to test the sharpness. He winced as the razor-sharp edge cut his callused thumb, then licked the blood off his skin and kissed the blade.

Hearing footsteps entering the antechamber, Amren turned to find Ferrex, one of the few guards he implicitly trusted. The lion-maned warrior had the same mindset as his—unadulterated hatred for the Romans and a hunger to avenge Vala's death. Though Ferrex was a commoner, he had qualities the king admired: undying loyalty, strong moral beliefs, and unwavering courage.

"Are you ready, my king?" asked Ferrex.

Amren nodded. "Has everyone been moved away from the vicinity of the makeshift cell? I don't want Rhan to possess another person as she did with Agrona."

"All people have been relocated elsewhere in the village or outside the fortress walls," Ferrex confirmed.

"Good. Then we're set." Perplexed that Ferrex came alone, Amren looked at the entryway and asked, "Why isn't Trystan with you?"

Ferrex shrugged. "I searched for him in his quarters, but he wasn't there."

Unsettled that Trystan was missing on such a momentous night, Amren spat and cursed beneath his breath.

"Should I look for him again?" Ferrex asked.

Amren shook his head. "No. I'll deal with him later. Stay with me until we reach the outside of Agrona's cell. Wait there until I've done the deed and carried her body outside. Then accompany me to the pyre the Druids have sanctified in the hazelnut grove. We'll burn the corpse and release her soul to the ancestral spirits that will take her to the Otherworld."

"Understood," Ferrex said and shifted his weight. "What if you don't come out?"

"Set the cell on fire."

Before Ferrex could say anything, Trystan bounded into the chamber and blurted, "My king, guess who I've found?"

Not in the mood for guessing games, Amren growled, "Spit it out!"

Wide-eyed with excitement, Trystan proclaimed, "The Roman traitor, Marcellus!"

Amren jerked his head back, not sure if he had heard his commander correctly. "Marcellus? Here?"

"I found him skulking through the village. When I threatened to flay him for killing Vala, he insisted Marrock acted alone."

Not sharing his commander's enthusiasm, Amren growled, "How did an enemy get inside the walls?"

The grin on Trystan's face turned downward. "He was disguised as an assistant to the Roman merchant, Cato."

"Cato?"

"He supplies you with wine," Trystan clarified. "We're now questioning him."

A shudder ran down Amren's veins. Of all nights, how could Marcellus breach the fortress unless he had reinforcements nearby?

"Did you check for Roman troops hiding outside the fortress?" asked Amren.

"After the gate is closed at night, the sentries always check for hidden enemies. There was nothing out of sorts."

With the forthcoming blood moon, Amren knew it would be difficult to discern hidden enemies in the shadows. Besides, his guards were un-nerved that wayward ancestral wraiths might also drag them back to the Otherworld.

"What do you want me to do with Marcellus? He requests an audience with you." Trystan said.

Amren cursed beneath his breath.

Bel's fire, Marcellus shows up tonight! This is a bad sign.

"Do you want me to kill him?" asked Trystan.

"No. I'll deal with the scoundrel tomorrow." Still suspicious that Ro-man troops were hiding near the village, Amren asked, "Are there adequate guards with Marcellus to counter any surprise ambushes to help him to escape?"

"Two guards are stationed outside the round house where he is shack-led."

"But he got in, didn't he?"

"He won't get away," Trystan reassured.

The sudden appearance of Marcellus angered Amren, reminding him of the rogue's reckless liaison with Catrin that had forced him to judge her for treason and to pound an iron fist to emphasize what happens to traitors.

He resolved to behead Marcellus for deflowering Catrin and for failing to release Vala. A sordid delight tickled the king's stomach as he imagined the Roman's head joining the other skulls of all his notable adversaries on the Great Hall's wall.

With a grim smile, Amren gestured for Ferrex and Trystan to follow him. Trystan grabbed a torch from a sconce at the entryway to light their way through the village.

Outside, the moon's cratered face greeted Amren, reminding him of the grotesque face of his son. The king inwardly prayed to the gods for strength and cunning to outwit the Dark Druidess and strike her dead with one blow. Rhan's previous ability to shapeshift when she was his queen haunted the recesses of his mind. He couldn't allow her even a blink of time to possess another human being as she had with Agrona.

As the three men approached the wood-spike fence encircling Rhan's dome-shaped prison, Amren's battle instincts heightened when he heard loud chanting in the strange tongue of the Ancient Druids when they conversed with their gods. The chants shifted into wolf howls. Purplish fog suddenly spilled over the spiked fence surrounding the cell.

Ferrex and Trystan exclaimed at the same time, "What is that?"

A shiver sliced down Amren's spine. At first, he suspected Rhan was escaping in a magical fog that rendered her invisible. He gripped his dagger tighter and gestured for them to charge.

As they dashed through the purplish fog, an eerie glow emanated from the torch Trystan held, making it difficult for them to discern what was ahead. Upon finally reaching the entrance gate, Amren took the torch while Trystan inserted a key into the padlock. The wood door creaked inward as if a force invited them to enter. Amren trampled ahead but slammed against what felt like a stone wall and shot backwards on his buttocks. Ferrex and Trystan also flew back and landed flat on their backs.

"Only Catrin can enter my domain," Rhan's craggy voice wailed.

Realizing he had lost his element of surprise, Amren pressed a finger on his lips to signal his men to stay quiet. He rose and cautiously stepped forward, waving his dagger in front of him. His hand jolted when the dagger hit something, but there was nothing but misty fog in front of him. A shudder coursed through his veins. The dark Druidess must have anticipated the ambush and created an invisible wall to stop them from entering.

"Rhan, where are you?" Amren bellowed.

Hearing the Druidess cackle, Amren surmised by the direction of her voice that she was still in the confines of the dome-shaped cell.

"Speak with me," Amren shouted. "Remove your invisible wall."

The woman's voice taunted, "Not tonight. Wraiths warn me of the intent of the dagger in your hand."

"What are you afraid of?" Amren challenged. "Why haven't you struck me dead yet, if your magic is that powerful?"

"In good time," Rhan replied with a wicked chuckle. "In good time, my war king . . . once Myrddin arrives."

Amren was not sure if he had heard the name clearly. He remembered the wild Druid Myrddin, who had wandered out of the deep forest to announce his father unfit to be king. Soon after, the people obeyed Myrddin's command to sacrifice his father so Amren could be anointed as king. Was this Rhan's tactic, he wondered, to make him question his own ability to rule?

Shaking back his self-doubt, Amren stretched his fingertips over the surface of the invisible wall to ascertain its height. No matter how high he stretched, he could only detect the rock-like surface of the invisible wall. Unable to reach the top of the wall, he released a heavy sigh in frustration.

Trystan whispered, "What shall we do?"

"If can't go forward, we must go back," Amren mumbled. "By dawn, the moon will escape the shroud of blood and the magic from the Otherworld will have dissipated. We'll try again to breach the wall tomorrow night after I hold the final trial for Catrin."

Though Amren maintained a steel mien, his heart stabbed with the thought he had to condemn Catrin for confiding in a Roman enemy. He feared Rhan's curse was uncoiling to strike. He had to be ready to wield his sharp wits and to pound his brutal force to counter any of her surprises.

29

CRUEL TEST OF LOYALTY

That morning, Catrin had to face her father for his final judgment. She had lost hope of winning back his trust. Standing in the gloom of the Great Hall, she gazed at the two thrones on the dais. She grimly recalled her father's threat prior to Mor's wedding.

Your pathway to redemption is based on the next decisions and judgments you make. If you make a wrong decision and fail as a ruler, you will never be granted another chance. If Marcellus betrays us, I will be hard-pressed to rescind your banishment—a punishment far worse than death.

How could Catrin continue living if her heart was split between Marcellus and her father? Losing Vala was the fatal wound in her already bleeding heart. She trembled, recounting her father's words. *Would you bet your own life on the gamble that Marcellus will release Vala?*

Catrin's love for Marcellus and his failure to release Vala had condemned her as a traitor in her father's eyes. She looked around the stark receiving chamber and stared at the skulls looking down on her in judgment. She remembered the dark tale that her father had told her when she was a child.

A mermaid, who had saved a sailor from a shipwreck, swam to shore, cradling his head above the water. Though she desperately wanted to stay with the sailor, she realized she was a sea creature and would die on land. Heartbroken, she stabbed herself in the breast with a knife and turned the water red with her blood. Grief-stricken, she floated on the waves until her body dissolved into its foam. As the sun's rays radiated on the cold foam, delicate fairies sparkled over its surface.

When Catrin asked her father what the story meant, he replied, "It is a cautionary tale that water and earth can only meet at the shore. Everyone must be true to who they are."

At the time, the king's answer did not make sense. Yet now, Catrin felt as if she were the mermaid. The prospect of her father accepting her back was dissolving into the sea's foam. She had given up hope that she would ever see Marcellus again, with the threat of Roman forces invading her homeland.

How could she rip Marcellus out of her heart without losing part of her soul?

She stared at the king's austere and unforgiving high-backed throne. Her gaze then shifted to the torches illuminating the skulls on the wall. Their empty eye sockets and jaws gaping open in silence in retribution for their past deeds.

As tears formed in her eyes, Catrin caught a glimpse of Ferrex approaching her. Swallowing back her emotions, she stiffened and didn't acknowledge him. When he nudged her arm, she turned to find his green-speckled, hazel eyes reaching to console her. She should be more kind to her loyal and true friend, but how could she give her heart to another man after experiencing such profound loss with Marcellus?

She couldn't.

Ferrex dropped his eyes, as if he had heard her thoughts. With uncharacteristic silence, he shifted his weight with a pathetic expression of dejection on his face.

"You don't need to be here," she said stiffly. "I can face my father alone."

Ferrex's gaze lingered on her for a moment. "I've tried so hard to support you. But still you shun me. I deserve better than this."

Catrin looked away with momentary regret that she had hurt him, but she could not find the words to apologize. How could she? She couldn't even forgive herself for Vala's death.

Vala was a valiant warrior who showed more courage than any warrior in the kingdom when she volunteered to take Catrin's place as a Roman hostage. Vala had all the qualities that Catrin admired—loyalty, trustworthiness, and bravery.

It should have been me who died . . . not Vala.

Trying to soothe her angst, Catrin stroked the base of her neck where the Apollo's amulet used to be. She questioned whether she had the strength to break her pledge to be Marcellus's wife and to remain loyal to him. Even though her father accused Marcellus of betrayal, she still believed he would have done everything in his power to release Vala. Marcellus knew she would suffer the ultimate sentence of death.

With conflicting emotions of love, hate, and shame whirling inside, Catrin reflected on her past like a pebble skipping over the surface of water. The first time Marcellus professed his love. The last time she saw him wounded at the prisoner exchange, forever taken away. When Ferrex volunteered to train her as a warrior and later proclaimed his love.

And finally, Vala's headless body, a harbinger of Rhan's curse.

The gods demand the scales be balanced for the life you take today. If you deny my soul's journey to the Otherworld by beheading me, I curse you to the same fate as mine. When the Raven rises out of Apollo's flames with the dark powers of the Ancient Druids, Blood Wolf will form a pack with the mighty empire and fulfill this curse. The Raven will then cast liquid fire into the serpent's stone and forge vengeance on the empire's anvil.

The altered curse confounded Catrin. Had Rhan cursed her to burn in Marcellus's fiery passion, as her father accused, and make her turn a blind eye on what he truly was—a Roman enemy? Had her decision to reweave his life thread on the Wall of Lives' tapestry to save him doomed Vala?

Ferrex's nudge drew Catrin back into her reality. She looked away so he wouldn't see her anguish.

He will thank me for sparing him the heartache of loving me.

After several moments of silence, Ferrex lifted Catrin's chin so she would look at him. "Do I mean so little that you won't talk to me?"

"I don't deserve you," Catrin blurted, but she immediately blushed with embarrassment for her outcry and dropped her watery eyes.

Ferrex interlaced his fingers into hers and said softly, "Let me be the judge of that. I know how hard it is for you to face your father again. I promise to stay by your side and remain loyal. Perhaps, it would lighten your load if you'd share your thoughts with me."

The warm touch of Ferrex's hand comforted Catrin, but how could she open up to him? Her heart still belonged to Marcellus.

The squeeze of Ferrex's hand prompted Catrin to reply. Her throat tightened as she explained, "I'm not sure how to describe how I feel. It is as if I'm a dry well where dust blows in its inner depths instead of water. I had hoped . . . at least for a brief moment . . . at Mor's marriage, we could be family again."

She forced back a sob, swallowing hard. "But now, everyone despises me for what I did. I want to prove them wrong. But, but—" The words, "I don't know how," clipped in her throat.

Ferrex grimaced. "I am a man of strong words and must speak the truth. You will never atone until you accept the truth about Marcellus. He is an enemy who ill-used you and preyed on your innocence. You can mope and feel sorry for yourself. Or you can climb out of the hole you have dug yourself into."

Catrin glowered. "And what you mean by that? You don't know my mind. Can't you see I'm grieving for Vala? All you care about is your hurt pride."

Ferrex's face grew red with anger. "You might be sad, Raven, but what does that have to do with how you treat me or view yourself? Your father showed you mercy by allowing me to train you. He wanted you to be a warrior so you know what it means to fight alongside your people who willingly sacrifice their lives for you. You have yet to rise out of the ashes of your betrayal and give him your undying loyalty. What if Marcellus was here and threatened your father? Would you kill him?"

"He would never threaten my father!" Catrin insisted. "Who are you, a commoner, to judge me? I thought you were my friend. Am I wrong about that?"

"I am your friend," Ferrex said adamantly. "But every time I try to help you, you swat me away"— he waved his hand in front of her face—

"like some horsefly on a pile of shit. I would never put up with this from a man."

"Then treat me like you would a man," Catrin said, raising her head in challenge. "I am no weak link in your chainmail."

Ferrex pushed Catrin back. "You never answered me, Raven. Where does your loyalty lie? Is it with Marcellus or with the king?"

Catrin stepped up to Ferrex and clasped his chin. "Do not touch me that way again! And don't question my loyalty!"

Ferrex leveled his eyes at Catrin. "If you're not a traitor, then why are you facing your father's judgment for treason again?"

The accusation from one of her most ardent supporters shook Catrin. Dumbfounded, she felt as helpless as when she was a little girl at the time Marrock tried to transform her into one of his she-wolves. Her stomach clenched as she relived the terror of being lost in the forest in the aftermath of her escape. Finally finding her voice, she whimpered, "Why are you so cruel to me?"

Ferrex blew out an exasperated breath and mumbled, "Someone should cut out my tongue."

Feeling awkward, Catrin clutched herself until she heard footsteps shuffling into the chamber. She turned to find her father entering the receiving chamber from the antechamber. Behind the king were her mother, Mor, Belinus, and Cynwrig, each of them with grim faces.

A chill ran down her spine. The king would not show her any mercy. She had lost the gamble with her father that Marcellus would release Vala.

Amren, taking the queen's arm in the crook of his elbow, assisted her up the three steps and to her throne on the dais. The others remained behind Catrin and Ferrex.

As Amren seated himself on the throne, he clenched the armrests with white-knuckled hands. Rhiannon's face was pale as a ghost. She slumped in her throne and gave the king a forlorn look, her red-rimmed eyes swollen with tears.

Amren averted the queen's gaze and instead glared at Catrin. He flew out of his chair, stomped to the front edge of the platform, and peered down on her like an eagle ready to swoop on its prey. She crumbled under his scowl as he pronounced, "Catrin, you stand accused as a traitor. Everyone in this chamber has beseeched me to show you mercy. But, before I can consider their pleas, I will ask you a series of questions about your training as a warrior with Ferrex. You must answer each question correctly if you have any hope of earning my benevolence."

Catrin slightly bowed to affirm she was ready.

"What are the three most important qualities a warrior must possess?" Amren started. "Answer this from your heart."

Catrin replied with the mantra Ferrex had taught her, "Courage, loyalty, and ferocity."

The king rubbed his jaw, appearing displeased with her answer. "What must you do before you can win a battle?"

"Study the enemy," Catrin said, the stratagem Ferrex drilled during her training. "Anticipate your enemy's next move and counter him with an unexpected flourish of your weapon."

Amren narrowed an eye to the point of an arrow. "Who is your worst enemy? Think before you answer."

Catrin mulled over what response her father sought. The obvious answer was the Romans, but her father would then hone on Marcellus and her liaison with him. She decided to divert her father away from Marcellus by proclaiming someone he considered more treacherous.

"Marrock is my worst enemy."

"Are you sure about that, Catrin?" Amren asked. "Did Marrock lead you astray from your duty to safeguard our kingdom from the Roman enemy, Marcellus?"

"Marrock has threatened to destroy you and our family," Catrin countered.

Amren remained firm. "Answer the question! Who led you astray from your duty to safeguard our kingdom from Marcellus?"

Catrin could feel her throat constrict as she uttered, "I made the choice to trust Marcellus. But he promised to aid us."

The king pressed his lips into a hard line. "If that is the case, are you not your own worst enemy? This is true for anyone misguided by blind loyalties. This is the weakness that will lead to your downfall unless you take appropriate actions to correct it. Do you understand why I hesitate to take you back into my fold?"

Catrin stammered for words. "Father, I . . . I do want to . . . to remain loyal to you. Yet, my heart is torn by the love I pledged to another."

"Tell everyone in this chamber who he is," Amren demanded.

Catrin quavered. "Marcellus."

"If I were to bring this Roman enemy into the chamber now, would you proclaim your loyalty is greater for me than it is for him?"

The realization that she had to rescind her loyalty to Marcellus, so she could win her father's favor, sank like a heavy anchor in her chest. "My love for him does not diminish my love and fealty to you."

The king leaned his head forward like a vulture ready to eat its carrion. "You can have only one ruler. Is it Marcellus or me?"

Catrin felt panic grip her heart as she noted the king's stare shifting beyond her to the entryway.

"Perhaps, I can help you make that choice," Amren said brusquely. "Last night, Trystan caught Marcellus slinking in the darkness toward the Great Hall. When your Roman lover was caught, he requested an audience with me. However, before I do so, I want everyone in this room to know he is outside waiting for me to summon him."

Catrin felt as if her stomach had plunged into a bottomless pit. A sudden cold breeze whirled around her and she heard a woman's voice whisper, "Apollo is coming."

Lips quivering, she glanced over her shoulder to see who the woman was, but nobody was there. Looking around the chamber, she observed that no one else seemed to have reacted to the women's voice.

After the king ordered, "Bring the Roman prisoner in," the woman's voice proclaimed, "Can you still rise out of Apollo's flames with the powers of the Ancient Druids?"

Catrin looked up and realized the voice was emanating from a shadow gliding in and out of the rafters. The dark mist uncoiled like a snake from the ceiling beam, then slid down the wall and slithered in and out of a skull's eye sockets. A deafening crack of thunder shook the chamber and the loud patter of rain followed.

Paralyzed with fear, Catrin watched the serpentine shadow transform into a gray fog that floated to her feet and emitted a chill through her legs, up her spine, and into her head.

She shuddered.

30

CATRIN'S CHOICE

The rain dropped like sheets on Marcellus's face as he waited outside at the Great Hall's entryway with Trystan and another warrior on each of his sides. Shivering, he wondered how much longer he had to wait without a cloak to cover his head.

A man could die of consumption in these weather conditions, he inwardly groaned.

Though he was no longer shackled, his swollen ankles still burned from the metal cuff rubbing his raw skin. His shoulder throbbed from Trystan's less than amiable treatment from the previous night.

Look on the bright side, he tried to cheer himself. *I should thank the gods that I am still alive after Trystan's untimely greeting.*

His teeth began clacking as he wrapped his arms around himself to keep warm. A chill sliced across his neck and Catrin's headless body appeared in his eye's mind.

Was he too late to save her?

King Amren had, after all, executed his former queen for treason. He stifled a laugh from his gallows humor.

Idiot! Put your head back on before your wits spill on the ground.

Closing his eyes against the rain, he struggled to keep his thoughts off the grim prospect that both he and Catrin would lose their heads. He inwardly rehearsed on what he would say to convince Amren otherwise.

My king, you must believe me that I grieve for the loss of your daughter, Vala. But alas, I never foresaw Marrock would ambush us. Don't blame Ca-

trin for his vile deed. If you must blame someone, blame me. I never intended Catrin any harm . . . I love her.

Marcellus slapped his forehead dripping with rain.

You idiot! Why would the king be swayed by my proclamation of love?

The entryway doors suddenly opened and banged against the inner walls from a gale wind. Marcellus felt the tip of Trystan's sword jab into his back, and he stumbled into the Great Hall. He wiped the raindrops from his eyes.

The first image that came into his sight was a spiked skull on the wall. The same skull had also welcomed him when he had first met the king earlier in late spring. He then focused on the king and queen, both of them seated on their thrones. The king snarled, leaning forward in his high-backed chair, like a wolf ready to pounce on its prey. In contrast, the queen slumped in her chair, appearing weary. He then caught sight of Catrin standing before the thrones, her back turned to him. He gasped in relief that she was alive. A single gold braid cascaded off her shoulder as she looked back at him.

He recalled the last time he had seen her at the prisoner exchange. The white raven had just taken the brunt of a death arrow targeted at his heart. As he lay there wounded, losing consciousness, he saw her disappear into the gloom of the forest like a star at dawn. At the time, he wondered if she had shapeshifted into the raven and sacrificed herself to save him.

Marcellus tried to connect to Catrin's thoughts. He wanted to reassure her that he was there to protect her and save her as she had saved him. He was disheartened when she didn't acknowledge him or give any indication that she had heard him. She turned to face the king.

Waiting for the king to gesture him forward, Marcellus studied the small gathering of people standing behind Catrin. He recognized Cynwrig—the acclaimed warrior against whom he had foolishly competed in a battle-axe contest on the first night he had been held as hostage. He shifted his gaze to Belinus, the sun-tattooed guard who had brutally taunted him when he was shackled. Next to Belinus was Mor, whose rounded belly clearly showed she was with child. Marcellus assumed Belinus was the father.

Marcellus studied the brawny man standing next to Catrin. At first, he did not recognize the coppery-haired warrior, but he seemed to be attracted to Catrin by the way he gazed at her. It finally dawned on him that he was the guard whom he had tagged as the "Lion" because his hair and beard looked like a mane around his face. The mean-spirited warrior had oftentimes punched him without provocation.

King Amren finally gestured for Marcellus to move forward. He could barely swallow, apprehensive that his pleas for Catrin's life might not succeed. Noting the king's glower, he tried to strike a brave demeanor, squaring his shoulders as he strode forward. He acknowledged the king with a slight nod and waited for permission to speak.

"Why are you here under a banner of truce?" Amren asked sharply.

Marcellus cleared his throat, but his voice still cracked when he started. "I have come here to extend my condolences for the loss of your daughter, Vala. No one is more grieved than me that Marrock brutally murdered her. However, he acted alone. Further, he ambushed four of my Roman guards charged with escorting her. Tribune Decimus Flavius, who barely escaped Marrock's ambush, tried to explain this to your commander as he approached the shore with the Roman prisoners. But alas, Trystan saw Marrock kill Vala, and he in turn cut off the heads of the Roman prisoners. My father construes this act as grounds for war, but I convinced him to reconsider. I am here to offer you a truce to avoid further bloodshed."

Amren rose from his throne, stepped to the edge of the platform, and bored his eyes into Marcellus. "I hold you personally responsible for breaking your promise to free Vala! Your guards should have anticipated such an ambush!"

"No one regrets more than me what happened," Marcellus quickly replied, "but what Marrock did was out of my control."

"You agreed to release Vala so Catrin would be spared for her treasonous liaison with you," Amren said coldly. "She will now be judged harshly for your failure!"

Marcellus's stomach clenched when he saw the angst in Catrin's eyes. He implored Amren, "I beg you not to judge Catrin for my failure. Grant me a private audience so I can present you with terms for a truce that is much to your favor."

Amren regarded Marcellus for a moment, then barked an order in Celtic. Marcellus flinched as the Lion placed a dagger into Catrin's hand. The weapon swayed unsteadily in her hand as she looked at her father with eyes as big as a doe cornered by a wolf.

The king shouted something in Celtic to the Lion. The coppery-haired warrior stomped forward and began arguing. Amren jerked his hand toward the entryway, but the Lion gave the king a defiant look. Bewildered, Marcellus watched Trystan ascend the three stairs to the thrones and proffer the crook of his arm to the queen. Visibly shaken, she rose and took the commander's arm. Leaning against him, she descended the stairs and stepped over to Catrin. The queen began to weep as she clasped Catrin's hand, but Trystan urged her on. The others followed them out of the chamber except for the Lion. The king barked and dismissed the warrior with the wave of his hand.

This time, the Lion reluctantly left.

A sense of dread crawled over Marcellus as King Amren told Catrin in Latin, "You changed your Roman lover's fate to die at the prisoner exchange, even though he is our enemy. You did this knowing only the gods have the divine wisdom to foresee the consequences of changing the future. You have angered the gods with your blasphemous deed!" The king pointed to himself. "And you anger me for overstepping my authority. As a result, the gods punished us all by your altering the curse inscribed on the dagger you hold. To assuage the gods, you must now claim Marcellus's life. Only then, will we have any hope of breaking the curse and bringing peace to our kingdom."

Alarmed by the king's flawed reasoning, Marcellus blurted, "Killing me will start a war! Isn't that what the curse foretold?"

"The altered curse now says that Marrock will slay me after Catrin rises out of the flames of your passion." The king's stare shifted to Catrin. "You must do as I command to show your loyalty to me."

To Marcellus's dismay, Catrin's expression hardened into stone as she studied the etched script on the dagger's metal surface and then faced him. He could barely swallow when she pressed the blade's sharp edge against his throat. Conflicting emotions wrenched him that he would meet his doom at the hands of the woman he loved and had resolved to save. He met her eyes and silently spoke to her.

Don't do this, Catrin! I am your Apollo. I am your protector.

Appearing to understand his thoughts, she hesitated, tears swelling in her eyes. He knew then, she would not kill him. He considered taking her weapon away, so he could overtake the unarmed king. But to do so, he jeopardized both his and Catrin's life with no possible way to escape the guards outside. If her act of killing him would absolve her, he decided to accept his fate with courage. He held his head higher so she could more easily cut his neck.

Catrin hesitated.

"Do it!" Amren shouted.

Marcellus held steady as she pressed the blade harder against his throat. A chill of death floated over him. He closed his eyes for her final blow.

The dagger pulled away from his throat. He opened his eyes to find Catrin glaring at her father with defiance.

"For the love of gods, Catrin, you must act now!" Amren ordered. "Where does your loyalty stand—with your king or with the enemy?"

31

SACRIFICIAL LOVE

Catrin's heart hammered against her ribs like a mallet striking an anvil. She raised the dagger to her eyes and silently read the inscription. Was this what the curse meant? Would aligning herself with Marcellus help Rome destroy her father? But how could she stain her soul by killing her Roman husband to demonstrate her loyalty to the king?

The image of Rhan taunting her with wicked mirth flashed in her head.

You'll suffer the same fate as me if you don't kill Marcellus. Headless! Soulless!

A fiery rage sizzled through Catrin that her father had put her into such a dilemma. She tightened her fingers around the dagger's handle. For an instant, her impulse was to turn the blade on her father, but she hesitated.

Patricide is as heinous as murdering a husband.

Feeling as hopeless as a snared animal ready to bite off its feet to escape, Catrin thrust the blade toward her breast, but was met with stiff resistance from Marcellus grabbing the blade with his bare hands.

"Don't do this, Catrin!" he demanded. "Look at me! Look at me!"

Refusing to yield, Catrin said fervently, "I am already doomed because I won't kill you."

Marcellus gripped the blade harder, his inner voice reaching out to her, his love pulling her closer to his heart.

Look into my eyes. I am your Apollo. I am your protector.

Rhan's grated voice burst into Catrin's mind. *Don't give him the dagger!*

Confounded by the woman's voice in her head, Catrin fought harder to plunge the blade into her chest.

Marcellus spoke softly, but sternly, as if calming a skittish mare. "Give me the weapon, Catrin. You don't want to do this."

Rhan's essence webbed into Catrin's mind and began entrancing her. *Join me. And together, we'll break the curse.*

Fighting for lucidity, Catrin cried out, "I will not join you."

Marcellus relaxed his hold. "Join who?"

Catrin finally caught sight of his blood smearing the dagger blade. She shuddered with horror that the dagger's sharp edge had sliced his hand. Sensing his pain, she slackened her hold and gazed into his violet-blue eyes, connecting her thoughts with his.

Catrin, look into my eyes. Behold your Apollo, Marcellus communed. *I hear voices in your head. Get rid of them. Give me the weapon before you harm yourself.*

Sensing his overwhelming love, Catrin relinquished the dagger to Marcellus. He wiped the blood on his tunic and dropped the weapon on the wooden floor, then pulled her into his arms and stroked her hair to comfort her.

"Everything will be alright, my love," he whispered reassuringly, his lips lightly touching her ears. "Please stand by me as I speak to your father."

Catrin looked past Marcellus and found her father's glacier-blue eyes frozen on them. Rage again flared in her chest that he could be so heartless. Did he have so little regard for her that he could execute her for refusing to kill the man she had pledged her love?

Marcellus's arms loosened around Catrin, and he reproached the king, "Don't make Catrin choose loyalty between you and me. I love your daughter. And she loves me. We pledged ourselves as husband and wife before the Mother Goddess. Her loyalty to me is as sacred as her loyalty is to you. By forcing her to show her loyalty by killing me, you have cast her into a tempestuous sea to drown. That is why she turned the blade on herself rather than darken her soul with the vile deed of murdering me. If you must accuse someone of treason, condemn me! If you condemn me, then you must execute me. Don't make your beloved daughter do this."

With the powerful emotion of abiding love for Marcellus overtaking Catrin's reason, she fell to her knees, clasped her beloved's hands, and entreated, "Don't do this! Do not exchange your life for mine."

As Marcellus held her shoulders to lift her, she noticed her blood-smeared sleeve. Tears of remorse that she had caused him so much pain swelled in her eyes. She rose on her own accord and silently stood by his side to demonstrate her utmost support for Marcellus as he again scolded the king.

"You, of all people, should know that murdering me will rain destruction on your kingdom. My death gives my father the excuse to attack your homeland. I thought you a wiser ruler. Should you not first consider my father's terms for peace?"

The king answered by stomping down the stairs of the platform, picking up the dagger from the floor, and pointing it at Marcellus. "Who are you to judge me as a ruler?" he said with growl. "How old are you, eighteen . . . maybe nineteen years old at best?"

Catrin clung to Marcellus's arm as her father stepped within a few feet of them and brandished his dagger.

"I am nearly twenty," Marcellus boldly said. "And I'm old enough to know where your reckless actions will lead!"

"Twenty?" Amren's brow reddened and creased into a deep furrow. "And you think of yourself as an honorable man? You gave no thought about satisfying your lust with my daughter and thus endangering her life."

Marcellus's throat constricted. He lowered his head and extended his blood-smeared hands in a conciliatory gesture. "Forgive me, my king. I regret that my actions have endangered Catrin. I hold your daughter dear to my heart and will do whatever you ask so no harm comes to her."

Emboldened by Marcellus's declaration of his love for her, Catrin proclaimed, "I also love Marcellus and hold him dear to my heart."

The king finally lowered his dagger and stared at them with an anguished look for several moments, then finally said, "If you love Catrin and hold her dear, as you so claim, then you must swear your fealty to me as your king. Do this and I will consider your father's terms for peace."

"I will do this," Marcellus said without hesitation, "if my allegiance will redeem Catrin in your eyes."

Amren regarded Marcellus. "It might. But first, tell me your father's terms."

Marcellus pulled out a scroll from beneath his belt and extended it to Amren. "It is with a reluctant heart that I present you with the contract you already sealed with your blood."

The scroll fell out of Marcellus's hand onto the dark oak flooring. The king quickly scooped the scroll into one hand while maintaining a hold of the dagger with the other. He fumbled to straighten the parchment. As he read, his eyes shifted downward. He stitched his eyebrows together and grimaced. "You offer this, even though you've declared your love for Catrin?"

"These are not my terms," Marcellus said firmly, then turned to Catrin and spoke with a softer tone. "My only desire is to protect you at any cost."

A sense of dread crawled over Catrin when she saw the anguish in Marcellus's eyes as her father said, "Don't keep Catrin in the dark. Tell her what it says."

Marcellus stared at Catrin for a few moments. His voice cracked with emotion as he revealed, "It is the nuptial pact your father previously agreed with Cunobelin, which betrothed you to Adminius. Cunobelin will honor the marital contract as long as Adminius is given sovereignty of the northern Cantiaci lands. My father also accepts these terms for peace."

Catrin felt as if her heart had shattered into a thousand shards and blown away in a gale storm. The nuptial pact had been the impetus to give herself willingly to Marcellus. The walls seemed to collapse on her as she gasped for breath. Everything she had sacrificed was for naught. The reality that she was again the bargaining tool to seal an alliance and would be forced to marry a foreign prince made her stomach churn. And Marcellus—the man whom she had given her body, heart, and soul—had proffered the terms.

She glowered at Marcellus, then turned to her father and said defiantly, "I will not marry Adminius!"

Amren regarded Catrin for a moment and then his eyes blazed at Marcellus. "What do I gain by accepting this marital contract?"

"Peace with Cunobelin and the Romans, as I said."

"Peace," Amren hissed. "Peace in exchange for my northern borders. How can I accept this when Marrock is bent on destroying me? Cunobelin and the Romans have yet to control this monster."

Marcellus's jaw tensed. "My father and Cunobelin promise to punish Marrock for what he has done."

Amren raged. "They broke their promises when Marrock butchered Vala! You broke your pledge to be a husband to Catrin when you presented me with this preposterous offer. No! Never! I can't trust any of you—the Romans, Cunobelin, Marrock . . . but most of all you!"

Mixed emotions barraged Catrin as she mulled over what her father had said. Though she was relieved her father was against her betrothal to Adminius, she could see fury in her father's eyes directed at Marcellus.

She sensed the Raven's omniscient presence. Scanning for her guide in the beamed rafters, she only found a stray white dove perched on a wooden beam.

A sudden rumble of doors crashing against the walls startled Catrin. She pivoted toward the entryway. A gust of wind blew her loose hair back. The next instant, the Raven burst through the entryway and knocked the dagger out of the king's hands. The weapon clanged on the floor as Catrin's eyes followed the Raven's flight. The black creature swooped to the rafters and chased the pristine white dove away.

Catrin watched the dagger spin wildly on the floor until it stopped and its tip pointed at her. She felt her jaw drop in awe as she visualized gold dust alighting on the glowing blade and melting into its etching, obliterating the inscription. She picked up the dagger. To her dismay, the curse etched on the blade had not changed. She must have envisioned the blade melting the curse away.

Then in the corner of her eye, she glimpsed a shadow moving in the back corner.

She cried out with a gasp, "Who's there?"

A man's hoarse voice from the direction of the shadow replied, "Myrddin, the wandering Druid, here to advise the war king, Amren."

Unnerved that the Druid had been hiding in the back during the tense discourse between her father and Marcellus, Catrin muttered, "Myrddin?"

Amren turned on his heels and ordered, "Old man, come forth."

The click, click of a wooden stick thumped the floor as the shadowy man lumbered toward them. Under the illumination of torches, Myrddin appeared, hunched in a white robe, his face obscured behind the cowl of his hood. His scraggly gray beard hung over his chest like a bird's nest. In his hand was a wooden staff with a handle shaped like a serpent's mouth biting a crystal orb.

A chill ran down Catrin's spine. This was the wandering Druid she had earlier met at Ferrex's family farm.

32

WILD DRUID

Dumbstruck, King Amren gaped at Myrddin, who pulled back his hood to reveal glowing amber eyes. Amren recalled Rhan's earlier threat that she would strike him dead after Myrddin arrived. Taken aback that the Druid was secretly there during the proceedings against Catrin, he cursed beneath his breath. The last time he had seen Myrddin was when he was an adolescent suffering lovesickness for Rhan, the same malady Catrin was experiencing with Marcellus.

Amren recalled stories told by bards at festivities that Myrddin was a wild hermit born of a mortal woman but sired by an incubus. From his demonic legacy, Myrddin inherited extraordinary knowledge of the past and present. The sun god Bel later bequeathed him with prophetic abilities. The staff in his hand rendered Myrddin magical powers. He wondered if the wild Druid's sudden appearance was a harbinger of his own imminent demise.

"Did Rhan summon you?" he asked Myrddin.

The wild Druid proclaimed in a croaky voice, "The gods sent me as their messenger to counsel you in your time of greatest strife."

Amren bristled. "What strife?"

"A week ago," Myrddin said, twisting the strands of his gray beard with his fingers, "I dreamt that I had wandered out of the old forest to meet you on a footpath near the Ancient Oak. You asked, 'Why have you come?' I answered, 'A demonic entity wants to exchange destinies with one of your daughters.' After that, I immediately journeyed here to shine the gods' truth on what you must do next to counter this iniquitous being. I hid in the back corner, so I could better understand the depths of your family's strife."

Wary of Myrddin's true intent, Amren scrutinized the Druid's weathered, crinkled face. "Have you come to help me break Rhan's curse?"

Myrddin gave a crusty smirk. "Perhaps . . ."

Annoyed with the Druid's vague answer, Amren snapped his fingers. "Directly answer my question or be off with you!"

Grinning slyly, Myrddin hunched over his staff like a gnarled oak branch and pounded it on the dark oak floor three times. The crystalline globe, embedded in the serpent's mouth at the end of the staff, lit up like a rising sun. The wild Druid squinted at the orb's brilliant surface. He intoned, "I see midday transform to night. Crickets chirp, but bees abuzz disappear. Frost hovers above treetops like death. Leaves fly as black ravens above forest moss. Blood moon shrouds the sun. Emerald hills turn barren. The diamond's flash crowns the sun. Bees again pollinate Mother Earth."

The grizzled Druid peered at Catrin through one eye while keeping the other shut. "Are you the keeper of the curse?"

She turned to Amren and raised a brow, seeking advice on how she should respond.

"Read the inscribed curse on the dagger," he instructed.

Catrin retrieved the dagger from beneath her belt. The blade glinted from the orb's illumination as she read the curse.

"The gods demand the scales be balanced for the life you take today. If you deny my soul's journey to the Otherworld by beheading me, I curse you to the same fate as mine. When the Raven rises out of Apollo's flames with the dark powers of the Ancient Druids, Blood Wolf will form a pack with the mighty empire and fulfill this curse. The Raven will then cast liquid fire into the serpent's stone and forge vengeance on the empire's anvil."

Amren shifted his eyes toward Myrddin. "The curse says Blood Wolf will ally with the Roman Empire, but how can this be after his heinous deed of butchering their soldiers?"

The wild Druid tilted his head back and violently shook the staff until the orb turned as dark as a solar eclipse. "The curse stands unless the Raven alters the future."

Amren dubiously cocked an eyebrow. "Tell me, old man, who is this Raven you speak of?"

Myrddin squeezed his eyelids shut and waved his staff in a circular motion. "I feel the Raven's essence in the chamber. Its shadow weaves in and out of itself like a knotted serpent. But . . . I can't tell if it is wraith or human."

"More riddles!" Amren grumbled.

Myrddin's eyes popped open. He pointed his staff at Marcellus and declared, "You hold the key for unlocking the curse's riddle."

Appearing alarmed by the wild Druid's gesture, Marcellus clasped Catrin by the arm and asked in Latin, "What did the old man say?"

Amren noticed how Catrin silently gazed at Marcellus, her eyes flitting back and forth, as if she was silently answering him through her thoughts. After a few moments, Marcellus's jaw relaxed as if he understood. The couple's connection disconcerted Amren, as did Myrddin's prophetic vision. Fixing his eyes on Myrddin, Amren asked, "What makes you believe Marcellus can unlock the curse's riddle?"

"For the curse to be fulfilled, you must be king," Myrddin answered, his eyes as brilliant as amber gemstones. "But what if . . . you weren't king?"

"Get to your meaning!" Amren snapped.

Myrddin smiled. "Declare another as king and break the curse."

Incredulous, Amren was not at first sure if he had heard the wild Druid correctly. "What? Declare another king?"

Myrddin pounded his staff on the wood floor and the orb flamed like a torch. "Look for Apollo in the curse."

"Speak plainly, old man," Amren growled, becoming increasingly vexed with the wild Druid's riddles. "Who is this Apollo?"

Myrddin struck the floor three times with his staff. The wooden floor splintered to Marcellus's feet. The wild Druid narrowed an eye at the staff's fiery globe and said hoarsely, "The Roman standing before us is Apollo. The Raven must offer Apollo a cup to incite an ecstatic state to bind his soul with the divine goddess. Once Apollo spills his seed, prosperity and peace will return to the kingdom."

Amren crossed his arms and huffed. "Doesn't the ancient ritual demand a king be sacrificed and his blood drained to lift the curse off the lands?"

Catrin interrupted with fevered pitch. "Father, you can't follow Myrddin's advice, not if it requires sacrificing Marcellus. Marrock must have sent Myrddin to trick you into believing the curse can be simply broken by your stepping down as king. That monster could ambush us during the drunken revelry at the fertility rite."

Eyes widening like a wild wolf under attack, Myrddin growled, "My king, I assure you no mortal sent me. I only deliver messages from the gods!"

Amren shook his head at the underlings trying to steal his lightning bolt as a ruler. "I make the final decisions here—not my lovesick daughter or a Druid older than rocks." He glared at Catrin. "You have yet to redeem yourself for treason."

Catrin recoiled as if she had been struck by venom. Marcellus, appearing concerned, clasped her hand and met her gaze. She again seemed to commune with him, her eyes shifting back and forth. The couple's silent interaction reminded Amren of Rhan's ability to transmit her thoughts to him after they had been declared king and queen.

Marcellus finally nodded, appearing to agree with Catrin. She turned to Myrddin. "I am the Raven foretold in the curse. I will offer Marcellus the cup to symbolize his union as a mortal king to the Earth Goddess. Based on the ancient ritual, Marcellus's sovereignty as king will be legitimized through our marriage. Hence, the curse will lift, as you so claim. But no harm can befall Marcellus."

A crooked smile stretched across Myrddin's leathered face, his eyes dancing with delight. "Yes, quite possibly, the Raven is you. As such, you can perform the ancient fertility rite before your people."

Amren hesitated, wondering if he was losing his wits to agree to such a preposterous scheme. The image of the Roman publicly mating with his daughter in the fertility rite made him cringe. Imagining the Roman's head joining other enemy skulls on the wall made his stomach tickle with sordid delight. Yet, he was still at wit's end on how he could counter Rhan, with the invisible wall blocking him from slaying her. He decided to be patient and consider all his options. Perhaps, he could do as Myrddin suggested and proclaim Marcellus king to test the wild Druid's credibility as a sooth-sayer. He could further explore using Marcellus as a game piece.

Amren could barely contain his contempt as he proposed to Marcellus, "If I recognize your marriage with Catrin, can you persuade your father and Cunobelin to accept a political alliance with me and release Marrock for my pleasure?"

"If you reject the marital pact with Cunobelin," Marcellus said, "what can I possibly offer in return as recompense?"

"Tell them both that I grant you sovereignty over my northern lands," Amren said while ruminating over ways he could break down the invisible wall to kill Rhan and break the curse. He would then renounce the Roman scum as king. Ferrex would make a more suitable husband to Catrin.

Marcellus's eyes widened. "Do you honestly believe this will stop the curse?"

"If I kill Marrock," Amren retorted.

Before the stunned Marcellus could reply, Catrin chimed in, "Father, al-low me to speak with Marcellus in private so he understands what is being asked of him. You must promise me to bless my marriage to Marcellus, which we already pledged to each other before the Mother Goddess. Then I will offer him the matrimonial cup that binds him to the goddess of these lands."

Amren's face flushed with anger that his daughter had the audacity to request this. He refrained from shaking sense into her. She would soon learn rulers must make sacrifices for the good of their people. The way his lovesick daughter gazed at Marcellus clenched at Amren's heart. He could tell by the longing in her eyes that Marcellus had blinded her to what he truly was. Like all self-serving, ambitious men, the scoundrel would surely lose interest in Catrin once he understood the ramifications of marrying a foreigner.

"Before I agree to bless your marriage," Amren finally said, "I must consult further with Myrddin and other close advisors. However, you can speak privately with the Roman in my meeting chamber."

A smile bursting on her face, Catrin clasped Marcellus's hand. As Am-ren watched the couple amble to the back chamber, he wrestled with his memory of how he had suffered the same lovesickness for Rhan as his daughter felt for the Roman enemy. After Myrddin had crowned him with the antlers of the horned god, Rhan offered him the matrimonial cup. Its contents transformed his senses into an ecstatic state of lust as he watched the priestesses undress Rhan and dye her skin crimson with bloodroot. She danced around him like a hot flame and engulfed him into her fiery passion. During the fertility rite, he thrust in rhythm with the pounding drums that sounded like a gigantic heart pumping blood into his hardened loins. The drunken celebrants cheered as he thrice implanted seed into Rhan, impregnating her with Marrock—the son he had once hoped would inherit his kingdom.

Shortly after the ritual, Amren discovered his father's body hung upside down from the Ancient Oak. Myrddin was holding the ceremonial knife. The wild Druid confessed he had slit his father's throat and allowed the blood to drain on the forest tundra.

Myrddin's words, "This is what the gods demand for you to be king," were still etched in Amren's memory. The wild Druid's advice could be a trick to dethrone him in favor of Marcellus, but could he take the chance that his suspicion might not be right? He had to consider Myrddin's counsel and proceed slowly to ascertain the best course of action.

Staring at Myrddin, Amren bluntly asked, "What will be the sign the curse is broken once Marcellus is declared king?"

"The invisible wall around Rhan will collapse," Myrddin said, studying the serpent's orb on his staff.

"If I slay her, is the curse broken?" Amren asked.

"Yes, that is a surety."

"To transfer the sovereignty, does it require a sacrifice like that was demanded at my coronation?" asked Amren, sensing a foreboding chill slicing through his neck.

"Yes. A change in kingship always demands a sacrifice to the war goddesses . . . even when no curse looms over your head."

"I thought so," Amren said, resolved not to let Rhan, Cunobelin, the Romans, or Marrock destroy him. If sacrificing Marcellus appeased the goddesses, as Myrddin insinuated, he would do it without hesitation.

33

PRIVATE MOMENT

Behind the chamber's bolted door, Catrin felt a sob clutch her throat as she gazed at Marcellus. His deep blue eyes were almost purple in the soft illumination of the candlelight. The room suddenly felt hot when he pulled her into his embrace and pressed his lips over hers. The kiss deepened and his wet tongue danced around hers. The touch of his flushed face gave her a fleeting illusion she was warm, safe, and secure in his arms—their bodies and souls forging in the heat of passion.

But then, the grim reality that it was impossible for them to stay together shook Catrin out of the moment; they could still lose their lives for their betrayal. Even now, she found it dubious that her father was willing to marry her to Marcellus and accept him as the new king. Suspecting Myrddin and her father had ulterior motives, she had an uneasy twinge in her stomach. Had her first instinct been correct, she wondered, that Myrddin would sacrifice Marcellus after the fertility rite to lift the curse?

Yet, at the moment, she couldn't find the strength to push Marcellus away . . . to tell him to save himself, to forget her and never return.

When he finally released her from his tight embrace, her knees weakened and a sob of joy caught in her throat. She leaned her head against his shoulder and felt his chest heaving.

He nuzzled her hair and inhaled. "I missed you so much—your touch, your scent. I thought about you every day and what I would do if you were ever in my arms again."

Fighting back tears, Catrin looked at Marcellus and finally uttered the words that her heart could not say. "You should have stayed away and never returned. Why would you risk yourself for me?"

"You are a part of me . . . in a way I can't explain. If I ever lost you"—Marcellus sighed and held her closer—"I would lose a part of myself. Not only can I hear your thoughts when you are near me, but also when we're apart. If you were ever harmed, how could I live with myself, knowing I was the cause?"

Catrin gazed into his eyes and silently communed with him.

Do not blame yourself. Everything I did was of my free will. I choose you.

"I want you to hear this from my mouth," Marcellus said in a hushed voice. "I had to see you again before I died to tell you how sorry I am for ever having doubted your love. The hurt on your face when I accused you of betraying me at the prisoner exchange has haunted me day and night. When the death arrow shot close to my heart, I felt your essence enter me. I again sensed your strength as I fought Marrock in his wolf form. And when your father sent the message threatening to kill you if I didn't do what he asked, I thought my heart would split apart. I readily agreed, fearing he would harm you. You have a special hold on me, Catrin. Only your love can fill my emptiness."

Overwhelmed with his heartfelt words, Catrin lightly stroked Marcellus's cheek with her fingertips. He placed her hand on his chest, where she felt his rapidly beating heart.

"I need to know something else about you," Marcellus asked, a lump forming in his throat. "Did you shapeshift into a white raven and sacrifice yourself by taking the brunt of my death arrow? Do you have the same ability as Marrock?"

Catrin hesitated, detecting the uneasiness in Marcellus's voice. She pondered how she could explain so he understood and accepted her mystical powers.

Marcellus's brow furrowed. "How could you perish as a raven but be here with me now, still alive?"

Trying to ease his discomfort, Catrin caressed his face with the back of her hand. "I am what Ancient Druids call a soul traveler. The soul is like fluid while the body is solid. My soul can enter the mind of another living entity like a wave on a beach, but it must always return from whence it comes. That is what happened when I connected with the white raven and ordered it to take the brunt of the arrow. At the instant the white raven died, a piece of my soul was left in its body as my remaining soul returned to my human form."

"What do you mean 'left a piece of your soul'?" asked Marcellus, lifting an eyebrow.

"A shadow fills the piece of my soul that I left in the raven's body," Catrin explained. "I'm not sure why this happens, but I sometimes fear my soul could disappear into a shadow by using the powers of the Ancient Druids. Without a soul, I cannot be reborn into another form after I die. Now that you know this about me, are you still willing to bind with me in marriage so I can confer sovereignty to you?"

Marcellus gazed at Catrin and cupped her face between his hands. "Your mystical abilities confound me. I feel as if I'm in a dream whenever I am near you. But I believe you can use your powers for a greater purpose. You are driven by loyalty and love to both your family and me. That is why your heart is split and that is why you can't forsake me for your father. I love you more than life itself. Your cause is my cause. I will do everything your father demands so you are redeemed in his eyes. I will even try to convince my father to make peace with Amren. But, but . . ."

Marcellus's eyes lowered and his fingers trembled against Catrin's face. She clasped his hands. "What are you afraid to tell me?"

He looked away for a moment, as if gathering strength to say his next words. He finally admitted, "My father will never recognize our marriage. He will disown me. After my great-grandfather, Mark Antony, declared his marriage to the Egyptian Queen Cleopatra, the Senate stripped him of all honors and banned his legacy from the empire's records. Do you understand what I am telling you?"

Catrin wrapped her arms around Marcellus's neck and pulled him closer. "You can stay here with me."

Marcellus tensed. "You are asking me to forfeit my heritage and family. I've been struggling with the reality that I can't keep my Roman birthright if I stay here with you."

Catrin kissed Marcellus tenderly.

"Don't you see our pathways have joined? My father will do whatever Myrddin advises to break the curse. I know father will ultimately accept Myrddin's advice for us to marry and declare you as the new king," she said, although doubts still plagued her mind about what her father might do to Marcellus once the curse was broken.

Marcellus frowned. "I don't understand the influence of Rhan's curse over your father."

"Rhan's curse foretells my father will be beheaded by Marrock. As king, my father will do whatever is necessary to block the dark prophecy that threatens to devastate our kingdom if Marrock ever took control."

"Is this Rhan an evil spirit—a demon, a dark sorceress?" asked Marcellus, narrowing his eyes. "Was that Rhan's voice I heard speaking in your head before you turned the dagger on yourself?"

Catrin's stomach knotted into queasiness. "I'm not sure what you heard, but Rhan is an evil Druidess who possessed Agrona as a little girl. And now she wants to possess me and displace my soul."

"What do you mean 'displace your soul'?" asked Marcellus, furrowing his eyebrows together.

"For Rhan's soul to possess Agrona's body, I assumed she had to displace Agrona's soul."

"Where is Agrona's soul now—in the Otherworld?"

The answer as to where Agrona's soul had gone gnawed at Catrin. She wondered if Agrona's displaced soul roamed the woods where Rhan had been executed. Perhaps it was Agrona's wraith that had haunted new mothers in the village a few years back and demanded their babies.

"I don't know," Catrin finally admitted. "I never gave it much thought . . . until now. Why do you ask?"

"Curious, that's all," Marcellus said offhandedly, but then he nervously shifted his weight. "Before I met you, I never believed in supernatural powers. But now, I know they exist. I saw Marrock's shapeshifted wolf form disappear before my eyes. You summoned hundreds of ravens to attack the

Roman soldiers at the prisoner exchange, thus saving yourself and your warriors. From what you have said about Rhan, I've sensed her black magic and am afraid she can harm you."

"Once we perform the fertility rite and you are declared king, I believe the curse will be broken," Catrin said, though doubts lingered in her mind that the dark prophecy could be thwarted.

"What exactly happens during the fertility rite?" Marcellus asked.

Catrin hesitated. "You must couple with me before my people."

Marcellus grimaced. "What? Openly make love to you?"

"Yes. Myrddin will prepare an elixir that I will give you in the matrimonial cup. It will heighten your desire for me."

Marcellus pulled Catrin flush to his chest. "Everyone knows we have already consummated our marriage vows. Why must I perform this again in front of voyeurs for their perverse pleasures?"

"The fertility ritual validates your kingship and symbolizes your contract with the Earth Goddess to make the lands fertile through crops and livestock."

Catrin tensed when Marcellus began nibbling her ears and whispered, "I want to experience this special moment when I have all my senses, not when I'm drugged by your Druid."

Suddenly realizing the "special moment" was now, Catrin protested, leaning back from his embrace. "No. Not here!"

"Yes here," he groaned, his lips almost touching hers as he pushed her against the door. Feeling his warm, moist breath on her face, Catrin muttered, "What if someone barges in?"

Marcellus gently clasped her throat. "The door is bolted."

Catrin could barely swallow. "But they will hear us . . ."

Marcellus pulled Catrin's head toward his lips so she couldn't say another word. Her heart pounded wildly, his reckless desire frightening her, but at the same time enthralling her.

"When I almost died," he said softly, "I promised myself if I ever held you in my arms again, I would take you in the moment. Don't deny me this now."

With his thoughts connecting with hers, Catrin could feel his burning desire—an ember ready to spark by her slightest touch. His fiery blue eyes consumed her as he clasped the back of her head and passionately kissed her.

"Not here. We must wait until the fertility rite," she said, pulling away, her body flushed with heat, yet her resistance melting away.

"Yes, here." Marcellus nibbled at her throat. "What if your father doesn't accept Myrddin's advice for us to marry? We might not get another chance."

Groaning softly, he enveloped her lips with his, deepening the kiss and tantalizing her senses with promised forbidden delight. She felt herself weakening as his hand wandered over her tunic to fondle a breast.

But then, Catrin's heart almost stopped when she heard footsteps approaching the door. She pushed Marcellus back, but her struggle seemed to arouse him more. Becoming panicked, she implored him to stop. "This is madness! My father—"

"Yes . . . madness," Marcellus whispered.

Catrin could sense his growing desire overwhelming any fear of the king's presence outside the door.

"I need you," he rasped. "Your father could kill me in an instant."

Catrin struggled against his tight embrace. "It isn't the right time."

His warm lips touched hers as he said, "There is never a right time except the present."

The rumble of the king's voice saying, "Why is the chamber locked?" finally diverted Marcellus out of the moment.

He released her.

34

SERPENT'S ORB

Standing a few feet from Marcellus, Catrin self-consciously smoothed the tunic over her breeches and rubbed her lips, still aching from the power of his kiss. Uncomfortably flushed, she unbolted the door and pushed it open to find her father's steely glare and Myrddin meekly standing behind him.

"Why was the door locked?" Amren asked.

"I didn't want any interruptions while we spoke," Catrin replied demurely, her heart pounding against her rib cage like a mallet on an anvil.

Amren's eyebrows abruptly lifted. He regarded Catrin for a moment, then bore his eyes into Marcellus. "I want to speak with you, Roman, in private."

"For what purpose?" Catrin blurted anxiously.

"This is none of your concern," Amren snapped.

Catrin could tell by her father's icy blue eyes that he still harbored deep resentment toward Marcellus. A foreboding chill prickled across her neck that the king had something else in mind than what the wild Druid had proposed.

"Remember, Father, I asked you to bless our marriage," Catrin said, softly touching her father's arm.

Amren clasped Catrin's hand and squeezed her fingers. "I have not forgotten."

The king's painful grip brought Catrin almost to tears, but she muffled her whimper and stared doggedly at him.

Marcellus interceded. "My king, I would be honored to speak with you in the adjoining chamber while Catrin waits here. I have something to offer that might interest you."

Amren gestured to the meeting chamber. "We'll talk in there while Myrddin keeps watch over Catrin. He can give her further instruction on the fertility rite."

Not quite sure if she had interpreted her father's meaning correctly, Catrin looked at him in bewilderment. "Does that mean you agree to confer your kingship to Marcellus through our marriage and the fertility rite?"

Amren did not reply, his face as emotionless as hard stone. Disquieted by her father's silence, Catrin apprehensively glanced at Marcellus, who then suggested, "I would like to speak with the king further about my conditions for the rite."

Amren smiled grimly. "You are in no position to make demands, but I will consider what you have to say."

Catrin felt an uneasy twitch in her stomach as she watched Marcellus and her father disappear into the chamber. A wicked-sounding chuckle startled her. She turned to find Myrddin swaying on his staff like a twig trying to gain support from a tree branch. She wondered if it was more than a coincidence that she had previously encountered the Druid before Mor's wedding.

"I wish I had your elixir for my aged bones," the wild Druid said with a sinister smirk.

Bewildered, Catrin stepped back. "What do you mean?"

"The heavy breathing inside the chamber . . . the whisperings, groans— hmm, let me say, it sounded as though you were already in the midst of the fertility rite."

Abashed, Catrin didn't know how to respond to the wild Druid's insinuation, so she instead changed the topic. "Do you know how long my father will be with Marcellus?"

Myrddin's leathered lips stretched into a reptilian grin. "Not long. I suspect he is making sure all the eggs boil in the same cauldron."

"So my father confirmed with you that I could marry Marcellus?"

"Perhaps . . ."

Unsettled her father might be cooking up other schemes, Catrin asked, "Then why did he tell me that you would further instruct me on the fertility rite?"

Myrddin scratched his head as if befuddled. "Oh dear me, was that so? Ahh, now I remember what I wanted to say. What animal do you want to be at the fertility ritual?"

Odd that he did not address my question, Catrin thought, but she said, "Am I not to be covered with black feathers to represent the Raven foretold in Rhan's curse?"

"Oh, that makes good sense." Myrddin chuckled and pointed to his head. "Old mind leaks like a sieve." He raked something out of his chest-length beard and showed the yellow clump to Catrin. "The egg yolk from my breakfast reminds me of another question. How should Marcellus be attired?"

Catrin winced, not sure if senility had replaced Myrddin's wits. "The curse says he is Apollo—the Roman sun god."

Myrddin shook his head. "No, no, the Roman can't be a god from the heavens. He needs to be an earth god to mate with Mother Goddess. The horn god . . . what's his name—oh yes, Cerrunos, the Stag God of the forest."

Becoming annoyed with the muttering Druid, Catrin said sharply, "Father said you were to instruct me on the fertility rite, so why am I answering your questions?"

Myrddin thumped his head. "Ahh . . . so did you explain to Marcellus what will be expected of him?"

"I told him a little bit. Is there something in particular he should be aware of?"

"Priestesses of the Mother Goddess will crown him with the antlers of a stag before you offer him the matrimonial cup as a symbol of his union to the goddess of the lands."

"I can instruct Marcellus on what to do during the ceremony."

"Good. I'll prepare a potion that will harden his oak before the fertility rite," Myrddin added matter-of-factly.

"As long as he believes it is wine, he will drink it," Catrin said, though she doubted Marcellus needed any aphrodisiac to enhance his desire.

"I'll hide the bitterness of the drink with sweet honey." Myrddin tapped a forefinger on his lower lip. "Let me see . . . there is one more detail."

"What is it?" Catrin snapped.

"Priestesses of Mother Goddess must sanctify a matrimonial hut where Marcellus will plant his seed in you."

"I thought we would perform the fertility rite in a public ceremony."

"No, no, you must wait to copulate on a sacred bed or the curse won't be broken. The king's guards will be there to confirm the Roman spills his seed in you."

Catrin recoiled with the prospect that Ferrex and other guards would watch them in the throes of passion.

"Marcellus will never agree to this," she argued.

"It is not necessary for them to witness"—Myrddin pumped his finger into the opening of his clenched hand—"but they only need to confirm you both entered the hut."

"Said that way, I feel more relieved that we'll have some privacy on our wedding night," Catrin said, tempering the bite of her tone.

There was a glint in Myrddin's serpentine eyes. "Oh, I almost forgot. The king wants me to determine the extent of your mystical abilities."

Catrin hesitated, wondering if the wild Druid had intentionally acted senile so he could garner more information on what really interested him.

Magic.

"Father already knows about my abilities," Catrin said, raising an eyebrow with suspicion.

"Well . . . how do I say this?" Myrddin stroked his ruffled beard. "We need many coins in our purse to pay the ultimate price."

"Get to your meaning."

"Everyone must sacrifice to break Rhan's curse. Amren must step down as king. Marcellus must relinquish his Roman heritage. And as for you, my sweet one, only the gods know. Still, we might need other coins to pay the price for breaking the curse."

"What other coins?"

"Your magical abilities combined with mine. But I can't price the coins if I don't know the weight of your powers."

Catrin hesitated, noting Myrddin's wry smile. "The purse is getting a little too heavy. What has my father already told you about my magical abilities?"

"He said you can see the future through the Raven's mind."

"It is true I can see what it sees as it flies overhead, but others can also do this," Catrin said, cautious not to reveal the full extent of her abilities. "Has Father told you anything else?"

Myrddin quirked his bushy eyebrows up. "He said you can shapeshift."

The wild Druid's comment surprised Catrin, for she had never revealed she could shapeshift to her father. She said hesitantly, "I'm reluctant to do so."

"Why is that, my sweet?"

"I'm not sure what the consequences are of changing forms."

The corners of Myrddin's lips twisted into a half-smile. "I can see by your expression that this magic frightens you. Unless you completely understand how it is done, you could be frozen forever in the shapeshifted form and never return to your own."

The orb at the end of the Myrddin's staff began to glow, mesmerizing Catrin with its brilliant yellow surface. Seeing blurred images in the center of the translucent globe, she lightly touched the hard surface. A burning shock emitted into her fingertips, momentarily dazing her.

"What just happened?" she asked, her lucidity returning.

"The Ancient Druids use the serpent's orb as a portal into the future. You must have connected, because you flinched as if whisked forward in time. Did you see images in the crystalline globe?"

Catrin studied the serpent's orb. "Yes, but they are blurry."

"Peer at the serpent's orb like this," Myrddin instructed, narrowing one eye while keeping the other shut.

Catrin peered through one eye as he instructed. Agrona's face suddenly came into focus in the midst of blurred images. "It's Agrona," she said, squeezing her left eyelid to a slit. "But I can't discern the other images."

"Be patient, my sweet. The images will soon clear."

Continuing to squint, Catrin focused on an elongated banquet table at the center of the orb. She discerned that the table was in the same Great

Hall she was standing in, except there were additional spiked skulls lining the upper stone walls. To her surprise, Agrona was nursing a swaddled babe while warriors around her heartily ate roasted ribs and gulped ale from horn-shaped vessels. The orb's edges suddenly brightened.

The image of Marrock strutting into the Great Hall came into focus.

In her mind, Catrin could hear the rumble of warriors pounding their brass goblets on the table like thunder from a gathering storm.

Agrona did not seem to notice Marrock stepping behind her, as she lovingly stroked her baby's strawberry-blonde hair that fluffed like down feathers. Marrock drew a longsword from his baldric, and he grasped the hilt with both hands. The blade glinted as he plunged it into the base of Agrona's neck. Her eyes were agape in shock as Marrock roughly gripped her hair with one hand while yanking the blade out with the other. He then brutally smashed her head into the table. Warriors jumped out of their seats and scrambled to the doorway.

Observing Marrock pick up the screaming baby, Catrin recoiled with horror that he might kill the infant. Marrock gently unswaddled the baby to reveal she was a girl. A shudder coursed through Catrin's veins as Marrock nestled the naked baby into the curvature of his arms as he wiped the blood off her skin with a piece of his striated blue-and-gold cape. As he continued cleaning the infant's face, his monstrous head transfigured into the striking, smooth-skinned face of him as a young man before Catrin's ravens disfigured him.

The serpent's orb suddenly darkened when Myrddin banged the staff on the floor.

"What did you see?" he asked.

Horrified, Catrin bit her lower lip to make it stop quivering. She mulled over what the vision could have meant. Surely, Marrock must have known that Rhan had possessed Agrona. Killing Agrona was the same as matricide—a heinous crime. Yet, something viler pricked at Catrin. She could not reconcile Marrock cradling Agrona's baby, except for the unspeakable possibility that Marrock was the father. The thought made her cringe with revulsion.

In the corner of her eye, Catrin noted Myrddin's twisted smile. She wondered if he had conjured the vision in the serpent's orb. If so, what was his purpose?

"Did you see the images in the globe?" she asked.

"The globe appeared dark to me," Myrddin replied, raking more egg yolk out of his white beard.

"That's odd you couldn't see what I did, particularly if you have prophetic abilities, as you proclaim," she remarked.

"The future only reveals itself to the one who can alter it."

Frustrated with Myrddin's vague riddles and still suspicious of his inquiry about her mystical abilities, Catrin asked, "Does the serpent's orb only reveal the future if the curse is fulfilled? If the curse is broken after I confer the kingship to Marcellus, would the orb reveal a different prophecy?"

"Yes, very insightful of you," Myrddin said with a wry grin. "The orb only reveals the future if the present remains steadfast."

The sounds of voices and shuffling footsteps in the direction of the adjoining antechamber diverted Catrin's attention. She turned to find her father, with his arm around Marcellus, striding into the Great Hall as if they had become close companions. She remembered her father using the disguise of friendship as a way of entangling enemies in his web before striking them dead.

Catrin suddenly felt ill, not knowing her father's true intentions toward Marcellus. She inhaled a deep breath as others entered the chamber: Queen Rhiannon, Trystan, Mor, Belinus, Cynwrig, and a handful of nobles. The last person through the entryway was Ferrex, who had a nasty scowl contorting every line on his face downward.

Marcellus joined Catrin at the base of the thrones and lightly touched her arm while Myrddin remained at her other side. Amren met the queen at the bottom of the dais and offered her his arm. He escorted her up the three stairs to the thrones, where they seated themselves.

Sensing someone's eyes on her, Catrin glanced back to see Ferrex's face ablaze as red as hot embers. Unnerved, she turned her head and met the king's icy stare. His white-knuckled hands appeared frozen on the armrests of his throne.

35

MYRDDIN'S RIDDLES

King Amren studied his daughter, Catrin, for a moment, then shifted his eyes toward Myrddin, who still unsettled him. He looked around and considered how he might manage the people around him as pieces in his game. His primary objective now was to glean from Myrddin's riddles whether he could break through Rhan's invisible wall without relinquishing his throne. His hankering to kill the Roman rogue would have to wait until he clearly considered the consequences of such an act. Once he killed Rhan and broke her curse, he could then maneuver the other pieces in the political game to make sure he was ultimately recognized as the legitimate ruler of the Cantiaci.

"Myrddin, step forward," Amren commanded.

The wild Druid thumped his serpent-head staff on the floor as he shuffled within a few feet of the base of the thrones.

Amren silently sat erect on his throne and assessed the growing tension of everyone awaiting his final decision on whether he would follow Myrddin's counsel. He smiled smugly as everyone stole glances at one another in perplexity. His formidable enemy, Rhan, was not visibly present, but he could sense her hatred lurking in the high-vaulted rafters. He scanned the rafters for shadows, but only spotted Catrin's raven gawking at him. Seeing the creature offered him hope that he could break the curse. He wondered how much of the Ancient Druids' powers had already transferred to his daughter.

Catrin had, after all, already altered the curse.

Shifting his gaze to Myrddin, Amren addressed the assemblage of his advisors in Celtic. "After meeting with everyone in this chamber, I have concluded that it would be reckless for me to step down and proclaim a foreigner as king—particularly if this act fails to break the curse."

"My king, I beg to disagree," Myrddin blurted.

"Don't interrupt me!" Amren shouted, rising to his feet. "Some of my advisors have voiced their concerns about replacing me with a foreigner. It might incite my people to revolt."

Myrddin stomped his staff on the wooden floor. "But there is no other way—"

"Hear me out!" Amren interrupted. "I recognize your divine ability to speak with ancestral gods and have carefully considered your counsel. But I need more clarification from you before I make my final decision. It is my understanding that the ancient rite requires the goddess of the lands to confer sovereignty to the next king, is that not so?"

Myrddin nodded in agreement.

"It is only through the symbolic marriage with the goddess taking the guise of a divine mortal woman that the mortal king can rule. Once the king joins with the Earth Goddess, he connects to the land and its people. Is this not true?"

"Yes, my king." Myrddin confirmed.

"Does Rhan's curse foretell the Roman sun god, Apollo, will be the next king when the Raven flies out of his flames?"

"No, no . . . the king is not a god, but a mortal."

"I thought you said the Roman represents Apollo in the curse."

Myrddin scratched his head. "Oh, indeed, I did say that, but the Roman is not a god."

Amren snapped, "I know that," while in the back of his mind he considered how he could demonstrate the Roman was unfit to rule once the curse was lifted. He recalled his father, whose arm was lost in battle, being forced to abdicate his throne so his disfigurement would not transfer to the land. After Amren's ceremonial mating with Rhan, his father was sacrificed as atonement to the goddesses of war. Perhaps, the Roman rogue could have an unexpected accident. He smiled at the thought and continued the discourse with Myrddin.

"The marital bed must be prepared in the shape of the wheel to symbolize Apollo's chariot and be sanctified, is that not what you told me earlier?"

"Yes. I foresaw this in my vision. As I privately told you earlier, I instructed the priestesses of the Mother Goddess, when I first arrived, to prepare a wheel-shape bed in the matrimonial hut. There, the foreign king will consummate the fertility rite and spill his seed. Then fertility and prosperity will return to our lands."

Amren stepped to the front of the platform, where he looked down on Marcellus and said in Latin, "I've told everyone in this room that a matrimonial hut is being prepared at an undisclosed location where you and Catrin can consummate your marriage vows. I assume this meets your condition that you'd be allowed to finish the fertility rite in seclusion with my daughter."

Whispers filled the chamber as everyone stole glances between each other. Marcellus clasped Catrin's hand and nodded his agreement.

"Let us go through this one more time, so I get this right." Amren said. "Once the fertility rite is completed, I can break through the invisible wall."

"Wh . . . what is your question?" asked Myrddin, appearing flustered.

Amren rolled his eyes. "Let me reword this into a question. Once Marcellus is crowned as king, will the invisible wall disintegrate?"

Myrddin peered at the brilliant orb. "It is certain . . . yes, I mean yes . . . the wall can be breached."

"Finally, a concise answer," Amren said sarcastically. "Once I break through the invisible wall, I can slay Agrona, is that not correct?"

Myrddin hesitated, studying the orb's surface which was darkening. "Yes, yes, that is certain. If Rhan is slain, the curse is lifted. But Apollo must first seed the Raven in the fertility rite."

"We have already established that Catrin will confer kingship to Marcellus in the fertility rite." Amren turned to Marcellus. "Once you become king of the Cantiaci, will you keep your pledge that you will demand that your father and Cunobelin release Marrock to me?"

Marcellus's mouth flung open. "I don't know how my father will react when I announce that I have become king. But I will do—"

Amren clipped Marcellus off. "Good, then we are all agreed. Let us move forward with the ceremony and explore whether Myrddin's counsel for stopping Rhan's curse rings true."

The king pondered his next move if Myrddin's proposal proved to be a trick. Surely, the sacrifice of the Roman enemy and the wild Druid to the Earth Goddess would lift the blemish of Rhan's curse from the lands.

36

CROWN OF HORNS

Later in the afternoon, Marcellus walked with Catrin and the entourage of the king's closest advisors and family members through the bustling fortress, where swordsmiths were casting liquid iron and hammering blades on anvils. The ludicrousness of proclaiming him as the new king to stop Rhan's dark prophecy sliced through Marcellus's thoughts like an executioner's axe. Though the Romans often sought omens from priests to help them make decisions, Cantiaci bent like marsh grass to the advice of their Druids, their authority more respected than their current cursed king.

He wanted to voice his concerns to Catrin about his fate in the upcoming ritual, but she seemed so naively blissful that her father had agreed for them to marry, even though celebrants around him would undoubtedly delight in eating his heart. A chill surged through his veins whenever he met the burning glare of Ferrex—a Lion ready to battle him for his feline. He wondered why he'd never noticed this warrior's affections for Catrin before, when he had been held hostage.

Marcellus and the others somberly followed King Amren through the fortress entry gates. A cool breeze whirled low-lying fog around their feet as they strode down the hillside.

"Where are we going?" Marcellus nervously asked Catrin.

"To a sacred oak grove," she said, reaching for his hand, "where the ceremony will be held."

Taking Catrin's hand, Marcellus noticed the naked sword hanging from Ferrex's leather baldric. The Lion's glower roared his contempt at Marcellus. Swallowing his fear, Marcellus clasped Catrin's hand tighter, reinforcing his claim over her. Her warmth radiated into him, but he couldn't shake the queasiness in his gut that he was being escorted to his sacrificial pyre.

At the bottom of the hillside, the entourage walked on a pathway alongside harvested wheat fields and into the woodlands. There, white-robed Druids and black-dressed priestesses danced and spread red-berried mistletoe at the base of a gnarled trunk.

Catrin gestured for Marcellus to halt and silently communed with him on what to expect at the ceremony.

The priestesses will strip you and layer your body with pelts. Myrddin will crown your head with the antlers of a stag. I will give you a cup to drink and choose you as the new king. We will then perform the fertility rite, symbolizing your marriage to the Earth Goddess.

Marcellus nodded, acknowledging he understood what Catrin had said.

How will the fertility rite be performed?

Catrin smiled demurely.

You will be dressed as the horn god of the forest. The drink I give you will induce an ecstatic state in which you will ritualistically mate with me. This symbolizes your marriage as a mortal king to Mother Goddess so she will fertilize the lands.

Marrock shook his head in confusion.

I thought it was agreed that I would make love to you in the matrimonial hut.

Catrin giggled, a rosy color blossoming on her face.

Dance around me and create the illusion you are rutting me like a stag. After that, we'll finish the rite at the matrimonial hut.

With the image of his making love to Catrin heightening his desire, Marcellus ignored the people around him and passionately kissed her. She slipped out of his embrace and wagged her finger. He lustily grinned.

Will we go directly to the matrimonial hut during the ceremony to finish the fertility rite?

Catrin shook her head.

We will each be escorted to a separate location for additional blessings before going to the hut.

The clamor of chanting and chiming bells broke their silent conversation. A shiver ran down Marcellus's spine as Druids and priestesses, each of them wearing animal headdresses, encircled and separated him from Catrin.

Myrddin, whose head was covered with a fox-headed pelt, poured dark liquid into a wide-rimmed goblet and offered it to Marcellus. Inhaling the sweet aroma, he was repulsed with the bitter taste of the ale but forced a couple of sips down. He gave the drinking vessel back to the wild Druid.

Raising the goblet, Myrddin announced, "King Amren will now bless the marriage between Marcellus and his daughter, Catrin. As such, she will be empowered to confer her father's kingship to the Roman Apollo."

The circle of Druids and priestesses surrounding Marcellus opened at one end to allow King Amren and Catrin into the inner circle, where she stood beside Marcellus. The king gestured for them to kneel before him. As instructed, they both fell to their knees.

Catrin stretched out the palm of her left hand. In the king's hand was the jewel-encrusted dagger with Rhan's curse inscribed on its blade. Amren carefully sliced a thin line below her thumb with the sharp edge. He gestured for Marcellus to stretch out his right hand.

Until that moment, Marcellus had ignored the pain from his swollen hand that had been cut earlier, at the time he had prevented Catrin from taking her own life with the dagger. He winced as the king clenched his wrist and cut a deep crimson line through his newly-scabbed palm. The stabbing pain almost brought Marcellus to tears, but he stoically bit his lower lip with determination not to show his agony.

The king's eyes appeared to dance with delight as he pressed the blade deeper and blood oozed over its metal surface.

Alarmed, Marcellus flinched with the prospect that the razor-sharp edge could slice his tissue to the bone. The king finally finished his torturous cut and handed the dagger to Ferrex, whose feral eyes bore into Marcellus. Averting the Lion's glare, Marcellus grimaced from the throbbing pain as the king placed his bleeding hand on top of Catrin's and bound them together with plaid blue-and-gold cloth.

The king raised his hand over the couple. "I recognize the marriage of my daughter, Catrin, and the foreign husband she has chosen. I bind their hands, blood on blood, bone on bone, his family bloodline mixed with mine."

For several awkward moments, Catrin gazed at her father as if expecting him to say something more. The king fixed his eyes on Marcellus as he said something incomprehensible in Celtic. Catrin's wistful smile turned downward into a disappointed frown. Marcellus tried to commune with her to find out what the king had said.

Thunderous beating drums broke their connection.

Myrddin untied the cloth from the couple's hands and gave Catrin a goblet filled with wine-colored liquid. She lifted the vessel to Marcellus's lips and proclaimed, "With this sacred cup, I confer kingship of the Cantiaci to you. Drink this to acknowledge your marriage as mortal king to the sacred goddess of these lands. The goddess will legitimize your rule and break the curse that looms over our kingdom."

Anticipating another bitter drink, Marcellus moaned with pleasure as the honey-flavored wine tantalized his palate and warmed his throat. He eagerly drank the liquid as Catrin held the vessel steady for him.

Priestesses ladled more of the alcoholic drink from a brass cauldron and filled flagons with the aromatic liquid. The celebrants held out their horned cups for the priestesses to fill, but King Amren drank from a skull cup.

The effects of the drink relaxed Marcellus and eased the throbbing pain in his hand. Another unanticipated effect was the swelling hardness in his loins. He asked Catrin for another goblet of the intoxicating drink, which he downed.

Scantily-dressed priestesses began dancing around him, their hips bumping against his. Slightly disoriented, he couldn't comprehend why animal-headed women were cutting his tunic away with knives and peeling the pieces off his chest like cabbage leaves. He dreaded that once they removed his braccae, everyone would discover the truthfulness of his *testis*. Would his manhood meet their expectations as their new king?

Marcellus's thoughts then mired on how he could tell his father he had been crowned as the king of the Cantiaci and had married one of the native Britons. And hence, there was no need for Rome to invade Britannia. Marcellus could only imagine his father shouting, *You idiot! Mark Antony declared himself as Bacchus and Cleopatra his Isis. I'll grant you the blessing of removing your head.*

The crackling and brilliance of the nearby towering fire jolted Marcellus back to the reality that he had been stripped of all clothing. Goose bumps erupted all over his skin in the chill of the setting sun. Yet fortune smiled on him as priestesses began layering his shoulders and hips with warm animal pelts, which they tied together.

Myrddin gestured for Marcellus to kneel. The wild Druid waved the serpentine staff over his head and blathered incomprehensible words. A bare-breasted priestess, placing a crown of antlers on Marcellus's head, inadvertently poked one of the tips into his eye. Cursing beneath his breath, he could barely discern through watery eyes the sword Myrddin had extended to him.

Not sure what to do, Marcellus scanned the people until he found Catrin standing next to the king. She silently connected with him.

Thrust the sword into the ground until it is embedded in the earth's womb.

Marcellus staggered to his feet and gripped the sword hilt with both hands. With all his might, he thrust the blade into the loamy dirt.

Jubilant cries broke out. Flames from a large fire shot to the heavens.

Although he had thought it madness that this gesture symbolized he was the new king, his head swam with a sudden exhilaration of having the right to take Catrin as he wished.

The drums beat harder and harder and harder.

The priestesses then removed Catrin's cloths to reveal her nakedness. They danced around Catrin, then dressed her in black-feathered breeches and a bodice that tied at the front, and crowned her with a raven-beaked headdress. She stretched her black-feathered arms like wings and ambled toward Marcellus. He thought he heard a woman's voice he did not recognize whisper into his ear:

Embrace the wildness of the horn god
Rub your antlers and leave your mark
Bring forth life from dark forces
Transform the curse into the Raven's destiny.

Catrin danced around Marcellus as if she was a raven in flight. The rhythmic drum beats and flickering flames mesmerized him. His arousal intensified as she moved her hips back and forth, arousing him to an ecstatic state.

He wanted to kiss her but was distracted by the raven's beak on her head.

The drums pounded louder and louder and louder.

Catrin's black-feathered wings brushed across his chest. Momentarily dazed, he felt as if he was floating into a star-lit sky that was swirling around him. The pandemonium of cheers, clapping hands, and drumbeats finally swept Marcellus into raw lust. He reached out to embrace the Raven, but she eluded him and waved for him to follow her into the woods. The throbbing in his groin intensified as he trailed the Raven through the woods, away from the celebration.

The drums beat faster and faster and faster.

Following the Raven, Marcellus wandered deeper and deeper into the woods away from the revelers shouting in drunken glee.

Amren soberly watched several people scramble into the forest, their pleasures heightened from the alcoholic brew prepared by Myrddin. Rhiannon and Mor had left the festivities, leaving him to suffer in his humiliation that he had willingly stepped down as king to a foreigner. Other uninvited guests had joined in the festivities, dancing around the towering fire, their faces obscured inside animal headdresses. With the chaos of the revelry, he had lost sight of Catrin and the Roman rogue whose lusty intentions had been on wild display as he mauled his daughter, emulating the sex act. Looking all around for the couple, he wondered if they had also wandered into the woods with the other sex-crazed celebrants.

A sudden panic sliced through him that they needed to consummate their wedding vows on the wheel-shape bed, as Myrddin mandated, or otherwise the invisible wall could not be breached. Adding to his trepidation was the memory of the night when Marrock ambushed his people at Mor's wedding. Becoming concerned that this could happen again, he weaved through the staggering animal-headed drunkards in search of Ferrex. He finally found Ferrex sitting glumly on a tree stump, speaking with Myrddin.

He asked both of them, "Have you seen my daughter and the Roman?"

They both shrugged.

"Myrddin, what did you put in the drink?" Amren inquired. "Most of the celebrants are behaving like animals in heat."

"It was an elixir to heighten their senses and to accept blessings from the fertility goddess," Myrddin said with a chuckle. "I gave the Roman double the amount so he could directly converse with the goddess in an ecstatic state."

"Unfortunately, that Roman's cock might be conversing with Catrin as we speak," Amren said.

Myrddin wrinkled his forehead in confusion whereas Ferrex's eyes blazed.

"Let me get to the point, Myrddin," Amren continued. "Can the curse still be broken if they don't consummate the fertility rite on the bed sanctified by the priestesses?"

Myrddin seemed to wake up to the dilemma. "No. They must finish the fertility rite in the matrimonial hut."

"That is what I thought." Amren gestured to Ferrex and ordered, "Go find Catrin and that Roman husband of hers. Stop what they are doing! Bring them back here so my guards can escort them to the matrimonial hut."

"Yes, my king, right away," Ferrex said and rushed into the woods.

A few moments later, the serpent's orb on Myrddin's staff began glowing. Surmising that this might be a favorable sign from the gods, Amen asked Myrddin, "Has the goddess of these lands connected with the Roman?"

Myrddin squinted at the orb's pearl-like surface. "Yes, yes, I believe the goddess has accepted the new mortal king."

The wild Druid vigorously rubbed the orb with the palm of his hand, and his eyes suddenly widened with alarm. "No, wait! Why didn't I see this before? The curse can only be broken after the Raven flies through the invisible wall."

"Speak plainly, old man," Amren grunted, unnerved with the new revelation. "You mean the raven perched on the Great Hall's rafters?"

Myrddin waved his hand back and forth over the serpent's orb until it shone as brilliant as the rising sun. "Only the Raven designated in the curse can break through the wall."

"You told me earlier that I could burst through the invisible wall once Marcellus becomes king," Amren said, raising his voice in ire. "Now you're telling me something different."

"Rhan's powers have been accentuated by the hate she has for you," Myrddin explained. "Only the Raven has the druidic powers to burst through the wall."

"Then why did you make me believe that I could break through the invisible wall and slay Rhan?"

Myrddin's eye narrowed to the point of an arrow. "The gods just now revealed only the Raven in the curse can slay Rhan."

"You mean only Catrin can do this?" asked Amren, becoming irate with Myrddin's contradictory statements.

"The curse does not specify whether the Raven is human or wraith." Myrddin raked a dead fly out of his straggly beard and flicked it away. "Only the gods know."

"For the love of gods, answer me yes or no. Does the Roman need to be proclaimed as the new king to lift the curse?"

"Apparently not," Myrddin said, shrugging his shoulders.

"Look what you've done, stupid old man!" Amren lashed. "That Roman has stolen my kingship and is now mating with my daughter."

Myrddin winced. "Forgive me, my king. I could gather some warriors to look for them. Why don't you stay here just in case Ferrex returns with Catrin and the Roman?"

"By the gods, I pray Ferrex finds my daughter before the Roman defiles her," Amren thundered, his chest heaving with rage. "If anything goes wrong, you will lose that head on your shoulders."

Myrddin gave a sly smile.

37

RED VIPEROUS MIST

In the cool breeze of the woods, Catrin first removed her headdress and bodice and then embraced Marcellus. He hungrily nibbled at her lips, then suckled her peaked nipples and tasted her below as he knelt and pulled her black-feathered breeches down her legs. She could sense his burning desire as she, in return, untied the pelts around his waist and jumped into his arms, wrapping her legs around him. The stars whirled around her as he guided her hips into his hardness. Closing her eyes, she envisioned herself rising into the heavens in ecstatic delirium until she was abruptly taken out of the moment by Ferrex's bellowing voice.

"What are you two doing?"

The next instant, strong hands yanked her away from Marcellus, and she crumpled to the ground. She heard a bone-crunching smack and Marcellus dropped close to her, flat on his back. Slightly disoriented from the effects of the elixir, she was dismayed to find Ferrex strutting up to her like a lion claiming his mate from a competitor.

"Why did you hit him?" she screamed, scurrying over to Marcellus to make sure he had not been harmed.

"I hardly touched him," Ferrex growled.

"Hardly touched him!" Catrin roared, her chest heaving with anger. "Look at him. He's unconscious, lost to this world!"

"That Roman was drunk, out of his mind," Ferrex retorted. "I brought him down like the rutting beast he is. You were to do this in the matrimonial hut. Otherwise, the curse can't be broken."

Catrin bounded to her feet and pushed Ferrex back. "You have no right to interfere!"

"Your father ordered me to find you and to bring you back before you . . . you—"

"Before I did what?" Catrin burst in. "Marcellus is my husband—the new king!"

"He is not my king," Ferrex said angrily, clenching her wrist. "I don't like this one bit. You lost your honor and almost your life because of him. My head spins trying to understand why your father declared him as your husband and the new king. I won't ever accept that Roman scum as my king. You belong to me. The king promised . . ."

Ferrex clamped his mouth and abruptly looked the other way.

"What did my father promise you?" Catrin demanded.

"It doesn't matter!" Ferrex spat. "But I ask myself, why does a foreigner get to bed you? Am I not good enough? I've shown my utmost loyalty to you, but you—"

"Not another word!" Catrin yelled, tempted to garrote Ferrex then and there.

"Bite my tongue," Ferrex said, then suddenly embraced Catrin, forcing her to kiss him. His foul, alcoholic breath assaulted her nostrils.

She shoved him back and slapped his face. "I don't belong to anyone. I choose my husband, not my father, and most of all, not you!"

Ferrex at first appeared stunned, but then gripped Catrin's wrist, pulling her closer. "Is that all I am to you? I risked life and limb for you. My reputation has been tarnished because I supported you when nobody else dared."

The stabbing pain of Ferrex's fingernails digging into her skin almost brought Catrin to tears, but she would not relent. "Take your hand off me! Or I'll lash you like a beast!"

Ferrex released her and laughed with contempt. "With what weapon? Even in the darkness, I can see you are naked of sword and clothes."

Suddenly feeling chilled and her skin erupting into goose pimples, Catrin backed away and crossed her arms to conceal herself.

Ferrex picked up her breeches from the ground and tossed them at her. "Get dressed," he ordered and turned his back to her.

Catrin fumbled to get her feet through the leg openings of her feathered breeches and pull them up over her hips. She leaned over Marcellus's motionless body to check he was breathing and then patted the base of the oak tree to find her feathered bodice. Finding the garment, she wrapped it over her shoulders and tied the front leather panels together over her breasts.

Anger again flamed inside her with the thought that Ferrex had rudely interrupted her amorous moment with Marcellus. She shoved the hard-muscled warrior in the back, hard.

"I'm dressed!"

He abruptly turned and raised a fist.

"Go ahead, strike me," she challenged.

Ferrex hesitated and shook his head. "What am I doing?" he muttered, lowering his hand. He took a step back and his voice cracked. "I don't want a fight. It's just . . . when I saw you with him . . ."

The remaining words clutched in Ferrex's throat almost like a sob. Though Catrin still seethed, she remained quiet to regain her composure and to allow him to do likewise. She could tell he was shamed by what he had done; he was looking down, his shoulders sunken.

"You idiot, what have you done?" he chastised himself beneath his breath. After a few more moments of awkward silence, he squared his shoulders. "The king has ordered me to take you back. Myrddin says you must finish the fertility rite in the matrimonial hut, or the curse can't be broken."

"What about Marcellus?" Catrin asked, kneeling to check if he had yet stirred.

"What about him?" Ferrex grumbled.

"We can't just leave him here."

Without a word, Ferrex lifted Marcellus and flung him over his shoulder.

"Let's go back," he grunted.

Adjusting her eyes to the darkness, Catrin cautiously stepped on the pathway leading back to the glade where she assumed the celebration was still underway. She could hear Ferrex's heavy footsteps behind her as she trekked a short distance but halted when she spotted torches flickering through the trees.

"Who is that?" she whispered.

"I'm not sure," Ferrex said, gesturing her to hide behind a tree.

The torches coming through the shadowy trees illuminated the faces of four warriors whom she did not recognize. Myrddin was behind them, shuffling with the aid of the serpent's staff in hand.

"Catrin, are you there? I have urgent news," the Druid cried out.

Catrin glanced at Ferrex, not sure if they should make their presence known. He touched her hand arm reassuringly. "It should be all right. Follow me."

Ferrex strode through the trees, with Marcellus bouncing off his back at each step, while Catrin trailed him. They met Myrddin and the warriors, their features obscured with blue woad painted on their faces. The wild Druid regarded Catrin, then lumbered around Ferrex and lifted Marcellus's head up to inspect.

"The elixir must have been too strong," Myrddin said with a dark chuckle. "You both ran from the ceremony like crazed deer in heat. I told Amren I would find the horned Roman and take him to the matrimonial bed."

Ferrex bristled. "The king ordered me to take the Roman directly to him."

Myrddin's lips contorted into a serpentine smile. "Change of plans. The Roman goes immediately to the sanctified hut, but the king wants to speak with Catrin." He gestured to the four warriors. "Take the Roman to the matrimonial hut. It is a short distance north of the Ancient Oak."

Not immediately recognizing the warriors, Ferrex moved closer to one of them. "Do I know you?"

The warrior glared. "I'm Arthfael, the son of Caderyn. And who are you?"

"Ferrex, the son of Bladud. Where do you come from?"

"I'm from a coastal village near the white cliffs. My friends and I were summoned to serve in King Amren's army."

Myrddin reinforced what Arthfael had said. "I've known these warriors for years and can vouch for them as loyal subjects to King Amren."

Catrin, suddenly sensing a foreboding chill that Marcellus might be harmed, touched Myrddin's shoulder with a shaky hand to gain his attention. "I'm concerned about Marcellus. He hit his head and has not awoken. I want to stay with him."

"He'll be fine," Myrddin reassured. "He'll only be in the ecstatic delirium a bit longer. I can assure you he will awake with oak hard enough to plant his seed after you join him at the hut."

"But he might be seriously hurt," Catrin argued. "Why can't he go with me?"

Myrddin twisted his mouth into a half-smile. "Trust me, my love, the grin on his face tells me he's in the midst of an ethereal dream. He is most likely with the Earth Goddess and must remain there until she has blessed him with her body."

"No, I want Ferrex to carry him back to my father," Catrin insisted.

Ferrex clasped Catrin's arm. "Do what Myrddin says. Marcellus can rest in the hut while we speak with your father."

Though Catrin still felt unsettled, she nodded her agreement. Ferrex transferred Marcellus's limp body over Arthfael's broad shoulder. He nudged her in the opposite direction from where the warriors were disappearing with Marcellus through the trees. She walked slowly beside Myrddin as Ferrex trailed behind them, holding a flaming torch to light the way. As thickening fog hovered over the landscape, the light from the torch became diffuse, making it difficult to see ahead.

The serpent's orb on Myrddin's staff suddenly lit up like a wintry supermoon. The wild Druid's face illuminated from the brilliant glow, and his black pupils slit like a snake's. He shook his staff and the words, "the curse," hissed from his mouth.

"What do you see?" Catrin anxiously asked, studying the swirling, pearl-white surface of the orb.

"The wall has crumbled," Myrddin proclaimed. "The Raven must fly through now!" He retrieved the gem-studded dagger from inside his cuff and handed it to Catrin. "You must do what the serpent's orb commands. Only you can slay Agrona. But you must hurry before the wall reforms."

"If I do this, will I break the curse?" Catrin excitedly asked.

Myrddin did not directly answer her question, but instead rasped, "Go! The Raven must fly tonight!" His face turned as white as curdled milk.

"Are you all right?" Catrin asked apprehensively, wrapping her arm around his shoulders to support him.

Myrddin uttered between breaths, his body starting to tremble violently. "Only you . . . can stop . . . Rhan's curse." He rasped, "Go," with his last breath and collapsed to the ground. The serpent's orb on the staff hit a nearby rock, shattering it into pieces of glowing shards.

With dagger still in hand, Catrin dropped to her knees beside the motionless body. She couldn't believe what she saw next.

The hooded cloak, covering Myrddin's head to toe, transformed into fog and disappeared. Flabbergasted, she gaped at the empty ground, unable to comprehend what she had just witnessed. She patted the ground to confirm he was gone.

Then suddenly, a shadow cast over her and began lifting her, scaring the wits out of her. She screamed and fought against the restraint of what she believed a wraith, as the image of Myrddin disappearing into a fog replayed in her mind.

"Stop it," Ferrex said sharply, embracing Catrin tighter. "It's me, Ferrex. I saw it, too."

Catrin leaned into his chest and shivered. "This is a bad omen. We need to get back to the fortress now!"

Ferrex hesitated. "The king ordered me to take you to him."

"You heard what Myrddin said. Only I can break through the wall now and slay Rhan," Catrin said fervently.

"What about your father?"

"I'll have one of the guards at the fortress summon him," Catrin said, pulling out of his embrace.

"I'm not sure about this," Ferrex said, grabbing her arm again.

Not wanting to argue with him any further, Catrin yanked away and strode down the pathway to the fortress. Ferrex caught up with her, and they both trekked through the woods.

After a while, they exited the woods and scrambled up the hillside to the fortress. On top, they waved at the tower sentry to let them in. The entry gate creaked open, allowing them both to enter. As Ferrex relayed the message to the sentry guard about fetching King Amren, Catrin studied the wooden-spiked fence ahead that obscured what was inside. A fortnight before, the area had been covered with pig pens, stables, and a thatched round house. After the wooden fence had been erected around the area, she was not sure if Agrona had been shackled in one of the stables or chained to a pole in the round house. The crisp air cut through her like shards of ice—or perhaps, it was the dark essence of Rhan encircling her.

Ferrex touched Catrin's arm. "Wait here for your father. I'll slay Agrona—or whatever that demonic spirit is."

Catrin showed Ferrex the dagger the wild Druid had given her. "The demonic spirit inside Agrona is Rhan. Myrddin told me that only I can kill her with this."

"Give me the dagger. I'll do it," Ferrex demanded.

Catrin held the hilt tighter, refusing to give it to him.

"I don't like this one bit," Ferrex grumbled. "Last night, I heard Agrona wailing and saw purple mist spill over the barricade, making my bollocks shrivel."

Even though his concerns mirrored hers, Catrin remained firm. "Only I can face Rhan."

Ferrex gripped Catrin's arm and squeezed hard. "Then I'm going with you."

Catrin finally conceded. "Come with me and we'll see what happens."

As they rushed to the fenced enclosure, Ferrex drew his sword. The guard on duty unlatched the fence gate and pushed it open for them to enter.

"Where is Agrona?" Catrin asked.

"She's in the round house," the guard answered. "The invisible wall is just a few feet ahead of you."

"Is Agrona shackled?"

"Yes. She's shackled to a long chain that gives her full range to roam within the domain. She has a cauldron to cook her own meals over a hearth—a mistake, I fear."

Catrin sensed Rhan's essence encircling and urging her into the barricade. She rolled her shoulders to loosen the tightness in her neck. In the night's dark silence, she recalled the loneliness of being shackled in the disheveled hovel where Agrona had forced her to drink hallucinogenic elixirs. In a moment of weakness under the influence of the drug, Catrin had allowed Rhan's essence to enter her mind so they could travel to the Wall of Lives. There, they both watched the Past project on Marrock's life thread. He had decapitated two children and transformed them into wolves for his pack. Catrin had been his next intended victim, but she escaped when her ravens attacked him and pecked his face with their sword-like beaks.

A foreboding chill noosed around Catrin's throat with the realization that Rhan may have captured a piece of her soul at the Wall of Lives before she could expunge her essence. Taking a deep breath, Catrin shook off the uneasiness, stepped forward, and extended her dagger to discern if the invisible wall still blocked the way.

She felt nothing but air.

More reassured, Catrin waved for Ferrex to follow her, but as she dashed to the dome-shape structure, she heard a loud thud. Glancing back, she saw Ferrex flat on his back just inside the wooden-spiked barricade.

Everything Myrddin had predicted had occurred. Only she could burst through the invisible wall.

And now she was utterly alone.

As Catrin entered the makeshift cell, she noted the central hearth with a cauldron hanging over its flames. Loud popping sounds emanated from a coppery mixture that was boiling over the pot's black-metal rim. On the other side of the fire was Agrona, her back turned, the cowl of her blood-red cloak covering her head.

Hiding the dagger at her side, Catrin stepped forward. She perceived Rhan's aura as a viper of hot embers coiling around the hooded Druidess. The viperous, red mist burst in mid-air, reared its head, and struck at her. Catrin lurched back to avert its venomous fangs and frantically thrust the dagger into what looked like black eyes in a bloodstream.

The red vapor disappeared, but something invisible wrapped around Catrin's throat, cutting off all air. Fighting for breath, she dropped the dagger and clawed at the invisible noose to pull it away. Unable to break the choke hold, she felt panic pump through her veins. With only an empty void in her lungs, her eyeballs felt as if they were ready to burst.

For what seemed like a lifetime, she frantically clawed at the invisible garrote strangling her, but then a surreal calm washed over her like soothing, warm water. Black dots appeared before her eyes as ravens flying into the distance. Cackles echoed, then faded in her ears.

She floated into a sea of darkness.

38

FIRESTORM

Amren paced back and forth in front of the diminishing ceremonial fire. A chill from the thick fog ran a shiver down his spine. He feared Rhan had stalked him and trapped him there, the site where they had married and he later executed her. For more than twenty years, Amren believed he could break her curse. But now, desperate to save his kingdom and family, he had recklessly given away his sovereignty to a foreigner. He could barely breathe, imagining the death mask covering his face and suffocating him. Trembling, he felt utterly alone without Rhiannon at his side in the night's crisp air.

Most of the celebrants had returned home. A few could be heard snoring or moaning from nearby trees. Only Trystan and a couple of armed warriors remained hidden and on alert for any unexpected surprises in the stillness of the woods. The horror of Marrock's ambush at Mor's wedding revisited Amren's thoughts. His initial anger that the lusty Roman had wandered off with his daughter had now transformed to a sense of impending doom.

Ferrex or Myrddin hadn't yet returned with Catrin.

Amren contemplated whether his remaining guards should search for Catrin and the Roman, but it would be difficult to maneuver in the thick fog, even with torches.

The sudden crunching of approaching footsteps jolted Amren out of his grim muse. He turned to find a sentry, not more than sixteen years of age, rushing toward him.

With a torch in hand, the young man said between breaths, "My king . . . you must return now . . . to the fortress."

Amren shuddered. "What has happened?"

"Ferrex and Catrin are waiting there for you."

Aggravated that Ferrex had disobeyed him and taken Catrin to the fortress, Amren felt his jaw tighten as he continued questioning. "Is the Roman with them?"

The sentry hesitated. "No."

"Where is he?"

"Ferrex didn't say. He only said they were ready to breach the wall."

"What wall?"

"Rhan's invisible wall, I believe Ferrex said."

Amren's chest heaved in anger. "Why would they do something that foolish?"

"I don't know. I'm only the messenger."

The king felt his heart tremor with the prospect that Ferrex and Catrin were in a dangerous situation they couldn't handle. The whereabouts of Marcellus was a mystery, but he'd deal with him later. "Trystan, guards come here now!"

Trystan ran through the trees, adjusting his belted sheathed sword, while four other guards rushed from various directions to join them.

"Retrieve torches and follow me back to the fortress," Amren ordered. "There is trouble brewing there."

With flaming torches in hand, Amren and his men weaved through the dense trees until they reached the pathway leading to the hilltop fort. They could only see a few feet ahead, the wraith-like fog swirling around them. Only their rapid footsteps could be heard as they ascended the steep climb to the fortress.

Then to his horror, Amren saw what appeared to be fiery stars raining down on the fortress. An instant later, an orange-red cloud billowed over the wooden-spiked fencing.

"Fire!" he yelled.

He sprinted up the steep ascent of the embankment until he glimpsed a shadow rushing toward him like a charging boar. Instinctively, he jerked sideways to avoid a collision and grounded his heels into the mud to halt. He waved his torch before the shadowy figure to illuminate the face of Ferrex. Catrin was not with him.

"Where's my daughter?" he asked.

"She's broken through the wall!" Ferrex rasped, breathing hard.

"Why aren't you with her?" Amren snapped.

Ferrex explained he had found Catrin and Marcellus, but on their way back to the ceremony, Myrddin and four men wearing animal headdresses had intercepted them. The men carried the drunken Marcellus to the matrimonial hut while Myrddin continued with Ferrex and Catrin to join the king. He concluded, saying, "Myrddin gave Catrin the dagger with the etched curse. He told her that only she could burst through the wall. The orb on his staff then shattered, and he disappeared into a fog."

Amren felt as if his heart had been splintered into two pieces. Disappearing into fog was a trick that Rhan had previously used when she was his queen.

"Why didn't you protect her?" he demanded.

Ferrex's voice cracked with emotion. "You have to believe me, I tried to get through . . . at various spots around the wall, but was thrown back each time."

"You mean Catrin is with Rhan?" Amren raged.

"Yes," Ferrex gasped.

Amren's impulse was to strike Ferrex for failing to protect his daughter, but his attention quickly diverted when he heard the blasts of carnyx horns and saw flames lapping the fortress wall. Fighting for composure, he asked Ferrex, "Are we under attack?"

"Not from an army, but something else," Ferrex said, his eyes agape in terror. "Fire fell like shooting stars from the sky."

"You mean enemy archers released flaming arrows?"

Ferrex's voice trembled. "No. These were demonic forces."

Suspecting Marrock had used his druidic powers to ignite the firestorm, Amren queried, "Did you search for any enemy inside?"

"My first concern was to find you."

Panic spiked into Amren's pounding heart. He ordered Trystan, "Get everyone still at the celebration to help us put out the fire."

The king scrambled up the embankment with Ferrex and other guards next to him. By the time Amren entered the fortress through the southern gate, he could barely engage his cramped legs.

What appeared as a firestorm had engulfed the northern wall. Red embers were shooting everywhere.

Chaos!

Men and women scurried back and forth, carrying buckets of water. Squealing pigs rammed against pens. Children were wandering aimlessly, wailing for their mothers. Stablemen held reins of rearing and kicking horses.

Catching sight of Belinus running with a bucket of water, Amren rushed over to him and commanded, "Organize a fire line to pass water buckets."

Belinus nodded and rushed off just as a soot-smeared swordsmith rushed up to Amren, screaming, "There's not enough water from the well."

"Gather runners to draw water from the river," Amren ordered and then turned to Ferrex. "Did you see Catrin escape?"

"No, my king," Ferrex replied. "I tried to break through to rescue her, but the heat was too intense."

"Did you hear any wails?" asked Amren, his throat clutching with emotion from the stark reality that his daughter might have perished.

"No, nothing . . . just the flames," Ferrex muttered, dropping his eyes. "It happened so fast. It was too late."

Amren fought back tears, refusing to accept Catrin was dead. He gestured for Ferrex to follow him to the northern gate to confirm with his own eyes the extent of the fire and his daughter's fate.

All of the structures were engulfed in flames. Amren, inhaling the thick smoke, could feel his lungs burn. The heat seared his face. A waft of burning skin assaulted his nostrils. Tears came to his eyes as he imagined Catrin being burnt alive. The thought of her last terrified moments of her skin melting away in the blistering heat almost brought him to his knees. Anguish consumed him like a wildfire that Catrin had been cursed to a horrific death. He was racked with guilt for earlier considering condemning Catrin to death for her betrayal.

And now, the fire had carried out that sentence.

For the first time in his life, Amren acknowledged he could not escape his fate. He had brought the curse on himself, believing the only way to maintain power as a king was through brute force. Duty-bound to judge his family the same as any of his subjects, he had executed his former queen and forced his son to watch without compunction. He might not deserve redemption, but the rest of his family needed his love and protection. He had to tell Rhiannon and Mor that Catrin had perished in the fire before they learned it from someone else. The burden of sharing the ill tidings again brought him to tears. He quickly wiped his eyes so no one would see his profound grief. He had to stay strong for his family and his people.

Amren ordered Ferrex to find Rhiannon and Mor and bring them to him.

As Ferrex weaved through the amassing villagers, Amren joined his people in the fire line to pass buckets of water to quench the fire. Overhead, flashes of lightning webbed across the sky, signaling an imminent storm. A raindrop splashed on Amren's forehead, quickly followed by another and another, until light rain fell upon everyone, bringing momentary relief from the fiery heat.

Yet, the fire raged on, even in the misty rain.

Sweat and raindrops beaded on Amren's face as he continued passing each bucket of water to the next person in line. Screams of terrified children and animals filled his ears. All he could feel was the raw pain gripping his arms as he rhythmically handed the life-saving water from one person to another.

Raindrops the size of pebbles then hurled down from the heavens. Gale winds blew rain like shards of shattered glass into Amren's face. With the deluge of rainfall, he could barely open his eyes and frequently had to stop his task. The wind finally calmed into a cool breeze, and the sky god mercifully poured sheets of rain on the blazing fortress.

At first, the stubborn fire hissed like a fiery serpent rearing its head to strike under the deluge, but gray smoke slithered out of the flames and quieted the beast. Soot-black clouds soon belched over the villagers. Amren's coughs joined the cacophony of violent hacking from other villagers as they retreated from the billows of smoke.

39

AFTERMATH OF FIRESTORM

At daybreak, the smoke had dissipated and the devastation on the northern side of the fortress was clearly visible. Weary men, women, and children, many of them wailing and weeping, wandered the scorched areas of the fortress. Some of them were rummaging through the charred structures.

Amren finally found his wife and Ferrex, both covered with soot, sifting through the ashes.

Rhiannon appeared in shock, her eyes vacant and face as pale as a corpse. Turning to Amren, she wailed, "Oh Mother Goddess, have mercy on Catrin!"

Anguished that he had not told her beforehand of Catrin's demise, Amren pulled Rhiannon into his arms and gently rubbed the top of her head to comfort her. He struggled to maintain a stoic façade but was heartbroken and weighed down with guilt that he had doomed his daughters with his curse.

But he couldn't quite yet accept that Rhan would willingly immolate herself along with Catrin to fulfill the curse. He asked himself who could have started the fire and why. Myrddin had mysteriously disappeared into a fog after telling Catrin that only she could break through the invisible wall. Perhaps Myrddin had summoned the fire from the sky, conspiring with Marrock or the Romans to trick him into proffering his sovereignty to Marcellus. He now wondered if Marrock's warriors had taken Marcellus to the Roman headquarters.

He had to find out the truth.

Amren wrapped his arm around his wife and escorted her back to the residential quarters, where Mor and Belinus were waiting for them. The queen collapsed into her daughter's arms and openly cried. Overcome with emotion, Amren embraced Rhiannon, kissed her, and said softly. "I love you."

A sob caught in his throat when he couldn't recall the last time he had told her that.

Rhiannon kissed him. "I love you, too. I've tried so hard to put on a brave face for you and my people. But I just can't believe…Catrin is dead."

As she gazed at Amren, tears streamed from her eyes. In that raw moment, the honesty of his wife's heartfelt emotions struck him, and he openly wept, kissing her for comfort.

"We don't know for sure," he tried to console her.

"Nobody could have survived that," Rhiannon said, sniffling. "The heat was too intense. Rhan is dead . . . and Catrin with her."

"We need to stay strong and not give up," Amren reassured his wife, while in the back of his mind he had accepted his inevitable fate that was foretold in Rhan's curse.

But he couldn't ask his family to give up hope.

Rhiannon choked back her sobs. "I will also show you that strength and fight by your side to avenge my daughters' deaths."

"No. I won't have you fight," Amren said adamantly.

Mor wrapped her arms around Amren. "Then I will fight for you."

Amren remained firm. "Mor, you carry the heir to my throne. I can't let either you or your mother risk your lives."

"You must do as your king commands and let me do the fighting. Mor, you must protect our child," Belinus interjected.

"Our child has no future until Marrock is defeated," Mor said fervently.

"Only Belinus will fight by my side," Amren said firmly. "You must leave for Gaul while I wage war. If I am defeated, at least both of you will live."

Mor gave Amren a stubborn raise of her brow. "I and my unborn child will fight as one. He will either be born in victory or die in the comfort of my womb."

Rhiannon burst in, "I will not abandon you, Amren. I made a vow that I would stay with you until my last breath."

Amren shook his head in exasperation. "I am outnumbered by two strong women. Before I take any action, I need to confront the Roman scoundrel who stole my kingship and lured Catrin into the woods. If I don't find him at the matrimonial hut, I know he is part of the conspiracy to dethrone me."

40

DEPTHS OF POSSIBILITIES

The first sensation Catrin felt regaining consciousness was the burning rawness in her throat and cool water embracing her body. Opening her eyes, she found herself floating in murky water. Above her were blurred, multi-colored threads weaving in and out of each other on the liquid surface. Disoriented, she gazed at the obscured images in the depths, wondering if she was in a nightmare.

A gurgled voice greeted, "Welcome. I've been waiting for you."

The cursed dagger suddenly appeared before Catrin's eyes, waving back and forth. Behind the blade was a shadowy face hidden in the cowl of a red cloak. A man's voice said more clearly, "Did you believe you could stop the curse by killing Rhan with this? Look around and tell me what you see."

Catrin observed what appeared to be a cavern under the surface of the water. It had several openings she assumed led to a network of tunnels. She inhaled water through her nostrils. She gasped as if taking her first breath at birth. The burning pain in her lungs dissipated as her breathing adjusted to the water world.

Bewildered that she was not drowning, Catrin asked the hooded essence, "Am I in a lake?"

"You are in another realm in your mind."

Catrin then recalled the horror of her last moments of Rhan choking her to death. And now it felt as if an evil essence was invading her mind.

"Are you Rhan?" she asked warily.

"I am you," the voice mimicked Catrin's voice.

Catrin panicked and rapidly fluttered her feet to propel herself to surface, but a force held her down. Unable to swim upward, she wondered if she was in the Otherworld of souls.

The man's voice seemed to have heard her thoughts. "You appear dead in the mortal world but yet still live. Your soul is frozen in the Past."

Catrin could feel her heart beating, but it was from somewhere else.

"What is this place?" she asked.

The shadow pulled back its cowl with a wing to reveal the shadowy head of the Raven. It said in a man's graveled voice, "You are beneath the Wall of Lives. This is known as the Depths of Possibilities. Everything that could have happened if you had made other choices live here."

"Why am I here?"

"I sent you here to escape Rhan's grasp and to figure out how to break the curse."

"Break the curse?"

"Haven't you wondered why you couldn't see how the life threads rewove on the Wall of Lives' tapestry in the Future after you had saved Marcellus's life and thus altered the curse?"

"Yes, but . . . but I never understand why."

"It's because you couldn't see below the tapestry into the murky Depths of Possibilities to view what happens after you made the choice. Were you aware that there were other choices you could have made in the Past that would have broken the curse?"

The revelation struck Catrin with awe. "Can I go back to the Past and now make those choices?"

"It's too late," the Raven said soberly. "But you can learn what choices to make in the Future by observing the Past and moving forward to the Present."

"Then show me those choices I could have made," Catrin demanded.

The Raven's shadowy figure pressed its wings on top of her head and chanted in an ancient, incomprehensible tongue. A light tunnel projected from the Raven's beak. Catrin entered a tunnel of brilliant silver light and walked to a mist-covered lake with reflections of people's lives rippling from the middle toward the shore.

"You'll be shown a ripple of the Future for each choice you didn't make." The Raven cocked its head and ruffled its feathers. "Ready?"

"Yes," Catrin said hesitantly.

"You never answered your father's question about what is the most important quality a person must possess to rule. Are you bound by duty or love?"

"That is not a fair question," said Catrin, apprehensive she would again be asked to choose loyalty between her father and Marcellus. "How can I do my duty if I feel with my heart?"

The Raven's chuckle disquieted Catrin. "Let us see if we can determine the answer to that question. The first choice you could have made to break the curse was to marry Adminius, but you chose not to fulfill your duty. Behold the Future if you had made that choice."

The Raven flew over the lake and transformed the water into ocean waves crashing against the white cliffs. On the emerald hillside, Catrin saw herself dressed in a gown on which gems sparkled like stars on the sky-blue sheer cloth. Standing beside her was Adminius, dressed like a Roman with a white tunic and purple-edged toga. In the distance, on the highest point of the cliff, a rectangular Roman villa and lighthouse had been erected.

Adminius held Catrin's hand as he led her up a white-chalk pathway to the palatial structure. At the entrance, he picked her up and carried her through its stone-wall corridor into a chamber where there was a bed covered with red-fox pelts.

Inside the dimly lit room, Catrin could feel her chest tighten as Adminius slowly untied her belt. His rough warrior hand stroked the base of her neck before he proceeded to disrobe her. He first loosened the lacing of her front bodice and spread the cloth flaps apart, then continued releasing her remaining garments, seemingly unaware of her pained expression.

He leered at her nakedness, and she could feel his eyes fondling her body.

Self-consciously, Catrin crossed her arms over her body, but he yanked them apart and slung her over his shoulder. She felt as helpless as when Marrock had lured her into the forest so he could transform her into one of his she-wolves.

Adminius threw Catrin down on the bed and pushed her face-down, his sinewy body covering hers. The fur pelts entangled her legs as he pressed his hips hard against hers like a rutting stag.

The vision disappeared.

Dumbstruck, Catrin gaped at the Raven in horror.

"Oh sweet child, I can see you are troubled," the Raven croaked. "This was the sacrifice you had to make to forge peace between the two kingdoms. If you had done your duty, Cunobelin would not have supported Marrock's claims to your father's throne. Instead, your father would have given Adminius sovereignty over the kingdom's coastline. It seems the Romans helped Adminius build the grand palace and lighthouse in exchange for . . . hmm, let's conjecture—his alliance with Rome to invade Britannia."

"So I could have broken the curse, but Adminius would have sold his soul to the Romans like a whore and spread our kingdom's shores to their invasion," Catrin said with contempt.

"A choice can be a two-edged sword," the Raven cackled. "You would have exchanged your father's curse for another outcome just as dire."

"What about my choice to marry Marcellus? Myrddin said if I conferred the kingship to him, it would break the curse. Why didn't this happen?"

The Raven gave a dark chuckle. "Oh yes, it seemed a perfect solution. You marry the Roman enemy you love and also stop the curse. The mistake you made is you didn't complete the fertility ritual as Myrddin instructed. You failed to consummate the marriage in the matrimonial hut. Instead, you went into the forest with Marcellus like an animal in heat to perform the fertility rite. Myrddin deceived you, then you confronted Rhan, and now you are here in the Past."

Catrin felt her stomach sink like an anchor into the depths of her regret. "What if I had consummated the marriage as Myrddin had advised?"

"Let us look at that possibility and see what the Future might have been."

The Raven flew over the white cliffs and transformed the crashing waves against the white cliffs into a glacial-blue lake. On its calm surface, Catrin saw a reflection of herself nursing a baby while Marcellus looked over her shoulders. His pallid face was gaunt and heavily bearded; his skin was sallow; and his bloodshot eyes sunken in his head. Dense woods, allowing little sunlight to filter through the thick canopy of leaves, surrounded them.

Marcellus tenderly took the swaddled baby from Catrin's arms and cradled its head against his chest.

The Raven sighed. "Nothing brings greater joy to a woman than to create a child with a man she loves."

Tears formed in Catrin's eyes. "Why do we both look so haggard even though he was declared king? You said if I had fulfilled the fertility rite as Myrddin instructed, the curse would have been lifted."

The Raven did not answer.

Catrin then recalled tales of newly crowned kings being sacrificed at the ancient Bel rituals once they fertilized the Mother Goddess. Their blood was sprinkled on the farmlands to assure good crops. Had this been her father's intent? She and Marcellus would have been forced to escape with their lives, neither family accepting their marriage.

Profound sadness washed over Catrin. "Are you telling me that no matter what I decide, I doom those I love or I doom myself? There must be another choice I can make so I can return to the Present and break the curse."

41

LUST FOR POWER

The Raven revealed to Catrin in a voice that eerily sounded like Myrddin, "What rulers want most is power and will do anything to get it. I must warn you that Marrock has discovered the key for unlocking dark forces. The only way you can now defeat Marrock and break the curse is to harness the dark magic of the Ancient Druids."

"How can I do that?" asked Catrin.

"You vowed your fealty as a warrior to your father, but never acted on it."

"Are you telling me if I fulfill my duty as warrior, I can defeat Marrock in battle and break the curse?

"Possibly." The Raven stretched its wings forward and drew in a whirling fog through the thick canopy of treetops. "Let us look into the Depths of Possibilities to see what your destiny is as a warrior."

Catrin saw herself at the bottom of the white cliffs, pointing the dagger with Rhan's inscribed curse toward clouds shaped like black wings.

The Raven intoned, "The dagger is a double-edged weapon that can both ignite the curse's dark forces and light your destiny. Gaze through the haze. Let raw strength surge into your arms. Feel the bursts of energy in your legs as you climb the sheer wall."

Catrin envisioned sheathing the dagger beneath her belt so she could reach overhead for a rope dangling from the top of the cliffs. She clamped the rope between her feet and pushed her legs up so she could reach for a higher grip, one hand at a time. Painstakingly, she continued climbing, repeating the muscle-grinding sequence of resetting her feet, pushing herself up with her legs while pulling upward with her arms. About halfway up the white cliff, she looked up and found Marrock standing on top of the cliff, waving his arms as if summoning the forces of nature.

Cracks of thunder rumbled the cliffside and rocks loosened beneath her feet. A bolt of lightning struck her legs, and its force flung her off the precipice. She plummeted to the crashing waves below, but just before smashing on the jagged rocks, she spread her arms like wings and shapeshifted into a black raven. The bird's dark silhouette cast a shadow on the chalk-white wall as it rose higher and higher until she soared over Marrock's head.

The raven landed near a palatial fortress, where she shifted back to her human form. She unsheathed the dagger from her belt and transformed the weapon into a sword. Its blade flashed brilliant white light as she circled and swung the sword in preparation for the death battle with Marrock.

He appeared through the mist in his shapeshifted wolf form.

Catrin's heart raced as she readied herself to confront him. He leapt at her with bared fangs. She thrust her sword into his underbelly, but he disappeared into the fog.

"Did I kill Marrock?" Catrin asked, puzzled.

"You must answer that yourself," the Raven replied.

This was not the type of answer her raven guide typically gave. She asked another question to help her resolve her current dilemma. "How can I move forward to the Present and stop the curse?"

"What did you just observe?"

The Raven's answer with another question frustrated Catrin. "I was a warrior in heated battle with Marrock, but it was not clear if I had defeated him."

"You must make your next choice based on the ripple of the Future I revealed to you," the Raven answered.

"If I choose to become a warrior, can I move forward to the Present and stop the curse?"

"Yes, Catrin, it is possible to return to the Present with that choice." The Raven paused and ruffled its feathers. "But you can only defeat Marrock with the cleverness of a raven."

"I don't understand."

"You couldn't tell from your vision whether you had defeated Marrock in your human form or not. What is certain is your powers were greatest after lightning struck you and you transformed into a raven."

"Are you telling me that I can only return to the Present in the shape of a raven?"

"Yes."

"But how?"

"You already have the gift to metamorphose into another form. It's like a caterpillar spinning a cocoon to become a moth," the Raven explained.

"I've never done that before," Catrin said. "My soul has always entered the minds of other living entities, but pieces of it are left whenever I return to my human body."

"Shapeshifting is different. You change your body into another shape like molten metal cast into a mold. Your soul never leaves the body as you solidify into another form."

Catrin shook her head, trying to grasp what the Raven had just told her. She also remembered Myrddin saying something similar about shapeshifting when she met him for the first time near the river. "I still don't understand why I can't return to the Present in my human form."

The Raven ruffled its feathers. "Why do you keep questioning me? You must return as a raven to the Present or be frozen in the Past in your human body."

Taken aback by the Raven's sharp response, Catrin hesitated. This was so unlike her animal guide. Yet, after further consideration, she didn't know how to resolve her current dilemma of getting back to the Present except to follow the Raven's advice. Taking a leap of faith, she finally agreed to return in the raven form.

"What must I do next?" she asked.

"Visualize yourself levitating from your human body. Latch onto the image of a raven in your mind. Sense the power of lightning striking you and heating your body. Then envision your human body melting and remolding into the shape of a raven as it cools."

Catrin did what the Raven instructed. As she visualized her soul latching onto a white raven, it felt as if her body was ablaze and her eyes ready to burst out of the sockets. The piercing pain of ivory-white feathers ratcheting into her skin made her cry out in pain. The burning pain eased as her body shrank and hardened into shape.

Everything went dark and she found herself entangled in what felt like clothing. Glimpsing some light filtering through some kind of opening, she clawed at the cloth and wiggled her tail feathers to push herself through the constrained fabric. It slowly dawned on her that she was in the human-size tunic that she had been wearing. If what the Raven had said was correct, she had successfully returned to the Present.

She poked her head through the opening of the tunic's sleeve as if she was a baby being born. With greater effort, she squirmed and twisted her feathered body until the fabric tore apart. Freeing herself from the sleeve, she landed sideways on the mossy ground. The awkwardness of her rounded breast contoured for flight made it difficult for her to turn herself upright on clawed feet. After a few painstaking attempts, she flipped herself up and looked around to get her bearings.

The dense trees looked familiar, like those near the wedding ritual site. The matrimonial hut where Marcellus was taken must be close by. She decided to check on him first then find her father. Unaccustomed to her new body, she clumsily flung herself into the air and flapped her wings, but only flew a few yards before she dropped to the ground. Before she could thrust up into the air again, she was clasped by two gnarly hands that abruptly lifted her up. To her shock, Myrddin's face appeared before her eyes. She wildly flapped her wings to escape, but the Druid clutched her feathered breast tighter with both hands and threw her into a large birdcage.

Catrin peered through the wooden bars to find Myrddin standing with a naked woman with her back turned. He handed a cloak to the mysterious woman, saying, "You can put this on to make yourself invisible."

"What do we do with Catrin, now that she is a raven?" the woman asked.

"She'll be trapped in her raven body unless you shapeshift back to your own body," Myrddin replied in a voice eerily similar to the Raven's.

The words, "shapeshifted back," blurted from Catrin's throat as an in-comprehensible shriek. She pressed her raven head against the wooden bars to get a better look at the woman. To her horror, the woman was a mirror image of Catrin's human form, holding the jewel-crusted dagger with Rhan's inscribed curse in one hand.

Rhan's distinct voice cackled with mirth as she smiled smugly at Catrin. "Foolish girl, Myrddin tricked you into believing he was the Raven. He showed me how to shapeshift into your human form as you transformed into the white raven, so I could fulfill my curse."

Catrin couldn't understand why it was necessary for Rhan to take her shape to fulfill the curse. Nevertheless, she recognized that she had been tricked by Myrddin to believe he was the Raven. She had to change back to her human form and get out of the cage. Replicating the steps she had utilized to transform into the raven, she visualized shapeshifting to her human form.

Nothing happened.

She again tried to shapeshift but to no avail. Frustrated, she recalled Myrddin's words from their first encounter.

There can't be duplicates of the same living entity at one time.

Catrin felt her heart hammer against her rib cage as she watched Rhan cut the palm of her hand with the blade and set the dagger on the ground near the bird cage.

"I leave this weapon to remind you that I am the Raven foretold in the curse, not you. As moon swallows day, light will extinguish glory on Amren. I will cast the first brimstone to ignite the firestorm of war."

Myrddin grabbed Rhan by the arm. "You shouldn't say this in front of Catrin."

"Why not? What do we have to fear?" Rhan mocked. "I will rise out of Apollo's flame with Marcellus's child in my belly. After I transfer Agrona's soul into our new creation, I will access the full powers of the Ancient Druids as foretold in the curse."

A sense of dread ruffled Catrin's feathers as she recalled the vision in Myrddin's orb. Marcellus must have been the father of the baby girl in

Agrona's arms.

Myrddin urgently tugged on Rhan's arm. "Quit taunting Catrin. We need to get to the matrimonial hut before Amren learns the guards he has stationed there have been massacred."

Taking Myrddin's arm, Rhan said, "Then let us go."

Catrin frantically smacked her body against the clasped door of the cage, but it didn't budge. In desperation, she tried to commune with Rhan to stop her.

Marrock will betray you if the curse is fulfilled!

The Druidess stopped and glanced back at Catrin.

I think not! Without food and water, you will die soulless in that cage.

The only words Catrin could rattle from her raven throat were "Kraa . . . kraa," as she watched both Rhan and Myrddin wrap cloaks around their shoulders and disappear into a fog.

The image of Rhan seducing Marcellus drove Catrin into panic. She had to find some way to warn him. She battered against the cage door again and again until she collapsed on her side in excruciating pain. For a while, she lay dazed, but finally found the strength to turn upright on clawed feet. She heard a raven shriek from above.

Looking up in the direction of the sound, Catrin watched the raven drop like an obsidian stone and land on a nearby tree stump. The raven bobbed its head and ruffled its feathers.

Catrin reciprocated with similar gestures, but to her consternation, she could not meld with the raven's thoughts.

The raven tilted its head upside-down and gawked at Catrin with beady, amber eyes.

Still nothing!

Catrin felt helpless, condemned to death in the confines of her raven body and the constraints of the cage. The raven must have sensed Catrin's distress. It hopped off the log, waddled to the cage, and emitted a spark from its beak.

Another spark crackled, then more sparks burned into her skin.

Finally a connection.

A force drew Catrin into the raven's mind. An instant later, a light flashed in her mind and she could see through the raven's eyes. She directed the creature to fly to the matrimonial hut, which had been erected in a forest glade near a wheat field, hoping Marcellus would heed her warning.

42

BLOOD AND SEDUCTION

Marcellus slept restlessly, dreaming Catrin was transforming into a white raven. She enfolded his body into her ebony-tipped, white wings and said in a sultry voice, "I have come to reclaim my soul."

He quavered. "If you take my soul, you must first peck out my heart."

Catrin cocked her raven-head. "I can do that." Restraining him with her wings, she thrust her beak into his chest.

Marcellus awoke with a start and jerked to a sitting position. His heart was beating so fast he thought it would burst. Disoriented, he massaged his throbbing temple and glanced around the dome-shape room. The cold mist creeping through the wattle walls made him shiver. He couldn't remember how he got there. His memory felt like seaweed drifting back and forth from reality to dreams. Unable to keep his droopy eyes open, he again nestled into the warmth of fur pelts and floated into a trance-like stupor.

The sound of footsteps and Catrin's voice saying, "I'm back," wrestled Marcellus out of his dream state. He looked in the direction of the voice and saw the fog-like figure of a woman standing at the flapped entryway. Groggy-headed, he tried to rub the blurriness out of his eyes, but when he opened them again, he was shocked to see the woman's naked figure floating toward him. Petrified, he jerked to a sitting position and gawked at the hazy face until it sharpened into Catrin's features.

"Did I scare you, my love?" she asked with a sultry voice.

Noticing what looked like blood on Catrin's breasts, Marcellus felt his mouth drop. She slowly rubbed the crimson liquid around her nipple between her finger and thumb as she ambled toward him.

"Don't be alarmed," she said.

Marcellus, ignoring the queasiness in his stomach, embraced her as she leaned over to give him a kiss. She pressed her mouth hard against his and thrust her wet tongue through his tight lips, awakening his loins with a jolt. As she slowly released the kiss, he could hardly breathe, noticing her red, plump nipples that he wanted to suckle.

Yet he hesitated. Her kiss had felt unfamiliar.

Catrin smiled with wicked delight. "Did I wake you from sweet dreams, love?"

"More like a nightmare," Marcellus said breathlessly. "But it feels like a dream now that you're here. It's odd, but I didn't hear you come in . . . and . . ." The words caught in his throat when he observed the blood dripping from her hands.

She spread her fingers apart and remarked, "I almost forgot about the cut on my hand in my eagerness to get here."

Marcellus recoiled in disgust when she dabbed a forefinger in her blood-soaked hand and tried to rub the red substance over his lower lip.

"What are you doing?" he blurted, dismayed.

Catrin's amused grin baffled him. "Blood sticks like sweet honey when it thickens," she said off-handedly. "Let me wash this off before I get in bed with you."

Good idea, he thought.

Catrin turned her back to Marcellus and sauntered to a bowl of water set on a long wooden top. He raked his trembling fingers through his hair and inspected his hand for any bloodstain.

"How did you injure your hand?" he asked.

"Don't you recall my father cutting the palms of our hands at the wedding ceremony?"

"No. I must have drunk too much," Marcellus said, rubbing his throbbing temple.

"The druidic potion you were given can play havoc with the memory. Do you remember us consummating our marriage vows just hours ago?"

Marcellus shook his head in disbelief that he had no memory of the special moment.

"We did?"

"You were quite vigorous," Catrin chuckled. "The good news is the curse is broken. I returned to the fortress and killed Rhan. I must have cut myself again with the dagger."

Trying to grasp what she had just told him, Marcellus stared at her in bewilderment. "What?"

Not answering, Catrin vigorously splashed water all over her face and breasts, then picked up a piece of linen from the table and pressed it against her face, staining the cloth to a crimson color.

Am I in a nightmare? Marcellus wondered, shaking his head.

Catrin must have heard his thoughts. "Don't fret, my love, I am flesh and blood."

Why can't I hear your thoughts? he asked, trying to connect with her mind.

She turned around, leaned her hands against the table edge, and provocatively arched her back as she asked, "How did you take my good news?"

Marcellus distractedly lowered his gaze from her breasts to inner thighs. "What news?"

"The news I killed Agrona. With the deed, I also destroyed Rhan's soul."

Marcellus jerked his head back. "Then everything Myrddin predicted has come true. But don't you think it a bit grim doing this after we had made love earlier?"

Catrin curled her lips into a wicked smile, disconcerting Marcellus. The unusual silence from outside the roundhouse now seemed foreboding as a crypt.

"Where are your father's guards?" he asked.

"They were only here long enough to see me enter the matrimonial hut," Catrin replied. "They returned to the village after we consummated our marriage. They're probably celebrating that Rhan is dead."

Growing more uneasy with the stillness, Marcellus asked with a shaky voice, "Why don't I hear drum beats from the festivities?"

"You only need to feel the beat of my heart . . ."—Catrin rubbed a perked nipple between her thumb and forefinger, then slowly moved her fingertips downward—"and feel my tightness pulsate with every thrust."

Marcellus gawked at Catrin in disbelief. This was so unlike her to speak bluntly about sex, unlike his Roman lover, who continually sought adventuresome foreplay. He wondered if Myrddin had instructed her on how to draw out his basic desires during their fertility ritual. He uneasily shifted to his side and directed the conversation back to Rhan's demise.

"What did your father say after you killed Rhan?"

Catrin grinned. "My father was there when I twisted the blade into Rhan's breast . . . or should I say Agrona's heart?"

Marcellus flinched. "Aren't you a least bit bothered by this?"

Catrin shrugged. "Why should I be? I got rid of a demon that had possessed an innocent, mute girl. By slaying Agrona, I lifted Rhan's curse. And now"—she licked her lips and her blue-green eyes reached out to his—"I am aching for you below. Why don't you take off your loincloth so I can have a closer look at you?"

Disquieted by Catrin's salacious stare, Marcellus pulled the pelt up over his waist. "What did Rhan say before you killed her?"

"She offered to lift the curse if I correctly chose one of three possibilities."

"And what were these?" Marcellus asked, tugging the pelt up to his chin.

Catrin gave a twisted smile as she unbraided her hair. "The first choice was to marry Adminius. Of course, I promptly rejected that out of hand. Rhan then gave me the option of becoming a fierce warrior so I could defeat Marrock. That possibility was most tempting, I have to admit. Nonetheless, I inquired about the third choice."

She shook her hair loose. The long strands cascaded over her shoulders like a golden waterfall at sunset. "Hmm. . . I love how my hair caresses my skin."

Breathing becoming ragged, Marcellus could hardly swallow. His hesitation about taking Catrin was melting away. He recalled making love to her in the cave just before she escorted him to the prisoner exchange. At the time, she was like a siren luring him to her dangerous waters with the promise that their ecstasy would alter his fate to die. In retrospect, perhaps he had idealized Catrin as a maiden who needed his gentle touch. But now, all he wanted to do was satisfy his lust.

And yet he hesitated. "You never told me about the third choice."

Catrin blew out the candle on the tabletop, making the room darker.

"Make a baby with you."

A baby!

He again wondered if he was dreaming. He answered his own question when she crawled under the pelt and snuggled her naked body against his. Hot blood rushed into his face as her hand began exploring his loin-clothed hardness. She deftly loosened the ends of the fabric and remarked, "This is quite an impediment."

Her fingers stroked the length of him, but a bang against the wall and raven's shriek distracted him from the heated moment.

"Did you hear that?" he asked.

"Hear what?" she said, slowly sliding her finger over his phallic tip. "Hmm . . . you are as hard as oak."

Marcellus moaned with delight. "Where did you learn to use such clever hands?"

"I've heard Romans worship the god Priapus with his oversized phallus and that they enjoy this," she purred. "You are indeed a god . . . the Apollo in Rhan's curse."

Another raven's shriek and Catrin's off-hand comment yanked Marcellus out of the heated moment again. He abruptly sat up and looked at her in bewilderment.

"Why are you acting this way?"

Catrin pulled him down flat on the bed. "Would it help if I stroked you harder?"

Marcellus sat back up. "No. I want to talk."

Catrin pulled the pelt off him. "Talk about what?"

Shivering with goose bumps, Marcellus said, "We've hardly spoken. And now you want me to take you like an animal in one of your barbaric rites. I don't see how our marriage . . . our consummation will stop a war. I only agreed to do this so you wouldn't be harmed."

"I thought it was because you desired me," Catrin said in a softer, sultry tone. "Not only do you get me, you also break the curse."

"What if I seed a child in you?" Marcellus said, not sure how he should tell his father about marrying a Celtic foreigner.

"Let us not speak of this anymore. Just make love to me."

Another thud against the wall and a raven's caw startled Marcellus.

"Did you hear that?"

"It is probably some silly bird," Catrin moaned, nibbling the base of his neck and melting away any resistance with the heat of her lips.

No longer able to resist this sensual goddess, Marcellus rolled on top of Catrin and pinned her arms over her head to make sure she knew he was the master of her heart. He conquered every curve of her body with his hands and mouth until she cried out in ecstasy. She then entwined his hips to maneuver him to his back and straddle him. As she rocked back and forth on his hardness, he felt as if he was Apollo rising higher and higher to the heavens—his reasoning plunging into raw lust.

After spilling his seed, Marcellus was shaken from his ecstasy with the grating shrieks of a raven and clicking metal from outside. Hearing men shout, "Get ready, grab your weapons," he yanked Catrin off him. He jumped to his feet and grabbed her wrist. He hurriedly swatted the pelted flap aside, but a blue-faced warrior greeted them, blocking their way.

43

MURKY POSSIBILITIES

Struggling to see through the raven's eyes, Catrin felt as helpless as if she were sinking into a bog. Even though the raven had not been able to get inside the matrimonial hut, she had sensed Marcellus's raw sexual desires through its walls. She told herself over and over that Rhan had beguiled him, yet she still felt the sting of betrayal that he had not heeded the raven's warnings. He should have sensed the woman in his arms was an imposter.

But now what she saw through raven eyes alarmed her more!

At the forest edge, Marrock lifted a burning torch in which warriors dipped their arrow tips. Each of the archers simultaneously notched a fiery arrow in the bow and let loose a shooting flame. The fiery arrows massed across the cloud-covered sky and landed on the matrimonial hut's thatched roof.

As the raven frantically waddled around the base of the dome structure, Catrin could hear the fire's crackle, but she couldn't clearly see the blaze on the roof. She directed the creature to fly overhead and get a better view.

The flames looked like red tongues lapping the roof. The fire devoured the straw-thatch and roared as it engulfed the dome structure. Charcoal-black smoke billowed to the height of the raven's flight. The acrid haze made it almost impossible for Catrin to see the area of the burning structure. Horrified that Marcellus was being burned alive, she told the raven to dive through the smoke in the hope that the bird could lead him to safety.

The choking haze made it almost impossible to see. Hot red embers singed the raven's feathers as it frantically flew through the firestorm. She sensed the creature's confusion as it inhaled the thick smoke and wheezed upon its exhale. So the raven wouldn't asphyxiate, she ordered it to fly out of the thick smoke for fresh air. The raven soared over the canopy of the treetops with an aerial view of the chaos below.

Catrin spotted her father and his warriors dashing through the trees toward the burning structure. Another volley of fiery arrows arced together in the sky, almost hitting the raven, and landed in the midst of the king's warriors. More than half the warriors dropped with arrows lodged in their chests, legs, or arms.

Glimpsing a couple of shadowy figures moving along the fringe of the forest, she directed the raven to fly lower for a closer look. The moon-cratered face of her half-brother came into her view. To her dismay, she recognized Marcellus hanging off Marrock's shoulder and Rhan, still in the form of Catrin, following him. Hobbled horses awaited them in the dense woods. Marrock flung the limp Marcellus over a gray plough horse.

Fearing Marrock was planning to kill Marcellus, Catrin felt as if her guts were being twisted out of her belly.

Only she could stop him now.

Catrin ordered the raven to attack. It swooped from the trees and clawed Marrock's scalp as it flew just over his head, drawing blood. He unsheathed the sword at his side and brandished it. She targeted his eyes to blind him on the next aerial assault. She sensed the raven's acceleration as it dove at his face.

Marrock abruptly tilted his head back and his blue-green eyes began to glow, switching to the color of amber gemstones. This was a sign he was drawing on his powers to incapacitate the raven, but Catrin wasn't sure how. She ordered the raven to pull up, but it was too late.

Its wings froze.

Light flashed in her mind, and she knew the raven had disconnected from her thoughts.

Catrin found herself as the white raven inside the cage again. She wasn't sure how much time had elapsed. Apprehensive that Marrock had killed the raven, she helplessly peered through the wooden rods of the cage.

Without food and water, she would die. To survive, she had to find a way to get out of her confines and shapeshift back to her human form.

She pecked at the latch to unlock the door. No luck. She rammed herself against the cage to force it open. After several more attempts, she collapsed in pain and in exhaustion. Even in her state of profound distress, she could not shed tears from her raven eyes. Almost giving up hope, she heard the raven's caws from an upper tree branch. She excitedly returned its call.

The raven, appearing unharmed, flew down next to the cage. Catrin nestled against the wooded bars so it could preen her white-feathered wings. Its beak emitted a burning spark, making her flinch. Another spark crackled, then another as the raven plucked her feathers until they finally connected.

Drawn into the Raven's mind, Catrin hurdled through a dark tunnel that led to the portal into the Otherworld. Just before she burst through the gateway, she somersaulted up, bounced off the multi-colored Wall of Lives, and floated up a bright-colored fluid tapestry with various hues of red, blue, and yellow flashing lights. She searched for Marcellus's life thread. Finding the crimp at the Present, she saw Marrock setting Marcellus's lifeless body next to a tree. Rhan, still in Catrin's human form, helped Marrock bind Marcellus's legs and arms. Although Marcellus appeared dead, Catrin assumed he was in a drug-induced stupor. She looked ahead to the Future of the life thread. To her horror, she saw Marrock stabbing Marcellus in the belly with a knife. A shudder ran down her spine. She contemplated re-weaving the life thread so Marcellus could escape Marrock in the Present.

But she hesitated.

Without the ability to control how the Future rewove the life threads of others, it could alter the curse in unexpected and possibly deadlier ways.

The Raven must have sensed her trepidation. "You have good reason to waver. You must first plunge below the tapestry's surface into the Depths of Possibilities and tell me what you observe."

Catrin dove below the liquid surface, but it was murky as to whether Marrock killed Marcellus or not. The foul substance she breathed in burned her lungs. She propelled herself upward, using raven wings as fish fins, through the tenebrous possibilities of what the Future would be if she rewove Marcellus's life thread. Finally reaching the surface, she bopped her head above the water and spewed the various possibilities out of her mouth. Every possibility resulted in the fulfillment of Rhan's curse. Marrock was destined to rule with a brutal hand.

"Reweaving Marcellus's thread will only have disastrous consequences," Catrin finally conceded. "Can I reweave *my own life thread* to change the Future?"

"You've always had the ability to change the Future by the choices you make," the Raven said.

"Then I must now make the right decision based on what I know has already happened in the Past." Catrin paused, trying to answer some gnawing questions. "There must be a reason that Myrddin tricked me into shapeshifting to a raven. The only reason I can surmise is Rhan took my human form to trick Marcellus into having sex with her on the matrimonial bed. She must believe that by doing so, she will acquire the powers of the Ancient Druids, am I not right?"

"Perhaps," the Raven croaked. "You must have gleaned this insight from the murky possibilities."

"What I don't understand is why Rhan wants to have a child with Marcellus."

"Haven't you ever wondered what happened to Agrona's soul when Rhan possessed her?" the Raven asked.

"I assumed Rhan displaced Agrona's soul."

"Remember when I first revealed the life threads for Rhan and Agrona twisted into one strand on the fluid tapestry?"

"Yes. That is how I learned Rhan had possessed Agrona."

"The twisted strand signified that Agrona's body harbors two souls," the Raven revealed. "Tell me, how can a soul reincarnate into another body?"

Catrin paused to consider the answer. "By exchanging bodies at the time another living being is born."

"Then you have your answer to the riddle as to why Rhan wants a child."

"You mean Agrona's soul will reincarnate into the child seeded by Marcellus?"

"Indeed, it seems so," the Raven croaked, ruffling its feathers.

A revelation inexplicitly planted in Catrin's mind, and she asked, "Must the child be born before Rhan can access the powers of the Ancient Druids?"

The Raven didn't immediately answer and gawked at her. It finally asked, "Is that what you saw in the Depths of Possibilities?"

"I couldn't see clearly; it was too murky. But I sense this is true," Catrin said thoughtfully. "I must get out of this cage and revert to my human form so I can warn my father about what has happened. I tried to do this before but couldn't. Myrddin told me that there cannot be duplicate forms at one time."

"This is true," the Raven confirmed. "You can only shapeshift back at the instant Rhan becomes Agrona again."

"But how can we make Rhan revert back to Agrona's shape?"

"You have already gleaned the answer from the Depths of Possibilities, have you not?"

Catrin pondered for a moment and the resolution to the dilemma came to her mind's eye as a reflection on a crystalline lake. "The moment the child seeds in Rhan's womb, she will lose all mystical powers until the baby is born."

"That means she will have to shift back to her original form at the time the seed takes hold," the Raven added.

"How long will it take for the seed to plant?"

"Five to seven days," the Raven croaked.

The prospect that she would be trapped in the cage that long shook Catrin to the core. Even if she could shift to her human form then, it might be too late to save Marcellus and possibly stop the curse.

44

DRINK OF OBLIVION

Marcellus could not distinguish between reality and memories of escaping with Catrin from the blue-faced warrior. His lucidity slowly returned with the discomfort of blood rushing to his head. His body was bouncing against something muscular that he surmised was a horse. Though he couldn't move his arms or legs, he could feel the misty air on his skin.

Opening his eyes, he caught a glimmer of light on the emerald moss sweeping below him. Ahead of him, he heard the droning voices of a woman and a man speaking Celtic. He managed to capture the names of Marrock and Catrin from their discourse. Not yet having full faculty of his senses, Marcellus struggled to piece together his last memory of Marrock's grotesque face before he fell into a paralytic dream state. His ears perked up as the couple began speaking in Latin.

The woman's deep voice said, "Myrddin is now with Senator Antonius to negotiate the terms of his son's release."

"I'd just as soon kill the Roman," the man said in a harsh, bitter tone. "He's caused me nothing but grief with the senator and Cunobelin. I still don't understand why you had sex with him."

"You heard what Myrddin said. I have to rise out of his flames as the Raven to harvest the powers of the Ancient Druids. I can't reap these full powers until I've ousted Agrona's soul into the child I conceive and give birth to," the woman replied.

"You could have fucked any man to get that child, including me," the man snarled.

"Don't take this personally. Myrddin said I had to conceive a child with the Roman—the Apollo in the curse," the woman replied in a more conciliatory tone.

Marcellus's head swam with confusion as he struggled to recognize the voices of the man and the woman. The man's voice eerily sounded like Marrock's, but he couldn't identify the woman's voice. Nothing they had said made sense to him.

Am I still in a nightmare?

His head smacked hard against the horse's flank, affirming his nightmare was indeed a reality. If only he could get off the horse, he could identify the riders ahead of him and escape. He grunted, struggling to move his dangling arms and legs, but they felt numb.

"We're almost at camp," the man remarked.

The jostling of the Marcellus's horse halted.

"Help me get him off the horse," the woman demanded, "so I can give him the final elixir to erase his memory of Catrin before we meet his father."

What in Hades?

A sense of dread crawled over Marcellus as he heard crunching footsteps approach him. Hot breath blew into his ears as the man growled, "I should cut out your intestines and eat them."

Marrock's threat jolted Marcellus to the danger he faced. His heart pounded so hard, he thought it would shatter his rib cage. Surging blood prickled his appendages. He twitched his arm then jerked his leg.

But could he galvanize his muscles to fling himself off the horse and escape?

In one massive effort, Marcellus jerked his torso downward and his body immediately dropped to the ground. He smacked the top of his head, knocking the breath out of him. Momentary dazed, he lay there gazing at the multi-colored dots dancing before his eyes until they were replaced by a man's blurred face.

A hammer fist to the jaw rousted Marcellus into the reality that he was now on his back staring at the pallid, pitted face of Marrock.

"The Roman is awake," Marrock bellowed. "You didn't give him enough of the drink."

"If I'd given him more, it would've killed him," the woman replied, approaching them.

To Marcellus's shock, he recognized the woman.

Catrin!

Dumbfounded, he felt as if his stomach had plunged into a pit of snakes. Raw emotions of love, hate, and betrayal coiled inside him, ready to strike. He quickly rolled to his side to escape, but felt a knee drive his shoulders flat to the ground. He wildly kicked his legs to get the hefty weight off him, but the bony kneecap kept him pinned down as his arms were cranked behind his back, first the left, then the right.

Marcellus yelled, "Get off me," but it was for naught, as the woman hustled to bind his ankles together with leather straps. Unable to grasp why Catrin was aiding Marrock, he rasped in anguish, "Why are you doing this?"

She didn't answer.

Raw agony sheared through Marcellus. His world had flipped on its head, his reality now a cruel jest. Should he laugh or cry at the comedy playing before his eyes? The woman he cherished, the woman he most trusted, was mysteriously colluding with her half-brother? How could this be? Did Catrin's vile half-brother have her under his spell with the use of sorcery?

Have I gone insane?

After Marcellus's wrists were bound, Marrock's massive hand turned him on his back. Marcellus felt his jaw drop as Catrin leaned over to whisper, "You are, indeed, as virile as Apollo. I will forever cherish that climactic moment you were inside of me. Unfortunately, that moment will disappear from your memory."

She rose and smiled thinly at Marrock. "I'll now prepare the drink of oblivion."

Panicked that they wanted to poison him, Marcellus asked, "What are you planning to do?"

Marrock chewed on a hangnail and spat it at his face.

"Return you to your father," Marrock grunted. "We've come to an agreement to combine our armies to destroy Amren and his family."

Marcellus asked the question that most plagued him. "Why is Catrin with you?"

Marrock curled his lips into a half-smile. "Is that who you think she is?"

The comment dumbfounded Marcellus. Profound sadness washed over him that Catrin might be under Marrock's black magic.

And there was nothing he could do.

It seemed like a lifetime before Catrin returned with a water skin bag. Marrock forced Marcellus's lips open as she poured the bitter-tasting liquid into his mouth. Marcellus frantically tried to spit out the drink, but the copious amount of liquid flooded his throat. He had to swallow to prevent choking to death.

The hallucinogenic effects of the elixir quickly overwhelmed his senses. He envisioned a tapeworm eating bits of his memory away.

Neighing horses awoke Marcellus, and he emerged from what seemed like murky water. His temples pounded as if he had been at a Bacchanal revelry, but he couldn't remember celebrating. Memories skipped rapidly back and forth while others fell like autumn leaves from his mind. At one moment, he was a boy in Gaul riding a horse into a river where they were both swept away. In another piece of his memory, he was having sex with his Roman lover for the first time as a nervous sixteen-year-old boy, but her ebony hair was blonde and chestnut-brown eyes were the blue-green color of the sea along a white shoreline.

Forcing his eyes open, he found himself lying under a canopy of green foliage with wisps of fog streaming through the treetops. It felt as if he were still in a dream.

Where am I?

Marcellus struggled to get up, but something was binding his legs and wrists. He yanked wildly against his restraints but couldn't loosen them. His heart almost stopped as the blue-painted face of a hideously scarred man with a knife clasped in his hand came into his vision. He asked in a gulp, "What are you planning to do?"

A woman's voice instead answered, "Greetings, Marcellus Antonius. We wish you no harm."

Suddenly panicked that he couldn't remember being called that name, he cranked his head backwards to see who was talking. The woman was a striking, athletic young woman about fifteen years old with turquoise eyes and gold-blonde hair freely flowing over her shoulders.

"Who are you?" Marcellus asked.

"I'm Agrona," the young woman said in a sultry voice. "The warrior beside me is Marrock. Do you remember us?"

Marcellus grasped at bits of memories which he seemed to have misplaced. "I was riding in the woods with my father and after that—" He clipped off his words, suddenly alarmed that he couldn't recall the last few days. He vaguely remembered traveling with his father in Gaul on the way to Britannia, but everything after that was hazy.

Agrona's lips twitched a smile. "You were held as a prisoner in King Amren's fortress. Do you recall us rescuing you?"

Marcellus shuddered. "King Amren? Rescue?"

Agrona knelt beside him and gently stroked his cheek, her touch oddly familiar. "You don't remember me, do you, my love?" She then said with a lewd undertone to her voice, "You have such a handsome face—almost god-like when your hardness was inside me."

Marcellus felt repulsed, but at the same time oddly attracted to the young woman.

Agrona, seeming to know what he was thinking, chuckled. "You should thank the gods for your good fortune. We were able to save you from a most horrific death. King Amren was ready to sacrifice you to the war goddesses."

Marcellus frantically tried to grasp what Agrona had just told him, but with no memory to anchor on, he felt adrift. All he could mutter was, "I can't believe this is happening!"

Agrona gave him a wicked smile. "You soon will. But now, you are our guest. Soon, your father will be joining us in our campaign to take revenge against King Amren for what he has done to you."

Baffled he could not recall this horrific event, Marcellus felt as if cobwebs were obscuring his mind. Even now, he wasn't sure if he could delineate between reality and fantasy. "Why am I bound, if I'm your guest?"

She didn't answer, but suddenly clutched her stomach and moaned. "The time is near for the seed to implant."

To Marcellus's utter shock, she unabashedly removed all of her clothes and lay down close to him, spreading her legs. She wailed in agony, as if in childbirth, flailing her legs and arms. Marrock leaned over and gently wiped the profuse sweat off her face with a wet cloth as she labored.

Then Marcellus's reality turned into a horrific nightmare.

Agrona's body disintegrated into colored particles and then coalesced to form another heavily tattooed woman about thirty years old, the same age as Marcellus's Roman lover. She had raven-black hair and amber-colored eyes. As she began shaking violently, Marrock covered her with a plaid, wool cloak, and he watched over her intently until she calmed, her eyes glazed on Marcellus.

After several moments, Agrona became coherent and groaned, "Help me up."

Marrock helped the woman to her feet and wrapped the cloak more securely around her shoulders. She leaned her head against his shoulder and said coldly, "Make sure the wound does not kill him."

Panic sheared through Marcellus as the massive, blue-faced Marrock released the tattooed woman and ominously waved a knife. The demon's mouth melted into a sadistic smile as he knelt and slowly sliced Marcellus's abdomen, just above the groin, with the blade.

Marcellus cried out in agony, his reality becoming a nightmare of burning pain racking his senses, as Agrona cauterized the bleeding wound with the red-hot metal of a sword blade.

45

DAMNATIO MEMORIAE

Lucius Antonius was shaken to see Marcellus as helpless as a newborn baby as the soldiers carried him on a stretcher into his headquarters. His son's face was as pallid as the chalk-white cliffs where Lucius had rapidly deployed his troops in preparation for the two-front assault on King Amren's line of defense. Marrock and Agrona had assured him that his son had not suffered a life-threatening gash to his belly, but he was not so sure. Marcellus was delirious, at times opening his fear-struck eyes and asking, "Where am I?"

A good question, Lucius asked himself. *Where have I been and how did I get to this point?*

The last time Lucius saw his son, he was the epitome of a vital, masculine Roman. Lucius felt a heavy weight in his heart that Marcellus, who had shown so much promise, had fallen to the wiles of a foreign sorceress. He had hoped his son would not claim the ill fate of his forefathers. The memory of Mark Antony—the ultimate soldier's commander, charismatic and strategic—had been erased from Rome's history by the act of *damnatio memoriae.* Iullus Antonius—a poet and shrewd politician—had been branded a traitor for his treasonous adultery with Julia, the married daughter of Emperor Augustus.

No father could have hoped so much for his son as Lucius had for Marcellus. Nevertheless, his son chose the same self-destructive path that had brought his great forefathers down.

A woman!

Lucius recalled that fateful day, as if it were yesterday, when he had to say good-bye to his father, Iullus. How could he have anticipated his father's precipitous fall from grace?

Iullus had risen to the upper political echelon and was beloved by Rome and Augustus, who treated him more like a son. Lucius's own mother, Marcella, was the daughter of Augustus's sister, Octavia. Marcella bore three children with Iullus, Lucius being the eldest. Iullus had always been a dutiful husband and father.

Or so Lucius believed.

As an eighteen-year-old man at the time, Lucius refused to believe the rumors that his father was having an affair with Julia. Tears now formed in his eyes as he recalled escorting his mother to view the corpse. Iullus had been a striking man, but the bluish tint of his corpse would forever haunt Lucius. The wiles of a powerful woman had brought his father down and shattered his own dreams of sharing political fortunes with the imperial power. Banished as a pariah to Gaul, Lucius had suffered for the sins of his forefathers.

And now, to Lucius's regret, Marcellus had also lost reasoning to passion for a foreign whore. He couldn't take the blame for his rebellious, headstrong son foolishly entering King Amren's den of wolves to be devoured. It was, after all, the king's daughter who had bewitched Marcellus and lured him to her dangerous shores where he willingly risked his life to save hers. Lucius would never forgive Marcellus for deceiving and betraying him.

And now it had come to this.

He had bartered a deal with a demon to rescue Marcellus. The monstrous-faced Marrock now awaited him outside so that together they could devise the final scheme for destroying King Amren.

Marcellus's anguished cry, "Father, where am I?" pulled Lucius out of his contemplation. He knelt beside his son, lying restlessly on the cot, and stroked his forehead as he had once done when Marcellus was a little boy and looked up to him as a role model.

"You are safe with me, son," Lucius said, his hand trembling with mixed emotions of guilt and hate.

Marcellus appeared more lucid, eyes brightening. "Why can't I remember the last few days?"

Lucius kissed his son's brow. "You've been wounded. Your loss of memory is temporary."

The answer did not seem to assuage Marcellus. He asked again, "When will my memory return?"

Lucius smiled. "What matters most is what I remember. Rome will honor your heroism in Britannia."

Marcellus appeared confused. "Britannia? Is that where I am?"

"Yes, you are in a nightmare in a foreign land, but you'll soon return home."

"Remind me again, who am I?" asked Marcellus, his voice full of distress.

His son's loss of memory was more than Lucius had bargained for. Sadness tugged at his heart that his son had to go through such misery. He told him proudly, "You are Marcellus Antonius. I am your father, Lucius Antonius. We are descendants of the greatest heroes in Rome. Your great-grandfather, Mark Antony, was a great general and consul of Rome. Your grandfather, my father, Iullus Antonius was a poet, politician, and almost like a son to Emperor Augustus. Always remember this. . ." He swallowed back a sob in his throat.

"Was I in battle?" Marcellus asked, widening his eyes as if he couldn't believe it.

"Yes, you killed several of the enemy," Lucius said to embolden his son.

"Why can't I remember this?"

"Rest, my son," Lucius said, clasping his son's hands. "Let me serve as your memory. In time, the pieces of your life will come together again."

Hearing someone entering the tent, Lucius turned to the doorway, where Decimus was standing. The tribune saluted and announced, "Marrock, Myrddin, and Cunobelin's son and advisors are assembled outside to discuss the final plans. Senator Marcus Licinius Crassus Frugi would like to speak with you now, in private."

"Let me have a few private moments with my son, then send Marcus in," Lucius requested. "I'll speak with Marrock and the others after that."

"Of course, Lucius, I understand. How does your son fare?" Decimus asked.

"He's disoriented with fever," Lucius said somberly. "Go fetch Marrock's healer so she can treat him."

Decimus saluted and left.

Lucius clasped Marcellus's hands. At last, his son appeared to be in a more restful sleep, although his soft moans could be heard with each breath.

The voice of Senator Frugi saying, "I am grieved that your son has returned with wounds," drew Lucius's attention. He turned to find Senator Frugi standing at the doorway.

Lucius rose and said ruefully, "It is at these times when you realize how important family is—especially sons."

"It took a lot of courage for Marcellus to meet King Amren under such dire circumstances. I'm sure Tiberius will understand our need for expedient political interference here. I wanted to assure you that you have my complete support. When we return to Rome, it will be my honor to finalize the marriage contract for Marcellus to marry my daughter, Licinia. It is more important than ever to seal our political alliance."

Lucius sighed. "Thank you, Marcus. I appreciate that."

Decimus entered the tent with a heavily tattooed woman and announced, "This is Agrona, the Druidess you summoned to treat Marcellus."

Lucius acknowledged Decimus with a slight nod. "Thank you, Tribune." He gestured for Senator Frugi to leave. "If you wouldn't mind, I'll join you outside with the others after I've had a chance to talk with the healer."

Senator Frugi left, leaving Decimus and Agrona behind. The Druidess knelt beside Marcellus and placed a palm on his forehead. Turning to Lucius, she said, "He is with fever. I'll further treat the wound for swelling and putrid pus. As you have requested, I'll give him some more of the potion that will help erase his recent memory of the torture he had to endure at the hands of King Amren."

"As I previously said, I don't want his memory completely erased," Lucius said emphatically. "I want him to remember his childhood in Gaul and his experiences as a young man in Rome."

"The elixir should not impact his long-term memory too much. Think of it this way"—a sordid smile beamed across Agrona's face—"you now have the chance to replace his recent memories with new ones you want him to remember."

"Will he forget that whore who bewitched him?" Lucius asked with a biting tone.

"I'll also give him a potion that breaks spells." Agrona leaned over to inspect Marcellus's neck. "If I remember correctly, he had an amulet of Apollo around his neck. That is what Amren's daughter used to bewitch him. Hopefully, it's still not in her possession."

"Should I be concerned?" Lucius asked.

"No. I can assure you she will soon be dead," Agrona said with mirth. "Go ahead and talk with Marrock as I treat your son."

Decimus interjected, "Is it a good idea to leave your son alone with her?"

Considering it further, Lucius decided it best that a guard be left with Marcellus at all times. Even though Marrock and Agrona had safely returned him, it was not so long ago that Marrock and Marcellus had been in a brutal fight, after which Cunobelin had announced his intentions to seal a political alliance with Amren through the marriage of Adminius and Catrin.

"Have a guard stay with him," Lucius commanded.

After Decimus returned with the guard, Lucius exited the headquarters to meet with Marrock and his supporters, including Cunobelin's rebellious son, Caratacus, and Myrddin. Other Roman patricians, including Senator Frugi, were already seated on foldable chairs under an open-ended tent that had been used by a local merchant to sell his wares. The cool ocean breeze signaled the sun would soon set although low-lying clouds obscured its radiance.

Marrock clasped Lucius's forearm in a friendly gesture. "Greetings, my friend."

Lucius winced from the tight grip and answered in Latin. "Salve."

After everyone was introduced, servants appeared with flasks containing liquid refreshment and platters of cheeses, dried meats, and wheat cakes.

"May I offer you some refreshments before we discuss the terms?" Lucius proffered.

"Not at this time," Marrock refused for himself and everyone in his group. "After we speak, I must quickly reposition my warriors and prepare for the ambush on King Amren. He is marching toward us as we speak."

Likewise, Lucius refused wine for himself, although other Roman nobles partook of the wine and food offered them. He started the final negotiations. "We have a cohort of legionaries on forced march to the Cantiaci capital. They should be there by dawn."

"Our spies tell us that very few able-bodied warriors have been left to defend the Cantiaci capital," Marrock informed everyone. "Just last week, at which time we rescued Marcellus, we burned half of the fortress down so we could easily breach their walls."

Lucius gave a tense smile. "I've arranged for ships to transport Cantiaci captives to sell into slavery. Let me be clear. I want the king and all of his family dead, but I want his warriors to sell as gladiators for a good price. The younger women with lighter features should also bring a good price from the brothels. Roman men particularly savor uncharted virgins."

"How is your son?" Marrock inquired.

Lucius grimaced. "He's not well, but your Druidess has assured me his wound is not life-threatening. I'm not pleased he was brought to me in that condition. That was not what I bartered for."

Marrock stared at Lucius. "He's lucky to be alive. Just as we arrived to rescue him, King Amren was ready to demonstrate his brutal power by cutting out your son's entrails to inspect for omens."

"This said from a man who butchered my men," Decimus interjected bitterly.

Marrock smiled thinly. "I understand we have an uneasy alliance due to unfortunate circumstances. But let us get past this and work together for our mutual benefit. This is what I have to offer to sweeten the deal. I have instructed my warriors to capture as many Cantiaci as possible for you to sell into slavery. Further, in the spring, I will allow Romans to build a fortress and lighthouse on the highest point of the white cliffs to assure the safety of their seafaring merchants. I am by nature a peaceable man and only want to share my good fortunes with you. Can I trust your tribune to do the same?"

Lucius noted Decimus's scowl directed at Marrock. He would have a stern word with him after the meeting. In the meanwhile, he said assuredly to Marrock, "Decimus is most loyal to me and understands the urgency of the political action to bring peace to your homeland."

"Then these are my final terms," Marrock said more brusquely. "Rome must recognize me as their client king and press this fact on Cunobelin. His son, Caratacus, supports me as well as some of his advisors, as you can see by their attendance here."

Lucius struggled to keep a stone face to hide his contempt. "Agreed, as long as you pay the yearly tribute we agreed to."

"Done." Marrock paused and his lips curled into a serpentine smile. "But I have only one small request."

"Which is?"

"I want Amren's queen and Mor brought to me for my pleasure."

Noting the absence of the king's youngest daughter among his demands, Lucius asked, "What about the king's youngest daughter?"

Marrock chuckled. "Agrona told me she died in the firestorm at the fortress."

Lucius smiled with the unexpected news and looked at Decimus. "Take note of that."

Decimus's eyes looked as if they were ready to throw daggers at Marrock.

Lucius resolved to deal with both the barbarian monster and Decimus in good time. For now, his prime focus was to destroy King Amren.

46

HUMAN FORM

For the last few agonizing days, Catrin had been trapped in the cage. They had been the most frustrating days of her life—constrained in her raven form and imprisoned in the wood-bar cell. She was beginning to doubt if she was right about Rhan losing her magical powers once Marcellus's seed implanted in her womb. Even if Catrin's assumption held true, how would she know the instant Rhan reverted back to Agrona's form? Would she automatically shapeshift back to her human form or would she have to initiate the process?

These questions and concerns about the safety for Marcellus and her family haunted her. She had lost connection with Marcellus's essence, making it harder for her to cling to hope that he was still alive.

And what of her family? Were they safe and searching for her?

Catrin had grown wearier by the day, even as ravens scrambled to bring her entrails, tissue, and blood vessels from carrion they had found. She could not stomach the dead creatures. Spiders, insects, or lizards, which occasionally crawled into the cage, did not taste much better. She finally settled on left-over human food left in garbage heaps and fresh-picked berries transported in the ravens' beaks. Unfortunately, her stomach often cramped, diarrhea creating another problem of keeping her cage clean.

One of the ravens had cleverly set broken egg shells in the cage to collect rain water or drops of condensed dew. Despite the bird's efforts to bring Catrin sustenance, the strain of being cooped in the cage was taking a toll on her. It now took too much strength for her to enter the Raven's mind.

Thus, they had come to an agreement that the Raven would alert her at the instant Rhan reverted to Agrona's shape.

But that could still take a few more days. And by then, it could be too late to save Marcellus and to warn her father that Myrddin had tricked them.

Catrin heard children's voices nearby. Perhaps she could gain their attention so they could unlatch the cage door. The ravens' attempts to pull the slide bar from the rivet to open the door had previously failed. With her remaining strength, she cawed, gurgled, and rattled to get the children's attention.

Finally, one curious, freckled-face boy about eight years of age began glancing around the trees. Catrin shrieked louder. The boy looked in the direction of the cage, which had been obscured by thorny bushes. He disappeared behind a tree and reappeared above the cage. He scrunched his face on the wooden bars to gawk in and shouted excitedly, "Come here! See what I found!"

The boy grabbed the sides of the large cage to lift, but the weight proved too heavy. He knelt and his sky-blue eyes peered through the ribs of the cage.

"Hello there," he said as if talking to a toddler. "Who left you here?"

Catrin ruffled her feathers. *Get me out of here.*

The boy thrummed the wooden bars with his fingertips to tease her. She had to figure a way to get the cruel, freckled boy to open the cage. She pecked at the latch with her beak as if beating a drum. The boy recoiled as if she were ready to bite him.

A prepubescent girl with waist-length brown braids and her younger, chubby-cheeked sister appeared above the cage. The older girl remarked, "I wonder who left the white raven in there. It doesn't have any food or water."

Catrin bobbed her feathered head and gurgle softly to lure the girls closer to the cage. She pushed her body against the cage in a friendly gesture.

The chubby-cheeked girl stroked her white plumage and giggled. "So soft. Let's get it out."

The older girl inspected the cage until she found the lock and tried to pull the bar out of the latch. It didn't move. She looked at the boy. "It's stuck. Get me something to jar it loose."

The boy scanned the area and picked up the gem-stone dagger where Rhan had left it. He excitedly handed it to the older girl. "Will this work?"

The older girl rotated the dagger to inspect its blade. "It looks like a rich man's weapon. I'll see if I can force the latch open with it."

In anticipation of being set free, Catrin could feel her heart pound wildly in her chest. However, she became disheartened when the side bar did not at first budge. The older girl repositioned the blade. After several loud grunts, she finally opened the latch, and the door swung outward.

Catrin popped her feathered head through the opening to get out, but the chubby-cheeked girl roughly grabbed her. She clutched Catrin tightly again her chest while screaming with delight, "Look, look. So soft and pretty."

Catrin considered pecking the girl's hand to get free, but the boy snatched her before she had a chance. Her head whirled as the boy whipped her raven body up and down to taunt the little girl.

"I'm going to eat the bird in a pie tonight!" the boy teased.

What, me? Catrin thought. *I'll make you puke.*

The chubby-cheeked girl screamed at the top of her lungs until her older sister interceded, ripping Catrin out of the boy's hand.

"Don't do that," the older girl scolded. "White ravens have mystical powers." She lifted Catrin to within a few inches of her face and her voice pealed, "It has blue eyes."

Enough of this torture!

Catrin squawked loudly, making her irritation known. The startled girl dropped her like a rock on the ground.

Somewhat dazed from the hard fall, Catrin lay there for a few moments before flipping herself upright on clawed feet. She frantically waddled away to escape, but the mean-spirited boy blocked her way.

She pecked at his toes to get him to move.

The boy's feet shuffled away.

She made a mad dash to the cover of bushes, hopping as fast as she could. Too late!

The dagger's blade thrust into the ground, within inches of her feathered breast.

Catrin froze with fright and lay her head down, hoping to elicit the girls' empathies. The chubby-cheeked girl screamed in anger and kicked the boy in the chin. He jumped on one foot and wailed like a baby. The younger girl retrieved the dagger and threatened him with it.

The boy screamed, "You'll be sorry for this," but then stepped back and hid behind an oak.

With a satisfied grin, the chubby-cheeked girl squatted and stroked Catrin's feathers. "So pretty and sweet."

Clever girl, Catrin thought.

The older girl took out some brown bread from a pouch that was tied to her belt and gently placed it in front of Catrin. She pecked at it and swallowed the tasty crumbs. Noticing the skin water pouch tied to the older girl's belt, Catrin gave a pitiable stare, hoping she would understand the hint. The older girl set the skin container on the ground and allowed the water to dribble out of its spout.

Catrin scooped the water into her beak and swallowed until her thirst was quenched. Now more satisfied, she allowed the girls to pet her while warily watching the boy behind the tree.

As the girls began to lose interest, Catrin flapped her wings to test whether she could fly. Her body lifted off the ground a few feet, but then it dropped as if she were a chick just learning how to fly. After several more attempts at flight, she felt a strong force pulling her from above.

The Raven's shriek alerted her that Rhan had reverted back to Agrona's shape.

Catrin took the next steps to shapeshift back to her human form. She felt herself levitate out of her raven body as she visualized her human shape. She latched onto the image and braced for the horrific pain of shapeshifting to her human form. The outward pressure intensified as her body began stretching out in all directions. A burning pain flamed over her skin as her body began to disintegrate. Hearing the children's shrieks echoing into her ears, she knew her body was ready to burst into fine particles from the increasing outward force. The pain reached the point that she could no longer bear it, and she dissolved into a dark calmness.

Delirious, Catrin felt strong hands grip and shake her shoulders. A sharp pain shot through her collarbone. Her ears buzzed from bees swarming above her.

"Wake up!" one of the black-and-yellow striped bees demanded, slapping her face with its stinger. And then, she felt another slap, then another, until she tired of the abuse.

"Stop it!"

The bees disappeared and she heard a man's voice say, "Catrin, it's me. Wake up!"

Catrin forced her eyelids open and found Ferrex pressing the edge of a wet metal cup against her parched lips. Tasting the cool liquid, she took a sip. He lifted her head higher so she could more easily drink until her thirst quenched.

Disoriented, she tried to comprehend what had happened. A sudden chill in the air made her shiver so forcibly that her teeth clacked. As Ferrex covered her naked body with a wool cloak, she slowly realized that she had successfully shapeshifted back into her human form.

Ferrex's kindly face finally came into focus as he stroked her hair like a father soothing a hurt child. "You will be fine, Catrin."

"Where am I?" she inquired.

"We're near the Ancient Oak," he said.

With her mind clearing, Catrin recognized the area where she had been caged, close to the matrimonial hut that had been burned down. She didn't know how much time had elapsed since she had reverted back to her human form and whether Ferrex had witnessed the transformation.

"What happened to me?" she asked.

"You gave us a scare," Ferrex said, widening his eyes. "We all thought you had died in the fire."

"Fire?"

"After you entered Agrona's cell, flames shot onto the thatch-roof like shooting stars and set it afire. No one saw you or Agrona escape."

Catrin tried to comprehend what Ferrex had just told her. "I remember . . . I was with Rhan. She put some kind of choke hold on me. I passed out and went into some kind of trance. Myrddin then tricked me into shape-shifting into a raven."

Ferrex gaped at her as if he didn't believe her. "Let me get you something to eat. Perhaps that will help clear your mind."

He leaned Catrin against the Ancient Oak in a sitting position and re-trieved some flat cakes from a saddlebag on his horse for them to eat. She nibbled on the cakes, but the food didn't settle her stomach. She asked for another drink of water and then eased into her story about how Myrddin had tricked her into shapeshifting into a raven so Agrona could take her human form. She described the firestorm at the matrimonial hut. Tears shed from her eyes as the image of Marcellus's limp body came to her mind. She ended the tale by saying, "I tried to stop Marrock, but he almost cursed me to the Otherworld. Somehow I survived and came back."

"How did you manage to get back in your human form?" Ferrex asked.

"The Raven alerted me Agrona had reverted back to her own form. That is when I was able to shapeshift back to my human form. I must have lost consciousness, though." She paused, realizing it could have been some time since that happened. "How long has it been since the fire at the fortress?"

Ferrex grimaced and stood up. "It's been more than one week. As we speak, your father is gathering warriors from outlying villages for a bat-tle with Marrock's forces. Your sister, Mor, and Belinus have been left in charge of defending the fortress."

The guilt of allowing herself to be tricked by Myrddin weighed heavily in Catrin's mind. Her decision to confront Rhan might have set off a cas-cade of events that had doomed Marcellus, her family, and her kingdom. The king had warned that she might not be given another chance if she made other bad choices. She wondered if Ferrex had been mandated by the king to carry out her death sentence if he found her.

"Did Father send you to execute me?" she finally asked.

Ferrex shook his head. "Why would you think that? Your father is racked with grief that you were burned alive in the fire. He would give anything to see you again."

"Then why are you here?" she asked.

"Your father charged me to return to the fortress and gather more warriors for a final battle with Marrock. On my way, I heard children screaming." Ferrex chuckled, shaking his head. "Can you imagine my surprise when I found you naked, curled next to a tree? I didn't believe the children when they said you had changed from a raven into a woman. I sent them away with a scolding that they should never lie again."

He pulled the gem-studded dagger with the etched curse from his baldric and handed it to Catrin. "I found the cursed dagger near what looked like a bird cage. I can't read the etching. Has it changed?"

Catrin raised the dagger to her eyes. A sob caught in her throat as she silently read the curse. "Sweet Mother Goddess, the curse hasn't changed," she said, fighting back tears. "Nothing I've done has set it right."

"You've done nothing wrong," Ferrex said, giving Catrin a reassuring hug. "You were misled by Myrddin and Rhan. And now, I fear spies have also misled your father. They've reported that Marrock's forces were assembling west of here to ambush the capital. And that Marcellus is allying with them—"

"That's not true," Catrin snapped as she tucked the dagger beneath her belt. "Marrock took Marcellus as prisoner!"

Ferrex quieted and turned as pale as a ghost. Suspecting that he was hiding something from her, she asked, "Is there something I should know?"

"Your father ordered me to sneak into the enemy camp and kill Marcellus in vengeance for betraying us, but I couldn't locate Marrock's camp where it was reported to be."

Abashed, Catrin asked, "Why would you risk your life like that?"

"My life was shattered on the day I believed you had died in the fire. I blamed Marcellus for this, thinking he had betrayed us. Most of all, I blamed him for stealing my chance to marry you, as your father had promised me."

"What are you telling me?" Catrin asked, struggling to grasp what Ferrex had just said.

"You father always intended to kill Marcellus," Ferrex said bluntly.

Tears streamed from Catrin eyes. "That can't be true. Myrddin promised Father that the curse would be broken if I married Marcellus and proclaimed him king. And now you're telling me that he had always planned to murder Marcellus?"

"Are you that naïve, Catrin?" Ferrex said with a grimace. "Your father would never step down as king for a foreigner. He only did this with the hope of breaking the curse. Once he broke the curse, he would have burned Marcellus on a pyre as a sacrifice to the Earth Goddess in accordance with the traditions of our ancient ancestors to get rid of an unfit king."

Catrin felt as if her heart had been split apart. "Father deceived me! He blessed my marriage, knowing full well he would burn Marcellus alive for loving me! If given the choice, I would have thrown myself into the fire alongside him!" She broke into sobs and stammered, "I led Marcellus into a trap. He could be dead now for trying to save me."

Ferrex lifted Catrin into his embrace, the cloak falling away from her body. "Don't throw your life away on that Roman scum. We have a battle to fight against Marrock. Your father needs to know you're alive. He loves you!"

"I hate Father for deceiving me!" Catrin raged, fighting against Ferrex's restraints. "I never want to see him again. I want him to think I'm dead and suffer the guilt for what he did to me. I need to find Marcellus! Gods above, I can't let Marrock murder him!"

"Stop that!" Ferrex said harshly. "Wake up! You were living in a dream, but now you must face the harsh reality of our nightmare. This is about our survival as a people against Marrock. You pledged your fealty as a warrior to the king when I volunteered to train you. So do it! And forget Marcellus! He is most likely dead!"

To Catrin's utter shock, Ferrex reinforced his words by clenching her arm so tightly, she thought the bone would break. Yanking herself out of his grip, she fell backwards on her backside. Dumbfounded, she grappled with conflicting emotions of anger, disbelief, and humiliation that her most loyal friend had hurt her like that. She dabbed the burning tears from her cheeks.

Ferrex staggered back and lowered his eyes. "I shouldn't have grabbed you like that, but I am so frustrated with your blind love for the Roman." He proffered his hand to help her up.

Catrin swatted his hand away. "I can get up myself." She staggered to her feet and brushed the dirt off. "I should flog you for that."

Ferrex smirked. "Perhaps later, but now put that rage on Marrock. We need to return to the fortress and gather more forces to join the king. Despite how you feel about your father, we must warn him that Marrock is maneuvering his forces in a different location."

"I understand that," Catrin grumbled, rubbing her face to ease the soreness. "But if you ever grab me like that again, I'll cut off your hands."

Ferrex twitched a smile as if he would not expect anything less from her. "We need to do something about finding you some clothes, 'cause I can't think straight." He pulled off his long shirt and handed it to Catrin. "Here, put this on."

Heat of embarrassment blossomed on Catrin's face as she hurriedly put the tunic on as he watched. "Do you have something I could use as a belt?"

"I'll find something in my saddle bag."

"I'm anxious to see Mor before we leave again tomorrow," Catrin said, wrapping the belt around her waist and clasping it.

"The king will be happy to see you again."

"As I told you, I'll never forgive him," Catrin said bitterly, "but I will do my duty and fight for the survival of my family and people."

47

FIRE-BREATHING EAGLES

The rising sun ignited the horizon into a red fire. Ravens shot like black ar-rows over the fortress. Catrin shuddered, watching the bird augury through the Great Hall's doorway. The previous night, she had dreamt fire-breath-ing eagles burned the town to ashes while interconnecting shields closed in on her. To escape the crushing red wall, she had to shapeshift into a raven. Apprehensive about joining her father's forces, she still broiled with rage that he had deceived her about blessing her marriage to Marcellus. Even so, she resolved to rise above her hatred and find the fortitude to fight as an untested warrior in battle to defend her people.

Catrin closed the entrance door and walked to the central blazing hearth where her sister, Mor, was warming her hands.

"I'm set to go," Catrin said.

"I wish you'd stay here to help defend the fortress," Mor said, staring at the fire.

Catrin knew her sister, a trained spear maid, was capable of defending the hill fort without her. "I can better serve the kingdom by joining our father's forces to battle Marrock. I regret, though, you've been left with too few warriors to defend the fortress with half of the walls burned down."

"You're right, you should be with Father. Belinus will be at my side," Mor said, finally looking at Catrin with tear-filled eyes. "Before you leave, I wanted to give you something that Belinus found near the matrimonial hut. I know this holds special meaning for you."

Mor extended her hand to reveal the Apollo amulet. Catrin, taking the figurine that was sculpted in Marcellus's likeness, fought back tears. The return of the amulet gave her hope that it was a sign her Roman protector was alive. She pulled a raven tail feather from her belt and attached it to the statuette with a thin leather band as a symbol of her love for him.

"Please put this around my neck and give me your blessing," Catrin requested, lifting her hair for Mor to tie the leather straps of the amulet behind her neck.

Mor secured the amulet and kissed Catrin on the cheek. "May the Mother Goddess bless you and keep you from harm."

Embracing Mor, Catrin felt her sister's hard, round belly. The image of Vala's headless shadow holding an infant just before Mor's wedding came to her mind. "Don't do anything that could jeopardize your unborn child. Let Belinus do the fighting."

Mor tightened the embrace and sniffled. "Don't be foolishly brave. I've already grieved your death once. Don't make me do it again."

Catrin sighed and released the embrace. "Take care of yourself."

Without saying another word, Catrin strode to the entryway, where the weapons were stored. She sheathed a sword in her leather baldric and adjusted the dagger with Rhan's etched curse beneath her belt. She strapped an oblong shield to her forearm, and grabbed a couple of spears from a rack before exiting the Great Hall to meet Ferrex at the fortress gate.

The hamlet was bustling with activities preparing for a possible attack. A tusk-mustached Celtic elder limped past Catrin, herding cattle to stables for safe-keeping. Farmers were loading wheat and barley from wagons into granaries. The air was saturated with the smell of bog-ore roasting in smelting furnaces, as metal workers hammered sword blades and spearheads on their anvils.

At the front gate, Catrin shielded her eyes with a hand from the morning glare. She spotted the bare-chested Ferrex swaggering up the hillside to the fort. The tattooed lion paws running down his arms displayed his ferocity as a warrior. The distinctive blue-and-gold plaid breeches of the king's clansmen matched hers. He carried a backpack of weapons over his broad shoulder. Strapped to his arm was the red shield with the gold insignia of the three-headed horse of the king's clan.

As he approached Catrin, his face glowed from the breaking sunlight. "Do you have all your weapons?"

"Yes."

"Do you need any help with them?

"I can carry them myself," Catrin said, somewhat annoyed that he offered. "Did you see the fire in the sky at dawn?"

He smiled. "I did. It's always a great day to see the sun after a night full of darkness."

"Why are you in such a jovial mood?" Catrin asked with a scowl.

"Why are you in such a dour one?" Ferrex retorted.

"We're heading into battle," she said sharply. "Last night, I dreamt fire-breathing eagles burned down our fortress."

"It must get tiresome seeing those ill-boding visions," Ferrex remarked. "I'd rather be inspired by a glorious morning to help me defeat the enemy."

"Always an optimist," she said, frowning.

"If I weren't, I would never have volunteered to train you," Ferrex said with a smirk. "Besides, you need to get your mind off defeat. The warriors need to see fire in your eyes."

"You should heed the omens," Catrin said, growing weary of sparring words with him.

"Do I have a choice with you?" Ferrex grinned.

Catrin glared.

"Have the warriors gathered at the rendezvous site?" she asked as they descended the hilltop over the defensive ramparts.

"Most of them have, but a few warriors are still straggling from their farms," Ferrex said, slowing to readjust the pack on his back. "They have other commitments, you know, other than being warriors."

Noting the sarcasm in his voice, Catrin snapped, "I know that!"

Ferrex had an annoying glint of mirth in his eyes. "Well then, let's join our warriors."

At the edge of the forest, they set their weapons near a towering oak. She stayed there as Ferrex greeted some farmer-warriors equipped with pitchforks, hatchets, and wooden-tipped spears.

The cloudless sky promised a brilliant day, but Catrin noticed the forest was strangely quiet. She didn't hear the *coo-coos* of long-tailed cuckoos or the melodic chirps of wrens.

After speaking with the men, Ferrex joined Catrin and dropped his shield on some red-spiked flowers near the tree. He cuffed metal bands around his wrists and motioned for Catrin to do likewise. "Those farmers told me about rumors that Roman warships have landed near the white cliffs. Marrock's army was also spotted there."

"What about my father's forces?"

"I don't know," Ferrex answered with concern written on his face.

A shriek pierced the silence, which only Catrin seemed to have heard. She scanned the treetop and spotted a silver eagle atop the highest branch. Flames burst out of its beak and lapped at the oak's serrated leaves. Terrified she was seeing an omen, she squeezed her eyelids shut. And when she opened them again, the apparition disappeared. She could feel her mouth drop as she exclaimed, "I just saw the fire-breathing eagle."

Ferrex grabbed a sword and handed Catrin a spear. "I suddenly believe those omens of yours."

The Raven's shrieks shattered the forest stillness. Catrin could feel a light tremor beneath her feet and the faint sound of clacking metal in the distance. A burning sensation shot into her arms, and she visualized her father's troops marching in the forested valley just east of the white cliffs. Marrock's forces were lurking on a ridge above him.

"What's wrong?" Ferrex asked. "You are as jumpy as a frog about to be eaten by an eagle."

Catrin's stomach clenched. "My father is marching into a trap! We need to get back to the fortress, now!"

The clatter of metal swords against shields grew louder and louder. Both Ferrex and Catrin turned toward the direction of Romans charging them. Interconnecting red shields hiding the enemies' faces were moving like a wall toward them; their sandaled feet were marching in tandem like centipede legs. Roman cavalrymen, slashing their swords at Cantiaci warriors, were defending the right flank of the infantrymen.

Catrin trembled at the sight of a foot soldier carrying a pole with a silver eagle on top.

The fire-breathing eagle!

Looking in the opposite direction of the attacking Romans, she noticed billows of black smoke rising from the fortress. The fire-breathing eagles must have ignited the remaining wooden walls with their flames. This was a two-front Roman assault on the fortress.

"Grab your weapons," Ferrex shouted. "Hide in the woods. We're outnumbered."

Catrin grabbed a shield, sword, and spear and scrambled into the woods. Hearing screams of terror, she peeked through the trees. Romans had swarmed the open field. She spotted Belinus and Ferrex defending Mor, who was on horseback. Belinus swatted Mor's horse and shouted, "Get out of here. Find Catrin!"

Mor galloped her mount into the forest as Ferrex and Belinus were swallowed by Roman shields and Cantiaci warriors, herdsmen, and farmers clashing swords, picks, and axes in the onslaught.

48

BLOOD WOLF

Marrock, standing with Myrddin at the edge of the white cliffs, sniffed the briny air from the ocean channel. The glow of the morning sun faintly lit the Roman warships harbored in the bay, their hulls ready to fill with slaves. At that moment, Marrock embraced his destiny as Blood Wolf—a predator whose glory had been banished to the night while others slept. Last night's new moon signaled he would soon rise as the new king foretold in the curse.

The damp coolness falling on the hilltop made Blood Wolf's raven-sculpted face ache for revenge. He said to Myrddin, "Tell me again what my mother's curse means."

"The curse has labyrinthine meanings," Myrddin explained, leaning on a rosewood staff capped with a yellow globe, its surface etched with the image of the sun god driving a two-horse chariot. "How you interpret the curse depends on where you are in its maze."

"Don't speak in riddles," Marrock snapped.

Myrddin rubbed the crystalline beryl orb until it glowed like the sun. "The curse foretells a king with the soul of a warrior wolf will rise in power with the aid of Rome—"

"I know that," Marrock barked. "Tell me who the Raven is."

"Ahh, it depends on which raven controls the future in the cauldron's maze."

"Is the Raven my mother?"

Myrddin squinted at the globe. "Perhaps . . . perhaps not. It is true Rhan is always cooking up new schemes in her cauldron. But alas, the crystal ball is murky. The Raven could be human, wraith, or celestial . . . any or all of these."

"So my mother is not the Raven foretold in her curse?" Marrock said, growing weary of the wild Druid's contradictions.

"Only Rhan truly believes that. I only confirmed Agrona's soul would reincarnate into the child she conceived with the Roman."

"The Raven could even be me," Marrock said sardonically, now believing Catrin was dead and no longer threatened to acquire the powers of the Ancient Druids.

Myrddin waved his staff back and forth. "Blood Wolf is an earthly creature, but today a celestial essence will cast a shadow on the sun and turn day into night. Once its shadow flies out of the sun's corona, you can unleash the powers of the Ancient Druids to control nature's forces."

Marrock lifted Vala's skull, which he had meticulously cleaned and polished. "I'll be able to collect the powers through the skull's empty eye sockets today?"

"Yes, if you do as I instructed. Lift the scull to gather the remaining sunlight right before day turns into night. After that, you have limited time to control nature's forces as the celestial essence unveils the sun," Myrddin clarified.

"How can I gain full access to powers without any limitation on when I can use them?"

"You must harvest the skulls of King Amren and his queen to add with Vala's for the magical number of three."

Marrock rubbed the smooth surface of the skull's eye sockets. "Three skulls, full powers."

"That is so." Myrddin paused and stroked his beard in thought. "But the soul must remain with the skull and not allowed to wander for you to reap these powers."

Marrock smiled. "Then I no longer need my mother to carry out her curse. That is good. I no longer trust her and no longer want to share my sovereignty with her."

"The moment your mother conceives a child in her womb, she ousts Agrona's soul. In doing so, she also loses her magical abilities, which you can take advantage of. You might say, the child is baking in the oven and the curse is almost cooked in the cauldron," Myrddin said with a twinkle in his eyes.

Sweet justice, Marrock thought to himself. The cat-like screams of his mother in climactic ecstasy with Marcellus still grated at him like claws scratching metal. At least he had given Marcellus the keepsake of a painful slash in his belly on his journey back to Rome. Although Marrock was somewhat disappointed the Roman scum would never recall he had made the cut, it was necessary to erase his memory of the deed so Lucius Antonius could be deceived into believing King Amren had inflicted the wound.

The touch of a wet tongue licking his hand drew Marrock out of his thoughts. He fondly looked down on his black she-wolf. The others in the pack had already dispersed through the thick woods in the valley to await Amren's forces. The wolves had been commanded to lunge at Amren's warriors and to hold them down long enough to be neck-collared and chained for slavery.

Marrock caught sight of a rider galloping up the grassy hillside. As the red-haired warrior approached, he recognized Caratacus—Cunobelin's rebellious son.

Halting his horse in front of Marrock, Caratacus reported, "Our spies have spread word to coastline villages that the Romans overtook the Cantiaci capital and are marching back with captives. As you predicted, your father's army is heading this way in the dense woods of the valley east of here."

"I knew my father would do this in an effort to rescue his people. Are all of the soldiers ready for the ambush?"

Caratacus nodded. "Both my warriors and Roman soldiers are waiting in trenches, which we dug out at strategic spots alongside the pathway."

"The Romans will be leaving after the fall equinox," Marrock commented. "Tides can play havoc with ships at this time of year. If they don't wreck, the cargo of Cantiaci slaves will offer Senator Lucius Antonius riches beyond his wildest dreams."

"If their ships sink, I say good riddance." Caratacus spat. "Rome has been nothing more than a thorn."

"Make sure the bitch queen and her bastard daughter are brought to me alive for my pleasure," Marrock ordered. "I've been told Catrin has already been sent to the Otherworld."

"We need to hurry to spring the trap," Caratacus said, reining his horse around.

Marrock climbed on his horse and rode alongside Caratacus, leaving Myrddin behind, down the hillside to the valley where he joined his warriors.

By mid-day, the chill in the air felt like dusk. Marrock dared not look directly at the sun, but he knew the celestial being was on its journey to shroud the sun. The chatter of daylight creatures gave way to the foreboding calls of creatures at twilight—crickets chirping, owls hooting, doves cooing.

The wild-haired Caratacus jumped into the trench beside Marrock and reported, "Amren has taken the trap."

Marrock asked, "Is the bitch queen riding with him?"

"One of my scouts reported she is at the back of the army with the king's commander, Trystan," Caratacus replied.

"I'll handle the king myself."

Caratacus nodded. "I'll make sure every warrior understands that."

"Good. Did you confirm whether Mor was captured at the capital?"

"Not yet, but we should know soon enough when the remaining Romans join us after this battle."

The air suddenly cooled and the gold hues of light streaked above the treetops. All of nature's creatures silenced as if waiting for the carnage. The trampling of boots and clicking of swords against shields could now be heard in the distance. The tree boughs and vines obscured Amren's army ahead. The creatures of the forest grew quieter as the crunching footsteps grew louder and louder.

The enemy was close, but Marrock still couldn't see them through the thick woods in the dimming sunlight. He would give the signal to attack once he saw the whites of his father's eyes.

Marrock turned to the sound of padding paws approaching his side. The black she-wolf bared her teeth and growled. Reading the wolf's mind, he learned his father was at the front of his army. He peeked over the top of the ditch in anticipation.

A few moments later, Amren appeared as a shadow coming out of the mist swirling around the base of the trees.

Marrock retrieved the polished skull of Vala from his leather pouch.

The temperature dropped again.

A chill spiked down Marrock's spine. His scarred face ached as if thorns were pricking his skin. The annoying pain aggravated him even more. He squinted and focused on Amren who was riding his beloved black stallion.

The fog rose like red ghosts in the fading sun.

Marrock then saw the whites of his father's eyes. He lifted Vala's skull over his head to capture the remaining sunlight filtering through the trees.

Yes, Father, this is your end.

A man's voice from Amren's forces echoed throughout the forest, "It's a trap!"

Marrock knew then he had lost his element of surprise.

The thickening mist obscured warriors now engaged in brutal combat, but the snarls of wolves, clacking metal of swords, and cries of men and women resonated through the forest.

Then everything turned pitch black.

The chill in the air pierced to the bone.

In readiness, Marrock clasped Vala's skull in the palm of his hand. The outer edge of the sun flashed, signaling the night was turning to day again. Vala's skull began to glow as brilliant as the full moon in a night sky. A spark crackled through Marrock's fingertips, empowering him to control nature's forces. He intoned in the ancient druidic tongue, "Make earth tremble as moon unveils the sun."

An earthquake rumbled the ground. Amren's horse reared on its hind legs, throwing him off. Marrock set the skull down and climbed out of the trench to challenge his broad-shouldered father, a head shorter than him. Grabbing the hilt of the naked sword from his belt, he met Amren's blade with so much force that sparks flew off the metal. The strength and agility of the king astounded Marrock. He barely escaped the tip of his father's blade as he stepped back and lurched sideways.

Amren pounced at Marrock like a lynx, swiftly thrusting his sword. The sharp tip sliced Marrock across his bare chest. Screaming from the pain, he stepped back to avert his father's next strike.

"Make the earth tremble," Marrock yelled.

The ground's shaking movement drove Amren to his knees before his son.

Marrock, gripping the pommel of his sword for the final deathblow, howled, "*Cathos!*"

Amren gaped at the thread-like glimmer on Marrock's blade. Time seemed to freeze as he watched the events of his life flash on the strand of light. He viewed his lifetime with the perspective of an omniscient god. He saw the reflection of himself in Rhan's eyes when they had first made love. They were soul mates, one and the same, each providing the elixir to maintain their kingdom through brutal force. A battle-hardened ruler, he depended on her to summon the dark forces of nature to overcome his enemies: strike them down with lightning, discover their schemes by shapeshifting into other forms to conceal herself, and erase their memories with druidic magic potions. Rhan always did his bidding, but the dark forces of the Ancient Druids twisted her mind. His mind. When he executed her, he also lost his soul and humanity. He had treated everyone he loved with the same brute force as he had treated his enemies. Even as he found love with his new queen, Rhiannon, he had never told her how sorry he was that he had forced her to marry him, even though Trystan was her true love. His curse, the king's curse, had condemned Vala, the bastard daughter he had embraced as his champion. And his curse also condemned the only daughter he had fathered.

The vision of Catrin reaching out to him was the last image in his mind before the cold-edge steel sliced through his neck.

Amren's mind went dark.

Upon awakening, he found himself floating over the battlefield. He felt peace at long last in the midst of clashing swords, bone-crunching blows, and screaming warriors.

But then, his calm turned to panic when he saw his son lift his bloody head above the storm of battle. The cheers and war cries of Marrock's warriors rumbled like thunder. The grassy pasture had transformed into a killing field covered with unrecognizable, mutilated bodies, and rivers of blood.

"Someone put my head back on so I can lead the charge against Marrock," Amren shouted.

"A raven will pick you up shortly," a warrior assured, floating by him.

Others warriors lifted off the ground and stretched their hands to the ravens circling above. One by one the creatures swooped down and picked up pieces of the warriors in their beaks and flew away.

But Amren was left behind.

Bewildered, he clutched his breast but could not detect a heartbeat. A powerful force emanating from his severed head was pulling on him. He sensed Vala's essence was entrapped in her skull near Marrock and was under his son's control. He inexplicably knew if his spirit returned to his skull, Marrock could then harness unspeakable powers from it. His soul would never enter the Otherworld without proper funeral rites for his head. He had to escape from Marrock to prevent his son from using the power from his soul for evil purposes.

Spotting a riderless warhorse fleeing the melee, Amren's spirit grasped onto its mane. As he held onto the horse's long hair, his soul flapped in the wind. He sensed the strain of the horse's muscles but felt no pain as his spirit hit the tree branches. The strength of the force from his head diminished as the horse distanced itself from Marrock, but Catrin's essence grew stronger and stronger. To his shock, he realized his daughter was not among the dead.

Catrin was yet alive, and she needed his love and guidance to help her survive his curse.

49

ESCAPE TO WHITE CLIFFS

Catrin saw wisps of fog dancing over motionless bodies near the forest edge where she and Mor were hiding. The omens they had just experienced frightened her. The day had turned to night and the ground had trembled beneath her feet. As she warily approached the corpses, on which ravens were feasting, tears filled her eyes. The fortress, the only home she had ever known, had been burned down to ashes. Most of her people were now gone, either captured by the Romans or killed in the assault. She had seen women threatened with rape turn their swords on themselves.

As Catrin approached the body of one warrior, she recognized the familiar tattoo of the sun on his arm. She wasn't prepared for the horror of seeing the warrior's slashed throat. His jaw was locked in silent scream, his eyes frozen open in terror. She jerked her head up and looked apprehensively at Mor. Emotions of rage, fear, and sorrow whirled inside her as she watched Mor throw her body over Belinus and wail. He had bravely sacrificed himself, fighting off the Roman soldiers, so they could escape.

Fearing that some Romans might have stayed behind to capture any stragglers, Catrin pulled Mor into her embrace. "Shh . . . we need to go and find Father."

Mor's lips quivered as tears streamed down her face. "We . . . we can't just leave him here."

"We need to go now. Or we'll meet his fate," Catrin said emphatically. She retrieved a nearby gelding while Mor mounted her horse.

They rode behind the cover of hedgerows that lined the roadway to the white cliffs, but evidence of Roman plunder and destruction made them reconsider their route. Several of the round houses had been burned down, many of the inhabitants missing or found dead, mainly the elderly. A couple of survivors wandering the area warned Mor and Catrin that Romans were capturing and collar-chaining the people. They had heard rumors that King Amren's army had been annihilated. Survivors were regrouping at a secret location.

Catrin surmised it was a cavern near the village of Dubris, which Britons had dug out before Julius Caesar's attack several decades earlier.

By the end of the day, Catrin's legs were cramped from the long ride and swollen from the thorns that had stabbed her as they were forced to hide from enemy soldiers behind blackberry bushes the closer they got to the cliffs.

At dusk, they finally reached the white cliffs, their visibility diminished with the thick fog. As Catrin rode along the cliffside, she heard the waves crashing below. She could barely see the pathway along the precipitous cliff edge that led to Dubris. Fatigue made her lightheaded. The horse's swaying motion made her drowsy.

Closing her eyes, she momentarily fell into a light sleep, until the sound of men speaking Latin jolted her awake. When she didn't recognize the area, her stomach clenched.

"Did we take the wrong path?" she asked Mor.

"Possibly . . ." Mor turned her horse. "I'm not sure where we are."

The men's voices became louder, but then silenced. Hearing the crunch of approaching footsteps, Catrin feared they had been spotted. The only way she and her sister could escape would be to drive their horses down the hillside in total darkness.

She searched the sky for the Raven and silently prayed for its help.

Show me the light to safety.

A shooting star flashed above and momentarily illuminated another pathway. Sensing the Raven, Catrin directed her horse toward the direction of its shrieks. Her sister followed as they pressed their nervous horses down the steep slope. When they entered a dense forest, Catrin heard a twig snap and halted her horse. Turning toward the direction of the sound, she could see no movement in the dark.

She froze to stillness and drew her sword.

A man called out, "Mor, Catrin."

Recognizing the voice of Trystan, Catrin exhaled in relief.

Five shadowy figures stepped out of the pines. Catrin could barely discern Trystan as he approached them and said, "Thank the gods you are safe."

Catrin dropped off her horse and steadied herself against its side. The horror of the previous days finally crashed on her like a wave. Her throat felt parched as she rasped, "Romans ambushed the capital two days ago. We barely escaped with our lives."

Trystan gawked at Catrin. "I can't believe you're alive. We thought you had perished in the fire. If only your father knew . . . but . . ." Trystan paused before his words could escape in a rasp. "He is dead."

Catrin felt as if the whole world had crushed on her. She dropped to her knees and the anguish she felt from her previous words—"I hate Father"— racked her with grief and guilt. She felt as if her stomach had been kicked by a horse. "How did he die?"

"We were caught-off guard and ambushed by Marrock's forces. Your father fought valiantly, but the forces of nature worked against us. The day turned as dark as a moonless night. The earth shook. In the ensuing battle, Marrock beheaded the king," Trystan said, widening his eyes as if he couldn't believe what he was saying.

Catrin felt numb—the Past, the Present, and the Future frozen in one time. What she had dreaded most, what she had fought so hard to break— Rhan's curse—was now in the Past. Every future she had seen in the Depths of Possibilities had come to this. The ramifications of Rhan's curse sunk into her mind—Vala dead, Father dead, Belinus dead. Marcellus and Ferrex were also most likely dead, as well as others she had cherished and loved. How could she live with the fact that her love for Marcellus had ultimately led to the fulfillment of the curse?

The sound of Mor's sobs finally broke down Catrin's steel façade, which she had struggled to maintain to survive. Grief and guilt overwhelmed her and she openly wept, barely able to catch her breath. As tears flooded her eyes, Trystan held Catrin's head against his chest and said softly, "Your father would not want you to weep. Take heart. Your mother yet lives and is preparing for the final battle for our survival."

50

SPIRITUAL WARRIOR

Catrin's spirits lifted, learning her mother was still alive. She asked, "Where is Mother now?"

"She is gathering forces in a nearby cavern," Trystan replied. "Other survivors from nearby villages have also escaped to its haven. We have nearly two hundred warriors ready to fight."

Not nearly enough, Catrin thought, her stomach dropping. "There must have been twice that number of Romans who attacked the fortress and took our people as captives. I only saw a few survivors on our ride here."

"Roman scum!" Trystan spat. "Your father was trying to rescue these captives before we were ambushed by Marrock's forces. Did you see the Roman encampment as you rode here?"

Catrin said, "We heard Romans talking on the other side of the hill, but it was too dark to determine how many there were."

"I fear the Romans are joining Marrock's warriors for the final battle. I will send scouts to determine the location of their respective forces. In the meantime, we should go back to our camp. Follow me."

The sisters quietly followed Trystan, weaving between the trees until they reached the mouth of the cave. Within the dimly lit cavern, several warriors were sharpening their swords while others slept on the chalky ground near the walls.

Catrin, noticing an unarmed young woman about her age, questioned herself as to why she hadn't fought to defend the fortress instead of hiding in the woods. Although she knew that she had to protect Mor and her unborn child, she nonetheless should have fought alongside Ferrex and Belinus.

She had let her people down.

Scanning the cave for her mother, Catrin tapped a warrior's arm when she was unable to find her. "Where's the queen?"

"She should return shortly from a nearby village where she is recruiting more soldiers and gaining more information." the warrior answered.

"I don't understand why the Romans attacked us," Mor said.

"Our spies said Marrock secretly allied with Rome to overthrow our kingdom," Trystan interjected.

"What do the Romans hope to gain?" asked Mor.

"Marrock must have agreed to provide our people as slaves to Rome. I suspect Rome has a more sinister plan of pitting tribal kings against each other for an excuse to invade Britannia—a conquest Julius Caesar left undone."

Catrin unsheathed her sword from her belt. "Marrock is a traitor! I will cut out his heart."

Trystan furrowed his eyebrows. "Strong words from a girl who is not battle-tested."

"I'm old enough!" Catrin declared. "Ferrex has taught me how to fight."

Trystan cracked a smile. "I have no doubt of your ferocity." Clasping Catrin's shoulder, he turned her toward the camp and nudged her forward. "Get some sleep. Marrock has vowed to kill everyone in your family. And that includes you."

Catrin was ready to protest, but Trystan squeezed her arm to silence her. In a fiery huff, she stormed away. *I am here to fight for my kingdom, not be hidden away!*

Mor ran after Catrin. "You shouldn't have stomped away from Trystan."

Catrin glared at her sister. "I am here to defend our kingdom. Trystan doesn't believe I can fight. I can and I will!"

"Nobody doubts your bravery," Mor reassured. "But now you need to think with a clear head. You have another gift that could help us in battle."

Catrin raised her brow. "What is that?"

Mor gestured Catrin toward the back of the cavern where they sat down in a more isolated spot where they could privately talk.

"The only way we can defeat the Romans is to take them by surprise," Mor said emphatically. "Only you have the gift of prophecy. Call upon the Raven so you can foresee the upcoming battle and study the enemies' weaknesses so we can turn the tide."

"But I can only foresee the future when I enter the Raven's mind and . . ." Catrin looked away and bit her lip.

"What's wrong?" Mor asked.

"I don't always understand my visions."

"Tell me why," Mor encouraged.

"I had a vision that an eagle breathed fire on our fortress and set it ablaze. Not until I saw Romans rallying around an animal-skinned soldier carrying an eagle atop a pole did I understand the meaning," Catrin said with the heaviness of regret in her heart.

"Don't blame yourself for failing to understand the meaning. We are in a desperate situation. Now more than ever, you need to call upon your raven guide to show us how to prepare for our next battle."

Catrin nervously crossed her legs and stared at the ceiling.

"What are you not telling me?" Mor asked.

"Whenever I tried to intervene in what will happen in the future, I've only made it worse. When I found out from Ferrex that Father wanted to kill Marcellus after we had married, I declared that I hated him. My hate cursed Father. That is the reason he is dead."

"Our father is dead because Marrock killed him," said Mor, clasping Catrin's arm. "This has nothing to do with you."

"If Father was here now, I would tell him how sorry I am and how much I love him." Catrin looked away, tears welling in her eyes. "Sometimes I fear I am a dark creature like Marrock. Whenever I fill with rage, I no longer feel human. I become the essence of my raven spirit that only wants to peck out the eyes of its enemies."

"You are a spiritual warrior. Use that rage to help us. War brings out the worst in all of us."

Catrin had a sick feeling in her stomach. "I will willingly die for my kingdom, but I fear losing my soul if I continue to use my raven powers."

"We are in dire straits. You have no choice but to use these powers if we have any chance to survive," Mor said fervently, ending the conversation.

51

RAVEN FORESIGHT

Sleep would not come to Catrin. She felt trapped within the musty-smelling walls of the cave. Images of the slaughter in her village streamed through her mind: soldiers tearing babies away from their mothers; women ripping away Roman shields with bare hands; horses stomping the elderly, women, and children.

Catrin turned on her side, but the woolen bedding did not cushion her from the frigid ground. Her mind sought a respite from the horrors of the day. Her fatigued body ached for sleep, but doubts still flooded her mind. She got up and rummaged through her satchel for the Apollo amulet. Finding it, she rubbed its smooth surface. She sighed. Marcellus could not protect her now. No one could protect her except herself. She remembered her father's words before Mor's wedding.

Your pathway to redemption is based on the next decisions and judgments you make.

She could no longer live in the past and what could have been. Her heart had been split between her father and Marcellus. Just when she thought she could have both of their love, she had neither. But she still had her mother and sister.

And she must protect them at all costs.

As she rhythmically stroked the amulet's polished marble, she gazed at the cave wall and fell into a trance. She visualized herself running through a battlefield with Marrock chasing her, brandishing his sword above his head. Her heart pounded as she sprinted up a steep incline, every muscle burning with every stride. Yet she could not escape Marrock. Terror gripped her chest when she reached the edge of the cliff edge. There was nowhere to escape except over the precipice. Looking to the blue sky, she saw Marcellus as the sun god, Apollo, in a golden chariot flying toward her. As Marrock swung his blade at her neck, Apollo transformed her into a raven. She soared over Marrock and prepared to attack him, as Apollo drove his chariot near her.

Suddenly, a loud screeching startled Catrin from her vision. Drowsy, she rubbed her eyes. She again heard the stentorian bird sounds from outside the cave and knew the Raven wanted to connect with her.

Mor stirred and mumbled, "Did you hear that raven shriek?"

"We need to go now," Catrin said urgently. "I must commune with the Raven on the top of the white cliffs. But we can't let Trystan see us leave. He will try to stop us."

"Are you crazy? The hilltop is swarming with Romans."

"I've seen a vision that gives me hope," Catrin said excitedly. "You were right. I need to use the Raven's foresight to help us prepare for battle. You need to be with me, though. I sometimes lose consciousness as I connect with the Raven."

Mor reluctantly agreed.

They fumbled for their weapons and walked quietly outside the cave. A few sentries were on guard. Nearby, Trystan could be heard snoring as loud as a growling bear. Catrin motioned to a guard that they had to relieve themselves. He pointed to nearby trees.

The breaking dawn provided light for Catrin and Mor as they ascended the pathway to the top. As they reached the summit, clouds in the eastern horizon flamed to a fiery orange.

Mor tied feathers into Catrin's golden braids and painted wings on her forehead, using blue woad.

"Stay close to me," said Catrin. "I'm always dizzy after I leave the Raven."

"Don't worry. I'll stay at your side."

Catrin took the red-jeweled sword from Mor and pointed the blade toward the Raven flying over the chalky cliffs. The brilliance of the sun escaping the cover of the horizon momentarily blinded her. She dropped her sword and spread her arms like a raven. The biting wind roared across the water as she beseeched the Raven, "Let me see my enemies."

She felt herself shoot like an arrow into a raven soaring overhead. A light flashed as she entered its mind. She felt sparks burned through her legs and into her spine and arms; her muscles contracted in synchrony with the raven's wings. Now she saw the world through raven eyes.

Catrin commanded the raven to fly beyond the cliffs. In the distance were several Roman warships equipped with oars and sails speeding toward a sparsely vegetated bay where heavily armed soldiers were disembarking. Waves crashed on the beach as Roman guards pulled on the collar chains of Cantiaci prisoners and waded to nearby ships. A gray-haired, hunched woman, whom Catrin recognized as one of her mother's attendants, stumbled and fell on the pebble beach. A Roman soldier slashed her throat with a dagger as if she were a sacrificial animal.

A chill ran down her spine as ghostly fog began blurring the coastline. Strong gusts pushed the raven down. Catrin raised her human arms and shifted her weight forward to lift the raven. Catching the breeze under its wings, the bird soared higher and flew back over the cliffs. At a stone wall on the hilltop, Marrock was near the cliff edge with a battalion of Roman soldiers.

Catrin ordered the raven to attack.

Pluck out his eyes!

Marrock's eyes widened in terror as the raven dove at him. But before the bird reached its target, Catrin felt cold metal shackle her wrists. Apprehensive that Marrock was freezing the raven's wings, she leapt out of its mind.

The next instant, she found Mor kneeling over her. "What happened?"

Head still spinning, Catrin stammered, "Mar . . . Marrock is with the Romans."

"Where?"

"On the hilltop overlooking the settlement of Drubis," Catrin answered. "There, they are loading captives on warships. We need to get back and tell Trystan."

Mor extended her hand. "Can you walk on your own?'

Catrin grasped her sister's wrist to stand. "Yes, I'm fine."

As Mor and Catrin approached Trystan at the bottom of the pathway, his eyes were ablaze. "I told you not to leave," he said sharply. "Roman scouts were sighted near our camp. You could have led them to our position."

Staring fixedly at Trystan, Mor said, "We left for a good purpose. Catrin called upon the Raven to find the Romans."

Trystan narrowed his eyes. "What did you see?"

"Roman warships have landed at the settlement of Dubris. They are taking prisoners aboard. Many of them are my father's warriors."

"How many Romans?"

"At least four hundred, if not more."

Trystan's jaw tensed. "We are badly outnumbered. Did you see Marrock's battle troops?"

"Marrock is with a Roman squadron at the fortress just above Dubris.

"Go back to the cave," Trystan ordered. "We are making arrangements for you to escape to Gaul."

Inside the cave, the sisters squatted by the fire and reached out to its warmth. The wind shifted and blew smoke at them. They both turned away, coughing. No matter how tightly Catrin wrapped the cloak around her, she could feel her cold muscles clamp tightly. Gazing at the cauldron boiling a stew of rabbit and dark grains, she recalled Marrock's terrified eyes as the raven swooped down on him. It was the same look Marrock had on that fateful day nearly seven years earlier when her father threw him on the ground and clenched him by the throat. The king should have killed Marrock on that day, but instead had shown his son mercy by banishing him.

Marrock's last words still resonated with Catrin. *I am the legitimate heir to the throne! Not your whore queen! Not your bastard daughters!*

Catrin felt her hate coiling like a snake in her body, ready to strike at Marrock—a family member turned enemy. She looked to Mor. "I'm not going to Gaul. I'm staying here to fight."

"So am I," Mor said. "Let us eat. This may be our last meal before battle."

Catrin handed some thick stew in a ceramic bowl to Mor. Catrin bit into a chunk of rabbit, but the meal did not slake her hunger as she thought about the upcoming battle against the Roman hoards and Marrock.

A man's voice blared into the cave. "The queen has returned with some warriors."

The sisters bolted to their feet and went outside to watch the fighters stagger into camp, some carrying blood-soaked bodies over their shoulders. As the battle-weary warriors shuffled past, Catrin could feel her stomach knotting as she searched for her mother.

Queen Rhiannon was behind the warriors, astride a thick-maned horse. Catrin ran to greet her mother but was suddenly swept into the stream of people surrounding the queen. Dried blood was streaked across her forehead and caked in her black hair.

Trystan stepped forward and greeted Rhiannon as *Caturiga*, warrior queen. The people huddled closer as the queen spoke. "Two days ago, your king and several of his warriors met death with honor in battle. They were welcomed as heroes in the Otherworld. King Amren died protecting his family, his people, and his homeland. Their bodies are still on the battlefield."

Wails echoed throughout the camp. Catrin could hardly breathe as she choked back her tears. She looked at Mor, whose face had paled.

The queen rode amongst her people as she spoke. "I, too, wailed and beat my chest in grief when I had to leave my dead husband behind. But we must now turn our sorrow into fury. As the Queen of the Cantiaci, I pledged my loyalty to the king when we forged an alliance between the Regni and Cantiaci kingdoms through our marriage. But today, the king's black-hearted son threatens to tear our kingdom asunder."

Cries of grief turned to outrage. Caught up in the whirlwind of tribal fury, Catrin shrieked, "Traitor! Scum!"

Rhiannon's glare burned into her loyal followers as she ignited their fervor with her words. "This dark prince wants to steal your kingdom by allying with a rival tribe and a foreign enemy. We are on the side of righteous vengeance to overcome our adversaries: the Romans who satisfy their greed by the sale of our flesh; the Catuvellauni who sate their appetites by stealing our lands; and the banished black prince who drinks our blood to quench his lust for power."

The queen paused and the warriors waited silently in anticipation of her words. Rhiannon's cry thundered through the camp. "Rain death upon the invaders who pillage our homeland! We must conquer or die!"

Battle chants echoed through the valley. In unison, the warriors shouted, "Conquer or die!"

When the queen finally met Catrin's eyes, she dismounted and weaved through the warriors to embrace her. "Oh, sweet Catrin, we thought you were dead!"

"I have resurrected as the Battle Raven," Catrin declared.

52

BATTLE RAVEN

Under the cover of night, Catrin and the Cantiaci warriors scattered over the hillside near the Roman encampment at Dubris. Morning mist rolled in from the ocean channel and crept over the coastline and hillside. Hidden in thick pines midway up the hill, Catrin and Mor wore leather chest protectors over their tunics; the other fighters donned chain metal shirts, breeches, and striped capes clasped about their shoulders. All the warriors were heavily armed with swords, spears, and shields displaying the animal emblems of their families: boar, horse, raven, stag, and hawk. Some rode horses. Most were on foot.

Catrin could hardly see Mor standing nearby, but she could hear the rhythmic footsteps of the Roman soldiers marching below. Rhiannon dismounted and walked over to Catrin. "Pray to the goddess of war. Tell me what she sees."

Closing her eyes, Catrin prayed to Bodua, asking for her help in the upcoming conflict.

Give my people courage. Make them fierce warriors. Send me the Battle Raven so I can see the enemy's weakness through its eyes.

Catrin heard screeches from above. Looking up, she found a raven and merged her thoughts with it. She commanded it to fly above the Roman formation in the valley so she could assess the conditions of the battlefield and see how the enemy soldiers were lining up. Swooping closer to the soldiers, she could hear the trumpets blare and see the soldiers' anxious stares as they began to march.

After disconnecting with the raven, Catrin told her mother, "I saw four columns of Roman soldiers behind a front wall of interconnecting shields. Horsemen are at the rear. I see fear in the enemies' eyes. Fog creates confusion. Bodua says charge now!"

Rhiannon raised her sword and galloped down the line of her followers. Roaring battle cries and pounding swords on their shields, the warriors worked themselves into frenzy. Her mother continued to gallop up and down the line.

As the Roman army marched up the hill, Rhiannon charged into the drizzling fog with her warriors, their war screams echoing over the valley. Blue-tattooed warriors sprinted down the hill as enemy spears and arrows whizzed through the air toward them. The mist swallowed the battling armies.

Catrin and Mor joined the next attack force led by Trystan on a chestnut stallion. Catrin's stomach knotted as she waited with spear in hand for the command to attack. She started to shake. Doubts assaulted her. She stroked the smooth surface of the Apollo amulet, which inexplicably soothed her. Taking several rapid breaths, she forged her fear into rage.

Trystan at last pointed his sword toward the left flank of the Roman infantrymen—the signal to strike. Catrin grasped her spear with both hands. Excitement rushed through her body as she ran alongside her companions into the fray. Reaching the Roman shields, Celtic fighters leapt over them and thrust their spears at the enemy soldiers. The wall of shields crumbled and soldiers fell back.

Catrin and Mor charged through the disintegrating enemy line and into the melee, where soldiers slashed blindly with their swords. Mor stabbed at a Roman's neck as Catrin thrust her spear into his chest. The soldier stared wide-eyed at Catrin as she forced the spear, using all her strength, through armor, muscle, and bone. His body jerked with a last breath.

Struggling to yank out her spear, Catrin saw all around her Romans thrusting their swords into Cantiaci warriors. After a Roman soldier slashed open the stomach of a nearby warrior, the odor of rotten eggs assaulted her nostrils as his intestines unraveled from a gaping wound. Her senses heightened and fight instincts took over.

She struck the face of another soldier with her spear. When he fell, she cracked his skull open with the spear tip, spilling spongy matter on the ground.

With her spear now embedded in the soldier's head, Catrin frantically drew her sword. All around her, fighters blurred as they battled away. Stepping on a headless body, she felt chills streak down her back. She wanted to escape, but the enemy kept coming at her.

She had no choice but to slash at every Roman near her and quickly lost count of those she killed or wounded.

The Roman soldiers fighting together as one unit behind their shields began to surround Catrin and her fellow fighters. She felt trapped. As the interlocking shields pushed against the frenzied warriors, the Romans used their short swords for the final kills. Blue-tattooed bodies covered with blood piled up on the ground.

Catrin weaved her way through the fallen bodies to escape, gagging from the stench of blood and excrement. A Roman shieldsman blocked her. She catapulted herself against his red shield, but he pushed her back. As she stumbled and fell, her shoulder struck a sharp rock. Pain shot through her chest.

Above her, a Roman suddenly raised his sword for the deathblow, but Trystan buried his sword in the soldier's neck. Blood splattered all over Catrin.

"Get out of here," Trystan yelled.

Catrin climbed to her feet. The Romans were now taking Britons as prisoners. Her only hope was to escape the enemy soldiers around her. A Cantiaci fighter screamed while three soldiers stabbed him in the back and chest. She felt paralyzed, disoriented in the fog. She thought she heard Mor scream, "Run," but couldn't find her sister in the onslaught.

To survive, Catrin had to escape the bloodbath.

She tried to jump over a body, but she stumbled, almost falling. She looked back, but still didn't see her sister. Ahead, she spotted a raven flying up a hill and deeper into the fog. She dashed in the same direction as the bird. Her legs felt as heavy as bronze. Her lungs burned.

Over and over again, she whispered to the beat of her footsteps, "Keep moving. Stay with the raven."

Catrin glanced over her shoulder. A Roman soldier was now chasing her. The iron on his chest armor flashed as he accelerated. Terrified, she thought her heart would burst as she ran faster. She stumbled over a rock, and the soldier grabbed her wrist, forcing the sword from her hand.

Fighting for her life, she kicked his knee and pounded her fist into his jaw. The blow hardly dazed him. He reached for her shoulder, but she jerked his hand backwards, pushing him to the ground while poking him in the eyes with her other hand.

A shield from another soldier rammed into her back, and she slammed on the ground. As the two Romans struggled to subdue her, she kicked, scratched, and jabbed at their eyes.

One of the Romans punched her in the jaw, shouting, "You bitch!"

The pain stabbed through Catrin's skull and her head buzzed.

A man's voice bellowed, "Quintus, hold her so I can cut her throat."

"No!" Catrin screamed.

The soldier called Quintus held her down with his knee. "I want her as a slave."

Catrin was determined not to be taken alive, but when she felt the sharp tip of a dagger at her throat, she gasped.

The soldier growled at Quintus, "That's how you control a lioness!"

Quintus pulled Catrin up, but she again punched his face. This time Quintus pressed his dagger to her throat, and she froze when she felt its cold edge.

"I swear the women fight more fiercely than the men," Quintus mumbled.

Out of the fog, the red-caped tribune Catrin recognized as Decimus rode up and ordered, "Let me see the captive."

Quintus pushed Catrin forward. She cringed as the commander closely examined her face. "She might be King Amren's daughter. Tear the tunic away from her shoulder and look for a brand."

Catrin felt the serrated dagger cut her back as Quintus ripped a jagged hole in her tunic. "She has the brand of a horse."

"It's the king's insignia. Take her to the fortress where Marrock is waiting. I will join you soon."

Decimus didn't seem to notice Catrin's alarm about facing Marrock as he turned his horse and disappeared into the drizzle.

Quintus held his dagger against her back as they climbed the hill. She felt her stomach clench as she approached the walled fortress atop the cliffs. She retched from the sight of decapitated bodies of warriors who had been sacrificed on stone altars.

Fearing she would meet their fate, Catrin fought fiercely against Quintus's restraints to get away, but he threw her against the stone wall, momentarily stunning her. Her head was yanked back by the hair so she could see her mother, who was restrained by two Romans. A shudder struck down her spine as Marrock, his wolf pack, and several archers approached the queen.

Red hair spiked angrily from Marrock's head. His amber eyes spewed hate as he grabbed Rhiannon's hair and spat into her face. "Whore! Behold your new king. It is my right to fuck you like my father did. I will not show you any mercy."

As his eyes shifted toward Catrin, his mouth dropped. "Dark gods below, you're still alive!" For a moment, he paused, but then his grimace contorted into an evil smile. He yelled in the queen's face. "I will now avenge the execution of my mother upon this imposter queen!"

Rhiannon did not cringe or show fear. Rather, she addressed her captors in the Roman tongue: "Behold Amren's treacherous son. He tricked Rome into helping him overthrow his honorable father. You shall now bear witness to the vile deeds of this demon you proclaim as king."

Two Romans threw Rhiannon against the jagged rocks of the fortress. An overwhelming feeling of helplessness hit Catrin like a brick as she heard her mother cry out. The soldiers ruthlessly slammed the statuesque queen like a carcass against the wall. Another burley Roman tried to subdue her legs, but she kicked and knocked him to the ground.

Everything seemed in slow motion as Catrin watched Marrock approach the queen with his mouth foaming like a rabid dog. His eyes ablaze, he punched Rhiannon in the temple with so much force, her head slammed against the stone wall with a sickening, bone-cracking noise. She collapsed on the ground and her body began convulsing.

The words, "Mother! Mother!" caught in Catrin's throat, which was constricted with panic.

Marrock ordered the two soldiers, "Hold her tight," as he dropped his breeches. Even in her worst nightmare, Catrin could not have imagined the abomination of what Marrock did next.

He cut the straps of the queen's leather armor and pulled it off. To Catrin's horror, he tore the burgundy tunic apart with his bare hands, revealing her naked breasts. As she lay limp on the ground, he pawed at her body like a ravenous wolf over its fallen prey, turning her face down.

Catrin clamped her eyelids shut, unable to watch the vile deed. A chill of dread crawled all over her as she heard her mother groan, then scream. Grunts of a rutting wolf echoed in Catrin's ears, and she slit her eyelids open to see her mother's body violently jerking from the motion of Marrock thrusting against her.

Rage filled every pore of Catrin's body. The Raven shrieked in her mind. An instant later, a light flashed in her mind, and she visualized herself manipulating Marrock's life-thread on the Wall of Lives.

Hundreds of black-feathered warriors led by the Raven streamed out of the Otherworld's dark portal into a whirling tornado above the white cliffs, its apex directed at Marrock. He released the queen and bellowed to the archers, "Shoot the ravens down."

The arrows shot into the twisting cloud of shrieking ravens. Several of them dropped, bounced off the sheer cliff wall, and plunged into the crashing waves below.

Before the remaining ravens could reach Marrock in their aerial assault, he severed Rhiannon's head in one quick stroke. He picked the queen's head up by the hair to show Catrin and the Roman soldiers.

Catrin gagged and fell to her knees. She wanted to wail, but her sorrow turned to rage again when she saw Marrock tie her mother's head to the neck of a horse. He covered his face with one of his arms to ward off the attacking ravens as he strode toward Catrin with a longsword in his hand. She dug into the depths of her courage to confront her half-brother.

As Quintus still restrained Catrin, Marrock lifted her chin with his blood-stained hand and forced her to look into his face. Her eyes burned vengeance at Marrock as he held the blade against her neck. Her rage uncoiled like a serpent and she hissed. "I will peck out your eyes."

A dark essence took hold of Catrin and she bellowed, "Battle Raven, conquer or die!"

Fast-moving shadows coalesced into a dark cloud and rained down as demented demons on Marrock. He yelled, "Loose," to his archers, who then released their arrows. A volley shot into the air and pierced the ravens, several of them dropping like obsidian stones. Another volley of arrows immediately released and more ravens plunged.

This time, Catrin felt a sharp pain in her chest as if she herself had been shot. She looked down in panic for the wound, but nothing was there. Her heart stopped as if she had been pierced by an arrow tip.

She gasped for air and was swept into darkness.

53

FATHER'S LOVE

Awakened by a man's commanding voice, Catrin found herself lying in a puddle of water near the fortress wall. Her head felt as though a spike had been pounded through it. She touched her swollen forehead and felt sticky blood on her fingers. Disoriented, she tried to remember what had happened. Her last memories were of ravens flying overhead and Marrock raising his sword. She wiggled her limbs to make sure she was unharmed. Looking up, she saw clouds streaming white across the sun. To her side was a blurry image of a man leaning over her.

The man she recognized as Decimus stood and barked, "What is the butchery here?"

"The sacrifices were performed by Marrock," a soldier replied.

"Where is Marrock now?"

"He's gone."

"I can see that," said Decimus. "Where did he go?"

"I don't know," the soldier quavered. "Ravens attacked him and he rode off."

"Ravens?"

"Yes sir."

Shaking from sudden chills, Catrin watched the red-caped tribune inspect the headless corpses, including her mother's. His mouth scrunched into a scowl. "What happened to their heads?"

"Marrock threw most of them over the cliff, but he tied the queen's head to his horse's saddle," the soldier said.

The crescent scar bulged on the commander's face as he spat. "And we allied with this butcher."

A sense of shame and guilt washed over Catrin. She had failed to stop Marrock. All of her family was dead. And now she was at the mercy of the Romans.

"Quintus, pull the captive up," Decimus ordered.

A thickset soldier with a bulbous nose pulled Catrin from the ground to face Decimus. Still shivering from chills, Catrin turned her head away from his icy stare.

"I remember your ferocity on the battlefield," Decimus said, pressing his fingers on a tender spot on her forehead. "A nasty gash. Did Marrock do this?"

Catrin noticed the shifting color of the tribune's eyes from green to amber brown in the changing light of the clouds streaming overhead.

"Do you understand what I am saying?" he asked.

She nodded.

He smirked. "Don't worry. I won't give you back to Marrock."

At first, Catrin sighed in relief, but her hackles rose as Decimus stroked her face with his callused hand and then fondled her breast. "Roman noblemen would take pleasure in you."

Catrin tried to squirm away from his hand groping between her legs. He lewdly said, "What a waste to kill a girl like you—ripe for the plucking. What's your name?"

Catrin's lips quivered.

Decimus clenched her by the chin. "Answer me!"

She barely whispered her name.

Decimus's lips twisted into a cruel smile. "Oh yes, Catrin, I know who you are. You are the king's sorceress daughter. You are to be sold as a whore into a brothel." He shoved her at Quintus and ordered, "Bind her."

Quintus snickered as he yanked her toward the fortress wall.

The thought of being violated jolted Catrin. She had lost everything— her family, her homeland, and Marcellus. All she had left to fight for was her dignity.

Spotting a raven flying above, she merged with its essence and ordered it to attack. The raven swooped down with outstretched talons that clawed at Quintus's head, diverting his attention. Seizing the opportunity, she retrieved the cursed dagger from her belt and sliced his thigh with it. She kicked at his wounded leg and he collapsed to the ground.

Two other soldiers rushed at Catrin, but the raven swooped at them. As the soldiers raised their arms to protect their faces, she fled past them and sidestepped the blow of another soldier. She leapt over a low stone wall and her legs felt like they were flying as she sprinted to the precipice.

"You idiots! Trap that rabbit before she escapes," Decimus roared.

Catrin sprinted at full speed, pumping her arms back and forth. Her heart hammered against her chest in anticipation that she would throw herself off the white cliff. Her legs felt aflame as she dashed closer and closer to the precipice. Grated breaths parched her throat. She focused on the gray waves crashing against the sheer white cliffs.

Freedom!

Then to her shock, a riderless warhorse passed and she suddenly found herself in her father's embrace, halting her. His warm essence radiated into her and tears filled her eyes when he told her that he loved her.

I never meant to betray you, she silently communed.

"I know that. But now, you must survive." Amren released her and instructed, "Lift the dagger with the curse toward the heavens."

Catrin unsheathed the dagger from her belt and pointed it toward the cloudy sky. The blade glinted as the sun broke through the dark clouds.

"Thrust the blade into the serpent's stone I create," Amren said.

What appeared next was not a vision.

The hilt in Catrin's hand grew hotter as the gray steel surface of the blade turned to a crimson color. Her father's spirit alighted like gold dust on the curved blade and melted into the etching, obliterating the curse. A large numbers of serpents massed together and their saliva hardened to form a stone that jutted from the chalky-white ground. Catrin, grasping the hilt with both hands, slid the blade into the hard stone. She imagined herself dissolving into the foam of the crashing waves below and felt the sun's warmth on her skin as she drifted away on the ocean currents.

The misty figures of her parents and Vala then floated over the precipice, but they faded when Roman soldiers surrounded her.

"Trap her!" one soldier yelled.

"Move over there!" another man's voice shouted.

"We won't harm you," the tribune said.

A burly infantryman tackled her and pounded her face on the ground. The bitter taste of chalk mixed with blood filled her mouth. Her head was yanked back by the hair and the sharp edge of a gladius pressed against her throat.

"You will regret running from us, bitch!"

Sandaled soldier boots scuffled around her. The blade whisked away from her neck as Decimus said with disdain, "You dishonor yourself with your stupidity."

The burley soldier yanked Catrin up to her feet to face Decimus. The tribune said, raising his voice, "How can you call yourselves Romans after this girl showed more fighting instincts than all of you put together? She had enough wits to disable all of you. Never will this happen again. Quintus, you will be lashed for your ineptitude."

Decimus suddenly widened his eyes at a raven landing on the serpent's stone. He muttered, "This is a bad omen."

The burley soldier gripped Catrin's wrist and forced her arm back until her shoulder was ready to snap. He pressed his forearm against her throat, making her gasp for air. "Do you want me to kill the witch?"

Decimus lifted the leather strap around Catrin's neck to reveal the Apollo amulet. "No, wait. Why is this around your neck?"

Catrin didn't answer.

Decimus drew her chin to his leathery face. The stench of his breath hovered over her like rotting meat. "Is the raven on the stone a messenger from Apollo?"

Catrin squirmed as Decimus grabbed her by the hair and his cracked lips touched her ear as he whispered, "If you order that raven to attack, I'll cut you into pieces for it to eat. Do you want to live?"

"Yes," she rasped.

"Then you'll show me how you summon Apollo's powers."

Catrin lightly nodded, not sure what the tribune expected of her.

Decimus pulled away and turned to his soldiers. "That raven is a warning from Apollo. If we execute her, the Fates will exact vengeance. This girl is my prisoner. Do not lay a hand on her." He motioned to a guard. "You there, take her to my ship. And don't let her escape!"

Catrin was overcome with emotion with the strange twist in fate that the Apollo amulet had protected her from certain death. As the guard shackled her wrists, she felt Marcellus's love and knew he was alive. She wept in relief that she no longer had to choose between her father and Marcellus. They were both with her now and had given her hope to survive the storm ahead.

The guard dragged Catrin, chained like an animal, down the hill toward the beach. With the devastating loss of her family, status, and identity, she looked forlornly at the familiar white cliffs before she was yanked into the water. Her teeth clattered as she waited to be stowed aboard the ship. Once on board, a guard ordered her down the stairs into the hull. Moans of wounded men echoed throughout the ship.

Entering the damp belly of the ship, she gagged from the stench of vomit on the wooden floor. A soldier grabbed her arm and yanked her to an isolated corner where he chained her ankles to a wall. Her stomach cramped and she vomited blood onto the floor. The scourge of her wounds, both physical and mental, and the use of the powers of the Ancient Druids finally racked her with agonizing pain. She burned with fever and her body went limp, all her strength washed away.

She cried out to her father in anguish.

Hovering between life and death, Catrin saw her spirit levitate above her body. She felt a warm light pulling her into a tunnel where she could see the shadow of a man. When he turned, she recognized her father with the dagger in his hand.

"Daughter, do not be afraid," he reassured her. "You must now begin a difficult journey into the Roman world."

"Father, please don't leave me!"

The Raven landed on Amren's shoulder. "You must be forged into a battle-hardened warrior on the empire's anvil before you can return home. It is only then, you can pull the dagger out of the stone and embrace my curse as your destiny. You will then access the full powers of the Ancient Druids to overcome Marrock and to reclaim my throne."

The king's next words thundered like a god's across the night sky. "Behold the Raven, the messenger of Apollo! Behold the sun god, your protector."

LIST OF CHARACTERS
(ALPHABETICAL ORDER)

Main Celtic Characters

Adminius—Pro-Roman Catuvellauni Prince; eldest son of Cunobelin

Agrona—Amren's spiritual advisor and Druidess; possessed by Rhan

Amren—King of the Cantiaci; biological father of Catrin and Marrock

Ariene— Catuvellauni Druidess; Marrock's wife and Cunobelin's daughter

Catrin—Cantiaci Princess; Celtic spiritual warrior; daughter of Amren and Rhiannon

Ferrex—Cantiaci warrior known as *The Lion;* Catrin's mentor and loyal friend

Marrock—Druid and wolf shapeshifter, also known as Blood Wolf; Catrin's half-brother; son of Rhan and Amren; Cunobelin's son-in-law through marriage with Ariene

Myrddin—Ancient Druid, also known as the wild Druid and wandering Druid

Rhan—Former Cantiaci Queen and powerful Druidess executed by Amren; possessed Agrona as child.

Rhiannon—Current Queen of the Cantiaci, formerly from the Regni Tribe; Mother of Vala, Mor, and Catrin

The Raven—Spiritual guide Catrin can access through a physical raven; powerful warrior queen and Druidess foretold in Rhan's curse

Trystan—Amren's second-in-command; Rhiannon's former lover and father of Vala and Mor

Minor Celtic Characters

Alfrid—Farmer/Neighbor of Marrock and Ariene

Arthfael—Warrior serving Marrock

Belinus—Amren's guard tagged as the *sun-tattooed warrior*; Mor's husband

Bladud—Father of Ferrex

Caratacus—Anti-Roman Catuvellauni Prince; son of Cunobelin

Cunobelin—King of the Catuvellauni; Father of Adminius, Caratacus, and Togodumnus

Cynwrig—Cantiaci warrior known as the *Red Executioner*

Mor—Catrin's middle bastard sister; daughter of Rhiannon and Trystan

Togodumnus—Anti-Roman Catuvellauni Prince; Son of Cunobelin

Vala—Catrin's eldest bastard sister; daughter of Rhiannon and Trystan

Roman Main Characters

Cato—Roman merchant

Decimus Flavius—Military tribune; protector of Lucius Antonius

Lucius Antonius—Roman politician, father of Marcellus; banished son of Iullus Antonius and Claudia Marcella; grandson of Mark Antony

Marcellus Antonius—Catrin's Roman lover; great-grandson of Mark Antony, grandson of Iullus Antonius; son of Lucius Antonius

Priscus Dius—Centurion; former gladiator

Mentioned Roman Characters

Augustus—First Roman Emperor from 27 BC until 14 AD; defeated Mark Antony in Battle of Actium in 31 BC

Claudia Marcella—Wife of Iullus Antonius; mother of Lucius Antonius; daughter of Octavia with first husband Gaius Claudius Marcellus

Cleopatra—Egyptian Queen; Julius Caesar's mistress; Mark Antony's wife **Drusilla**—Wife of Lucius Antonius; mother of Marcellus Antonius

Gaius Druses—Nobleman and Mentor to Lucius Antonius; Father of Drusilla

Eliana—Marcellus's older Roman lover

Iullus Antonius—Roman Consul, senator, and poet; second son of Mark

Antony and his third wife Fulvia; executed for adultery with Julia, daughter of Augustus

Julia—Augustus's only daughter; wife of Tiberius; banished for adulterous affair with Iullus Antonius in 2 BC

Marcus Licinius Crassus Frugi: Praetor, Consul, and senator; political ally of Lucius Antonius

Mark Antony—Roman consul, triumvir, and general; Cleopatra's lover and husband

Octavia—Third wife of Mark Antony; sister of Augustus

Ovid— Roman poet during the reign of Augustus

Tiberius—Roman Emperor from 14 AD to 37 AD, succeeding the first emperor, Augustus

Mythological Deity

Apollo—Roman god of the sun, healing, music, truth, and divination

Bodua—Celtic Goddess of Victory

Dea Matres—Divine Mother Goddess

Mother Goddess—Goddess of nature, motherhood, fertility, creation, and destruction

Jupiter—Supreme god in the Roman pantheon of gods

Raven—Celtic goddesses of war are linked with ravens, which are associated with death and war; messenger of the Roman god Apollo

Taranis—Celtic god of thunder

Vulcan—Roman god of fire, metalworking, and forging

ACKNOWLEDGEMENTS

I am indebted to many people who supported me on my adventure of writing Book 2: *Dagger's Destiny* in the *Curse of Clansmen and Kings* series. A special thank you is extended to my writing coach, Doug Kurtz, for his invaluable advice on the plot, character arcs, and theme of balancing duty with love. I am grateful to Kate Anderson, Tom Goodfellow, and Ryanne Buck for their insightful suggestions and thought-provoking questions that inspired me to create some additional twists in the storyline. My copy editor, Jessica Knauss, made some great suggestions for revisions and did a thorough job of line editing.

I also greatly appreciate the advice from my husband, Tom, for fine-tuning some of the passages as I read the book aloud to him. And finally, I'd like to acknowledge Kathy Meis and her team at Bublish, Inc. for their invaluable input on the overall vision of the *Curse of Clansmen and Kings* series which is reflected in the book cover.

AUTHOR'S NOTE

The *Curse of Clansmen and Kings* series is a blend of historical fiction and mythology of southeast Celtic tribes in Britannia before the invasion of the Roman Emperor Claudius in 43 AD. The biggest challenge in researching this project is the ancient Celts left almost no written records. Historical events had to be supplanted by Greek and Roman historians and medieval writers who spun Celtic mythology into their Christian beliefs. Archaeological findings from this time period also help fill in some of the gaps.

The political background used in this series is based on my research of southeast Celtic tribes in Britain which evolved differently than those in Wales, Scotland, and Ireland. After Julius Caesar's military expeditions to southeast Britannia in 55–54 BC, there was strong Roman influence over politics and trade in the area. Rome demanded hostages from this region to ensure treaty agreements were met. Hostages were frequently young males, although taking females was not unheard of, and they came from royal families. They were allowed to move freely in public places with minimal security measures to prevent their escape. The Roman patrician watching over them could serve as patron, father, and teacher. Many of the first century British rulers were educated in Rome and adopted the Roman taste for luxury goods. To support their extravagant lifestyles, pro-Roman kings warred with other tribal territories to supply the Roman Empire with slaves. Powerful Celtic kings expanded their territories and minted coins.

Although there is no written account of any Roman expeditionary forces sent to Britain before Claudius's invasion in 43 AD, there are recorded incidents of British kings pleading for Rome's help to intervene on their behalf. Britannia was considered a client state where British kings and queens paid tribute to Rome, but they ruled independently over their kingdoms, similar to Cleopatra's reign in Egypt. Archaeological evidence now supports the Claudius's invasion was nothing more than a peace-keeping mission to halt the expansion of anti-Roman factions led by Cunobelin's sons, Caratacus and Togodumnus. There may have already been a Roman military presence that protected the areas of Britannia vital to trading with the empire. The tribal names in this novel are based on Ptolemy's map of Celtic kingdoms generated in 150 AD.

The Celtic characters in this novel are fictional except for Cunobelin, referred to as the King of Britannia by the Romans, and his sons— Adminius and Caratacus. Several of the Celtic characters in the series could speak Latin because of their formal training in Rome or through their interactions with Roman merchants. Although the Celtic society was becoming more paternalistic, women were still held in high regard and could rule. The most famous warrior queen was Boudica, who united the Britons in 61 BC and almost expelled the Romans. She was also known as a powerful Druidess who Romans claimed sacrificed some of her victims to the war goddess Andaste.

The Roman characters are fictional except for Lucius Antonius, the son of Iullus Antonius and grandson of Marcus Antonius (Mark Antony). Marcus Licinius Crassus Frugi, who is briefly mentioned in this book, came into favor with Claudius and may have been involved in diplomatic negotiations with British rulers during the Roman invasion in 43 AD. Very little is known about Lucius Antonius except that he was banished in 2 BC to Gaul after his father, Iullus Antonius, was accused of treason and forced to fall on his sword. It is unclear whether Lucius had any children, but it is coincidental that another famous Roman general, Marcus Antonius Primus, was born in Gaul about 30 AD.

The fantastical elements in this novel are based on mystical powers of heroes and heroines from the Celtic legends of Ireland and Wales. Most interestingly, ancient historians and Julius Caesar wrote that Celts believed in the reincarnation of the soul. This philosophy is consistent with the Greek philosopher, Pythagoras, in 500 BC. I have freely expanded on the concept of the soul as a way to explain Catrin's mystical powers. There are over three hundred documented names of Celtics gods and goddess, but only a few of the more popular names referred to by the Romans are presented in this story. Also of note, several Celtic healing sites are named after Apollo, probably a consequence of the blending of religious beliefs.

The inaugural rite of the king described in this book is based on Celtic mythology and traditions. The term *sovereignty goddess* denotes a goddess who can confer sovereignty upon a king by marrying or having sex with him. A sacred marriage was considered the ritual union of the goddess of the land with the mortal king. The key element of the sacred marriage—and kingship—was the consummation between the king and the goddess of the territory he was to rule over. The goddess only enters this marriage if the king is suitable, and even after marriage, she can reject a weak ruler in favor of a man who is better suited. One of the best known figures in Irish mythology is the queen of Connacht, Medb, from the Ulster Cycle. A man became king of Connacht only by participating in a ritual drunkenness that opens him up to an ecstatic state to contact with the divine.

Interestingly, there is also evidence that the Celts ritually sacrificed their kings to the gods if the times turned bad under their reign. The king had great power but also great responsibility to ensure the prosperity of his people. Through his marriage to the goddess of the land, he was meant to guarantee her benevolence. He had to ensure the land was productive. If the weather turned bad, or there was plague, cattle disease or losses in war, he was held personally responsible. By using a range of methods to kill the victim, the ancient Irish sacrificed to the goddess in all her forms. This manner of the horrible death is unique to the ritual killing of Celtic kings.

It should be noted the Raven is capitalized when it represents a spiritual guide that Catrin can access through an actual physical raven. Also the Raven predicted in Rhan's curse is capitalized. *Cathos* means detestation or hatred in the ancient Celtic language.

ABOUT THE AUTHOR

Award-winning author, Linnea Tanner weaves Celtic tales of love, magic, adventure, betrayal and intrigue into historical fiction set in Ancient Rome and Britannia. Since childhood, she has passionately read about ancient civilizations and mythology which held women in higher esteem. Of particular interest are the enigmatic Celts who were reputed as fierce warriors and mystical Druids.

Depending on the time of day and season of the year, you will find her exploring and researching ancient and medieval history, mythology and archaeology to support her writing. As the author of the *Curse of Clansmen and Kings* series, she has extensively researched and traveled to sites described within each book.

A native of Colorado, Linnea attended the University of Colorado and earned both her bachelor's and master's degrees in chemistry. She lives in Windsor with her husband and has two children and six grandchildren.

AMULET'S RAPTURE
BOOK 3 OF CURSE OF CLANSMEN AND KINGS SERIES

Follow Catrin and Marcellus in their Epic Celtic Tale of Forbidden Love, Magical Adventure, and Political Intrigue in Ancient Rome and Britannia. Don't miss the next installment of the **CURSE OF CLANSMEN AND KINGS** series coming soon.

Linnea Tanner's
AMULET'S RAPTURE
Read next page for a preview . . .

The Celtic warrior princess, Catrin, is in the worst of circumstances. After witnessing the slaughter of her family in battle, she is lucky to be alive, but is enslaved and disguised as a boy in the Roman Legion. Marcellus—the great-grandson of Mark Antony—is haunted by the loss of his memory after being wounded in Britannia and drugged by a dark Druidess. When Marcellus reunites with Catrin in Gaul, he is shocked to discover the dark secret that she is the woman he married in Britannia. He again becomes enraptured with Catrin and is her ally and lover as she struggles to survive the brutality of her Roman master. Though they believe they are destined to be with each other, they encounter resistance to their love at every turn. They will have to sacrifice almost everything to be together. But can Catrin balance her strength and destiny to retake her kingdom as a warrior queen with her role as the lover of a man who considers her subservient?

To keep up-to-date with the latest news on the upcoming books in the *Apollo's Raven* epic series please visit and sign up for the FREE e-Bulletin:

http://www.linneatanner.com

PROLOGUE

Everything I am has disappeared and what could have been will never be. My father's curse has transformed into my destiny as the Battle Raven. I hunger for vengeance and feast on the carrion of battle, turmoil, and war. My heart fills with rage. Will I ever again taste the sweet nectar of love as memories of my true self and identity fade away?

— Catrin in Roman slave ship

The impenetrable white cliffs in a foreign land summon me to return. I left my soul and heart on the emerald hilltops as memories sweep away from its shores in a crashing wave and plunge into the ocean depths.

— Marcellus, sailing away from Britannia

I

RAVEN FLEDGLING

Early Spring, 25AD, Northern Gaul

Catrin, a slave in the Roman Legion, scooped the raven fledging that had fallen out of the oak into her hands. She hid behind the tree so the soldiers guarding her would not see her with it. She could feel the bird's rapid heartbeats through its feathery breast. Stroking the raven's head, she whispered, "You have nothing to fear. I have a raven spirit."

The blue-eyed raven chick relaxed and quietly peered at Catrin as she checked for any injuries it might have sustained. Finding none, she mulled over whether to take it to the Roman encampment and watch over it. Though the raven's wings displayed short-tipped feathers for flight, it moved awkwardly and had fluffy feathers on its head—signs it might have been too young to leave the nest. Most fledglings, she knew, could hide from predators until they were strong enough to fly, but they still depended on their parents to feed them.

Unfortunately, one of her cruel guards had just killed the raven's parents.

Tears swelled in Catrin's eyes as she sensed the baby raven's distress. This was the same anguish she had felt after being torn from her homeland of Britannia, where her parents had been brutally slain. Now enslaved in northern Gaul, she had lost her identity as a Cantiaci princess. She was as powerless as the fledgling, but she held out hope. Her dead father showed her in a dream that a young raven would teach her how to gain more powers from the Ancient Druids.

"Marius, are you done?" a soldier's voice called out.

Catrin winced from the sound of the Roman name that her master, Tribune Decimus Flavius, had given her. "Give me a few moments to gather more herbs for the medicus."

"Don't take too long. We need to get back."

Looking down at the raven chick again, she felt light-headed from the effects of a head wound inflicted in a battle almost six months ago in mid-autumn. She was bald like a newly-hatched bird, her thick gold-blonde hair shaven off to ward off infection and lice.

The raven nestled in the palms of her hands and opened its beak wide, shrieking for a meal. She found a caterpillar and stuffed it into the chick's throat. The meal did not seem to assuage its hunger, though. The fledgling opened its beak wide again and squawked, expecting another tasty morsel. She snatched a butterfly alighting on a violet blossom and stuffed it into the raven's red-throated mouth. It seemed at first surprised by the texture of its meal, but then heartily gulped it down.

Catrin stroked the raven, sensing a mystical force emanating from its soft plumage, as her father had promised. A charge burned into her skin, and a bright light flashed in her mind. Her thoughts then connected with her spiritual guide, the Raven, who could take her to other realms in her mind. She envisioned hurtling through a dark tunnel to the Wall of Lives—a multi-colored archway that transitioned from the mortal world to the Otherworld. The life thread of every mortal weaving in and out of the wall's fluid tapestry determined a person's fate. There, she would search for the thread of her Roman husband, Marcellus, to connect with him through her thoughts. Even though his family would never accept their secret marriage, he might help her escape enslavement.

Just before she burst through the portal into the Otherworld, she somersaulted up to the Wall of Lives where Past, Present, and Future merged into one time. She looked for the crimp in Marcellus's vibrant red life thread at the Present to commune with him. Images of him strolling with another young nobleman flashed on the thread. They were both in the midst of white-stone structures towering around them. A throng of people of all skin tones and manner of dress milled around them. Marcellus's violet-blue eyes appeared lifeless, unlike the mischievous glint she remembered when they were last together in the fall. To connect with his essence, she lightly touched his life thread, careful not to displace it and inadvertently change his future. The strand felt cold to the touch. She recalled her vision that his memory of her had been erased after the Dark Druidess forced the drink of oblivion down his throat. How could she connect with him if he had no memory of her on which to anchor?

A man's voice shouting, "Marius," roused Catrin out of the Raven's mind. The sudden switch from the Wall of Lives to the mortal world at first disoriented her. She struggled to maintain balance on her feet as she found herself in the forest again. The Roman guard, Gallus, was within inches of her face, staring into her eyes.

"Why didn't you answer when I called for you?" he demanded.

"I was in another world" she replied. "My mind sometimes wanders ever since I hurt my head."

"You know the commander will have my head if you escape. I've been too lenient, allowing you to gather herbs without shackles."

The anger in Gallus's voice disquieted Catrin. He was the only Roman soldier who had treated her kindly, watching over her like a brother. Most of the other soldiers were cruel, disgruntled their commander, Tribune Decimus Flavius, ordered the medicus to treat her life-threatening wounds with the same care as for any Roman. It still puzzled her why Decimus had spared her and taken such valiant efforts to save her life.

She lowered her eyes. "Forgive me. It won't happen again."

The raven's sudden squawking diverted Gallus's gaze to her hands. "Is that a bird?"

Catrin opened her hands to reveal the raven fledging that immediately opened its beak wide for another meal. "I saw it fall from its nest and found it hiding under a bush. Its parents are dead . . . so I thought I could keep it."

"Throw it away!" Gallus barked. "The men will think it is a bad omen."

Another soldier whom Catrin recognized as Quintus approached them. He was a stout spearman with a hawkish nose and a penchant for prying in other people's affairs.

"What do you got in your hands, Eunuch?" he demanded.

"I'm a boy," Catrin said emphatically, wary of what the vile soldier might do if he ever discovered she was a young woman. "I am called Marius."

"You're a eunuch slave with nothing between your legs," Quintus retorted. "I don't care if Decimus keeps you around as his pet. Answer my question. What do you have in your hands?"

"A baby raven I found for the medicus to use in his healing rituals," Catrin said, holding the fledging tighter.

Quintus cocked an eyebrow. "A raven?"

"The medicus uses ravens to cast out evil spirits of sick men when everyone is asleep," Catrin said, hoping the explanation would put a stop to the infantryman's advances.

Quintus regarded Catrin for a moment, then gave a twisted smirk. "Is that so? Drop your braccae. I want to see what is between your legs."

Protectively clutching the raven with one hand, Catrin shoved Quintus in the chest with the other. "Decimus has given strict orders that no soldier is to lay a hand on me."

"Brash words from a slave!" Quintus lashed. "I want to see what attracts Decimus to you."

"Leave him alone," Gallus barked, gripping Quintus's arm. "Decimus told me this slave can cast evil spells. Decimus takes Marius to Apollo's temple so he can speak with the sun god."

"What? This eunuch?" Quintus said, his anger turning on Gallus. "I want to see this magic you speak of."

"If you insist," Catrin said, fearing she might be raped.

Gallus gawked at Catrin. "Are you sure about this?"

"I'm sure." Catrin said, stretching out her hand to reveal the raven to Quintus. "Touch the bird."

Quintus jerked his head back. "What for?"

"So you can see my magic. Are you afraid of a little raven?" Catrin asked.

"No! I'll snap its head off!" Quintus said, reaching for the fledging, but sparks shot from the bird's beak into his hand.

"Dark gods below!" he screamed in pain.

"The raven curses your man parts to shrivel," Catrin said, "unless you leave me alone!"

Gallus shoved Quintus in the chest. "You heard Marius. Leave him alone or you'll also feel my wrath. We need to get back."

"I'll tell Decimus that you left Marias unshackled."

Gallus pressed up to Quintus. "If you do, we'll have words."

Quintus backed down and stomped away.

Relieved, Catrin put the baby raven on an upper branch of a tree with the hope it would not be eaten by a predator, but could survive on its own as she had been forced to do.

2

ROMAN WORLD

That night, in the infirmary, where Catrin had been assigned to sleep and to assist the medicus, she plunged into the dark abyss of a recurring nightmare. She again relived the horrific moment when her half-brother, Marrock, held his blade against her neck. With shivers shooting through her body, she escaped the deathblow by transforming herself into a raven.

Rough hands then abruptly lifted her shoulders and jolted her awake. She gasped for air like a newly born baby. The room reeked of mold. Her head felt as though it had been hammered by a nail as the timbered walls whirled around her. A white-haired man as wide as a sapling came into focus. He touched her tender forehead.

"Oww!" she yelped.

"You need to get up," the medicus said in Greek, helping her to sit on the edge of the cot. "Your master wants to see you."

"Tribune Decimus Flavius?"

The medicus nodded and handed her a curved strigil and oil. "Clean with these. Dress in fresh clothes…over there on the table."

Dizzy, Catrin struggled to maintain her balance as she removed her tunic. Tears welled in her eyes as she touched her fuzzy head, suddenly morose her hair, which had hung over her shoulders, was gone. The medicus was the only person, except for Decimus, who knew she was a woman. She rubbed oil on her skin as the Medicus prepared some medicinal ointments. She fumbled to dress into the oversized garments—red tunic, trousers, and cape. No matter how tightly she buckled her belt, the itchy trousers slipped down her hips. After she dressed, the medicus signaled for a guard.

As she followed the stocky soldier outside, he warned, "Keep your mouth shut unless the tribune orders you to speak."

The damp air pricked Catrin's face, and she snuggled into her woolen cape. Walking alongside the guard, she studied the spiked wooden wall surrounding the encampment. Heavily armed sentries posted at the four towers made escape almost impossible. In the middle of the camp, soldiers huddled around fires, where they gnawed on gristly ribs or scooped porridge from bronze cups with their hands to eat.

As she approached the camp's center, she noticed the fledging raven peering down at Decimus from atop some wooden barracks. The sight of the young raven encouraged her that it was indeed the guide and protector sent by her dead father. Even though she could feel its essence reaching out to her, she hesitated to project herself into its mind. The bird gawked at her for several moments before shifting its eyes toward Decimus and unexpectedly croaking in a man's voice, "Get in line!"

Decimus, whom Catrin knew to be a highly superstitious man, waved his arms at the raven and shouted, "Get out of here, you evil spirit!"

The raven calmly preened its feathers. With a red face, the commander turned to a soldier. "Get rid of that cursed bird now."

The soldier threw a rock at the bird but missed its target. Catrin inwardly chuckled, and the raven mimicked a woman's laugh. She smiled, watching Decimus jump.

"Did you order that raven to do that?" he shouted at her.

She nervously shook her head.

"Tell that damn bird to go away!"

Before Catrin could speak, the young raven unexpectedly swooped down at Decimus.

"Damn you, black demon!" he shouted and shook his fist in rage.

After the raven flew away, Decimus pushed Catrin forward and shoved her through the entryway of his headquarters onto the floor. Trembling, she staggered to her feet and looked around the musky room, sparsely furnished with a crudely made wooden table, a bench, and some chairs. In an adjoining room was an ebony chest and a cot covered with a blanket.

Catrin stared at the crescent scar on Decimus' face as he stepped over to her and ordered, "Remove your cloak."

She unwound her cloak and looked humbly down.

"Not nearly as striking as when I first captured you." Decimus remarked, raising her chin and forcing her to look into his close-set, hazel eyes which reminded her of a wolf's. "The medicus tells me you speak and read both Latin and Greek. How did you learn these tongues?"

Catrin shrugged.

Decimus squeezed her jaw with his fingers. "Did your father teach you?"

"My father often talked to me in the Roman tongue, but I was schooled by someone else."

"By a priest of Apollo?"

Catrin looked at Decimus with puzzlement. He released her and motioned for her to sit across the table from him.

"Tell me about Marrock?" he began questioning.

"Why do you need to know?" Catrin asked, bitterness burning inside that he had mercilessly killed her parents and sister.

"Rome considers your brother as its client king."

"Marrock is my half-brother," Catrin hissed. "We have the same father but different mothers."

Leaning forward, Decimus narrowed his eyes at her. "Why did Marrock kill your parents, but not you?"

Catrin wilted under the tribune's burning stare. "I don't know."

"Is he afraid of your powers?"

"Is that what you think?" Catrin blurted.

"Why did you have the amulet of Apollo around your neck when we captured you? This is a Roman god."

Catrin did not reply, wondering if the tribune knew Marcellus had given her the amulet as a symbol of his love. She sensed the tribune's underlying fear of her as he shot off his next questions in rapid succession.

"Did Apollo send that raven to curse me? Did a Roman priest train you to be a warrior priestess?"

Catrin silently hardened her stare at the tribune to mask her angst.

Decimus slammed the table with his fist and shouted, "Answer me, you defiant wench!" He pushed away from the table and drew his sword. "Do you remember how you used this weapon on my men before you were taken captive last fall?"

Decimus tossed the sword to Catrin, and she caught it by the handle. Galvanized by his unexpected gesture, she bolted to her feet. When he grabbed another sword, her heart hammered against her ribs. Fight instincts took over as she anticipated his next move.

The tribune stepped around the table and thrust his gladius at her, but she parried with her blade. When she swung her weapon at him, he countered with his sword and grabbed her wrist, forcing the sword from her hand. She kicked his knee and he keeled over. As she reached for her sword, he grabbed her from behind and wrapped his leg around her.

"Stop!" he barked. "Or I'll slash your throat!"

Petrified, Catrin froze.

Decimus loosened his grip. "I'll let you go, little rabbit, but I don't want to hear any further stories about you cursing my men through a raven."

She nodded, her lips quivering.

"Centurion, come in here now," Decimus called out.

Catrin cringed when Centurion Priscus, who had more facial scars than Decimus, entered the quarters. Almost a head taller than Decimus, he had the light skinned features of a Gallic warrior. The blue tattoo flaring down the entire length of his arm gave him a fierce appearance. She had heard rumors that he had been a gladiator who Decimus had freed.

Decimus jerked her face toward the centurion. "This is your new trainer, Priscus. He'll train you to be a special type of warrior. You must obey his commands."

"Train me to do what?" Catrin blurted.

Decimus slapped her across the face with the back of his hand. "Don't question me in that tone, slave! Obviously, you were already trained to fight in battle against my soldiers."

Taken aback, Catrin lowered her eyes as Priscus circled her, his grotesque scars appearing to leap out of his face. The centurion turned to Decimus.

"I can't see his muscles. Have him remove his garments."

Catrin looked at Decimus with aghast. He glowered. "Do as Priscus tells you."

"But . . . but, he'll know . . ." The words, "I'm a woman," clutched in her throat. Fighting back tears, she sat on the plank floor and pulled off her sandaled boots. After loosening the drawstring to her baggy trousers, she pulled them down and tried to tuck the tunic between her legs. She stood with the hope she would not have to undress completely.

Decimus gestured for her to remove her tunic.

Catrin, remembering her mother saying, "Don't let any Roman defile you if you are caught," defiantly shook her head.

"If you don't take that tunic off, I will tear it from your body! And I'll lash you until your skin peels off."

Horrified, Catrin reluctantly removed her tunic and clutched it against her chest. As Priscus leered at her, she cringed when he rubbed her back and pinched her shoulder and arm. She held her breath as his eyes wandered down her buttocks and upper thighs. He yanked her tunic away. She squeezed her eyelids shut as he stroked her breasts and abdomen, his scaly hands scratching her skin. As his spidery fingertips crawled between her inner thighs, she jerked away to escape his sharp fingernails. He pushed down on her shoulder to hold her still.

"Careful how you touch her," Decimus warned with a growl to his voice.

"I don't believe she has the strength or stamina to endure the training of a gladiatrix," Priscus said as he released her.

Feeling violated, Catrin stepped away and crossed her arms to hide her nakedness.

Decimus shook his head. "Granted, she's lost some muscle mass due to injuries. By Celtic standards, she is small. Still, she is almost the height of a Roman soldier. I saw her fight in battle like a lioness. In Britannia, I witnessed other women like her who were the equal of any Roman soldier in hand-to-hand combat. Our women pale in comparison to these Celts. Don't underestimate her. This slave possesses special fighting skills—skills that may be gifts from Apollo. Train her in single combat."

Priscus scratched his head. "Let me think a moment."

Decimus cast a glance at Catrin. "Put your clothes back on."

Catrin stared, stupefied.

"Put your clothes on," Decimus repeated.

Catrin fumbled with her tunic and pulled up her trousers. She cradled herself like a baby while these cruel men continued to speak about her as though she was not there.

"I'll do as you order," Priscus said, "but females aren't allowed to condition in the Roman legion. I fear the men will discover she's a woman."

Decimus placed his hand on Priscus's shoulder. "The men already believe she is a boy. How will you train her?"

"It makes more sense to exercise her with the soldiers and train her in single combat with them. She could spar with me. Or with any slave you procure to become a gladiator. That way, we can test everyone's skills before consigning them to a lanista."

Trembling, Catrin struggled to understand what lanista meant.

"Do as you see fit," Decimus said. "However, make sure the men don't learn of her true gender. They are already crazed from the long winter months. Make sure no one lays a hand on her. I want her chaste. No complications."

Priscus looked at Catrin. Feeling his piercing stare, she cradled herself tighter.

"I don't want her training with the men when she is bleeding," he demanded.

Decimus nodded. "I've been told hard conditioning sometimes stops the cycle."

"Possibly," Priscus said. "It's best she's moved from the infirmary and kept in your quarters to avoid any unexpected surprises from the men."

"Agreed. She can serve my personal needs."

Catrin flinched. *What personal needs?*

Priscus cocked an eyebrow. "The soldiers will keep their hands off her if they think she is a boy who sleeps in your bed."

Decimus scowled at Priscus. "Let their tongues wag."

"Forgive my bluntness," Priscus said. "What you do with her is none of my business. At least, get her some clothing that fits her and doesn't impede her movement—a loincloth to hide her cunni and something to bind her breasts down."

Decimus nodded.

Priscus raised his eyes toward the ceiling. "Only with the help of the gods can I forge her into a warrior."

"You focus on your task. The gods will do the rest," Decimus snorted.

"As you command. If you have no further need of me, I'll take my leave."

"You're dismissed."

Priscus saluted and left.

Decimus grabbed Catrin's arm and pulled her up to his face, alarming her. "You will learn your place as my slave. Remember, I could have slit your throat in Britannia. Instead, I showed you mercy and spared your life. If you run away, you will be stripped, raped, and crucified. If you show any self-pity or weep, I'll sell you as a whore."

Catrin tightened her trembling hands into fists and stiffened her shoulders. "I am a warrior and will prove it so."

Decimus pressed on her shoulder, forcing her to kneel. "Make sure you do. You now live in the Roman world and have no choice but to accept your fate as my slave."

He pushed his fingertips against Catrin's tender head until she cried out. The chamber walls seemed to crush on her as she lowered her head in deference as he continued speaking.

"You must never let anyone know you're a woman. If any of my men finds out, they'll do far worse than what Priscus just did to you. Do exactly what I say. Do not speak unless I say so."

Catrin's thoughts were rushing down a river of despair and dashing against the rocks. Not only had the Romans stripped her of clothes, they had stripped her of her name, her gender, her identity, her heritage, her birthright, her family.

Is it my fate only to know Roman brutality? What of my destiny to retake my kingdom?

Decimus jerked Catrin to her feet and dragged her over to the table where he untied a pouch and pulled out the amulet of the marble figurine of Apollo. "I only spared you because of your divine connection to Apollo."

He handed her the statuette that he had taken from her when he captured her. This was the only possession she had from Marcellus as a symbol of his love. To soothe herself, she stroked its marble surface as Decimus said, "I was told by Marcellus that you have prophetic abilities."

Catrin nervously nodded, taken aback that her Roman husband had revealed her abilities to Decimus.

The tribune curled his lips into a thin smile. "I thought so. If you beseech Apollo to foretell my future and to keep his cursed raven messenger from me, I will not lay a hand on you nor will I allow any of my soldiers to do so. A priest has told me that you must remain celibate as the warrior priestess of Apollo."

The commander's motivations perplexed Catrin, but she would do anything to keep him and any soldier away from her. Lie about his future and manipulate him, if need be.

"I'll do as you command," she said, humbly dropping her eyes.

"Good girl. My bedchamber is in the other room." He pointed to the corner of the main headquarters. "And you can sleep over there."

She cringed with the thought that he might not keep his word to leave her alone.

But that night, Decimus retired to his bed without any further incident.

Somewhat relieved, Catrin sat down on her wool-blanket bedding on the floor and held her knees against her chest as she caressed the Apollo amulet with her fingertips. The white cliffs of Britannia beckoned to her, but she did not know how she could cross the ocean channel. Her hatred of the Romans burned in the pit of her stomach like a firestorm. Every muscle in her body longed to escape, but what choice did she have other than to yield to her master's commands? There was no honor in dying by crucifixion as a runaway slave. She had seen naked bodies rot on the crosses and eaten away by ravens. She had to survive her slavery and overcome her master to fulfill her destiny to overthrow Marrock. Yet to survive in the Roman world, she could not show any weakness or reveal her true intent to return home. Instead, she must show the stealth of a warrior and cunning of a raven.

She could not falter.

Gazing at the Apollo statuette, she listened to the raven fledging crying out to her in the distance. Sensing its essence, she stared at the wooden wall and fell into a trance. The room lit up with a yellow glow. Marcellus, driving a gold-rimmed chariot, slowly came into focus. He extended his hand to her. "Come with me. I am Apollo, your protector."

She envisioned herself climbing into his chariot. He snapped a whip over the heads of the black stallions and drove the vehicle into the sky.

"Where are you taking me?" she asked, gazing into his deep-set, blue eyes that reflected her golden hair tumbling over her shoulders.

"I am taking you on a journey," he replied, his hand gently touching hers.

Yet, she was uneasy with the realization that Marcellus was now a stranger with no memory of her. "Didn't you promised to protect me and to take me back to my homeland?"

Marcellus caressed her face and drew her to his warm lips. "You must first burn in my fire in Rome."

The Raven's screeching startled Catrin from her vision, and she gasped. How could Marcellus protect her if he was in Rome? She had to find a way to lure him to northern Gaul, so she could enrapture him again with her love and convince him to help her escape to Britannia.

*****

Please leave a review for DAGGER'S DESTINY

Keep up-to-date with the latest news on the development of
the *Curse of Clansmen and Kings* series
at *https://linneatanner.com*

CPSIA information can be obtained
at www.ICGtesting.com
Printed in the USA
LVHW111922030519
616613LV00001B/15/P

9 780998 230054